Archduke Rudolph, Beethoven's Patron, Pupil, and Friend

Frontispiece. Archduke Rudolph in 1812 Aquarelle by Jean-Baptiste Isabey
(Rollettmuseum, Baden)

Archduke Rudolph, Beethoven's Patron, Pupil, and Friend

His Life and Music

by
Susan Kagan

PENDRAGON PRESS
STUYVESANT

Library of Congress Cataloging-in-Publication Data

Kagan, Susan.
　Archduke Rudolph, Beethoven's patron, pupil, and friend : his life
and music / by Susan Kagan.

　　p.　　cm.
　Bibliography: p. 265
　"Thematic catalogue of the compositions of Archduke Rudolph" : p. 313
　Includes index.
　ISBN 0-945193-45-9
　1. Rudolph, Erzherzog von Österreich, Cardinal, 1788-1831.
2. Composers—Austria—Biography. 3. Rudolph, Erzherzog von
Österreich, Cardinal, 1788-1831—Criticism and interpretation.
4. Rudolph, Erzherzog von Österreich, Cardinal, 1788-1831—Thematic
catalogs. 5. Beethoven, Ludwig van, 1770-1827. I. Title.
ML410.R896K3 1988
780'.92'4—dc19
[B]　　　　　　　　　　　　　　　　　　　　　　　　88-17859
　　　　　　　　　　　　　　　　　　　　　　　　　　　CIP
　　　　　　　　　　　　　　　　　　　　　　　　　　　MN

Contents

Acknowledgements   vii

List of Illustrations   ix

Introduction   xiii

Chapter
   I.   The Composer's Life: An Overview   1

  II. Archduke Rudolph's Studies in Music Theory   53

 III. The *Forty Variations on a Theme By Beethoven*   69

 IV. Variations and Other Works for Piano   119

  V. Variations for Clarinet and Other Woodwind Works   151

 VI. Sonata Compositions   183

VII. Other Music for Instrumental Ensembles   213

VIII. Compositions for Voice   233

 IX. Conclusion   263

v

Bibliography   265

Appendices
   1.   Archduke Rudolph's Music Catalogues   267
   2.   Original Texts For Translated Material and Vocal Music   297
   3.   Thematic Catalogue of the Compositions of Archduke
       Rudolph   313

Index   347

Acknowledgements

Many individuals and institutions contributed greatly to the realization of this publication, and it is with deep pleasure that I acknowledge their assistance. My first thanks go to the committee of distinguished scholars who oversaw the dissertation on which this book is based: Barry S. Brook, my advisor, who guided me through the years of my graduate studies at the Graduate School of the City University of New York and my dissertation research with unflagging interest, patience, and encouragement, who has been both mentor and friend, and who has supported this project from its inception and provided me with the benefit of his vast knowledge and experience; L. Michael Griffel of Hunter College, who insisted on absolute clarity of thought and expression, and consistently provided constructive criticism of great value; and Edward O. D. Downes of Queens College, who proved especially helpful with the perspective he brought from his many years as teacher and critic.

The cooperation of archivists and librarians here and abroad has been of crucial help; I am grateful to William Shank of the Graduate School library of the City University of New York, and to Elliott Kaback of the Hunter College library; the staff of the music archive of the Gesellschaft der Musikfreunde in Vienna—Hedwig Mitringer, former director, and Otto Biba, present director, and Peter Riethus, Dorothea Chavanne, and Christa Stracke; Franz Dirnberger of the Haus-, Hof- und Staatsarchiv, Vienna; in Czechoslovakia, Theodora Straková, former director, and Jiří Sehnal, present director of the music archive of the Moravian Museum, Brno; Antonín Lukáš, curator of the Kroměříž Castle archive; Antonín Jirka, art historian; and Miloš Kouřil of the State Archive in Olomouc.

Numerous institutions furnished documents and pictures: in Vienna, the Gesellschaft der Musikfreunde, the Haus-, Hof- und Staatsarchiv, the Wiener Stadt- und Landesbibliothek, the Historisches Museum der Stadt Wien, and the Musiksammlung, Handschriftensammlung, and Bild-Archiv und Porträt Sammlung of the Österreichische Nationalbibliothek; in Czechoslovakia, the Státní Zámek Hudební Archiv in Kroměříž, and the Statni Oblastní Archiv in Olomouc; the Deutsche Staatsbibliothek in Berlin, DDR; the Beethoven-Archiv in Bonn; the Thuringische Landesbibliothek in Weimar; and the Forschungsbibliothek in Gotha.

For their reading of the manuscript in whole or in part, and their helpful suggestions and comments I am indebted to Rufus Hallmark, Richard B. Kramer, William S. Newman, Maynard Solomon, Eric Werner, and especially Siegmund Levarie, who in addition to his perceptive and meticulous attention to matters of editing, assisted me greatly in providing accurate translations. I have very special thanks for Alan Tyson, who took time from his own scholarly activities to go through my manuscript with scrupulous care and to make invaluable suggestions for its improvement.

Friends and colleagues with expertise in many areas who gave generously of their time and assistance are Theophil Antonicek, the late Max Block, Mortimer H. Frank, David Goldberger, Walburga Litschauer, Carl Schachter, Richard Wernick, and Robert Winter.

To Martin Bernstein I have a gratitude that cannot be acknowledged with a mere thanks; mentor, informal teacher and advisor, musical colleague, close and cherished friend, he first brought Archduke Rudolph's music to my attention and is thus, in a sense, the spiritual father of this book.

The contribution of my family—their patience, moral support, willingness to sacrifice, and belief in me—I have saved for last. My husband Gerald gave his enthusiastic encouragement to my work, and aided me in many of its technical aspects, as did my sons, Justin and Andrew. To them, and to my late parents, I lovingly dedicate this work.

List of Illustrations

Frontispiece. Archduke Rudolph in 1812 Aquarelle by Jean-Baptiste Isabey (Rollettmuseum, Baden) ii

Plate 1. Archduke Rudolph's signature on the manuscript of the *Forty Variations on a Theme by Beethoven* xii

Plate 2. Archduke Rudolph in early childhood with his brothers Rainer and Ludwig xxiv

Plate 3. Page from Vatican publication announcing Archduke Rudolph's appointment as coadjutor 4

Plate 4. Letter from Beethoven to Archduke Rudolph, 1816 (autograph) 24

Plate 5. Letter from Beethoven to Archduke Rudolph, 1817 (autograph) 25

Plate 6. Archduke Rudolph, 1805 (oil painting by J.B. Lampi the Elder) 38

Plate 7. Archduke Rudolph as a youth 39

Plate 8. Archduke Rudolph in uniform (engraving by Höfel after Schiavoni) 40

Plate 9. Archduke Rudolph in uniform (bust) 41

Plate 10. Archduke Rudolph, Archbishop, 1819 (engraving after Giangiacomo) 42

Plate 11. Archduke Rudolph, Archbishop, 1819 43

Plate 12. Archduke Rudolph, Archbishop, 1819 (lithograph by Kunike) 44

Plate 13. Archduke Rudolph, Archbishop, 1819 (oil painting by Amerling) 45

Plate 14. Archduke Rudolph, Cardinal-Archbishop, 1822 (oil painting by Dittman) 46

Plate 15. Archduke Rudolph, Cardinal-Archbishop, 1823 (engraving after Suchy) 47

Plate 16. Archduke Rudolph, Cardinal-Archbishop, 1823 (lithograph after Lanzedelly) 48

Plate 17. Archduke Rudolph, Cardinal-Archbishop (miniature by Teltscher) 49

Plate 18. Archduke Rudolph, plaque in Gesellschaft der Musikfreunde 50

Plate 19. Archduke Rudolph, Cardinal-Archbishop, ca. 1825 (oil painting by J.B. Lampi the Younger) 51

Plate 20. Kroměříž Castle, Kroměříž, Czechoslovakia 52

Plate 21. Page from Archduke Rudolph's contrapuntal exercises (autograph) 58

Plate 22. Page from Archduke Rudolph's transcription of the Minuet from Beethoven's Septet (Opus 20) for clarinet, viola, bassoon, and guitar (autograph) 64

Plate 23. Title page of S.A. Steiner edition (1819) of Archduke Rudolph's "Aufgabe": Forty Variations on a Theme by Beethoven 68

Plate 24. Beethoven, "O Hoffnung" (WoO 200) [autograph] 70

Plate 25. Beethoven's sketches for corrections in the Forty Variations (page 1) [autograph] 112

Plate 26. Beethoven's sketches for corrections in the Forty Variations (page 2) [autograph] 113

Plate 27. Beethoven's sketches for corrections in the Forty Variations (page 3) [autograph] 114

Plate 28. Beethoven's sketches for corrections in the *Forty Variations* (page 4) [autograph] 115

Plate 29. Beethoven's sketches for corrections in the *Forty Variations* (page 5) [autograph] 116

Plate 30. Beethoven's suggested title for the *Forty Variations* (autograph) 117

Plate 31. Detail from the manuscript of the *Forty Variations* with Beethoven's corrections in the margin (autograph) 118

Plate 32. Page from Archduke Rudolph's *Variations in G* for piano (autograph) 122

Plate 33. Title page, Archduke Rudolph's *Variations for Czakan* (autograph) 168

Plate 34. Page from miscellaneous sketches, with Archduke Rudolph's doodles (autograph) 232

Plate 35. Page from Archduke Rudolph's duet, "Ich denke dein" (autograph) 254

Plate 36. Archduke Rudolph memorial monument, Bad Ischl, Austria 262

Plate 37. Archduke Rudolph commemorative silver medal struck in 1820. 268

Plate 1. Archduke Rudolph's signature on the manuscript of the
Forty Variations on a Theme by Beethoven (Kroměříž, Czechoslovakia).

Introduction

Within the wide circle of personages in Vienna surrounding the central figure of Beethoven during the early nineteenth century, many have been immortalized almost solely because of their association with him. The names of such individuals as Razumovsky or Diabelli are familiar not only to Beethoven scholars but also to countless musicians and music-lovers, primarily because they figured significantly in Beethoven's life. The Beethoven circle included patrons and friends, in whose palaces and homes the composer's music was often performed; the musicians who played his works; the many publishers with whom Beethoven had dealings; and, of course, the dozens of ancillary friends and acquaintances, high and low born, who played some part in his life. Among all these, one person in particular who emerges as a uniquely important individual, for his association with Beethoven was so multi-faceted, is the Archduke Rudolph, who was Beethoven's most loyal patron, his most generous friend, and his long-term student in piano and composition.

Child of the Imperial Habsburg family, son of one emperor and brother of another, Archduke Rudolph was born in 1788, and received the thorough musical education that was considered part of the traditional wide-ranging course of studies for children of the aristocracy.[1] His ability was far above average; by the age of fifteen his accomplishments as a pianist were well known in the aristocratic salons of Vienna frequented by Beethoven, whose acquaintance he made at that time, around 1803. Shortly thereafter, Archduke

[1] Full details on Archduke Rudolph's ancestry, education, and other biographical particulars can be found in chapter 1.

Rudolph became Beethoven's pupil, first in piano, then in composition,[2] and the two established a relationship that was to have crucial consequences for both. Although Rudolph's career as a pianist was cut short in his early twenties because of a painful arthritic condition that affected his fingers, he continued to compose under Beethoven's tutelage until close to the latter's death. His musical interests extended far beyond his own music-making; from as early an age as thirteen, he was a passionate collector of music—manuscripts and printed editions—and books on music, as well as a compulsive cataloguer of his vast collection.[3]

The Archduke's place in Beethoven's life has not been ignored; no substantial work on Beethoven fails to acknowledge Rudolph's significance in Beethoven's life, paiticularly as a patron. As a personality in his own right, however, Archduke Rudolph has remained a shadowy figure, relegated to the footnotes of musicological literature. No biography of the Archduke has yet been written, and few primary source materials have been uncovered.

The principal reason for the obscurity surrounding Rudolph's life is probably his relative lack of importance in the Imperial Habsburg family. He was one of the sixteen titled children born to Emperor Leopold II (reigned 1790-1792) and his wife, Princess Maria Ludovica. Rudolph's eldest brother, Emperor Franz (1768-1835) ruled the vast domains of the Austrian Empire.[4] The historical events of the time—the Napoleonic wars, the Congress of Vienna, the political and social reshaping of Europe—were of a magnitude that dwarfed all but the major figures involved; hence the activities of one member of the Imperial family whose career was neither military nor political have been considered of little importance. In addition, Archduke Rudolph's positions in the church hierarchy—first as Archbishop, then as Cardinal Archbishop—ensured a certain amount of privacy. Rudolph's name occurs infrequently in published writings of people involved in the Viennese music world during his lifetime. His frequent attendance at concerts and the theater is confirmed by numerous comments on performances in his correspondence, and

[2]See chapter 1, p. 3.
[3]Archduke Rudolph's catalogues are discussed in Appendix 1.
[4]When Emperor Franz succeeded to the throne in 1792, he was titled Franz II, Emperor of the Austrian Empire and ruler of the Holy Roman Empire. Following the dissolution of the Holy Roman Empire during the Napoleonic wars, Franz took the title (in 1804) of Franz I, Emperor of Austria.

his appearances at these public places were occasionally noted in the press; but the sparse number of reports mentioning his name in such contemporary sources as *Der Sammler* and the *Allgemeine musikalische Zeitung* suggests that his appearances were simply not newsworthy. Similarly, his frequent arrivals and departures to and from Vienna, his official residences in Olmütz (now Olomouc) and Kremsier (now Kroměříž),[5] and the spas in Baden and Teplitz, although documented in his correspondence, usually went unrecorded in the press.

The most comprehensive information about Archduke Rudolph was assembled and published over one hundred years ago by Alexander Wheelock Thayer in the first three volumes of the first German edition of his great biography of Beethoven;[6] Thayer used previously published material of other individuals conversant with details of Beethoven's relationships, as well as the collected Beethoven correspondence and some of the Conversation Books. Since then, only one other author has attempted to describe Rudolph as other than a satellite orbiting the Beethovenian planet: Alexander Novotny, in a Viennese periodical (1961), delves into the Archduke's significance for Vienna.[7] Drawing upon such important unpublished sources as archival documents in the Haus-, Hof- und Staatsarchiv in Vienna and in the Wiener Universität, Novotny sheds light upon the early education of the Imperial children. By examining the philosophy and principles of the educators, Novotny illuminates the relationship between Archduke Rudolph's education and the cultural milieu of early nineteenth-century Vienna.

Two other articles concerning Archduke Rudolph are in print: the first is Donald W. MacArdle's thorough documentary survey of Beethoven's personal association with Rudolph, "Beethoven and the Archduke Rudolph,"[8] which at the time it was published brought together in English all available information in published sources; the more recent article is by Jan Racek, "Beethoven's Beziehungen zur mährischen Musikkultur im 18. und 19. Jahrhundert."[9] Both articles,

---

[5]Olomouc and Kroměříž are cities in present-day Czechoslovakia. The nineteenth-century names will be used when historical references are made.

[6]Alexander Wheelock Thayer, *Ludwig van Beethovens Leben* (Berlin: Schneider, 1866; Weber, 1872, 1879). These volumes had been translated into German by Hermann Deiters from the original English manuscript.

[7]Alexander Novotny, "Kardinal Erzherzog Rudolph (1788-1831) und seine Bedeutung für Wien," *Wiener Geschichtsblätter* 4 (1961) 341-47.

[8]*Beethoven-Jahrbuch 1959-60*, iv (Bonn, 1962) 37-58.

[9]*Beethoven-Jahrbuch 1973-77*, ix (Bonn, 1977) 377-93.

as one can deduce from their titles, are limited principally to matters related to Beethoven.

A rich source of information is the extant correspondence of Archduke Rudolph, both published and unpublished, the largest of which is the collection of Beethoven's letters to him.[10] Over one hundred in number, each of these letters, no matter how brief or how trivial the content, was carefully preserved by the Archduke. Taken together with Beethoven's letters to others in which he makes references to Rudolph, they throw light upon the complex relations between the two men. Even more valuable in furnishing information about the Archduke's private life and everyday activities is a collection of letters he wrote to Joseph Anton Ignaz Baumeister, who was Rudolph's childhood tutor and, until his death in 1819, his personal secretary and librarian. Fifty-three of Rudolph's letters to Baumeister, written during the years 1809 to 1818, are preserved in the Haus-, Hof- und Staatsarchiv in Vienna.[11] Fourteen of these letters were published in 1845 in the Viennese journal *Sonntagsblätter*;[12] the many errors in the editor's transcriptions, however, make the published texts unreliable. In addition, there are two smaller collections of Rudolph's letters, unpublished and previously unreported, to various individuals, Beethoven and Baumeister among them: nine are in the Wiener Stadt- und Landesbibliothek,[13] and fourteen are in the Handschriftensammlung of the Österreichische Nationalbibliothek.[14] In addition, there are several letters scattered through the vast archival materials of the former Archbishopric of Olmütz, now located in the Státní Oblastní Archiv in Olomouc; these letters, for the most part, are to members of the clergy, and concern matters relevant to Church business. Four other letters of the Archduke's, not among those mentioned thus far, were published.[15]

[10]Emily Anderson, ed. and trans., *The Letters of Beethoven*, 3 vols. (London: Macmillan, 1961).

[11]Karton 52.

[12]17./18. Heft (387-89, 417-19).

[13]Catalogue numbers I. N. 118, 8218, 8219, 8220, 10662, 25430, 25436, 39471, 68557.

[14]Catalogue numbers 33/88 (1-12), and 442/31 (13-14).

[15]Two are to Beethoven: one in George Marek, *Beethoven: Biography of A Genius* (New York: Thomas Y. Crowell Co., 1972) 324; the other in A.C. Kalischer and Theodor Frimmel, eds., *Beethovens sämtliche Briefe*, 2nd ed.. 5 vols. (Berlin & Leipzig: Schuster & Loeffler, 1980-11) IV, 300-01. One is to Baumeister, in *Beethoven-Jahrbuch* II (1909) 321; the fourth is to Prince Lobkowitz, in A.W. Thayer, *Ludwig van Beethovens Leben*, 2nd ed., ed. and enl. Hermann Deiters and Hugo Riemann, 5 vols. (Leipzig: Breitkopf & Härtel, 1907-08) III, 492.

These various biographical sources all alluded to Archduke Rudolph's composition studies with Beethoven, but although Thayer and the others were fully aware that Rudolph was Beethoven's *only* composition student, little attention was given to Rudolph's own compositions, undoubtedly on the assumption that his efforts as an amateur did not merit more than cursory notice. The three compositions by the Archduke published during his lifetime—*Forty Variations on a Theme by Beethoven* (S. A. Steiner, 1819), *Sonata in A for Clarinet and Piano* (S. A. Steiner, 1822), and a *Fugue* on a theme by Diabelli (Diabelli, 1824)— are mentioned in almost all these sources, but more as curiosities than as representative examples from a larger oeuvre.

Part of the ignorance about the extent of Rudolph's output is attributable to historical and geographical circumstances. From the year 1805, when he was appointed coadjutor[16] to the Archbishop of Olmütz, and especially after 1819, when he was ordained Archbishop, Rudolph spent most of his time in Olmütz and in Kremsier, where the principal residences of the Archbishopric were located. The library of the palace in Kremsier held the contents of Rudolph's music collection, and it was in Kremsier that Rudolph appears to have done most of his composing. When, after his death in 1831, by the terms of his will his music collection was sent to the Gesellschaft der Musikfreunde in Vienna, his own compositions remained behind in Kremsier. How the exclusion of his own works from the bequest came about is not clear, as the wording of the will does not suggest such a separation. The relatively few compositions by Rudolph that are in the archives of the Gesellschaft der Musikfreunde were in all likelihood already in Vienna at the time of Rudolph's death.

The collection of manuscripts in Kremsier remained in obscurity for several decades, until in 1919, following the establishment of the Czechoslovakian State, Czech musicologists, under the direction of Vladimír Helfert, began to systematically catalogue the music holdings of various archives in the Moravian District. Among them were Archduke Rudolph's compositions in the Kremsier palace library.

In 1921 Paul Nettl, in a preliminary report,[17] gave a brief description of Archduke Rudolph's compositions in the Kremsier archive, in which

---

[16] A position in the church; see chapter 1, p. 6, n. 13.
[17] Paul Nettl, "Erinnerungen an Erzherzog Rudolph, den Freund und Schüler Beethovens," *Zeitschrift für Musikwissenschaft* IV (1921) 95-99.

he noted particularly the presence of faded, scarcely legible pencil corrections in Beethoven's hand on several pages of manuscripts. This was followed five years later by another article in the same journal by Karl Vetterl[18] with a more comprehensive description of the materials in the archive. Of great interest was Vetterl's disclosure of a previously unreported Beethoven autograph among Rudolph's manuscripts—five pages of unclear sketches, some in ink, some in pencil. In addition to including incipits of all the completed works and several that were just fragments, Vetterl described the catalogues he found in the library. These registers, in the Archduke's handwriting, recorded the entire contents of his music collection (through the year 1810): manuscripts, printed music, and books on all musical subjects, amassed by the Archduke from the time he was thirteen years old. Vetterl's conclusions were that Rudolph's compositions revealed true musical talent, and he emphasized the need for a thorough scholarly investigation.

Nothing further concerning the Archduke's works appeared in print until 1970, when the Austrian musicologist Gerhard Croll, in an article published in a collection of Beethoven studies,[19] expressed surprise at the continued neglect of this body of music by Beethoven scholars and reiterated Nettl's warnings about the extremely faded condition of Beethoven's corrections. Croll's article, actually written in the late 1960's, appeared at a time when the political situation created a climate that effectively precluded attempts on the part of musicologists from the West to examine archival materials in Czechoslovakia. This difficulty was unquestionably heightened when the materials involved failed to represent the Czech "cultural heritage" (as one official expressed it), and also were associated with an individual who, as a member of the Habsburg monarchy, symbolized nineteenth-century political oppression. In the last several years, however, a relaxation in the official attitude toward the West changed matters significantly so that, although direct information from governmental sources was still difficult to obtain, access to the archives themselves was made possible in 1976. At that time Dr. Jiří Sehnal, then assistant director of the music division of the Moravian

[18]Karl Vetterl, "Der musikalische Nachlass des Erzherzogs Rudolf im erzbischöf-lichen Archiv zu Kremsier," *Zeitschrift für Musikwissenschaft* IX (1926-27) 168-78.
[19]Gerhard Croll, "Die Musiksammlung des Erzherzogs Rudolph," *Beethoven-Studien* (1970) 51-55.

Museum in Brno (formerly Brünn), had just completed a new inventory of Archduke Rudolph's music and drawn up a detailed catalogue with incipits of Rudolph's compositions, including many of the unfinished sketches and fragments. Permission was readily granted to the author to examine and photograph every manuscript and many other documents pertaining to Archduke Rudolph's works.

The collection of autographs in Kroměříž, along with the two dozen or so manuscripts of the Archduke's compositions in the archive of the Gesellschaft der Musikfreunde (most of them copies, but a few important autographs also), indicates that Rudolph's output of finished works was not very large. The thematic catalogue in Appendix 3 of this study gives incipits and details for Rudolph's total oeuvre, but his two dozen-odd completed works can be summarized here: there are five sets of variations for piano (one for piano four hands), among which are the *Forty Variations on a Theme by Beethoven*, published in 1819 by Steiner, Beethoven's principal publisher at that time; several sets of variations for clarinet or other woodwind with piano, one for violin and piano, and two for chamber ensemble; two sonatas in the traditional Classical four-movement structure, one for clarinet and piano (published in 1822 by Steiner), and one for violin and piano; a fugue written for Diabelli (published in 1824); several sets of *Ländler* or other dances for piano solo, piano four hands, and orchestra; arias and one duet for voice with piano accompaniment, among which is a vocal canon on the *Lebewohl* theme from Beethoven's Sonata in E-flat, Opus 81a ("Les Adieux"), composed for and dedicated to the Archduke. Rudolph's unfinished works number in the dozens; these include some that appear to be missing one or more pages to be complete. In addition to the works listed above, there are transcriptions and arrangements of works by other composers; theoretical exercises; and hundreds of miscellaneous sketches.

In the process of examining and classifying Archduke Rudolph's compositions in Kremsier, the palace archivists were faced with a mass of manuscripts—some on loose sheets, some sewn together in small booklets; some were in ink, some in pencil; some were seemingly complete works, some brief sketches of a few measures. Each item was assigned a catalogue number rather loosely according to genre. Since the Archduke had sometimes used manuscript paper that had been sewn together into gatherings of various numbers of sheets, many compositions were preserved intact; in other cases, where sketches clearly fit together, the archivists were able to assemble parts of a work into a whole. Complicating this undertaking was Rudolph's infrequent use of clef signs, key signatures, or instrumentation in his sketches. Hence hundreds of pages of sketches of seemingly disparate parts could not be classified and were bundled together into miscellaneous assortments under the title *Membra disjecta* (disjoint elements).[20] Most of these sketches are rough drafts—some the briefest of fragments (a few measures), others continuing for several pages. All had been jotted down, often rather incoherently, in a kind of shorthand devised by Rudolph, with numbers, large X's, and other puzzling signs dotting the manuscripts.[21] If any proof of Beethoven's influence on Rudolph was needed, it is well supplied by the appearance of these sketches, which demonstrate much similarity in working methods between pupil and teacher.

The most immediate problem involved in a study of Archduke Rudolph's music is the establishment of an accurate chronology for his compositions, which, with two exceptions (both in 1810), were not dated. One method of dating—by paper watermark study—is of limited value, because Archduke Rudolph used a wide variety of papers from many sources, and there is insufficient data available for most of them.[22] Two other means of arriving at dates for his works have proved useful: his handwriting, both of music and script, and his music catalogues. The dating of individual compositions will be discussed chapter by chapter in relation to the works themselves, but the significant points of evidence may be summarized here.

To begin with, the Archduke's compositions can be divided roughly into two periods: an "early" period, from ca. 1809 to 1814, during which time most of his music was composed, and a later, more mature period, from 1814 to ca. 1824, after which Rudolph's composing appears to have ceased. This division is based on one firm

[20]KRa A 4433-38. Other collections of miscellaneous sketches and fragments are catalogued under KRa A 4431, 4432, 4385-86, and 4387-88.

[21]It was possible for this writer to identify and classify a number of sketches in the *Membra disjecta* that belong to specific works of Rudolph; these will be noted in discussion of those works.

[22]I am indebted to Robert Winter, who shared with me his extensive knowledge of watermarks on Viennese papers used by Beethoven and Schubert during the first quarter of the nineteenth century and aided me in identifying the watermarks on several of Rudolph's manuscripts.

piece of evidence—Rudolph's notation of the bass clef, which until 1813 or 1814 he made exactly like Beethoven's:

In a work known to date from 1814, and in all the music written after that, Rudolph made his bass clefs in the manner more commonly used today:[23]

The treble clef sign was generally consistent in both early and later manuscripts:

As a rule, there is a difference in the physical appearance of Rudolph's early and mature works. Although one must account for differences in writing rough drafts and fair copies, in the early manuscripts Rudolph's writing tends to be careless, usually with complete disregard for the alignment of parts, whereas in the later manuscripts the appearance is much neater and the writing more controlled in all aspects.

One other feature of writing style involves the spelling of certain words that turn up regularly in Rudolph's music, notably the words "allegretto" and "polacca." Rudolph's spelling of these and other words is not always consistent (in a period when spelling in general was not standardized), but in the early manuscripts one most often reads "alegretto" and "pollaca," while in the later manuscripts one finds "allegretto" and "polacca."

The most significant aid in establishing chronology is the largest and most comprehensive of the Archduke's music catalogues, preserved in the Gesellschaft der Musikfreunde—the *Musikalien-Register*,[24] containing 410 pages, most of it in Rudolph's hand. This

---

[23]On a few manuscripts which from all appearances may be ascribed to an even earlier period, possibly predating Rudolph's study with Beethoven, one finds still another form of clef signs, both treble and bass; see chapter 2 for fuller discussion and examples.

[24]The *Musikalien-Register* (Wgm 1268/33), divided into two alphabetical collections (A-K, L-Z) and housed in two large boxes, is fully described in Appendix 1, along with Archduke Rudolph's other catalogues.

catalogue, probably begun around 1810, is invaluable for the information it supplies, because as the Archduke acquired a new work, he entered it in that order in the catalogue; the entries (involving many composers and publishers) thus are chronological, as can be verified by publisher's catalogues of the period. Fortunately, the Archduke included in his catalogue one page on which he listed most of his own finished compositions; like the entries for other composers, these are listed in chronological order, presumably the order in which they were composed.

The handwriting of the catalogue entries also offers important clues for dating; Rudolph's penmanship underwent drastic changes from one period to another. The evidence presented by the handwriting changes and the order of entries is confirmed by the other pieces of evidence offered by his notation and spelling.

There are seventeen entries for the Archduke's compositions, not all of which are listed (for example, a set of piano variations that may have been his first large-scale work [discussed in chapter 4, p. 120-125], and a few works composed after 1819). The handwriting of his early entries (numbers one through ten), for music composed through ca. 1812, is fairly uniform. In entry number eleven, dated 1814, the handwriting is somewhat different, and the two succeeding entries, ca. 1816, show a handwriting that is markedly distorted—undoubtedly the result of the arthritic condition that crippled his fingers around that time; the way the entries slant, in fact, may reflect writing while bedridden. Entries fourteen and fifteen, dating from ca. 1818-19, are in another hand, suggesting that the pressure of Rudolph's duties in connection with his appointment as Archbishop prevented him from keeping up with his catalogues. The final two entries, numbers sixteen and seventeen, are for the two works published in late 1819 and in 1822—the *Forty Variations* and the Clarinet Sonata. Again for reasons unknown, the Archduke ceased to enter his own new compositions in the catalogue after 1822, although he continued to list the works of other composers until 1826-27.

In sum, the chronology we have been able to establish accounts for almost every work Rudolph composed. In some cases, the date can be only roughly determined, e.g., before 1812, or after 1814; in other cases, drawing on the evidence provided by several factors, it can be fixed more precisely.

This book is an attempt to provide a complete biographical picture of Archduke Rudolph; to survey and assess his total oeuvre, examine significant works in detail, and furnish a thematic catalogue of his compositions; and finally, to present and scrutinize Beethoven's suggestions and corrections as Rudolph's teacher.

The biographical overview in chapter 1 brings together information from all available sources—those already published, as well as new archival material in Rudolph's letters and catalogues. A comprehensive portrait of the Archduke—his background and milieu, his many interests, his ecclesiastic career, and the significant relationships in his life—helps to flesh out the rather one-dimensional picture of him that has emerged from previously available information and allows us to view him as a person in his own right.

In chapter 2, devoted to the surviving materials of the Archduke's theoretical studies, and in the ensuing six chapters, Rudolph's music is surveyed and evaluated, by discussion of the genres used, the manner in which he wrote for specific instruments, structure, and harmonic procedures. For the most part, this survey is limited to completed works, but in a few cases, some special feature in an incomplete composition proved of sufficient interest or importance to warrant its inclusion in our discussion. The thematic catalogue in Appendix 3 contains all pertinent information relevant to each of Archduke Rudolph's compositions.

Finally, there are Beethoven's written corrections and suggestions in several of Rudolph's manuscripts—annotations which afford us the opportunity of perceiving Beethoven in the unaccustomed role of teacher and critic. Beethoven studies have brought out Rudolph's importance as a patron; now, a study of Rudolph reveals some significant aspects of Beethoven as a teacher.

Archduke Rudolph's music, while not, perhaps, of major consequence, is the work of a gifted, industrious, and capable craftsman, not simply an influential dilettante. The time has come, finally, to look at Rudolph in the light of his own achievements.

Plate 2. Archduke Rudolph in early childhood with his brothers
Archdukes Rainer and Ludwig (Miniature in mezzotint)
(Österreichische Nationalbibliothek, Vienna).

CHAPTER I

The Composer's Life:
An Overview

Archduke Rudolph Johann Joseph Rainer was born on January 8, 1788, in the Pitti Palace in Florence, Italy, the sixteenth and youngest of the twelve sons and four daughters born to Leopold, Grand Duke of Tuscany,[1] and Princess Maria Ludovica of Spain.[2] Upon the death of Leopold's eldest brother, reigning Emperor Joseph II, in 1790, the family moved to Vienna, where Leopold succeeded to the throne. His reign lasted just two years; both he and his wife died in 1792, and he was succeeded by his eldest son, Franz. Along with the responsibility of ruling an enormous and powerful empire, the twenty-four-year-

---

[1]Leopold and his brother, Emperor Joseph, were the two eldest sons of the sixteen children of Empress Maria Theresia and Emperor Franz I (of Lorraine). Since Joseph died childless, his younger brother was next in line to the throne. Both Mozart's opera *La clemenza di Tito* (K. 621) and Beethoven's *Kantate auf die Erhebung Leopolds II. zur Kaiserwürde* (WoO 88) commemorated Leopold's coronation.

[2]Of the sixteen children born to Leopold and Maria Ludovica, fourteen reached adulthood. Thayer's reference to Archduke Rudolph as Emperor Franz's half-brother (Thayer-Deiters-Riemann, *Beethovens Leben* II, 543: see also *Thayer's Life of Beethoven*, rev. and ed. Elliot Forbes [Princeton: Princeton University Press, 1967] 364) appears to be erroneous.

1

old Emperor was in charge of the upbringing and supervision of his orphaned siblings.

Although many details about the early education of the Imperial children are lacking, some information in the palace archives, as reported by Novotny,[3] reveals a highly conscientious attitude on the part of Emperor Franz toward his responsibilities in rearing the children, particularly the boys. He expressed the desire to be an adequate substitute father to his siblings and chose the personnel who were to supervise their training with surprising flexibility. Emperor Franz involved himself personally in their education, issuing directives to their tutors regarding their instruction, the development of mind and character, physical care, and methods of punishment—all to be carried out in the right measure, without excess or disorder.

The education of the Imperial children was wide-ranging, in order to prepare them for the duties entailed in the various positions they would hold in the monarchy, either in governmental, military, or religious offices. The daily routine of Habsburg children, documented in letters and directives in the palace archives, was crammed with instruction in many areas. Lessons in three foreign languages (Latin, Italian, and Spanish), German grammar and writing, religion, history, court protocol, fencing, dancing, and music filled their days. The children were allowed no unsupervised time alone, and discipline was strict.[4] Emperor Franz's active interest in music assured it a prominent place in a curriculum that emphasized cultural subjects.[5] The Emperor, an amateur violinist, enjoyed playing Haydn string quartets; his second wife, Empress Maria Thérèse (1772-1807), daughter of the Queen of Naples, sang the soprano solos when Haydn's *Die Jahreszeiten* and *Die Schöpfung* were performed at the court in 1801.[6]

---

[3]Novotny, "Kardinal Erzherzog Rudolph," 342-44.

[4]Novotny, "Kardinal Erzherzog Rudolph," 343.

[5]MacArdle, "Beethoven and the Archduke Rudolph," 37. MacArdle also traces Archduke Rudolph's musical heritage in the Habsburg ancestry; among composers were his great-great-grandfather, Leopold I (1640-1705), and great-grandfather, Karl VI (1685-1740), and his two uncles, Joseph II (1740-1790) and Maximilian Franz, Elector of Cologne (1756-1801).

[6]Dorothy Gies McGuigan, *The Habsburgs* (Garden City, New York: Doubleday and Co., 1966) 278-79. The Empress was the dedicatee of Beethoven's Septet, Opus 20, as well as of Haydn's *Theresienmesse.*

Of the three educators who oversaw Archduke Rudolph's early studies, the first was General Freiherr Haager von Altensteig (1722-1812), who was appointed "Ajo" [Italian: tutor] to the young Archdukes in 1792, when he was seventy years old, and whose importance in their lives was so great that Archduke Johann remarked in later years, "We had no real father, our father was General Haager."[7] A second educator was Sigismund Anton Graf von Hohewort (1720-1820), an ecclesiastic who later became Prince-Archbishop of Vienna, officiating at the numerous weddings and baptisms in the Imperial family. Most significant for Archduke Rudolph was the third educator, Joseph Baumeister (1750-1819), a distinguished jurist, historian, and man of letters, who became the tutor of the two youngest Archdukes, Ludwig and Rudolph, in 1792, and later served Rudolph exclusively as chamberlain, personal librarian and secretary, and friend. More will be learned of this individual later.

Neither Köchel, who made a thorough investigation of court records relating to music, nor Novotny appears to have found anything in those records that reveals when Archduke Rudolph began his music studies, or how extensive his early studies were. The foundations of his education in this respect remain a mystery. The first known music teacher of the Archduke (and his brothers) was the Court Composer, Anton Tayber (1754-1822), a thoroughly trained musician who had learned composition under Padre Martini and played clavier in the Imperial orchestra. A similar and far more important puzzle concerns the precise point at which Archduke Rudolph became Beethoven's pupil, since court records also lack that information; indeed, there are no records whatsoever of payments made to Beethoven for lessons. Thayer, knowing that previous researchers, including the "indefatigable" Köchel,[8] had been unable to establish the exact date of Beethoven's engagement, believed it was during the winter of 1803-04, around the time the Archduke was given his own retinue of Court personnel. Thayer based this conclusion at least partly on Anton Schindler's assertion that

---

[7]Novotny, "Kardinal Erzherzog Rudolph," 342.
[8]Thayer-Deiters-Riemann, *Beethovens Leben*, II, 544.

SANCTISSIMI DOMINI NOSTRI

PII

DIVINA PROVIDENTIA

PAPÆ VII.

ALLOCUTIO

HABITA IN CONSISTORIO SECRETO

Die IX. Septembris MDCCCV.

IN PROPOSITIONE COADJUTORIÆ

ECCLESIÆ OLOMUCENSIS

PRO REGIO PRINCIPE

RUDOLPHO ARCHIDUCE AUSTRIÆ.

ROMÆ MDCCCV.

Apud Lazarinum Rev. Cam. Apost. Typographum

Plate 3. Page from Vatican publication announcing Archduke Rudolph's
appointment as coadjutor of Archbishopric of Olmütz, 1805.
(Statní Oblastní Archiv, Olomouc).

4

Beethoven had written the piano part of the Concerto for Piano, Violin, and Violoncello ("Triple" Concerto) for Rudolph.[9] If such was the case, the Archduke, at age fifteen, was a pianist of considerable skill, and the reports that he performed to general satisfaction ("zu allgemeiner Befriedigung")[10] in the salons of Prince Lobkowitz and other music-loving members of the Viennese aristocracy would support Beethoven's willingness to entrust Rudolph with such demanding music. It seems reasonably certain that it was through such musical occasions, very probably at the Lobkowitz palace, that Archduke Rudolph first met Beethoven, an encounter which developed into a relationship—first as pupil, then also as friend and patron—that was the most enduring and least problematical that Beethoven ever maintained with anyone close to him.

Archduke Rudolph, like his brothers, was at first prepared for a military career; in 1804, at the age of sixteen, he was given the rank of *General-Feld-Wachtmeister*.[11] Shortly thereafter, however, he changed his direction, entered into training for a religious career, and in 1805 took the minor vows of the Catholic Church, with the rights of succession to the Archbishopric of Olmütz. The eminent historian of the Austrian Empire, Constantin von Wurzbach, attributed Rudolph's move toward an ecclesiastic life to his weak health and pious nature ("schwächliche Gesundheit und frommer Sinn").[12] The Archduke inherited the Habsburg predisposition to epilepsy and suffered frequently from seizures that left him an invalid for several days thereafter; in addition, he was subject to attacks of gout and rheumatism which crippled his hands and prevented him from playing the piano as early as 1814 when he was only twenty-six. These health problems necessitated repeated courses of treatment at the health spas of Baden and Teplitz. As for his pious character, this is

---

[9]*Anton Schindler's Beethoven-Biographie*, ed. A.C. Kalischer (Berlin und Leipzig: Schuster & Loeffler, 1909) 190. See also Anton Schindler, *Beethoven As I Knew Him*, ed. Donald W. MacArdle, trans. Constance S. Jolly (London: Faber & Faber, 1966) 140. Schindler's veracity has come more and more under suspicion in recent research developments, especially in connection with his forgeries in the Conversation Books. Although he would seem to have little reason to fabricate this particular assertion, one must approach all his statements with caution.

[10]Thayer, *Ludwig van Beethovens Leben*, II, 543.

[11]This rank, which has no precise equivalent in the United States Army, is roughly similar to a sergeant of field artillery; the title of "general" is in the nature of an honorary title.

[12]*Biographisches-Lexikon des Kaiserthums Österreich* IV (1861) 145.

borne out by contemporary reports of his gentleness and good nature as well as by the content of his surviving letters.

In June 1805 Rudolph was appointed coadjutor[13] of the Archbishopric of Olmütz with the then Cardinal Archbishop, Anton Theodor von Colloredo (1762-1811),[14] and given his own apartments in the Imperial palace, the Hofburg.[15] In the retinue of stewards and servants who attended him were Count Ferdinand von Laurençin d'Armont, who was his *Obersthofmeister* or Chief Steward; Joseph Freiherr (Baron) von Schweiger; and the two brothers, Counts Ferdinand and Franz de Troyer, who served as *Kammerherren*, or chamberlains. Both Ferdinand de Troyer (1781-1851),[16] who eventually became *Obersthofmeister*, and his brother Franz were skilled woodwind players; Rudolph dedicated his compositions for czakan[17] and piano to one or both of them. Ferdinand, who had studied clarinet with a then well-known performer, Joseph Friedlowsky,[18] at the Vienna Conservatory, was the dedicatee of Archduke Rudolph's Clarinet Sonata, published in 1822; he was also the person for whom Schubert composed his Octet in F, D. 803, in 1824.

Most important among the members of Archduke Rudolph's entourage was the aforementioned Joseph Baumeister, who devoted himself to the Archduke as a personal secretary and overseer of his constantly growing collection of music and books. Baumeister's ancestry included several individuals who had served in official government posts; his own father had been Court Chamberlain. Baumeister's scholarly credentials were impeccable; he had advanced degrees in law and history and was the author of several published works.[19] In addition to the intellectual services Baumeister performed for Rudolph, he was the Archduke's close friend and confidant.

[13]The position of coadjutor is held by a bishop who assists a diocesan bishop, and often has rights of succession.

[14]Not to be confused with the Archbishop of Salzburg, Count Hieronymus Colloredo (1732-1812).

[15]According to Schindler, it was in Rudolph's private apartments that Beethoven was introduced by Prince Razumovsky to Czar Alexander and other members of the Imperial Russian family in 1814. (See Schindler, *Biographie*, 98).

[16]The dates for d'Armont, Schweiger, and Franz de Troyer are unknown.

[17]The czakan was a type of flute. See chapter 5.

[18]Joseph Friedlowsky (b. 1775) played in the orchestra of the Theater an der Wien and performed several of Beethoven's works, including the Trio in B-flat for Clarinet, Cello, and Piano, Opus 11, and the Septet, Opus 20.

[19]These included a six-volume didactic history, *Die Welt in Bildern*; a political history of Styria; and genealogical tables of the Habsburg and Lorraine ancestral lineage.

Rudolph's letters to Baumeister, covering the period from 1809 to 1819, are rich in information about the Archduke's social relations, habits, interests, and everyday activities, and reveal a shared intimacy on many levels. Owing to the closeness between the two men, the letters, through their informal and familiar tone, convey those character traits of good nature and gentleness mentioned earlier, which are reinforced by anecdotes related by some members of the Beethoven circle.[20]

Rudolph regaled Baumeister with accounts of his visits and visitors, of hunts and country entertainments, and especially of the theater productions and concerts he attended. Much in these reports is amiable small talk—of the weather, of births, marriages, and deaths. The Archduke, who loved the theater and went as often as his health and the weather permitted, reported his views on the performances and requested reports from Baumeister on *his* reactions to theater events. References to plays, operas, and operettas attended, and to the actors and singers performing, are scattered throughout the letters written from Kremsier and Baden, particularly the latter, where so many of the Viennese arisocracy vacationed: "I am going this evening to *Johann von Paris,* which is being given for the first time,"[21] Rudolph wrote in June, 1813, and a few days later, "*Johann von Paris* was performed very well here last night."[22] During the same month, he wrote: "Yesterday we saw a very good performance of *Aline,*"[23] and in another letter, "I am glad that Mme. Grünbaum has met with your approval, and I am very curious to hear her soon

---

[20]Two anecdotes on this subject have often been repeated in the Beethoven literature. Schindler stated that Archduke Rudolph's soft and gentle voice enabled Beethoven to hear him with the aid only of his smallest ear-trumpet, at a time (1818) when he was forced to resort to conversation books as a means of communication (Thayer-Deiters-Riemann, *Beethovens Leben* IV, 151). Ferdinand Ries related an incident in which Archduke Rudolph, following Beethoven's angry objection to observing all the rules of court protocol regarding dress while visiting the palace, gave orders that the rules were to be overlooked when Beethoven came to give Rudolph lessons (Franz Wegeler and Ferdinand Ries, *Biographische Notizen über Ludwig van Beethoven* [Coblenz: 1838] 133).

[21]Letter in the Haus-, Hof- und Staatsarchiv, Vienna, Karton 52. This and all the following translations of Archduke Rudolph's letters are by the author, unless otherwise noted. Original German texts of passages quoted can be found in Appendix 2. *Johann von Paris (Jean de Paris),* a comic opera by Boieldieu, was written in 1812.

[22]*Ibid.,* letter of 11 June 1813.

[23]*Ibid.,* letter of 21 June 1813. Boieldieu's comic opera *Aline* was written in 1804.

myself."[24] In 1816 Rudolph wrote from Baden, "You will have gone to the theater today, and I expect a description of the performance of *Sargino* through Mlle. Teyber."[25] While at Kremsier in 1817, the Archduke wrote to Baumeister, "With pleasure I received . . . your letter and discovered that you are better, and were perhaps meanwhile at *Don Giovanni*."[26] In 1818, again from Baden, Rudolph wrote, "Have you heard Catalani, and how did you find her? They say she will sing here also."[27] In the same letter, Rudolph added that he was sending Baumeister the first part of a work by Caroline Pichler, which "will certainly amuse you, it pleased me also very much."[28] Earlier (in 1814) Rudolph had written to Baumeister at some length about Caroline Pichler's play *Rudolph von Habsburg*, which the author had evidently sent to the Archduke: "Give the poetess my thanks, and assure her that I have read this new work with much pleasure, and that I express the wish that it be performed soon with music on the level of the poetry."[29] Among other well-known performers seen by Archduke Rudolph and mentioned in his correspondence with Baumeister were the Viennese actors Ignaz Schuster (1779-1835) and Ferdinand Raimund (1791-1836), the latter very famous for his plays.

On other occasions, the Archduke expressed interest in Baumeister's hobbies, which seemingly had to do with various scientific devices. In one letter, for example, after telling Baumeister that he should "use the remaining money left over for a purpose of your own choosing," he added, "I am pleased with that 'cronographickum,' the more so because I wished for the contents with all my soul."[30] And in a letter

[24]*Ibid.*, letter of 29 June 1813. Theresa Grünbaum, née Müller (1791-1876), was a noted actress and singer.

[25]*Ibid.*, letter of 4 July 1816. *Sargino*, a "dramma eroicomico" by Paer, was written in 1803.

[26]*Ibid.*, letter of 17 September 1817.

[27]*Ibid.*, letter of 27 June 1818. Angelica Catalani (1780-1849), the famous Italian soprano, was touring Europe at the time this letter was written. In another letter from July, 1818, Rudolph enclosed a poem about Catalani which he had apparently written himself (the poem is not extant). Among the papers found in the Kremsier archive was a biographical history of her career.

[28]*Ibid.* On Caroline Pichler, see note 29.

[29]Letter in Stadt- und Landesbibliothek, I. N. 118, 12 June 1814. Caroline Pichler (1769-1843), well-known Viennese poetess and playwright, had offered Beethoven her play *Mathilde ou les Croisades* in 1814 for an opera libretto. Beethoven, although unable to use it, expressed a favorable opinion of it.

[30]Letter in Haus-, Hof- und Staatsarchiv, 18 July 1813. This oddly named instrument may have been some kind of metronome; Maelzel's metronome was originally called a "chronometer" (*Thayer's Life*, p. 545).

from 1819, Rudolph wrote: "Since I know your predilection for thermometers, I write to tell you that the heat in the shade drove it up to 29 degrees [centigrade]."[31]

While most of Archduke Rudolph's letters to Baumeister were written from Baden, especially during the summer months, a few from Kremsier contain several references to his contacts with the Catholic clergy. It is clear that when he was away from Vienna, much of Rudolph's time was occupied with clerical duties connected with the Archbishopric; these, too, he shared with Baumeister, who seemed to be acquainted personally with the clergymen. In letters from 1809, written from Ofen (Buda) where the Imperial family was living in exile, the Archduke sent his regards through Baumeister to various priests. In the years 1817-1819, when his elevation to Archbishop was approaching, his contacts with the Cardinal and other high-ranking clergy are mentioned frequently: "The Cardinal, who has all kinds of messages for you, is much better than in former years,"[32] Rudolph wrote from Kremsier in 1817; and in another letter ten days later, "The Cardinal yesterday ordained the new Bishop of Brünn, Stuffler, at which people from all over convened . . . Bishop Kollowrat was also there, in the company of Canon Souppé, who sends you greetings."[33] In 1818, from Baden, Rudolph wrote to Baumeister: "I can easily imagine that the unexpected visit of the Archbishop of Lemberg has given you much pleasure; it will please me also to see this worthy man again."[34]

Baumeister's health in his last years was as fragile as the Archduke's, and the letters are a virtual chronicle of the illnesses, sufferings, and convalescences undergone by both. Rudolph spent a good deal of time in bed because of ill health, took long courses of curative baths, and described vividly on several occasions the epilectic seizures he endured, which usually left him weak and in pain for many days afterward. One such attack was described in a letter to Baumeister written from Kremsier on November 4, 1818:

---

[31]*Sonntagsblätter*, 18. Heft, 419.
[32]Letter in Haus-, Hof- und Staatsarchiv, 12 September 1817. The Cardinal was Maria Thaddäus Graf zu Trauttmannsdorf (1761-1819), Archduke Rudolph's immediate predecessor.
[33]*Ibid.*, letter of 22 September 1817.
[34]*Ibid.*, letter of 24 July 1818.

Dearest Baumeister!

I would have written sooner, had I not, after the completion of 40 days, on the 27th of October in the morning, had an attack of my nervous condition [epilepsy]; but I must render thanks to the Almighty, because this time he let me off much more lightly. For, after two attacks, which were by themselves weaker than usual, I slept a good deal, and the head was not so dizzy, the cramps were much weaker, and today I shall again appear at the table. I then hope, with God's help, to be let off at least for another 40 days.[35]

With all his own suffering, however, Rudolph showed the utmost solicitude and devotion to Baumeister and *his* state of health. The sentiments expressed by the Archduke are touching and genuine; their tone of deeply-felt affection, respect, and gratitude suggests that, in fact, Baumeister filled the role of father-surrogate to Rudolph. He addresses Baumeister as "Dearest Baumeister," signs himself "Your grateful pupil" or "grateful friend," and unfailingly inquires about the members of Baumeister's family. In 1809, for example, after the treaties with Napoleon had been signed, the Archduke wrote to Baumeister: "You know what my thoughts have always been, hence you can easily imagine how happy I am to have peace, but how completely content I will finally be when I can assure you in person how much I will always be your grateful pupil."[36] In later years, especially in 1817-18, Rudolph wrote to Baumeister more frequently than ever. A large portion of a letter written in 1817 from Baden is given below to illustrate the caring, considerate expression that permeates all of Rudolph's letters to Baumeister:

Dearest Baumeister!

As sorry as I was to learn from your last letter that you have ended your country life, and that your new residence in the city at first did not suit you as well, I still hope that you will soon get accustomed to it, all the more as I believe that you would not have enjoyed it in those days anyway, as they were exceedingly hot, and since yesterday evening it has been raining continuously. I have been quite well since my last stay in Vienna and also went to the theater, where I made the acquaintance of a very good actor at the Josephstädter Theater, Herr Raymund, one

[35]Letter in Handschriftensammlung of Österreich Nationalbibliothek, 442/31-1.
[36]Haus-, Hof- und Staatsarchiv, no date or place.

of the better comedians in such roles I have seen . . . This morning I finished my cure with the 25th bath, and only wish, with God's help, to be as satisfied this coming winter with the results as I was last winter. I think I will come to Vienna September 4th, and hope to find you there quite well, as to my great joy you were already in much better condition the last time I saw you. I will stay there a few days to assure you once again in person how much I am forever

Your most devoted pupil, Archduke Rudolph

Give my regards to your children, and I hope the country air has a good effect on them too. My brothers and chamberlains always ask me about your health, and send you their regards.[37]

In one of his last letters to Baumeister, three months before the latter's death in October 1819, the Archduke wrote:

How often throughout the extraordinary heat that has plagued us for the last five days have I thought of you, my good Baumeister, how much you must be suffering; now that it is cooler again, you will be all the better, if God has heard my ardent prayers.[38]

While Archduke Rudolph was away from Vienna, Baumeister was in charge of maintaining his music library, and Rudolph relied on Baumeister to send him music or books from the collection as needed or desired, and to receive and catalogue new items acquired by the Archduke. There are continual references to the collection in the letters to Baumeister,[39] some samples of which follow:

I ask that you send me the Trios of Prince Louis Ferdinand of Prussia . . . I believe there are three or five Trios.[40]

At the next opportunity, please send me the Quartet of Prince Louis Ferdinand of Prussia, the one dedicated to Rode, with the parts; and the works of Domenico Scarlatti, but only those bound in blue.[41]

Please send me the variations on the March from Aschenbrödel by Hummel; the 3 Beethoven Sonatas dedicated to Salieri; of the works in

[37]*Ibid.*, letter of August 1817. "Raymund" is Ferdinand Raimund.
[38]*Sonntagsblätter*, 18. Heft, 419.
[39]Six of Beethoven's published letters are to Baumeister, most of them concerning the loan or return of the composer's manuscripts in the Archduke's library.
[40]Haus-, Hof- und Staatsarchiv, no date or place.
[41]*Ibid.*, letter of 25 August 1814.

strict style, the two volumes of Fugues and Sonatas by Händel; the *Anthologie musicale*, all volumes; and *Der Volkommene Kapellmeister* of Mattheson. [42]

Thank you for the music you sent; everything was correct except for one work by Jomelli—I asked for a *Missa* in manuscript, and received a printed *Miserere*. I am sending back to you more works which I no longer need, for you to file when you have the opportunity ... Also, when your health permits, please send me the enclosed list of works ... and also the catalogue of works for 4 hands, which I now need. [43]

Many of the letters quoted were written from Baden; evidently, while taking the curative baths, Archduke Rudolph devoted much of his time to studying different works, perhaps as a relaxation from his clerical duties. The variety of compositions requested indicates that his tastes and interests were wide-ranging, and his precise descriptions of individual items reveal his intimate knowledge of his vast collection.

The Archduke's ecclesiastical career had begun in 1805 with appointments first as domestic prelate of Olmütz, and shortly after as coadjutor to the Archbishopric, with rights of succession. [44] But when Cardinal-Archbishop Colloredo died in 1811, Rudolph chose to forego his rights, and Colloredo's seat was taken by Archbishop Maria Thaddäus Graf zu Trauttmannsdorf. A material factor in Rudolph's decision to postpone his succession could possibly have been the importance he attached to his involvement with Beethoven and his composition lessons with him. The twenty-three-year-old Archduke was beginning to develop his composition techniques in earnest, if we can judge from two works he composed in 1810, [45] shortly after the Imperial family's exile in Hungary (following the siege of Vienna) had ended. The assumption of the position of Archbishop, with its manifold and time-consuming duties, would surely have severely limited the time Rudolph needed for the perfection of his craft.

The critical events in Austrian history during this period—the

---

[42]Stadt- und Landesbibliothek, I. N. 118, letter of 12 June 1814.
[43]Haus-, Hof- und Staatsarchiv, letter of 1 July 1818.
[44]See note 13.
[45]The two compositions for czakan and piano (see chapter 5), a set of variations and a Divertissement dated respectively March and May 1810, and dedicated to Ferdinand and Franz de Troyer.

advance of the French army into Austrian territory, several important battles (in which Rudolph's brother, Archduke Karl, was involved as a military leader), the siege of Vienna, and Napoleon's occupation of the Imperial palace Schönbrunn—are only scantily alluded to in several letters written by Archduke Rudolph to an unnamed friend from the Imperial family's place of exile in Ofen (Buda), Hungary.[46] The letters, dated August 1809, contain chatty, inconsequential news, with numerous references to individuals who were apparently familiar to both the writer and the recipient of the letters. Rudolph describes guests, excursions, and visits taking place in and around the vicinity in precise detail. Familiar names of the aristocracy—Erdödy, Lichtenstein, Esterházy, and Schwarzenberg—are mentioned, as well as many references to "their Majesties," "the Emperor," and "my brothers." Napoleon is mentioned twice, so casually that one can infer that the Archduke was—perhaps by choice—quite isolated from State matters.

Although there are no allusions in these early letters to the Archduke's composing, he was in contact with Beethoven. In a letter to Baumeister dated December 1809, Rudolph wrote: "Give my New Year's greetings to Dobenz, Parkar, Zeiler, Lany, Teyber, and Beethoven, whom I thank for the Fantasie he sent, which I like very much."[47] In all the letters written to Baumeister in 1809, Beethoven's name is included with this group of individuals to whom Rudolph wished to be remembered.

The progress of Archduke Rudolph's relationship with Beethoven from the winter of 1803-04, when Rudolph presumably began to study with the composer, to the crucial year 1809, is not documented, as has been noted earlier, either by palace archival records showing payments to Beethoven or by letters.[48] Alan Tyson has pointed out

[46]These letters, addressed "Bester Freund," are in the Stadt- und Landesbibliothek (see Introduction). Their similarity to the letters to Baumeister, in content and in style, suggests that they were also written to him.

[47]Haus-, Hof- und Staatsarchiv, letter of 28 December 1809. Parkar and Lany were members of the clergy whose names occur frequently in Rudolph's early letters to Baumeister. Franz Zeiler (1751-1828), a renowned jurist, tutored all the Archdukes in law. The *Fantasie* for piano, Opus 77 (composed in October 1809), was a manuscript copy, according to a notation in Rudolph's catalogue. The catalogue entries of both the *Fantasie* and the Sonata in F-sharp, Opus 78, in fact, provide the sole evidence that the two works were completed that very month.

[48]The earliest letter with a reference to lessons is one Beethoven wrote to Baron Ignaz von Gleichenstein in February 1810 (Anderson, *Letters*, 264).

that the first unequivocal link between the two men can be assigned to 1807, when Beethoven decided to dedicate the Piano Concerto in G, Op. 58, to Rudolph.[49] Certainly by 1809 a strong bond existed between pupil and teacher, attested by several significant events. First and foremost was the joint annuity contract of March 1, undertaken by Archduke Rudolph, Prince Ferdinand Kinsky (1781-1812), and Prince Josef Lobkowitz (1772-1816) to counter the offer to Beethoven of the position of Kapellmeister at the court of Jerome Bonaparte, King of Westphalia. The agreement guaranteed Beethoven the annual sum of 4000 florins as long as he made his home in Vienna; Archduke Rudolph's portion of the annuity was 1500 florins, which he began paying immediately after the contract was signed.[50] When the Austrian currency was devalued in 1811 because of the effect of the recent wars on the economy, Rudolph promptly began paying Beethoven in so-called redemption bonds, which ensured that the new paper money (*Wiener Währung*) was equal in purchasing power to the promised amount in florins, and he continued these payments without fail until Beethoven's death. The defaults of the other two patrons—one through death, the other through bankruptcy—created difficulties for Beethoven for many years in his attempts to collect the annuity payments from their estates—difficulties which were resolved on more than one occasion through the intervention of the Archduke. The history of the annuity contract and its subsequent problems for Beethoven need not be detailed here;[51] the significant point is that Rudolph's act in retaining Beethoven for Vienna was not only the gesture of a generous patron of the arts—it also guaranteed for Rudolph the continuation of the flourishing musical relationship between the two men.

The departure of Archduke Rudolph and the Imperial family from Vienna in early May 1809 during the siege and occupation of the city

[49]Alan Tyson, "The 'Razumovsky' Quartets: Some Aspects of the Sources," in *Beethoven Studies 3* (Cambridge: Cambridge University Press, 1982) 107-140.

[50]Some useful statistics on living costs in Vienna at that time were cited by Alice M. Hanson in an unpublished paper, "Schubert's Position in Viennese Musical Life: A Social and Economic Perspective," delivered before the American Musicological Society in November 1981 in Boston, Mass. These indicate that a single man could live extremely well on 2000-4000 florins per annum; it then becomes evident that Beethoven's annuity, which constituted only a portion of his total income, was generous indeed.

[51]See Thayer-Deiters-Riemann, *Beethovens Leben* III, 116ff.

by the French army was commemorated by Beethoven in his Piano Sonata in E-flat, Opus 81a ("Les Adieux"). Beethoven's genuine sense of loss can perhaps be seen best in the projected title for the first movement that he noted down on one page of his sketches for the sonata: "Der Abschied—am 4ten Mai—gewidmet und aus dem Herzen geschrieben S. K. H. [Seiner Kaiserliche Hoheit]."[52]

If Archduke Rudolph needed proof of Beethoven's gratitude and devotion, it was abundantly provided over the next two decades by the number of dedications the composer made to him, more than to any other person. The quantity alone is noteworthy, but even more meaningful is the quality of these dedicated works, all of which are among Beethoven's choicest compositions. On more than one occasion Beethoven expressed himself on this subject: for example, in May 1809 in a letter to Breitkopf and Härtel requesting that the dedication of the two Piano Trios, Opus 70, be made to the Archduke, Beethoven said:

> I have noticed once or twice that when I happen to dedicate to someone else a work which he likes, he seems to be slightly aggrieved. He has become very fond of these trios. So no doubt he would again feel hurt if they were dedicated to someone else. But if it has already happened, there is nothing more to be done.[53]

Beethoven reiterated these sentiments in a letter to Rudolph concerning the dedication of the Piano Trio in B-flat, Opus 97 ("Archduke"), composed in 1811:

---

[52]Georg Kinsky and Hans Halm, *Das Werk Beethovens: Thematisch-Bibliographisches Verzeichnis seiner sämtlichen vollendeten Kompositionen* (Munich and Duisberg: G. Henle, 1955) 216. Beethoven presented Rudolph with the autograph of the sonata on the return of the Imperial family to Vienna early in 1810.

[53]Anderson, *Letters*, 230-31 (emended). On occasion, translations from these volumes have been emended by the present author in accordance with the German originals. In such instances the citation will include the word (emended). Original German texts of this and all other quotations from Beethoven's letters can be found in Appendix 2. Regarding the dedication of Opus 70, Beethoven's request did in fact come too late; the trios were published with a dedication to Countess Erdödy, following instructions Beethoven had given earlier to the publisher.

I am sending herewith the dedication of the trio to Y. I. H. It is stated on this work; but indeed all the works on which your name is stated and which are of any value whatsoever are intended for Y. I. H.[54]

The dedications to the Archduke had begun in 1808, with the publication of the Piano Concerto No. 4 in G, Opus 58. The Piano Sonata, Opus 81a, and the Piano Concerto No. 5 in E-flat, Opus 73 ("Emperor"), composed in 1809, were published in 1811, with dedications to Rudolph. According to Kinsky,[55] the cadenzas of the first four piano concertos, as well as the cadenza for the piano transcription of the Violin Concerto, had been written out by Beethoven in 1809 for Rudolph. Subsequent dedications of published works by Beethoven, in chronological order, were: the piano arrangement of the opera *Fidelio*, Opus 72b (by Moscheles), in 1814; the Sonata for Violin and Piano in G, Opus 96, and the Trio for Piano, Violin, and Violoncello in B-flat, Opus 97, in 1816; the Piano Sonata in B-flat, Opus 106 ("Hammerklavier") in 1819; the Piano Sonata in C Minor, Opus 111, in 1823;[56] the *Grosse Fuge* for String Quartet, Opus 133, and Beethoven's arrangement of it for piano four hands, Opus 134, in 1827; and finally, the work Beethoven himself referred to as his greatest achievement, the *Missa Solemnis*, which was completed in

[54]Anderson, *Letters*, 612 (emended). Beethoven habitually abbreviated the Archduke's title ("Your Imperial Highness") with initials. In the originals, he wrote "I. K. H." ("Ihro Kaiserliche Hoheit") or, on occasion, "E. K. H." (Euer Kaiserliche Hoheit").

[55]Kinsky-Halm, 36.

[56]The statement by Theodor Frimmel in his *Beethoven-Handbuch* (Leipzig: Breitkopf & Härtel, 1926) I, 86 to the effect that the dedication of Opus 111 was not made by Beethoven is incorrect, although the dedication of the sonata involved some conflicting directions on Beethoven's part. In May 1822 he offered to the Paris publisher Schlesinger the liberty of dedicating it to whomever he chose (Anderson, *Letters*, 944)—instructions he contradicted three months later, in August, 1822, telling Schlesinger that the sonata was to be dedicated to "His Imperial Highness, the Cardinal," and adding that he had already told Rudolph about the dedication (Anderson, *Letters*, 965). In a letter to the Schlesinger firm dated February 1823, Beethoven instructed them to make the dedication to Antonia Brentano, née Birkenstock (Anderson, *Letters*, 1003). The London edition published by Clementi & Co. was dedicated to Antonia Brentano, the Vienna edition of 1823 by Cappi & Diabelli to Archduke Rudolph. The same summer, Beethoven wrote to Rudolph: "As Y. I. H. seemed to enjoy hearing the C minor sonata, I thought that I should not be too presumptuous if I gave you the surprise of dedicating it to Your Highness". (Anderson, *Letters*, 1054).

1823 but not published until 1827.[57] The complete story of the Mass—its composition, Beethoven's attempts to acquire subscribers among European royalty, his negotiations with various publishers— is fully covered by Thayer and other biographers. For the present purposes, however, only Beethoven's own words to the Archduke need be quoted; they are from a letter Beethoven wrote in June 1819 to congratulate the Archduke on his elevation to Cardinal-Archbishop the previous April:

> The day on which a High Mass composed by me will be performed during the ceremonies solemnized for Y. I. H. will be the most glorious day of my life; and God will enlighten me so that my poor talents may contribute to the glorification of that day.[58]

The dedication of one other work, the music to *Egmont*, Opus 84, was also intended for Archduke Rudolph, but like the Trios, Opus 70, Beethoven's instructions to Breitkopf and Härtel, in a letter dated August 1810, came too late.[59] Completing this list of published works dedicated to the Archduke are several brief song-themes and canons: a four-voice song, "Seiner kaiserliche Hoheit . . . Alles Gute, alles Schöne (WoO 179), which has a choral introduction followed by a four-part canon; "O Hoffnung" (WoO 200), composed for Rudolph's use as a theme for variations (see Chapter 3); and the short parody Beethoven wrote in a letter using the "O Hoffnung" theme, "Erfüllung" (WoO 205e).

The letters of this period (from 1810 until 1819, when the Archduke became Archbishop) show that the close relationship between Rudolph and Beethoven went beyond that of pupil and teacher. Beethoven relied on Rudolph for far more than the annuity payments, and the Archduke extended his patronage in several ways. Although court records do not show payments to Beethoven for lessons, two of his letters contain references to some kind of compensation. In 1814, for example, Beethoven gave the Archduke "My most profound thanks for your gift,"[60] possibly a monetary one.

---

[57]See letters to C.F. Peters (5 June 1822) and Ferdinand Ries (6 July 1822) in Anderson, *Letters*, 947 and 953.
[58]*Ibid.*, 814-15.
[59]*Ibid.*, 287-88.
[60]*Ibid.*, 476.

Much later, in 1824, Beethoven complained in a letter to the publishing firm Schott & Söhne about the number of lessons he was required to give Archduke Rudolph during the summer months: "Yet," he added, "I cannot live on my income; and my pen is my only other means of support."[61] The implication is that indeed Beethoven was receiving remuneration for the lessons, and for financial reasons was forced to continue them. In 1823 in a letter to Ferdinand Ries, Beethoven wrote of the obligation toward the Archduke: "If I don't go to him, my absence is regarded as a *crimen legis majestatis*. The additional payment I receive consists in my having, moreover, to draw my miserable earnings by means of a *stamped form*."[62] Again, this appears to signify that Beethoven was being compensated by the Archduke specifically for lessons.

Another instance of Archduke Rudolph's generosity involved payments for Beethoven's lodgings. Rudolph wrote to Beethoven from Baden in 1813, "If your stay in this healthful and beautiful place has the same good effect on your condition, my intention in taking care of your lodgings would be completely fulfilled."[63] And in 1816, in a draft of a letter, Beethoven wrote to Rudolph, "I took the rooms thinking that Y. I. Highness would refund me to a small extent. Otherwise I would not have taken them."[64]

On at least one occasion the Archduke underwrote the copying costs of a Beethoven score.[65] Thayer reported, "It was already in 1809 his [Beethoven's] practice to grant manuscript copies of his new works for the collection of Archduke Rudolph,"[66] and it would seem likely that Rudolph willingly defrayed some of the copying costs as a form of payment to Beethoven.

The importance of Archduke Rudolph's music collection to Beethoven personally as well as to Beethoven scholarship cannot be overstated; not only did Rudolph's library contain an amazingly

[61]Anderson, *Letters*, 1150-51.

[62]*Ibid.*, 1032-33. The words *crimen majestatis* refer to an act of treason. The "stamped form" (*Stempel*) was the official document requiring a special stamp, available for purchase in tobacco stores, that had to be hand-cancelled. Apparently Beethoven found this requirement humiliating.

[63]This letter is printed in full in *Anton Schindler's Beethoven-Biographie*, 232. (See also Schindler, *Beethoven As I Knew Him*, 164).

[64]Anderson, *Letters*, 583.

[65]The Symphony No. 7 in A, Opus 92, which was to be played in a charity concert in Graz in 1812. (Anderson, *Letters*, 382).

[66]*Thayer's Life of Beethoven*, 469.

comprehensive assemblage of printed music (mostly works from the late seventeenth through early nineteenth centuries), along with hundreds of works in manuscript, but it served as a safe repository for all of Beethoven's music. The chaotic condition of Beethoven's household and the resultant disorder in his music manuscripts necessitated countless requests to the Archduke (or his librarian) to "borrow back" from the Archduke's well-ordered library specific works which the composer needed. Just a few examples from letters Beethoven wrote to Baumeister illustrate this point: "Will you please be so kind as to lend the Sonata in F for pianoforte *with horn* obbligato [Opus 17] just for today . . . I will send it back at once tomorrow morning";[67] "Most politely do I request you to lend me just for today my two trios for piano, violin, and violoncello [Opus 70] . . . If I remember rightly, His Imperial Highness has *copies of these works* in his library";[68] "I request you, Sir, to send me the parts of the Symphony in A [Opus 92] and *my score as well.* His Imperial Highness can always have this music again."[69] That Beethoven felt free to utilize the Archduke's library at will is demonstrated by a letter he wrote to Rudolph in 1819 while the latter was in Baden: "I was in Vienna [in order] to collect in Y. I. H.'s library what was most useful to me."[70]

In one instance, Archduke Rudolph's enthusiasm for a certain composition by Beethoven—the Piano Sonata in E Minor, Opus 90—was so great that he made his own manuscript copy of it from Beethoven's autograph. Rudolph's copy is identical in every detail down to the title page, including Beethoven's date of composition.[71] Beethoven's difficulty in retrieving his original manuscript from Rudolph is revealed in two letters from 1814 and 1815: "It would be very nice too if Y. I. H. would send me back the manuscript in my own handwriting of the last sonata";[72] and "Please be so gracious as to have the E minor sonata sent to me. I need it for proof-reading."[73] In addition there are several letters to the publisher Steiner, in one of

[67]Anderson, *Letters*, 304.

[68]*Ibid.*, 372-73.

[69]*Ibid.*, 435.

[70]*Ibid., Letters,* 822.

[71]The Archduke's own autograph of Opus 90 is in the Nationalbibliothek in Vienna (Wn COD 16570). Despite Rudolph's obvious affection for this sonata, Beethoven dedicated it to Count Moritz Lichnowsky.

[72]Anderson, *Letters*, 466.

[73]*Ibid.*, 506.

which Beethoven wrote, "If you no longer require the manuscript of the pianoforte sonata, please *lend* it to me, for the Archduke Rudolph had it from me some time ago and now wants it again."[74]

Another way Archduke Rudolph helped Beethoven professionally was in allowing him the use of palace rooms for rehearsals and performances of his new compositions. Several letters from Beethoven in 1811[75] and 1813[76] refer to such arrangements involving the hiring of musicians to play certain orchestral works, including the Overtures to *King Stephan*, Opus 117, and *Ruins of Athens*, Opus 113, at Archduke Rudolph's Hofburg apartments. Other requests called on the Archduke's influence; for example, in securing the University Hall for a concert ("My most humble request is that Y. I. H. would be so gracious as just to send word through Baron Schweiger to the former Rector Magnificus. Then I shall certainly secure this hall.")[77] Beethoven also suggested that the Archduke provide lodgings for the cellist Anton Kraft (1752-1820) at the palace in exchange for musical services,[78] and he asked Rudolph to furnish a recommendation for a position for the Kapellmeister Joseph Drechsler (1782-1852) in 1823.[79]

In personal matters, Archduke Rudolph, by virtue of his position in the Imperial family, was able to exercise considerable influence on Beethoven's behalf, and did so willingly. The earliest documented example of such aid pertained to Beethoven's problems with collecting the annuity payments from the estates of the two other benefactors who had signed the annuity contract, Prince Kinsky and Prince Lobkowitz, after the death of the former in 1812 and the bankruptcy of the latter in 1813. Numerous letters attest to Beethoven's attempts to obtain the promised payments, and he turned to Archduke Rudolph for help in 1814. There are a number of references to the Archduke's intervention in letters from that year, and in one, dated December 1814, Beethoven wrote to Rudolph: "You are indeed very gracious to me, so much so that I shall in no wise be able to deserve

---

[74]Anderson, *Letters*, 505.

[75]*Ibid.*, 344.

[76]*Ibid.*, 414.

[77]*Ibid.*, 428-29. Beethoven gave two concerts at the University Hall (on December 8 and December 12) with Johann Maelzel (1772-1838).

[78]*Ibid.*, 432. Until 1813, when this letter was written, Kraft had been in the service of Prince Lobkowitz.

[79]*Ibid.*, 1070.

your kindness. I render to Y. I. H. my most humble thanks for your obliging intervention in connection with my affair at Prague."[80]

In 1819, when the complexities of the fight over the guardianship of Beethoven's nephew Karl were causing Beethoven great anxiety and occupying much of his time, Rudolph proved equally helpful, interceding with his brother, Archduke Ludwig, and even with Emperor Franz, as Beethoven had requested. Unquestionably, the Imperial influence had great bearing on Beethoven's success in the litigation.

Beethoven was well aware of the value of his friendship with Archduke Rudolph, and took full advantage of this connection, as can be seen in his requests for other favors, such as asking the Archduke to guarantee loans.[81] In a letter of October 1819 to Dr. Johann Baptist Bach, Beethoven asserted with confidence, "His Imperial Highness, Eminence, and Cardinal, who treats me as a friend and not a servant, would, if necessary, promptly produce a testimonial about my moral character."[82] Again, in a letter to Karl Winter written in 1820, Beethoven stated, "My relations with His Imperial Highness the Archbishop of Olmütz entitle me to hope for several desirable favors from him."[83]

In the light of these examples of Archduke Rudolph's generous and admiring attitude toward Beethoven, one might feel bewildered at reading some of the composer's remarks about the Archduke in letters to other individuals. At various times, particularly after Rudolph had become Cardinal Archbishop, he was described by Beethoven as "weak,"[84] "niggardly,"[85] and the cause of his [Beethoven's] being "reduced to beggary."[86] The apparent ambivalence of Beethoven's attitude toward Rudolph had its roots in two matters: the position the composer had hoped (in vain) to obtain at the Court, and his dislike of the unremitting obligation of teaching the Archduke.

[80] Anderson, Letters, 478.

[81] Ibid., 907.

[82] Ibid., 851. Johann Bach (1779-1847), a lawyer, was Beethoven's consultant on legal matters, and executor of his will.

[83] Ibid., Letters, 879. Karl Winter (d. 1827) was an official involved in the litigation over the guardianship of Beethoven's nephew.

[84] Ibid., 906 (letter to Franz Brentano, 1820).

[85] Ibid., 956-57 (letter to Johann van Beethoven, 1822).

[86] Ibid., 760 (letter to Ferdinand Ries, 1818).

In the first case, it is clear that from the time the annuity contract was signed, Beethoven expected an official appointment at the Court as Imperial Kapellmeister—the very position he had been offered at the Westphalian court. His good friend Baron Ignaz von Gleichenstein (1778-1828) had drawn up a list of "conditions" for the contract, the third of which stated Beethoven's desire to have a Court position and his willingness to give up the annuity payments for the salary accompanying such a position.[87] The final document lacked any specific mention of a Court appointment, but Beethoven still expected one; two weeks after the contract was signed, he wrote to Gleichenstein:

> You will see from the enclosed document, my dear, kind Gleichenstein, how honorable my remaining here has now become for me— Moreover, the title of Imperial Kapellmeister is to follow.[88]

But the appointment never materialized, although Beethoven continued to entertain hopes that it would. Even in 1820, in a letter to the publisher Nikolaus Simrock, Beethoven referred to himself—perhaps unwittingly, perhaps satirically—as Archduke Rudolph's "chief Kapellmeister," while complaining that Rudolph "has not yet got enough money to pay me what is right and proper."[89] Letters from 1819 (to Ferdinand Ries) also made references to changes in Archduke Rudolph's position, from which Beethoven expected to profit somehow, although exactly how is not clear.[90] Surely the fault was not the Archduke's, for it would have been to his advantage to have Beethoven situated at the Court, where his presence would have assured Rudolph steady contact; but in this one area, the Archduke failed to be influential on Beethoven's behalf.

The other cause of Beethoven's frustration was his responsibility toward Rudolph as his teacher, a situation which engendered continual ambivalence in Beethoven's feelings, if one can take his letters as evidence. Of the hundred or so letters Beethoven wrote to Archduke Rudolph (and the several more to Baumeister), over half are explanations and apologies for missing lessons. The first of these

---

[87] Thayer-Deiters-Riemann, *Beethovens Leben* III, 124.

[88] Anderson, *Letters*, 219.

[89] *Ibid.*, 873.

[90] *Ibid.*, 793-805, letters of March 8 and March 20. In the first of these, Beethoven wrote, "At last the Archduke is assuming his office of Archbishop of Olmütz. But it may be a long while before there is an improvement in my situation."

was written in December 1810 to Baumeister ("During the last few days I have had a headache and today it is very severe . . . But I hope that it will be better tomorrow; and if it is, I will certainly wait upon His Highness in the evening.");[91] the last was in November 1824 ("Being ill when I returned from Baden, I was prevented from visiting Y. I. H. as I desired . . . Tomorrow morning I shall have the pleasure of waiting upon you.")[92] The pattern of postponing, apologizing, and asking to be excused is continued throughout the intervening years, and most of the time the explanations do not ring true. In short, it appears that Beethoven used any and every excuse to put off the obligation which he found increasingly onerous as time went on. A few samples from his letters to Rudolph over the years illustrate the rather hollow-sounding reasons Beethoven gave him for his absences:

(1812)
Since Sunday I have been ailing, although mentally, it is true, more than physically. I beg your pardon a thousand times for not having excused myself earlier.[93]

(1814)
I am still exhausted by fatiguing affairs, vexations, pleasure and delight, all intermingled and inflicted upon me at once. But I shall have the honor of waiting upon Y. I. H. in a few days.[94]

(1816)
I crave your indulgence for having stayed away so long. Notwithstanding my healthy appearance, I have all this time been really ill and suffering from nervous exhaustion.[95]

(1820)
I wanted to hasten into town tomorrow in order to wait upon Y. I. H., but no carriage was to be had.[96]

(1821)
How said I am that *jaundice*, from which I am suffering, prevents me from hastening immediately to Y. I. H.[97]

---

[91] Anderson, *Letters*, 300-301.
[92] *Ibid.*, 1150.
[93] *Ibid.*, 395.
[94] *Ibid.*, 476.
[95] *Ibid.,Letters*, 636 (emended).
[96] *Ibid.*, 897.
[97] *Ibid.*, 921.

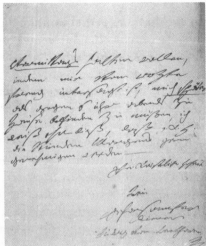
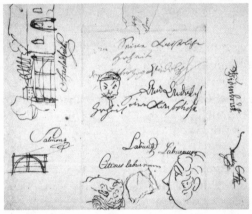

Plate 4. Facsimile of letter from Beethoven to Archduke Rudolph with
Rudolph's drawings on reverse (1816)
(Gesellschaft der Musikfreunde, Vienna).

Ihre Kaiserliche Hoheit!

Ich bin wieder genöthigt das Zimmer zu hüten, so unangen-
ehm es mir auch ist, deshalb nicht die Gnade bey I.K.H. zu
erscheinen zu haben, so muss ich mich doch mit Geduld darin
ergeben Unterdessen werde ich die gnädigste Nachsicht
I.K.H. night gar zu lange in Betreff meiner in Anspruch zu
nehmen genöthigt seyn, da ich recht bald hoffe ihnen aufwarten
zu können, so wie ich I.K.H. die beste volkommenste Gesundheit wünsche.

Ihro Kaiserliche Hoheit treu gehorsamster Diener
Ludwig van Beethoven

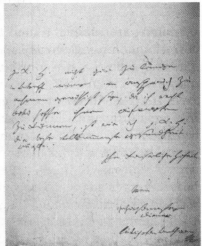

Plate 5. Facsimile of Beethoven letter to Archduke Rudolph with Rudolph's drawings on reverse side (1817) (Gesellschaft der Musikfreunde, Vienna).

Ihro Kaiserliche Hoheit!

Ich danke ihnen recht lebhaft für Ihre Gnädige Theilnahme an mir. Es geht mir wirklich besser und ich werde mich morgen selbst bei I.K.H. anfragen können, wie Sie es mit Ihren Stunden *vormittags* halten wollen, indem mir von Arzt streng untersagt ist, *mich später* als gegen 6 Uhr abends zu Hause befinden zu müssen. Ich weiss ohnedies, dass I.K.H. die Stunden morgens gern genehmigen werden.

Ihro Kaiserliche Hoheit treu gehorsamster Diener
Ludwig van Beethoven

There are remarks in some letters indicating that Beethoven was expected to give Rudolph several lessons a week at times—a schedule that makes Beethoven's many cancellations and excuses understandable. In 1816, for example, Beethoven referred to teaching the Archduke" at least three times a week."[98] Similar mentions can be read in letters from 1820[99] and 1822;[100] and in 1823, in a letter to Ferdinand Ries, Beethoven complained that during Rudolph's four-week stay in Vienna, he had been required to give him a lesson every day, sometimes lasting two-and-a-half, sometimes three hours each.[101] This kind of schedule was not the rule, of course, since the Archduke was away from Vienna for long periods of time, particularly after assuming the Archbishop's seat in 1819. Evidently, however, when he was in Beethoven's vicinity, he attempted to make up for lost time. It must have been extremely oppressive to Beethoven to find himself forced, even for a short period of time, to adhere to a rigid teaching schedule—an obligation that apparently brought him little personal satisfaction.

While Beethoven gave free expression to his negative feelings toward the Archduke in letters to intimates (see notes 84, 85, and 86), his letters to Rudolph are models of servility. In most of this correspondence, the language is artificial, and the exaggerated sentiments he expresses, like his excuses quoted earlier, have a hollow ring. To be sure, this was to some extent the accepted manner in which one addressed royalty; but Beethoven's writing style in his letters to the Archduke, aside from the conventional expressions, is unlike that used in his letters to others, even including members of the nobility. For example, Beethoven wrote to Archduke Rudolph in 1811:

> I am always desperately worried if I cannot be zealous in your service and if I cannot be with Y. I. H. as often as I like. It is most certainly true to say this privation causes me great suffering.[102]

And in 1816:

[98] Anderson, *Letters*, 567, letter to Archduke Rudolph.
[99] *Ibid.*, 905-906, letter to Nikolaus Simrock.
[100] *Ibid.*, 956-57, letter to Beethoven's brother, Johann.
[101] *Ibid.*, 1026.
[102] *Ibid.*, 317.

26

My warmest wishes begin with the New Year for the welfare of Y. I. H. With me, it is true, these wishes neither begin nor end. For every day I cherish these same wishes for Y. I. H. If I may add another wish for myself, then I should like Y. I. H. to allow me to grow and thrive daily in your grace and favor. The master will constantly strive not to be unworthy of the favor of his illustrious master and pupil.[103]

As if aware that Archduke Rudolph might entertain suspicions about his sincerity, Beethoven attempted to reassure him in a letter from 1820:

I do beg Y. I. H. to pay no attention to some reports about me. I have already heard in Vienna several remarks, which one might describe as gossip, with which people fancy that they can be of service even to Y. I. H. Since Y. I. H. calls me one of your precious possessions, then I can say with confidence that Y. I. H. is to me one of the most precious objects in the whole world . . . God keep Y. I. H. in perfect health for the benefit of humanity and, especially, of those who admire you.[104]

There were occasions, however, when Beethoven expressed positive and affectionate feelings towards Rudolph in letters to other individuals, and because these were unsolicited remarks, and Beethoven had nothing to gain from making them, they must be regarded as sincere utterances revealing genuine fondness for Rudolph. In 1810, for example, Beethoven referred to the Archduke as "an amiable and talented prince" in a letter to his friend Gleichenstein,[105] and in the same year he wrote to Breitkopf and Härtel, "There are no people *more small-minded than our great ones.* But I must make an exception in the case of Archdukes."[106] In 1823 Beethoven wrote to the publisher Nägeli regarding a proposed dedication to Rudolph, saying, "He understands music and is quite absorbed in it. He is so talented that I am sorry not to be able to take as much interest in him as I used to." And in a postscript, he added, "You need not approach him for permission for the dedication, because thus he will and ought to be surprised."[107] Beethoven's ambivalent feelings about Rudolph are summed up perfectly in a letter to his brother Johann written in 1822:

[103] Anderson, *Letters*, 626 (emended).
[104] *Ibid.*, 887.
[105] *Ibid.*, 265.
[106] *Ibid.*, 287.
[107] *Ibid.*, 1139 (emended).

The Cardinal Archbishop is here and I go to him twice a week. I have no hope of generous treatment or money, I admit. But I am on such a good, familiar footing with him that it would hurt me exceedingly not to be pleasant with him. Besides I do believe that his apparent niggardliness is not his fault.[108]

As for Archduke Rudolph's feelings toward Beethoven, no greater expression of his admiration and affection can be seen than in his good-natured tolerance of Beethoven's actions. The plain fact is that he willingly overlooked the negative side of Beethoven's attitude toward his lessons, and accepted his myriad excuses with indulgence. His belief in Beethoven's greatness, and his humble devotion to him as teacher, are revealed in a letter he wrote to Beethoven in 1820: "If only I were capable of producing something that would be worthy of you!"[109] For the Archduke, insofar as his music studies were concerned, Beethoven was certainly, as he himself put it in the letter quoted earlier (see page 27), a "precious possession." Under Beethoven's tutelage, Rudolph developed his skills as a pianist, studied music theory, and worked industriously to perfect himself in the craft of composition.

As a pianist, Rudolph must have been on a fairly high level by the time he first met Beethoven at Lobkowitz's palace in 1803-04. The earliest references to keyboard performances by Rudolph date from 1808 and 1809. Josef von Spaun (1788-1865), Schubert's close friend and colleague, told in his memoirs of being invited in the summer of 1808, while a student at the K.K. Stadtkonvikt and a member of the school orchestra, to perform at Schönbrunn before Archduke Rudolph. Beethoven was also present, and after the orchestra had played symphonies by Tayber and Haydn, Spaun related:

> The Archduke, who was very pleased, announced that he would also like to play something for us and that if we would undertake the difficult orchestral part he would play us a Mozart concerto in B-flat Major. We expressed our readiness at once and the Archduke played excellently.[110]

---

[108] Anderson, *Letters*, 957.

[109] Letter in Beethoven-Archiv, Bonn, dated 25 March 1820. The letter is translated in full in Marek, *Beethoven*, 324.

[110] *Schubert: Memoirs by His Friends*, ed. O.E. Deutsch (New York: Macmillan, 1958) 352-53. The Mozart concerto could have been either K. 450 or K. 456; both were in Rudolph's music collection.

In 1809, while Johann Friedrich Reichardt (1753-1814), composer, court conductor, and critic, was visiting Vienna, he heard Archduke Rudolph play on three separate occasions at Prince Lobkowitz's, and he commented on the concerts in his *Vertraute Briefe*, published in 1810. After the concert, in early January, he wrote:

> After dinner at Prince Lobkowitz . . . a great concert, in which the Archduke Rudolph, the Emperor's brother, played several of the hardest works of Prince Louis Ferdinand and Beethoven on the fortepiano, with much skill, precision, and feeling. Further, the Archduke is so modest and unassuming in his whole demeanor, and so informal, that it is easy to be near him.[111]

About three weeks later, another letter revealed the following:

> At a grand concert at Prince Lobkowitz's we again wonder at so rare and outstanding a talent in a Prince as has Archduke Rudolph. The Archduke played the most difficult concertos by Beethoven and sonatas by Prince Louis Ferdinand with great self-possession, repose, and accuracy.[112]

And the third, dated March 1:

> At Prince Lobkowitz's the beautiful quartet and evening concerts for Archduke Rudolph continued . . . Seidler distinguishes himself at each concert with his own concerto movements and with his excellent manner of accompanying the Archduke in the difficult Trios by Beethoven and Louis Ferdinand.[113]

Reichardt's enthusiastic appraisal of Rudolph's playing, which we have no reason to doubt was sincere despite its superlatives, was borne out by a report in 1813 by Franz Xaver Glöggl (1764-1839), who was the editor of the Linz *Musikalische Zeitung für die Oesterreichischen Staaten*. Glöggl heard the first performance of Beethoven's last violin sonata, Opus 96, dedicated to Archduke Rudolph, and

---

[111]J.F. Reichardt, *Vertraute Briefe auf einer Reise nach Wien und den Oesterreichischen Staaten zu Ende des Jahre 1808 und zu Anfang 1809* (Amsterdam, 1810) I, 294.

[112]Reichardt, *Vertraute Briefe*, 357 - 58.

[113]*Ibid.*, 467-68. Ferdinand August Seidler (b. 1778) had been a first violinist in the Königlichen preussischen Hofkapelle in Berlin. He settled in Vienna in 1811.

played by him with the famous French violinist Pierre Rode (1774-1830). The sonata was played twice—on 29 December 1812 and again on 7 January 1813—at Prince Lobkowitz's. Shortly before the first performance, Beethoven wrote to Rudolph about the sonata:

> The copyist will be able to begin work on the last movement very early tomorrow morning. As I am meantime writing some other works, he didn't press me very much with the last movement just to be punctual, the more so as in view of Rode's playing I have had to give more thought to the composition of this movement. In our Finales we like to have fairly brilliant passages, but R[ode] does not care for them—and so I have been rather held back.[114]

Beethoven's views on Rode's playing are not very clear; it appears, however, that he felt it was necessary to offer an explanation of why he was late in finishing the sonata in time for the performance. Perhaps there were still some rough spots in the sonata, for before the next performance Rudolph asked Beethoven to come to another rehearsal:

> Dear Beethoven,
>
> The day after tomorrow there will again be music at Prince Lobkowitz's . . . and I shall repeat the sonata with Rode. If your health and business permit, I would like to see you tomorrow at my place in order to play over the sonata.[115]

Glöggl, in reporting on the concert, had words of praise for Archduke Rudolph's performance:

> The great violinist Rode today played a new duet for pianoforte and violin with His Imperial Highness the Archduke Rudolph at Prince Lobkowitz's. The performance as a whole was good, but we must mention that the piano part was played far better, more in accordance with the spirit of the piece, and with more feeling than that of the violin.[116]

---

[114]Anderson, *Letters*, 391-92 (emended).
[115]Letter in Stadt- und Landesbibliothek, I. N. 25436 (n.d.).
[116]*Musikalische Zeitung für die Oesterreichischen Staaten*, II:4 (1813) 16.

It can be seen that Rudolph's interests and abilities as a pianist covered a wide range of repertoire and that he was at home in chamber music as well as solo music.

The Archduke had been plagued with physical problems affecting his hands since 1814; that year, in a letter to Prince Lobkowitz, who was an amateur violinist, Rudolph wrote:

> In my three-month-long illness . . . to my great sorrow . . . these gouty pains robbed me for a long time of the use of my hands, and thereby, of my greatest pleasure, piano-playing.[117]

Performances by Rudolph are not mentioned in any of his correspondence after that, but he evidently continued to practice and play when he was able to. A touching letter to Beethoven in 1816 confirms Rudolph's devotion to the piano; writing to thank Beethoven for sending him a copy of the newly engraved publication of Opus 96, he added:

> I am trying now to practice it well in order to add the art of the player to the art of the composer and the publisher, who by a really beautiful edition paid a well-deserved tribute.[118]

The painful arthritic ailment was undoubtedly a contributing factor in causing the piano to take a secondary place to composition in Archduke Rudolph's life after 1814. An additional factor in Rudolph's increased dedication to composing, which goes back at least to 1810,[119] must surely have been the inspiration and stimulation that resulted from having Beethoven as a teacher. Despite the many cancellations of lessons and excuses by Beethoven, he continued to teach Rudolph conscientiously and, for the Archduke, with beneficial results.

The evidence for this, of course, is the sizable number of works Rudolph composed and the hundreds of pages of manuscript

---

[117]Thayer, *Beethovens Leben* III, 492.

[118]Letter in Stadt- und Landesbibliothek, I. N. 68557 (16 July 1816).

[119]The earliest dated works are the two for czakan (a type of flute) and piano referred to earlier; however, the title page of a set of piano variations in the Kroměříž archive reads: "Premier composition de son A.I. Monseigneur l'Archiduc Rodolphe d'Autriche," suggesting an earlier date of composition than 1810. See Introduction for discussion of the dating of other early works.

sketches that attest to the diligence with which he struggled with the creative process—sketching, discarding, and working through his musical ideas.

Exactly when Archduke Rudolph's lessons with Beethoven came to an end is uncertain; letters from Beethoven to Schott at the end of 1824 (like the one to Ferdinand Ries from 1823 cited earlier) mention concentrated periods of teaching the Archduke every day while both were in Vienna,[120] but I have found no documentation about lessons subsequent to that year. The work accomplished in the personal meetings between teacher and pupil must have been substantial, for there was rarely any communication of instructive advice in Beethoven's letters to Rudolph; for this reason, the two instances of such advice on the procedures of composing preserved in letters from Beethoven to the Archduke are of special interest. The first was written in July 1823, while Beethoven was in Hetzendorf for the summer months; his letter asks Rudolph to "be patient a little longer about Y. I. H.'s variations," which the Archduke had evidently given him earlier for his examination and correction.[121] Beethoven then proceeds with his advice:

> Y. I. H. must now continue, in particular, your exercises in composition, and when sitting at the pianoforte you should jot down your ideas in the form of sketches. For this purpose you should have a small table beside the pianoforte. In this way not only is one's imagination stimulated but one also learns to pin down immediately the most remote ideas. You should also compose without a pianoforte; and you should sometimes work out a simple melody, for instance, a chorale with simple and again with different harmonies according to the laws of counterpoint and even beyond the latter. This will certainly not give Y. I. H. a headache; nay, rather, it will afford you real enjoyment when you thus find yourself in the very swim of artistic production.[122]

It is noteworthy that Beethoven's instructions to Rudolph seem aimed at providing him with a good deal of latitude—to experiment with harmony, and to pass from strict to free counterpoint. Earlier in the same year (3 March 1823) Beethoven had given some different

---

[120]Anderson, *Letters*, 1054-56.

[121]This refers to Rudolph's *Variations in E-flat for Clarinet and Piano* on a theme by Rossini (see chapter 5).

[122]Anderson, *Letters*, 1054-56 (emended).

instruction to Rudolph by letter; after first apologizing for his delay in writing, Beethoven wrote:

> I have noted the progress in Y. I. H.'s exercises; still, unfortunately, misunderstandings can be found there. The best method is to realize figured basses by good composers, and now and then to compose a four-voice song, and until I have the good fortune to be again with Y. I. H., even to compose in four voices for the piano; it may have good results, although it is more difficult, as the ascending and descending of the voices is not so natural as in vocal music.[123]

In view of the fact that two large-scale compositions of Archduke Rudolph had already been published, this detailed advice and the critical remarks on errors in exercises seem rather elementary. But the Archduke certainly put Beethoven's suggestions into practice; there are abundant sketches for the compositions which Rudolph was working on at this time. In fact, the Archduke's methods of working out his ideas, in very rough fashion, using his own system of notational shorthand, with large X's to mark passages to be changed or discarded, are very similar to those used by Beethoven in his sketchbooks.

Archduke Rudolph's development as a composer can be traced through his compositions, beginning with his earliest works ca. 1809-1810, and ending with those from his maturity, ca. 1824. The methods used to arrive at a chronology for his works have been described in the Introduction; the dating of individual works and their relationship to Beethoven's teaching is discussed in chapters 2 through 8. All evidence points to the conclusion that, in the main, Rudolph's compositions are the products of his studies with Beethoven.

As a patron of music, Archduke Rudolph maintained one other connection of significance—that with the Gesellschaft der Musik-freunde in Vienna. This institution, whose aims were to further the preservation and performance of music in the city, was established in 1812 at that critical juncture in Austrian history when the nation was devastated by war and economic failure. In order to ensure the survival of the Gesellschaft, Imperial support was sought in 1814, and it was to Archduke Rudolph, the most prominent musical member of

---

[123]From a letter printed in full in the J.A. Stargardt auction catalogue (No. 601) of 20/21 February 1973 (Morgan Library). Translation by author.

the Habsburg family, that the founders turned. With Emperor Franz's permission, Archduke Rudolph became the first Protector of the Gesellschaft, an act of patronage that did not involve financial support but which provided the necessary governmental aegis. More importantly, the Archduke bequeathed his vast music and music book collection to the library of the Gesellschaft upon his death. In paragraph twenty-two of his last will and testament, dated 9 October 1827, Rudolph gave:

> To the Vienna Musikverein, of which I am Protector, my entire music collection, including the music library, as it is laid out in the music room at Kremsier.[124]

While this directive seems to have no exclusions, the collection that went to Vienna in 1834, three years after Rudolph's death, did not include his own compositions. Except for a handful of manuscripts (some autographs, some copies), which had probably been either in private hands or already in the Gesellschaft library prior to the Archduke's death, the bulk of his compositions and all of his sketches remained in the castle archive in Kremsier.

To round out the picture of Archduke Rudolph's life, certain other creative interests deserve mention. One of these, an occupation to which he apparently devoted considerable time, was copperplate engraving; he also did sketching, drawing, and painting. Two letters to Baumeister contain references to his art work; in one, written from Prague in 1812, Rudolph asks Baumeister to send him "a piece of black chalk,"[125] and in the other, from Baden in 1816, Rudolph wrote, "Yesterday for the first time I once again began to sketch, which is going passably well."[126] In the tenth paragraph of his will, following bequests of various personal items to his brothers Karl, Joseph, Anton, Johann, Rainer, and Ludwig, Rudolph bequeathed to his eldest sister, Maria Theresia (1767-1827), "the portrait of Empress

---

[124]Haus-, Hof- und Staatsarchiv, ÖMaM, carton 226, etc.
[125]Letter in Haus-, Hof- under Staatsarchiv, 14 June 1812.
[126]*Ibid.*, 5 August 1816.

Louise which I myself painted."[127] Unfortunately, the whereabouts of any examples of Rudolph's art works are unknown; his productivity as an artist, however, is documented by a large catalogue in the Kroměříž castle archive, imaginatively designed and handsomely illustrated by him, in which he recorded a collection of books on various subjects, maps, and engravings.[128] On each page, a large painting depicts a standing bookcase with the contents of the shelves laid out (see illustration on p. 287). On one page, under the heading "Handzeichnungen S. Kais. Hoheit," is a depiction of six shelves of art works in different categories:

I. *Verschiedene Handzeichnungen*
II. *Köpfe, Figuren, Historische Stücke*
III. *Portraits*
IV. *Thiere, Landschaften, Ansichten*
V. *Blumen, Vignetten, Billets*
VI. *Miscellen*

When Rudolph became Cardinal Archbishop in 1820, his clerical duties, and probably the ceremonies connected with his State duties as well, took up a great deal of time. A few casual comments in his letters refer to the pressure from these activities, even before his enthronement took place; for instance, in a letter to Baumeister from Prague in 1812, Rudolph wrote, "I cannot write more from being fatigued by taking rides, from formalities, climbing stairs, and changing clothes."[129] And in a letter to Beethoven in 1820, the Archduke wrote, "I will send you something as soon as I have finished it (until now I haven't had a moment for it) for the correction of my mistakes and my instruction."[130]

After his enthronement, aside from the time spent at the spas taking curative baths, Archduke Rudolph's principal residences were in the Kremsier castle and, when performing duties related to the

---

[127]Maria Theresia was the wife of Anton, Prince (later King) of Saxony. Between the writing of the first draft of his will, at Bad Ischl on 6 August 1827, and the final one written in Vienna on 27 October 1827, Maria Theresia died, and Rudolph added a note that the portrait was to go to Anton instead. Empress Louise was Rudolph's niece, Marie Louise, daughter of Emperor Franz, who was married to Napoleon in 1810.

[128]Sign. Ž/b I 525.

[129]Letter in Haus-, Hof- und Staatsarchiv, 14 June 1812.

[130]Letter in the Beethoven-Archiv, Bonn, 25 March 1820 (see note 109).

Archbishopric, in Olmütz. Since his contacts with Beethoven were necessarily limited to those times when he visited Vienna or Baden, the lessons became less frequent, but they continued, as was noted earlier, at least through November 1824. Undoubtedly the poor health of both pupil and teacher, combined with the demands made on the Archduke's time by his clerical duties and other activities, brought about a gradual end to the teaching relationship, and with that, an end to the Archduke's activity as a composer. His name comes up fairly frequently in Beethoven's Conversation Books, and in the latter's correspondence with publishers after 1824, principally in references to the dedication of the *Missa Solemnis*. Friedrich Wieck (1785-1873) visited Beethoven in Vienna in 1826 and later reported, without giving further details, a conversation in which Archduke Rudolph was discussed.[131] That Beethoven still gave thought to the Archduke's musical development can be seen in a moving letter he wrote from his deathbed in 1827 to Johann Andreas Stumpff in London, thanking him for his gift of the newly published complete Handel edition; in the letter, Beethoven added, "In regard to supplying Handel's works to His Imperial Highness the Archduke Rudolph, I have nothing exact to say till now. In a few days I will write to him and draw his attention to this suggestion."[132] If Beethoven did write to Rudolph, the letter is lost; but the London edition of Handel's works, in forty calf-bound volumes, was in fact in Rudolph's library, and remains today at the Gesellschaft der Musikfreunde as part of the Archduke's bequest.

Immediately following Beethoven's death on March 26, 1827, Rudolph paid one last act of tribute to his teacher: he gathered the obituary notices and memorial articles from various newspapers and journals, and carefully copied them out word for word. In the Handschriftensammlung of the Österreichische Nationalbibliothek are two pages of notices from the *Österreichischer Beobachter, Der Wanderer,* and the *Allgemeine Zeitung,* including a description of Beethoven's funeral.[133] The four closely-written manuscript pages in the archive of the Gesellschaft der Musikfreunde contain, in addition to similar notices, the lengthy Necrology by Friedrich Rochlitz that

---

[131]Thayer-Deiters-Riemann, *Beethovens Leben* V, 342.

[132]Anderson, *Letters,* 1332-33 (emended). Stumpff (1769-1846) was a harp manufacturer who seems to have served as a middleman in deals involving music.

[133]Siglum 125/71.

appeared in the *Allgemeine musikalische Zeitung,* and two poems published in the *Allgemeine Theaterzeitung:* a "Fantasie an Beethoven's Grabe" and another titled "Louis van Beethoven's Sterbetag."[134]

In his last years, Archduke Rudolph busied himself with projects far removed from music. In 1827, he was instrumental in bringing about the return to Ölmutz of the Hochschule from the city of Brünn (now Brno), to which it had been transferred in 1778. In addition, he participated in founding the Witkowitzer Iron Works in 1829, where, for the first time in Austria, a modern English method of "puddling," or converting pig iron into wrought iron, was adopted.[135]

On 23 July 1831, while taking a cure in Baden, Archduke Rudolph died suddenly of a cerebral hemorrhage. He was forty-three years old. His body was interred in the Habsburg family crypt in Vienna, but his heart, removed earlier, was buried in the walls of the Cathedral of St. Wenceslas in Olmütz, seat of his archbishopric. Commemorating the site in a niche of the Cathedral wall there is a small bust of Rudolph; beneath it, an inscription reads:

RUDOLPHI

Archiducis • Purpurati • Antistitis

Olomucensis

COR

Quo• vivus• suos• erat• amplexus

Hic • Servatur

Perpetuum • Caritatis • Symbolum[136]

---

[134]No catalogue number. The authors of the two poems were Heinrich Börnstein and Paul Friedrich Walther, respectively.

[135]Novotny, "Kardinal Erzherzog Rudolph," 345. The Archduke added a codicil to his will, dated 14 August 1830, pertaining to the disposition of his considerable share in the ironworks after his death.

[136]"Of Rudolph, Archduke, Cardinal, Archbishop of Olmütz, the heart, in which when alive he lovingly held his [people], here will serve as a perpetual symbol of his benevolence."

Plate 6. Archduke Rudolph, 1805.
Oil painting by Johann Baptist Lampi the Elder (Kroměříž, Czechoslovakia).

Plate 7. Archduke Rudolph as a youth. Miniature
(Österreichische Nationalbibliothek, Vienna).

Plate 8. Archduke Rudolph in uniform. Engraving by Blasius Höfel after a painting by Natale Schiavoni (Österreichische Nationalbibliothek, Vienna).

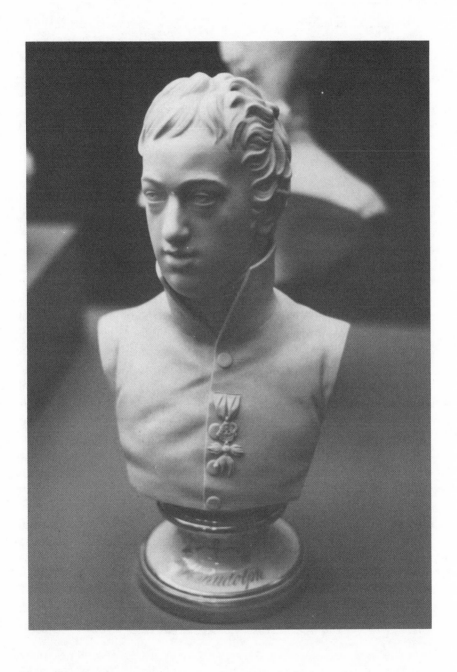

Plate 9. Archduke Rudolph in uniform. Bust in Österreichisches Museum für angewandte Kunst (Vienna).

Serenissimo Ridolphus Joannes Josephus Rainerius
Archidux Austriae Archiepiscop: Olmutiensis in Moravia
Tituli S. Petri in Montorio, S.R.E. Presbyter Card. venunciatius à SS.
D.N.PP. PIO VII. in Consist. secreto Palatii Quirinali die 4 Junius 1819.

Plate 10. Archduke Rudolph, Archbishop of Olmütz, 1819. Engraving after a
drawing by Giangiacomo (Österreichische Nationalbibliothek, Vienna).

42

Plate 11. Archduke Rudolph, Archbishop of Olmütz, ca. 1819.
(Gesellschaft der Musikfreunde, Vienna).

Plate 12. Archduke Rudolph, Archbishop of Olmütz, 1819.
Lithograph by Kunike (Kroměříž, Czechoslovakia).

Plate 13. Archduke Rudolph, Archbishop of Olmütz, 1819.
Oil painting by Friedrich von Amerling (Laxenburg Castle, Vienna).

Plate 14. Archduke Rudolph, Cardinal-Archbishop of Olmütz. Oil painting
by Johannes Dittmann, 1822 (Kroměříž, Czechoslovakia).

Plate 15. Archduke Rudolph, Cardinal-Archbishop of Olmütz.
Engraving after a painting by Adalbert Suchy
(Österreichische Nationalbibliothek, Vienna).

47

Plate 16. Archduke Rudolph, Cardinal-Archbishop of Olmütz, 1823.
Lithograph after an engraving by Lanzedelly
(Gesellschaft der Musikfreunde, Vienna).

Plate 17. Archduke Rudolph, Cardinal-Archbishop of Olmütz.
Miniature by Joseph Eduard Teltscher
(Österreichische Nationalbibliothek, Vienna).

Plate 18. Archduke Rudolph (Plaque in Gesellschaft der Musikfreunde, Vienna).

Plate 19. Archduke Rudolph, Cardinal-Archbishop of Olmütz.
Oil painting by Johann Baptist Lampi the Younger, ca. 1825
(Historisches Museum der Stadt Wien, Vienna).

Plate 20. Kroměříž Castle (Kroměříž, Czechoslovakia).

CHAPTER II

Archduke Rudolph's Studies in Music Theory

The lack of precise knowledge about Archduke Rudolph's early formal training in the fundamentals of music theory is a hindrance to a complete understanding and assessment of his development from music student to full-fledged composer. As was noted in chapter 1, his first teacher was the Court Composer, Anton Tayber, who taught all the Imperial children the rudiments of music, and it is believed that Tayber was followed by Beethoven, possibly around 1804. That by 1810, or slightly earlier, Rudolph has mastered fundamental precepts of music composition, including harmony and counterpoint, is demonstrated by two compositions dated March and May, 1810, respectively.[1] This presupposes a series of progressive lessons involving exercises in writing out four-part harmony, realizing figured bass melodies, and contrapuntal pieces following basic rules; it is particularly puzzling, therefore, to find that despite Rudolph's preservation of seemingly every scrap of paper on which he sketched, only a scant seventeen pages of theoretical exercises are

[1]The two compositions for czakan and piano, composed shortly after the Imperial family returned from exile in Hungary, are discussed in detail in chapter 5. A set of piano variations and a group of *Ländler* for piano, both of which appear to predate the czakan compositions, are discussed in chapter 4.

extant among his manuscripts, and these are undated and devoid of any corrections.

While nothing as comprehensive as the course of study Thomas Attwood pursued under Mozart[2] exists in Rudolph's papers, there is evidence in other sources that his theoretical studies were quite thorough, continuing throughout his relationship with Beethoven. These studies apparently began to be systematic after the summer of 1809 when, according to Thayer, Beethoven occupied himself during the difficult months while Vienna was under bombardment and siege by the French army and the Imperial family was in exile in Ofen (Buda), Hungary, "selecting and copying in order extracts from the theoretical works of C.P.E. Bach, Türk, Kirnberger, Fux, and Albrechtsberger for subsequent use in the instruction of Archduke Rudolph."[3] This collection of extracts, in five thick packets, had been purchased by the Viennese music publisher Tobias Haslinger at the auction of Beethoven's *Nachlass* in October 1827.[4] Haslinger turned them over to Ignaz von Seyfried (1776-1841), who published them in 1832 as the products of Beethoven's own studies in thoroughbass, counterpoint, and composition.[5] In 1872 Nottebohm made a searching investigation of the Seyfried publications and established that a good part of Beethoven's "studies" were, in fact, a comprehensive and methodical course in the fundamentals of music theory, prepared by him, Nottebohm surmised, for the instruction of his only student,

---

[2]Thomas Attwood (1765-1838), an English organist and composer, studied with Mozart during the years 1783 to 1787. See Erich Hertzmann *et al.*, *Thomas Attwoods Theorie- und Kompositionsstudien bei Mozart* (Kassel: Bärenreiter, 1965).

[3]*Thayer's Life of Beethoven*, 467. Thayer took his view of Beethoven's purpose in assembling the extracts from Gustav Nottebohm, whose investigation of these materials led him to connect their didactic nature with Beethoven's teaching of Rudolph. I am grateful to Richard Kramer for his helpful comments on and clarification of this subject.

[4]The report on the auction published in the *Harmonicon* in April 1828 noted that the sale of the extracts provoked considerable interest: "But by far the most interesting article of the whole sale fell to the lot of M. Haslinger—the collection of contrapuntic exercises, essays and finished pieces, which Beethoven wrote while under the tuition of his master, the celebrated Albrechtsberger, all in his own handwriting, with the interlineal corrections of that master, and his remarks on the margin ... We are happy to be able to state that this collection of studies, so interesting to the whole musical world, is immediately to be placed in the hands of Kapellmeister Seyfried, who is to prepare it for press." (*Thayer's Life of Beethoven*, 1071).

[5]Ignaz Ritter von Seyfried, *Ludwig van Beethovens Studien im Generalbasse, Contrapuncte, und in der Compositionslehre* (Vienna: T. Haslinger, 1832).

Archduke Rudolph.[6] Since these extracts were in Beethoven's possession at the time of his death, it is probable that he copied them out as a guide or outline to deal with specific problems in Rudolph's work as they arose.[7]

Another area of instruction involved counterpoint. In a letter to Haslinger from 1822, requesting a copy of Kirnberger, Beethoven wrote, "At the moment I am teaching counterpoint to someone and have not been able to find my own manuscript on this subject among my untidy piles of paper."[8] The "someone" was most likely Archduke Rudolph,[9] and the lessons in counterpoint, even as late as 1822, may well have been prompted by Rudolph's work on a fugue variation on Diabelli's waltz theme (see chapter 4). From these specific references to Beethoven's teaching, along with the recurrent mention of lessons in Beethoven's correspondence with the Archduke and others, we can surmise that Rudolph's studies with Beethoven embodied, over the course of the years, continual work in the fundamentals of theory and composition.

1. THEORETICAL EXERCISES

The seventeen extant pages of exercises in the Archduke's hand are divided between the Gesellschaft der Musikfreunde and the archive in Kroměříž. The Gesellschaft manuscripts consist of eight pages (Wgm VII 42287), and those in Kroměříž of nine pages scattered through the various sketch miscellanea (KRa A 4429, 4431, and 4385).

---

[6]Gustav Nottebohm, *Beethoveniana* (New York: Johnson Reprints, 1970 [reprint of 1872 edition] 154-203). Seyfried may have been justified in his belief that the extracts were Beethoven's student exercises, since they were in his hand; however, as Nottebohm points out, changes and omissions by Seyfried constituted misrepresentation on his part.

[7]One page of Beethoven's autograph is in the Library of Congress in Washington, D.C. (see Otto Albrecht, "Beethoven Autographs in the United States," in *Beiträge zur Beethoven-Bibliographie,* ed. Kurt Dorfmüller [Munich: Henle Verlag, 1978] 1-11).

[8]Anderson, *Letters,* 974. The date of 1817 for this letter is given erroneously by Georg Schünemann, "Beethovens Studien zur Instrumentation," *Beethoven-Jahrbuch* (1938) 146-61, following Nottebohm, *Beethovenia,* 200. Evidence for the 1822 date is provided by Beethoven's reference in the letter to a performance of the Overture to *King Stephan,* Op. 117, which took place in October of that year in Baden.

[9]The same letter is printed in MacArdle & Misch, *New Beethoven Letters,* 389-90. In a footnote, the editors identify the "someone" as Beethoven's nephew Karl.

The Gesellschaft manuscripts are titled *Elementi del Contrapunto*; on the first two pages, seven rules relating to first species counter-point are written out in Italian in neat script. The remaining six pages contain a series of fundamental chord layouts: the seven chords of each scale, in root position, first inversion, and second inversion; a simple chord progression (I-V-I-IV-I-IV-V-I) in every key, and with different bass lines; and finally, two pages of two-voice contrapuntal-harmonic exercises, in which one voice is labeled "canto fermo" and the other "Nota contra nota," with chord numbers between the two lines (Example 2-1):

Example 2-1. Archduke Rudolph, *Elementi del Contrapunto* (transcription)

At the bottom of the final page is a heading: "Seconde specie di Contrapunto," with the first rule given; the rest is apparently lost.

Among the similar materials in Kroměříž are two pages of four-stave harmonizations (soprano, soprano, alto, bass) over a figured-bass line; four other pages contain piano-score realizations of figured-bass progressions. On one page Rudolph did a considerable amount of doodling (there are examples of costume sketches and caricatures of faces on several other manuscripts of the Archduke's); there is a rather crude sketch of a house, such as a child might draw, and the word *Degenschild* written out several times.[10] One other page, partially filled with chordal exercises, has a sketch for a variation on Diabelli's waltz theme—one that bears no resemblance to the fugue Rudolph composed for the Diabelli set (see chapter 4). The final page is crowded with figured-bass exercises; one is a complete section of an unidentified Baroque composition; the other is the bass line only, with chord numbers beneath it, of the accompaniment to the opening measures of the slow movement of Beethoven's Piano Sonata in F Minor, Opus 57 ("Appassionata").

[10]This may refer to the name of a woman composer (Fanny von Degenschild) who is listed in one of Archduke Rudolph's music catalogues.

One other item, not related to composition but still classified as an exercise, bears mentioning—two pages with fingerings for chromatic thirds, for each hand (Example 2-2):

Example 2-2. Archduke Rudolph, Sketches (KRa A 4431)

None of these manuscript pages can be dated with certainty, but to judge from the clef signs, many appear to have been written after the Archduke began his studies with Beethoven. Little seems to have survived from Rudolph's earliest lessons with Tayber, perhaps because Rudolph did not think them worthy of preserving.

The seventeen extant pages of exercises do not offer much in illuminating Archduke Rudolph's development as a student of composition, but fortunately, his compositions—from the earliest to the last—along with hundreds of sketches, provide the material to witness his development as a composer. It is to these compositions that we now turn.

2. TRANSCRIPTIONS AND ARRANGEMENTS

The time-honored method of perfecting one's craft as a composer by copying out and arranging the works of master composers was practiced extensively by Archduke Rudolph. Along with his own compositions in the Kroměříž archive one finds copies, transcriptions, and arrangements, largely hitherto unidentified, of works by Beethoven, Mozart, Handel, Gluck, J.S. Bach, C.P.E. Bach, and Spontini. Most are complete sections or movements from larger works, and the remainder are fragments of varying lengths. A few of these, according to the handwriting and clef signs, are from an early period—that is, before 1814; most of them, however, were done at a more mature stage of Rudolph's career.

Several of these exercises in transcriptions were probably the result of assignments from Beethoven, who had made known to

Plate 21. One page from Archduke Rudolph's counterpoint exercises
(Vienna, Wgm VII 42287).

Rudolph his high regard for Bach, and especially for Handel, as models. He wrote to the Archduke in 1819, while the latter was preparing the *Forty Variations* for publication, the following words:

> The older composers render us double service, since there is generally real artistic value in their works (among them, of course, only the *German Händel* and *Sebastian Bach* possessed genius.)[11]

Handel is well represented in Archduke Rudolph's transcription exercises (after Mozart and Beethoven), with selections from *Messiah, Saul,* and the *Water Music.* The *Messiah* excerpts, none identified by title, are in two bundles of miscellaneous sketches in the Kroměříž archive (KRa A 4431-32) and consist of figured-bass settings of the Sinfonia, the recitative "Comfort ye," and the arias "Ev'ry valley shall be exalted" and "The people that walked in darkness." In all of these, Rudolph supplied figured-bass numbers and chordal realizations that were not provided by Handel in the score.[12]

The Sinfonia is in three versions, all complete. One, with figured bass, is a realization of the keyboard part that is strictly accompaniment; the other two are keyboard arrangements of the orchestral score. Unlike the simple, unimaginative chord realizations of the vocal excerpts, the settings of the Sinfonia are transcribed skillfully for keyboard solo, and the fugal passages, although a little awkward technically, are laid out for two hands in a playable manner. The two settings are basically alike, but not identical; one, a fair copy, has changes that, by re-positioning chords and doubling the bass notes, provide a richer and more soloistic sound. The presence of these different types of transcription suggests that they were exercises in harmonic realization rather than for the Archduke's personal use. To judge from the writing and clef signs, they were written out ca. 1812-13.

The other Handel transcriptions, all fragments, are exercises in score reduction, written out on two staves in piano score. One is an excerpt from *Saul* (the opening twenty-two measures of the "Dead March"); the other, two pages from the *Water Music;* both are in a collection of miscellaneous fragments (KRa A 4385-86). While the

---

[11]Anderson, *Letters,* 822.

[12]In "The people that walked in darkness," only the bass line, with chord numbers above it, is written out. The two other vocal pieces have numbers as well as simple chordal realizations of the accompaniment.

Water Music transcription dates from a later period (after 1814), the *Saul* fragment, in a primitively simple setting, is one of several manuscripts with clef signs not seen in any of Rudolph's music after 1809. The treble and bass clefs, distinctively different from those illustrated in the Introduction (see p. xxi), are written thus in the excerpt from *Saul*:

The manuscript with these clef signs are mostly fragments; a few are copies of other works, but there are also some piano compositions (discussed in chapter 4) which are clearly student-like works. It is likely that all these pre-date Rudolph's studies with Beethoven.

The special place Mozart's music occupied in the Archduke's music collection is documented not only by the sizable number of Mozart's compositions in all genres recorded in Rudolph's catalogues (including the autograph of the Piano Concerto in D Minor, K. 466) but especially by the unique thematic index of Mozart's piano concertos Rudolph made in one early catalogue (see Appendix 1). Musical influence can be seen in the thematic similarity between the first movement of Mozart's Quartet in G Minor for Piano and Strings (K. 478) and Rudolph's Violin Sonata (see chapter 6); a quotation from Mozart's Quintet in A for Clarinet and Strings (K. 581) in one of Rudolph's works for czakan (see chapter 5); and finally, transcriptions he made of certain works of Mozart, namely, the overtures to *Don Giovanni* (K. 527) and *Die Zauberflöte* (K. 620), the Fugue from the Kyrie of the *Requiem* (K. 626), the first movement of the above-mentioned Piano Quartet, and the first and third movements of the Sonata in F for Piano Four Hands (K. 497).

The transcriptions of the overtures to *Don Giovanni* (KRa A 4430) and *Die Zauberflöte* (KRa A 4429) are arrangements for two pianos, both fully edited with phrasing and dynamic markings, and notated accurately in ink, with few calligraphic errors.[13] In both transcriptions, the two piano parts are evenly divided in pianistic interest and faithfully reproduce the orchestral score. The piano parts are written

[13]Both arrangements date from Rudolph's maturity, ca. 1818. The transcription of *Die Zauberflöte* is entered in the Archduke's catalogue in the list of his own compositions (entry no. 14), one of the two entries in another hand. There are a few minor changes in pencil on the manuscript, probably by Rudolph himself.

out in score, *piano primo* and *piano secondo*, suggesting that the arrangements were exercises in score reduction, made perhaps in conjunction with studies in orchestration, rather than for performance.

A similar reduction was made of the first movement of the Piano Quartet in G Minor, which is on five pages, in ink (KRa A 4387). In this arrangement, only the string parts were transcribed in piano score, apparently intended as an accompaniment to the solo piano part.

Two other Mozart transcriptions are of the fugal section of the Kyrie from the *Requiem* (KRa A 4441), one for piano solo, the other for two pianos; both are complete, in ink, and comprise five pages altogether. They were not written at the same time, however; the writing indicates that the two-piano version was made some time before 1814, the one-piano version later.

The final transcriptions of Mozart works are of the first and last movements of the Sonata in F for Piano Four Hands, arranged for woodwind octet consisting of two oboes, two clarinets, two bassoons, and two horns (KRa A 4420 and 4416); each is on four pages, in ink, and neither manuscript is complete.[14] Rudolph's transferral of the piano parts to woodwinds proceeds logically: the oboes and clarinets share the themes of the *piano primo*, the bassoons take the bass lines, and the horns fill in the middle range. Large X's in ink, in a hand which is impossible to determine, appear in several places in the first-movement transcription, especially in the horn parts, but their meaning is unclear, since there are no obvious errors in the parts. The handwriting on both manuscripts places their dates at around the same time as the two-piano version of the Fugue from the *Requiem*, ca. before 1814.

Of primary interest among these examples of the Archduke's work in making transcriptions are his arrangements and copies of music by his teacher. None is identified by title, but there are transcriptions for piano solo or piano duet of the overture to *Egmont* (Opus 84) and Clärchen's *Lied* from *Egmont*; the overture to *König Stephan* (Opus 117); and the *Marsch für Militärmusik in F*, No. 2 (WoO 19). For various instrumental ensembles, Rudolph arranged the first movement of the

---

[14]The first movement appears to have once been completed, since the extant manuscript of the transcription begins at the top of one page in the middle of the Adagio introduction, lacks indications of clefs or instruments, and breaks off abruptly at the end of the fourth page.

Quintet in C for Strings (Opus 29) and the Minuet from the Septet (Opus 20).

The Archduke made two transcriptions of the *Egmont* overture (KRa A 4428). One version, notated in score, is incomplete and appears to be a preliminary sketch for the other, which is complete and, furthermore, is the only four-hand transcription written down in conventional duet style, with the *primo* and *secondo* parts on opposite pages. This version is carefully written, includes all dynamic markings from the original, and demonstrates Rudolph's knowledgeable handling of technical problems involved in adapting instrumental music for the piano. Repeated pairs of notes in the string parts, for example, which are ubiquitous throughout the overture, are transcribed as rapid two-note alternations (Examples 2-3 and 2-4):

Example 2-3. Beethoven, *Egmont Overture*, measures 29-31.

Example 2-4. Archduke Rudolph, *Egmont* transcription, measures 29-31.

As with the Mozart overtures, the *Egmont* transcription probably originated as an exercise, one that Archduke Rudolph also intended for playing. The other transcription from the *Egmont* incidental music, Clärchen's *Lied* (which follows directly after the overture), is a two-page reduction of the orchestral parts scored for piano solo; it is in the *Membra disjecta* (KRa A 4433).

Rudolph's transcription of the *Marsch für Militärmusik*, also in the *Membra disjecta*, is for piano solo. This march for military band, one of two composed in 1810 by Beethoven for the Horse Ballet, or Carrousel, at Laxenburg Castle,[15] was dedicated to Rudolph's brother, Archduke Anton. Rudolph apparently had a special love for this work, and in response to his request, Beethoven sent him the autograph, which was in the Archduke's music collection.[16]

Another arrangement for piano in this group is a setting of part of the first movement of Beethoven's Symphony No. 5 in C Minor (Opus 67), again seemingly an exercise in reduction rather than a practical piano solo. The transcription, on two pages, breaks off at the end of the second theme; both pages are marred by a large ink-blot. Finally, there is a fragment of a two-piano arrangement of the overture to *König Stephan*, also in the *Membra disjecta*; neatly written in ink, it ends after some seventy measures.

Among transcriptions for different chamber ensembles is one the Archduke made of the first movement of Beethoven's Quintet in C for Strings (Opus 29), originally for two violins, two violas, and cello, which Rudolph arranged for piano, violin, and cello (KRa A 4390).[17] In transcribing the five string parts, Rudolph avoided the simple solution, i.e., keeping the first violin and cello parts more or less intact and adapting the other three string parts for the piano, doubling the cello line where appropriate. Instead, he often divides melodic phrases between the violin and the right hand of the piano part, giving them equal importance; similarly, he divides the cello part of the Quintet between the cello part in the trio and the left hand of the piano part and allocates most of the viola part to the cello. This arrangement succeeds in making each instrument in the trio equally important and melodically balanced.[18] In Rudolph's trio transcription, the

[15]Laxenburg Castle, in the suburbs of Vienna, was one of the Imperial family's summer residences. The Carrousel, a spectacular event, developed from the medieval tournament. The celebration on 24 August 1810 was in honor of Maria Ludovica, third wife of Emperor Franz.

[16]The earliest extant letter from Beethoven to Archduke Rudolph concerned the marches. In a postscript, Beethoven wrote, "The music for horses which you have asked for will be brought to Y. I. H. at the fastest gallop." (Anderson, *Letters*, 292).

[17]This transcription is erroneously listed in the Brno card catalogue as a composition for piano four hands. The error is understandable because of Rudolph's placement of the piano part on the middle two of four staves, with the violin above and the cello below; the four staves, reading treble, treble, bass, bass, thus give the appearance of a four-hand piano score. More importantly, it is not identified as a Beethoven composition.

[18]Beethoven did much the same thing in arranging his Septet (Opus 20) for piano trio, reassigning parts so that the violin part, which is the most soloistic part in the Septet, is reduced in importance and the piano part made more prominent.

Plate 22. Transcription for clarinet, viola, bassoon, and guitar of the Minuet from Beethoven's Septet.

piano is given the most demanding music, with the writing quite virtuosic at times; examples 2-5 and 2-6 illustrate a passage in which the two string parts must be played as rapid consecutive thirds and sixths in the right hand of the piano part:

Example 2-5. Beethoven, *Quintet* (Opus 29), 1st movement, measures 21-23.

Example 2-6. Archduke Rudolph, Quintet transcription, measures 21-23.

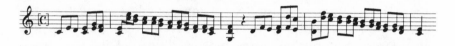

The score of the Quintet was not published until 1828, but the manuscript copy in the Archduke's library undoubtedly served to make the transcription.

The final Beethoven transcription made by Rudolph is of the well-known Minuet movement from the Septet [Opus 20] (KRa A 4527).[19] This three-page fragment is another of the Archduke's works for the ensemble of clarinet, viola, bassoon, and guitar, which are discussed in chapter 7. In arranging this work, Rudolph avoided a literal transcription, instead treating the guitar part quite freely by providing an Alberti bass figure which was not in Beethoven's original score.

We have seen (chapter 1) that Archduke Rudolph's library served as a repository for Beethoven's manuscripts, and his catalogues attest to his acquisition of every Beethoven publication as it appeared, including all the various arrangements and transcriptions. It was noted earlier that Rudolph made his own manuscript copy of a work he seems to have treasured, Beethoven's Piano Sonata in E Minor, Opus 90. Perhaps the copy was for his own use or, more likely, an

[19]This transcription is not listed in the Brno card catalogue. See Plate 22 for facsimile.

expression of homage; in either case, his copy of the Beethoven autograph is exact in every detail, even to the inclusion of the date of composition entered by Beethoven on the title page (16 August 1814) and the imitation of Beethoven's distinctive notational style—a style that Rudolph did not use in any of his own manuscripts.[20]

Archduke Rudolph's liking for the music of Spontini—specifically, his opera *La Vestale*—resulted in his using parts of the opera both for an original composition and for transcription. One of Rudolph's best-crafted works is his set of variations for two pianos on a theme from Act I of *La Vestale* (see chapter 4); in addition, he made an arrangement of the overture to that opera for two pianos, probably around the same time.[21] The manuscript (in handwriting similar to that in other works dating from ca. 1812-13) is in two parts in the Kroměříž archive; eleven pages are included with several other fragments (KRa A 4387-88), and four other pages are in the *Membra disjecta*. Like his other two-piano arrangements, the two parts share evenly in pianistic interest. This manuscript begins neatly, with phrasing and dynamics included, but becomes progressively less tidy, with crossed-out measures and no editing details.

The remaining transcriptions made by the Archduke are of two excerpts from Gluck's *Orfeo ed Eurydice*, set for piano solo, dating from different periods. A simple, primitively realized setting of the first twelve measures of "Che farò senza Eurydice" (KRa A 4385) is written down in Rudolph's earliest notation, with the same clef signs as those found in the setting of the "Dead March" from *Saul*. The other transcription, also a fragment, is of the music of the Furies from Act II, Scene I (KRa A 4387); on five pages, it dates from ca. 1812.

A march for piano from a Singspiel (*Der Kapellmeister*) by J. Ellmenreich[22] (KRa A 4384) was copied out by Rudolph, also in notation ca. before 1809.

One work by J.S. Bach—part of the Fugue in F Minor from Book II of the *Well-Tempered Clavier*—was copied out by the Archduke (KRa A 4438). More in the nature of exercises are copies he made of two short

---

[20]Some examples of Beethoven's notation that differ completely from Rudolph's are the sign "in 8va" and the use of a period dot following dynamic abbreviations.

[21]The variations were probably composed ca. 1812.

[22]Two marches from *Der Kapellmeister* were published by Franz Anton Hoffmeister in 1805 in various arrangements besides the piano version. Johann Baptist Ellmenreich (1770-1816) was a singer and actor in comic roles as well as a composer of *Singspiele*.

keyboard works by C.P.E. Bach—an Allegro in G and an Allegro in A.[23] Both of these had been published in Marpurg's *Anleitung zu Clavierspielen* (Berlin, 1765) with fingering for every note, as was suitable for the didactic purpose of the work. It is clear that Rudolph copied the two pieces directly from Marpurg, since he methodically duplicated every fingering in his own manuscript.

Lastly, Archduke Rudolph made a copy of Diabelli's waltz theme (see chapter 4), in which all editing details are incorporated. This copy, in pencil on a single sheet (KRa A 4431), was undoubtedly a working manuscript for Rudolph's use in composing his variation for the Diabelli publication of fifty variations on that theme.

[23]Wotquenne catalogue nos. 116/117. Rudolph's copies are in KRa A 4431.

Plate 23. Title page, the *Forty Variations on a Theme by Beethoven*, S.A. Steiner and Co., 1819.

CHAPTER III

The Forty Variations on a Theme by Beethoven

(1818-19); THEM. CAT. NO. 10

At the very heart of Archduke Rudolph's oeuvre is an ambitious and lengthy set of variations—forty in number—on a short, simple theme composed by Beethoven for Rudolph. These variations, published in 1819 by S.A. Steiner & Co., were not only the work that brought the Archduke before the public as a composer but also the culmination in print of his years of study with Beethoven.

The genesis of the Forty Variations was a four-measure song, or *Liedthema*, "O Hoffnung" (WoO 200),[1] written out by Beethoven in the spring of 1818 apparently as an assignment for Rudolph in variations composition. The autograph of "O Hoffnung," now in the archives of the Deutsche Staatsbibliothek in East Berlin (Bds Mus. ms. autogr. Beethoven 52), is on a single loose sheet in small format, with the staff lines drawn in roughly by hand. Beethoven's autograph is shown in facsimile in Plate 24.

---

[1]"O Hoffnung" was inadvertently omitted from the work-list of Beethoven's compositions in *The New Grove Dictionary of Music and Musicians*, 20 vols., ed. Stanley Sadie (London: Macmillan, 1980) II, 394-410. This error has been rectified in Joseph Kerman and Alan Tyson, *The New Grove Beethoven* (New York: Norton, 1983).

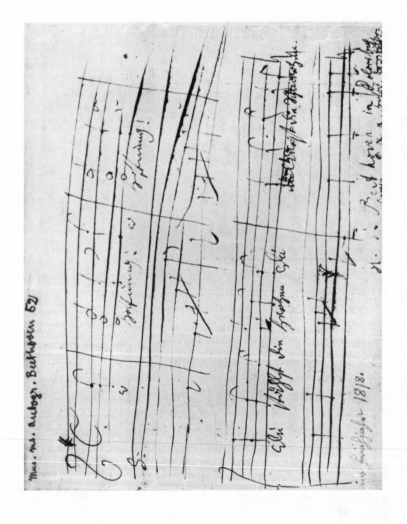

Plate 24. Beethoven, "O Hoffnung". Facsimile of autograph
(Deutsche Staatsbibliothek, Berlin, DDR).

Example 3-2. Beethoven, "O Hoffnung" (transcription)

The brief text ("O Hope! O Hope! You steel the heart, you soften the pain") is in Beethoven's hand; the confusion of words and music in the final measure suggests that the bottom notes of the right hand chords were added after the text was entered. The words in the lower right hand corner, written by Beethoven, are as follows: "L. v. Beethoven in Doloribus/causa S. k. k. Hoheit dem Erzher-/zoge Rudolph."[2] The date in the lower left corner, "im Früjahr 1818" appears to be in Rudolph's hand.

The scholarly literature concerning Beethoven's manuscript, which to my knowledge has never been reproduced in facsimile before, contains several errors that would have been apparent had the writers examined the autograph. Hans Boettcher, for example, listed the vital particulars about "O Hoffnung" in chart form in his book *Beethovens als Liederkomponist,*[3] citing A.B. Marx's *Beethovens Leben und Schaffen,* first published in 1859, as his principal source. Among the errors in Boettcher's description, the text is misquoted, with the word "vertreibst" substituted for "milderst"; Beethoven's additional words beneath the music are given wrongly, as "L. v. B. in doloribus komp. für Seine kaiserl. Hoheit, den Erzherzog Rudolph"; and finally, the text of the song is attributed to Christoph August Tiedge's *Urania,* a collection of lyrical poetry from which Beethoven drew the text for "An die Hoffnung." The similarity in titles undoubtedly accounts for the confusion, but since the text of "O Hoffnung" is not to be found in Tiedge's collection, and its origin is uncertain, there is the strong possibility that Beethoven himself wrote the words.[4]

[2]The Latin can be translated as "The reason (or theme) [is to be found] in sorrows." The "sorrows" may have been occasioned by an impending departure for the summer months by Beethoven or Rudolph.

[3]Hans Boettcher, *Beethoven als Liederkomponist* (Augsberg: Dr. Benno Filser Verlag, 1928) Plate XII/7.

[4]Hans Volkmann, in *Beethoven in seinen Beziehungen zu Dresden* (Dresden: Literatur Verlag, 1942) 237, points out the misattribution and proposes that Beethoven himself wrote the text.

These mistakes were perpetuated in later works, for example by Georg Kinsky, who in his discussion of "O Hoffnung" offered another misquotation of Beethoven's annotation, to wit: "componirt im Frühjahr 1818 von L. van Beethoven in doloribus für S. Kais. Hoheit den Erzherzog Rudolph."[5] Kinsky evidently did not see a facsimile of the Beethoven autograph, for he cites Nohl as the source for the annotation. Another error appearing in Kinsky concerns the music: the incipit has the wrong rhythm in the bass line in the first two measures (see Example 3-16 later in this chapter).

Two of these errors can perhaps be ascribed to changes made by Archduke Rudolph himself in Beethoven's theme, which he copied out several times in his sketches of the variations, as well as on the final page of another composition (see chapter 8, p. 234). These changes will be noted as they come up in the discussion of the variations.

After receiving Beethoven's theme, Rudolph apparently set to work composing the variations with great enthusiasm, for he sent off a draft to his teacher some time in the late fall of 1818. In his New Year's greeting to Archduke Rudolph on 1 January 1819, Beethoven alluded to personal problems concerning his nephew Karl as the reason he had not seen Rudolph in person:

> To this alone you must ascribe the fact that I have not called upon Y. I. H. in person nor reported on the masterly variations of my highly honored and illustrious pupil who is a favorite of the Muses. I dare not express my thanks either verbally or in writing for this surprise and for the favour with which I have been honored . . . In a few days I hope to hear Y. I. H. himself perform the masterpiece you have sent me; and nothing can delight me more than to assist Y. I. H. to take as soon as possible the seat on Parnassus which has already been prepared for Your Highness.[6]

---

[5] Kinsky-Halm, *Das Werk Beethovens*, 700. Both Thayer and Kinsky after him appear to have confused the text of "O Hoffnung" with those of the two Beethoven songs entitled "An die Hoffnung," Opus 32 and Opus 94, which are from Tiedge's *Urania*. In an additional reference in the notes on "O Hoffnung," Kinsky wrote "Vgl. 'An die Hoffnung.' "

[6] Anderson, *Letters*, 789. The "favour" Beethoven refers to is Rudolph's dedication of the variations to his teacher. In this letter and the others following on the variations, Beethoven repeatedly alludes to the names of persons and places in Classic antiquity.

Some time during the spring he wrote again to the Archduke:

> Only yesterday I wanted to bring you the variations. They really should be brought boldly to the light of day.[7]

In June, while at Mödling, Beethoven wrote to congratulate Rudolph on his appointment as Cardinal Archbishop of Olmütz; in his letter, he parodied his own "O Hoffnung" theme, substituting the word "Erfüllung!" for "O Hoffnung!", and changing both the meter (from 4/4 to 3/4) and the tonality (from G to D) [Example 3-3]:

Example 3-3. "Erfüllung!" (WoO 205ᵉ)

The letter is replete with Beethoven's unusual obsequities and also some didactic comments:

> As for Y. I. H.'s masterly variations I gave them the other day to be copied. I noticed several little slips and I must remind my illustrious pupil 'La musica merita d'esser studiata.' In view of Your Imperial Highness's truly fine talents and exceptional gifts of imagination it would be a pity not to press forward to the *very source of Castalia*; and on this expedition I offer to be your companion, as soon as Your Imperial Highness's time permits. Y. I. H. can thus create in two ways, both for the happiness and welfare of very many people and also for yourself. For in the present world of monarchs creators of music and benefactors of humanity have hitherto been lacking.[8]

It is doubtful that Beethoven spent any time during the summer months working on the variations with Archduke Rudolph; the latter was ill and recuperating at Baden, while Beethoven, more obsessed

[7]Anderson, *Letters*, 807.
[8]*Ibid.*, 813. In another letter (also 1819, but no day or month indicated), Beethoven wrote, "I have the honor to send you herewith by the copyist Schlemmer Y.I.H.'s masterly variations." The manuscript copy in the Gesellschaft der Musikfreunde (Q 15075) is not in Schlemmer's hand.

than ever with the mounting problems over his guardianship of Karl, stayed in Mödling. From there he continued to advise Rudolph on musical matters. In a letter dated July 29, after giving some thoughts on Bach and Handel, and art in general, he wrote:

> My eminent music pupil, who himself is now competing for the laurels of fame, must not bear the reproach of being one-sided ... Here are three poems. The Austrians are now aware that the *spirit of Apollo* has come to life again in the Imperial dynasty. From all sides I am receiving requests to obtain something composed by you.[9]

One month later, on August 31, Beethoven again wrote to congratulate Rudolph, who had just received the Grand Cross of the Order of St. Stephen from Emperor Franz. After promising to have the *Missa Solemnis* ready for the ceremonies to accompany Rudolph's enthronement as Cardinal (scheduled for March 1820), Beethoven returned to the subject of the *Forty Variations:*

> In regard to Y.I.H.'s masterly set of variations I think that they could be published with the following title, namely:
> Theme or exercise set by L. v. Beeth[oven] on which forty variations have been written and dedicated to his teacher by *His Excellency the Composer.*
> There are so many demands for this work; and in the end this very creditable composition might be sent into the world in garbled copies. So, in the name of Heaven, in addition to the many sacred orders which have been bestowed on Y. I. H. and made public, let the order of Apollo (or, to use a more Christian term, the order of St. Cecilia) be made public. No doubt Y. I. H. may perhaps accuse me of *vanity.* But I can assure you that, although I am really proud of it, that alone is certainly not my chief object ... Well, the question now is whether Y. I. H. is *satisfied with the title?* As to whether the variations should be published, I think that Y. I. H. should certainly close your eyes to it.[10]

There is an implication here that the publication of the variations had been discussed previously, perhaps in person, particularly since Beethoven mentions that three publishers had expressed interest in engraving them at their own expense, among them Steiner and

[9]Anderson, *Letters*, 822.
[10]*Ibid.*, 833 (emended). In the autograph (pictured Kalischer) Beethoven encircled the suggested title with a sort of cage.

Artaria. In a letter to Steiner dated October 10, written from Mödling, Beethoven said:

> I have told the Honorable Little Tobias [Haslinger] about some var[iations] composed by the Archduke. I proposed *you* for this purpose, because I do not think you will suffer any loss and because it is always an honor to engrave something composed by such a Principe Professore.[11]

A final reference to the publication was made in a letter dated October 15, in which Beethoven discussed the use of a nom de plume for the Archduke:

> ... Steiner has now received Y. I. H.'s var[iations] and will himself express his thanks to you. By the way, it has just occurred to me that Emperor Joseph travelled under the name of Count von Falkenstein because of the title ... [12]

When the variations appeared in print at the end of 1819, the title page differed considerably from previous suggestions. It read: "AUFGABE/von Ludwig van Beethoven gedichtet,/Vierzig Mahl verändert/und Ihrem Verfasser gewidmet/von seinen/Schüler/ R. E. H."

The idea of using a nom de plume had evidently been abandoned, and initials (Rudolph ErzHerzog) employed to disguise the royal identity of the composer—a disguise that the Viennese music public, knowing full well Rudolph's relationship with Beethoven, could not fail to see through. Beethoven's role in the composition, its publication, and its dedication, is displayed so prominently on the title page, the clear inference is that he took some pride in the end result. Following the appearance of the publication, two highly laudatory reviews appeared in the *Allgemeine musikalische Zeitung*—one in January 1820, the other in June 1820.

In their final published version the *Forty Variations* were thirty-one pages long, with an overall structure of large scope. After an extended, fantasy-style introduction, Beethoven's four-measure theme is presented, followed by thirty-four of the forty variations in the

---

[11]Anderson, *Letters*, 848.
[12]*Ibid*, 850 (emended).

same four-measure scheme (one other, No. 20, is six measures). The harmonic pattern of "O Hoffnung" is also maintained, including the C-sharp of the secondary dominant in measures three and four of the theme (see Example 3-2). Despite, or perhaps because of, the constricted limitations of this structure, the wealth of ingenuity and invention in the short variations is striking; each is composed with a fresh idea, in meter, tonality, figuration, or tempo, or combinations of these. Beginning with the thirty-sixth, the variations are composed freely, in varying lengths and styles, culminating in a multi-sectional finale capped with a four-voice fugue.[13]

The manuscript sketches for the *Forty Variations* are preserved in the Kroměříž archive; they encompass two earlier versions of the work and include six pages of Beethoven's autograph sketches for emendations. Under the library sigla A 4372-75, this group of manuscripts consists of:

A 4372 Version I, 26 pages;

A 4373 Version II, 41 pages;

A 4374 "O Hoffnung" theme, ink; crossed-out pencil sketches, 5 pages;

A 4375 Beethoven sketches, ink and pencil, 6 pages (5 pages of emendations, 1 page of a suggested title).

Both Versions I and II were corrected and emended in detail by Beethoven—sometimes directly on Rudolph's work (additions and deletions of notes, accidentals, rhythmic changes, etc.) or sometimes in the nearest margin. Version II is clearly a revision of Version I, since it incorporates the changes indicated by Beethoven in the earlier manuscript and most closely approximates the edition published by Steiner. Version II also underwent many changes, and it is to this manuscript that Beethoven appended the five pages of his own sketches, all of which are suggested emendations corresponding to certain passages in the body of the manuscript—passages which Beethoven marked with large pencilled X's or with numbers. The two pages of Beethoven's autograph in ink contain the corrections relating to the marked passages; they are strewn in seeming

---

[13]In the overall structure of the *Forty Variations* and the treatment of the theme, the work has at least one unique aspect: although there are other variation sets on brief themes in which the length and harmonic structure remain unchanged, there appears to be no other set of variations on a theme this short which maintains through as many as thirty-four variations its original four-measure length.

confusion onto the two crowded pages with no identifying marks such as clef signs. It is possible, with careful study, to decipher them and recognize their application to specific places in Rudolph's work, and they can then be seen to have been notated with the utmost precision. The difficulty of deciphering Beethoven's sketches suggests that he went through the manuscript himself, perhaps during the summer months when he was not giving Rudolph lessons, marked the offending passages with his pencilled X's, and then, when with the Archduke, wrote out each correction on the separate pages for Rudolph's clarification.[14]

The remaining three pages of Beethoven's autograph contain numbered corrections in pencil, extremely faded, which correspond to numbered passages in the closing fugue of the variations. The sixth page contains another suggested title for the work: "Veränderungen/ über ein Thema von/L. v. Beethoven/verfasst von Sr Kaiserliche/ Hoheit den/Erzherzog Rudolph/Erzbischof."

The dozens of corrections and emendations by Beethoven reveal his scrupulous attention to detail. Many of the suggested revisions deal with elementary compositional errors of a technical nature, such as exposed and hidden parallels, poor choice of doubling in chords, or awkward voice-leading—the same type of errors that were made by Rudolph and corrected by Beethoven in several other compositions; in all likelihood, it was to this type of mistake that Beethoven referred in his letter when speaking of "little slips" he had noticed. Very few of these technical faults escaped his eye, as can readily be observed in the corrected manuscripts. More significant, perhaps, than these technical errors, are revisions that reveal Beethoven's thinking about syntax and structure. Selective examples of both types of Beethoven's corrections—those dealing with minor errors and others concerned with changes of a larger scope—will be illustrated in the following description and discussion of the *Forty Variations*.

---

[14]Beethoven's illegible writing misled the Beethoven scholars who originally examined this material (notably Vetterl, "Der musikalische Nachlass," and Racek, "Beethoven's Beziehungen") into believing that Beethoven was composing his own original ideas for Rudolph's variations. It was only after this writer began memorizing the variations for performance that Beethoven's notation became decipherable and each correction could be related to its place in Rudolph's manuscript. Facsimiles of the Beethoven autographs are reproduced following page 111.

The opening movement of the *Forty Variations* is a long Adagio introduction (88 measures with a metronome marking of ♩ = 84) set in G minor, instead of the G major of the "O Hoffnung" theme. This tonal plan—a slow movement in the parallel minor preceding a theme in the major—bears a striking resemblance to Beethoven's variations for piano trio on the theme "Ich bin der Schneider Kakadu," Opus 121a.[15] In that work, too, a slow opening in G minor is followed by a simple, folk-like theme in G major (Example 3-4):

Example 3-4. Beethoven, *Variations for Piano, Violin, and Cello on "Ich bin der Schneider Kakadu"* (Opus 121a), measures 1-2, 47-49.

In Archduke Rudolph's Introduction (the first four measures are shown in Example 3-5), the prominent motivic elements of the "O Hoffnung" theme—the eighth-note upbeat, the *Seufzer* motive in the melody, and the dotted-rhythm scale in the bass—are developed in an improvisatory manner.

Example 3-5. *Forty Variations*, Introduction, measures 1-4.

The Introduction rambles somewhat, modulating after twenty measures to a new key area (A-flat) and a new theme, which is repeated later in B-flat. The movement is held together by the frequent

---

[15]The "Kakadu" Variations were not published until 1823, but they were composed much earlier. In 1816 Beethoven had offered them to Breitkopf & Härtel, stating that although they belonged to his "earlier works," they were not "poor stuff" (Anderson, *Letters*, 586). Rudolph probably had a manuscript copy in his collection.

recurrence of the dotted-rhythm scale figure, both ascending and descending.

Some of Beethoven's corrections in the Introduction are very slight and are typical of the dozens of similar emendations throughout the variations. Two such suggested changes are shown in Examples 3-6 and 3-7:*

Example 3-6. *Forty Variations* (Version I), Introduction, measure 9.

Example 3-7. *Forty Variations* (Version I), Introduction, measure 20.

In Example 3-6, the reinforcement of the dotted-rhythm figure in the left hand strengthens the melody and also preserves the subdominant harmony through two beats instead of Rudolph's variant on the second beat of the measure. The alteration in Example 3-7 is one of many Beethoven made with the object of making the passing note more piquant.

A change in melodic contour was indicated by Beethoven in the new theme in A-flat (measure 23); in fact, Beethoven changed Rudolph's original melody at each of its occurrences (Example 3-8):

---

*Beethoven's corrections, shown above or below the staff according to whether they concern the right-hand or left-hand parts, will be identified by the letter "B." Archduke Rudolph's original versions will be indicated by the letters "A.R."

Example 3-8a. *Forty Variations* (Version I), Introduction, measure 23.

Example 3-8b. *Forty Variations* (Version I), Introduction, measure 48.

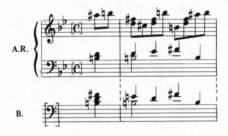

As Beethoven reshaped the melodic line, he provided more interest by placing the dissonant *D-flat* (Example 3-8a) and *E* on the downbeat and producing contrary motion against the bass accompaniment.

Three important structural revisions occur in the Introduction—two involving the interpolation of additional material, and one the excision of several measures. In the first of the two interpolations the addition of several measures was probably Beethoven's suggestion, since he wrote a correction above the staff, indicating his concern with the passage in question. Example 3-9 shows the original passage of Version I, with Beethoven's correction over the fourth measure; Example 3-10 shows the final version. In this passage, which serves as a transition from the second-theme key area of A-flat back to the tonic, the additional measures make the harmonic change less abrupt and build more tension toward the resolution on I $^6_4$ (measure 35).

Example 3-9. *Forty Variations* (Version I), Introduction

Example 3-10. *Forty Variations* (published edition), Introduction, measures 27-35.

The other example of added material occurs toward the end of the Introduction; in Version I (Example 3-11), the progression from the dominant chord at measure 83 to the dominant at the double bar (the final measure) takes place in four measures:

Example 3-11. *Forty Variations* (Version I), Introduction

The diminished seventh chord in the second measure, functioning as a second dominant, is extended in the revision another two measures with arpeggiated figuration; again, the purpose is to make the harmonic change less abrupt and, in making the figuration more brilliant, to stress the drama of the whole passage and its resolution (Example 3-12):

Example 3-12. *Forty Variations* (published edition), Introduction, measures 83-88.

The Introduction is rather long, and Rudolph's development of the basic motivic material is somewhat limited; indeed, this movement seems overextended and repetitious. One important revision, occurring in another modulatory passage (following a repeat of the new theme in B-flat), involves the excision of several measures. In Rudolph's original (Example 3-13), the transition from B-flat to the dominant chord takes place over twelve measures; it can be compared with the published version (Example 3-14), which was shortened to eight measures. In Example 3-13, a change of a whole measure Beethoven wrote above the staff in Version I is shown above the system:

Example 3-13. *Forty Variations* (Versions I and II), Introduction

Example 3-14. *Forty Variations* (published edition), Introduction, measures 69-76.

The weakness in Archduke Rudolph's original passage is its static harmony, which meanders around B-flat and arrives abruptly at the dominant chord without convincing preparation. The elimination of four of the twelve measures effectively tightens the structure.

The final two measures of the Introduction were altered by Beethoven in small but telling detail (Example 3-15):

Example 3-15a. *Forty Variations* (Version I), Introduction

Example 3-15b. *Forty Variations* (published edition), Introduction, measures 87-88.

The addition of the ninth (*E-flat*) to the dominant chord on the penultimate beat enriches the harmony and stresses the *Seufzer* motive. The other added note (the upbeat *A* at the end of measure 87) matches the rhythm of the "O Hoffnung" theme.

We mentioned earlier that Rudolph made changes in the theme—three in the music, one in the text. The first change was in the rhythm of the bass line in the first two measures (Example 3-16):

Example 3-16. "O Hoffnung," bass line, measures 1-2.

In both versions of the sketches, the theme is given with the altered rhythm, which is identical with the bass-line rhythm Rudolph wrote in the opening of the Introduction. But when Rudolph copied out the theme on the last page of the manuscript of his aria "La partenza" (see chapter 8, p. 234), it was exactly as Beethoven had written it; this was probably the first copy he made of the theme, before composing the variations.

The two other changes in the music are the addition of notes in two places—an *A* to the last eighth-note chord (right hand) of measure 1 (Example 3-17) and a *B* accompanying the sixteenth-note *G* (right hand) in measure 3 (Example 3-18):

Example 3-17. "O Hoffnung," measure 1

Example 3-18. "O Hoffnung," measure 3.

All of these minor alterations to Beethoven's theme must have met with his approval, since he had ample opportunity to "correct" them but did not do so.

The textual changes—a substitution of the word "vertreibst" for "milderst"—occurs in all three copies of the theme. In the "La partenza" manuscript and in Version I of the sketches, the word "du" precedes "vertreibst," bringing about an awkward accent on the first syllable of "vertreibst" (Example 3-19a):

Example 3-19a. "O Hoffnung" (Archduke Rudolph's copy), measures 3-4.

Du stählst die Her- zen, du ver - treibst die Schmer-zen.

In Version II, the text is written out the same way, but above the notes Beethoven wrote out a different text, omitting the word "du" to produce the proper accentuation (Example 3-19b):

Example 3-19b. "O Hoffnung" (Archduke Rudolph's copy), measures 3-4.

We can conclude then that Beethoven at least approved the change in text, or, more likely, may have suggested it himself.

Rudolph's first variation on the theme ingeniously combines half of Beethoven's treble melody with parts of the alto and bass lines in a unison setting for three voices (Example 3-20):

Example 3-20. *Forty Variations*, Variation 1, measures 1-4.

The next three variations build on this initial variant of the theme by adding one voice at a time. In the second variation (Example 3-21), Rudolph decided to change the explicit E-minor chord on the third beat of the second measure of Beethoven's setting by eliminating E in both chords:

Example 3-21. *Forty Variations*, Variation 2, measures 1-2.

In the sketch of Version I, Rudolph had originally kept Beethoven's harmonic plan, ending the second phrase in E minor (Example 3-22):

Example 3-22. *Forty Variations* (Version I), Variation 2, measures 1-2.

By chance, the change Rudolph made in the published version (Example 3-21) was questioned by Johannes Brahms, who was given a copy of the Steiner edition of the *Forty Variations* in 1856.[16] In Brahms's copy, now in the Gesellschaft der Musikfreunde (Wgm Q 15076), Brahms made his own "correction" in the score with his editorial blue pencil (Example 3-23):

[16]Brahms wrote to Clara Schumann on 15 January 1856: "Somebody else has sent me forty variations by Archduke Rudolph (R.E.H.) on a theme by Beethoven (on account of their curiosity)." *Letters of Clara Schumann and Johannes Brahms*, Vol. I, ed. Dr. Berthold Litzmann (New York: Vienna House, 1973) 62.

Example 3-23. *Forty Variations* (Brahms's copy), Variation 2, measures 1-2.

Variations 3 and 4 continue to build on the theme, each adding another voice, so that the fourth variation is a four-voice setting in which the treble and bass voices of the original "O Hoffnung" theme are inverted (Example 3-24 and 3-25):

Example 3-24. *Forty Variations*, Variation 3, measures 1-4.

Example 3-25. *Forty Variations*, Variation 4, measures 1-4.

At this point, the Archduke had gone as far as possible using inversion technique to vary Beethoven's chorale-like setting, all the while adhering to the style and character of the theme. Beginning with the fifth variation, marked by a change in tempo and an immediate departure from the chorale style, Rudolph uses an imaginative and resourceful array of musical styles and techniques to produce variety within the confines of the four-measure format and harmonic scheme set down by Beethoven. Rudolph's ingenuity in exploring these styles can be seen in a selection of brief excerpts from several representative variations.

Two variations, for instance (numbers 10 and 22 [Examples 3-26 and 3-27]) are imitative:

Example 3-26. *Forty Variations*, Variation 10, measures 1-2.

Example 3-27. *Forty Variations*, Variation 22, measures 1-2.

Three (numbers 13, 23, and 25) feature florid figuration in the right hand part (Examples 3-28, 3-29, and 3-30):

Example 3-28. *Forty Variations*, Variation 13, measures 3-4.

Example 3-29. *Forty Variations*, Variation 23, measures 3-4.

Example 3-30. *Forty Variations*, Variation 25, measures 1-4.

Some variations (numbers 19, 23, 25, 29, and 33) are technically demanding, even virtuosic (Examples 3-31, 3-32, and 3-33):

Example 3-31. *Forty Variations*, Variation 19, measures 1-4.

Example 3-32. *Forty Variations*, Variation 29, measures 1-2.

Example 3-33. *Forty Variations*, Variation 33, measures 1-4.

Chromaticism in the melody can be heard in several variations (numbers 6, 9, 21, 23, and 25); two excerpts are shown in Examples 3-34 and 3-35:

Example 3-34. *Forty Variations*, Variation 6, measures 1-2.

Example 3-35. *Forty Variations*, Variation 9, measures 1-2.

Changes in meter are infrequent (numbers 14 and 32 are in 12/8, and number 20 is in 6/8) [Examples 3-36 and 3-37]:

Example 3-36. *Forty Variations*, Variation 14, measures 1-2.

By using a variety of rhythmic devices such as triplets and syncopation, and especially by varying tempi, Rudolph creates an impression of metrical diversity, reinforced by the brevity of each variation.

Beethoven's dozens of corrections throughout the variations range from the most minimal (a change of one or two notes, or a slight rhythmic alteration) to emendations involving a whole measure or

92

Example 3-37. *Forty Variations*, Variation 20, measures 1-6.

two. In the first thirty-five variations Beethoven's corrections are mostly of the minimal type, and they fall into various categories: changes in melodic lines, in harmony, or sometimes in texture or rhythm; often one change involves two of these types. In the last five variations, which will be discussed later, there are larger structural changes as well as small ones.

Several representative corrections from Variations 1 through 35 have been selected to illustrate Beethoven's thinking on such matters as voice-leading, harmonic syntax, texture, and rhythm.

A change affecting both voice-leading and harmonic function, for instance, was made by Beethoven in Variation 11 (Example 3-38);

Example 3-38. *Forty Variations* (Version II), Variation 11, measures 3 (second half) and 4 (first half).

The descent of the bass voice (*A-G-F-sharp*) is more logical and smoother, and the chord on the last beat of measure 3 is made more explicit as a secondary dominant with *C-sharp* and the seventh added.

A similar change affecting dominant function was made in Variation 29 (Example 3-39):

Example 3-39. *Forty Variations* (Version I), Variation 29, measure 3 (second half).

Here the secondary dominant is sharpened by placing it on the strong beat and reinforcing it in the bass line with the same harmony.

In a passage in Variation 10, Beethoven made a change that affected texture; filling out Rudolph's thin, harmonically ambiguous chords both enriches the sound and makes the harmonies explicit. Beethoven also corrected Rudolph's spelling of the leading tone (Example 3-40):

Example 3-40. *Forty Variations* (Version II), Variation 10, measure 4.

One last correction shows a small rhythmic change (Example 3-41):

Example 3-41. *Forty Variations* (Version I), Variation 14, measure 1.

Beethoven's emendation preserves the momentum of the eighth notes throughout. In some of the last variations—particularly the long Finale—he made several such corrections where Rudolph had left a similar rhythmic gap.

In the last five variations, greater contrasts are achieved by variety in length, in style, and, even more, in modulations to different keys. Variation 36 is the only "slow" movement in the work (except for the Introduction): an Adagio in G major (with a middle section in E), it is quiet and reflective in mood, fantasy-like, with an improvisatory-sounding cadenza at measure 8 (Example 3-42):

Example 3-42: *Forty Variations*, Variation 36, measures 1-8.

A variation in "Tempo di marcia," with brisk dotted rhythms and driving motion, follows; there are no changes in key signature, but modulations to F and D-flat occur in the middle. A few measures are shown in Example 3-43:

Example 3-43. *Forty Variations*, Variation 37, measures 25-35.

Variation 38 offers sharp contrast tonally; in G minor (Allegro molto), it is in rounded binary form. In the second half there is some brief but piquant modulation, to the submediant first, then through the lowered supertonic to an augmented sixth chord before the final cadence (Example 3-44):

Example 3-44. *Forty Variations*, Variation 38, measures 1-32.

The penultimate variation reverts to G major; a serene, graceful minuet, it modulates toward the end to E minor, ending on a dominant and a measure's rest to anticipate the Finale, which storms in (Allegro agitato) in E minor (Example 3-45):

Example 3-45. *Forty Variations,* Variation 39 (last three measures) and Variation 40 (opening measure).

The Finale, Variation 40, is almost unremittingly energetic. It is an extended rondo with long sections in E major and C major. The thematic material is familiar, based on the "O Hoffnung" motive or a variant of it in each section (Example 3-46):

Example 3-46a. *Forty Variations,* Variation 40, measures 1-4.

Example 3-46b. *Forty Variations,* Variation 40, measures 33-36.

Example 3-46c. *Forty Variations,* Variation 40, measures 113-120.

After the return to the rondo theme in E minor at measure 195 (with a new, faster tempo—Più Allegro, ♩ = 120) and a brief modulation into E-flat, the Finale arrives at a stretto-like recapitulation of the "O Hoffnung" theme, ending with a ritardando to a fermata (Example 3-47):

Example 3-47. *Forty Variations,* Variation 40, measures 224-230.

Before we look at the conclusion of Variation 40, the fugue, some examples of Beethoven's emendations in this last group of variations bear mention. In the area of rhythm, for instance, the Finale has many corrections. The difficulty of sustaining interest in such a lengthy movement, in which melodic changes are minimal, is to some extent overcome by the propulsive momentum and energy of the tempo and style of writing; Beethoven's corrections are aimed at ensuring the maintenance of momentum by adding rhythmic figures where Rudolph left gaps (Example 3-48):

Example 3-48. *Forty Variations* (Version I), Variation 40 (measures 120-121 of published edition).

This particular passage from the C major section recurs several times, and Beethoven added the same dotted-rhythm filler on the fourth beat at each occurrence.

Beethoven's ferreting out and correcting parallel intervals is illustrated in two measures toward the end of the section in C major (Example 3-49):

Example 3-49. *Forty Variations,* Variation 40 (Version II) [measures 179-180 in published edition].

Beethoven's additions to the dominant seventh chord on the third beat succeed in camouflaging the parallel fifths in measure 179; in measure 180, he eliminated the more obvious parallels between the soprano and bass lines, but allowed them to remain between the soprano and tenor voices, where they are not so apparent to the ear.

A more complicated rhythmic change was made at a key point in the stretto-like section of Variation 40 just preceding the fugue. Here the additional figuration written in by Beethoven (Example 3-50) increases the rhythmic activity and adds contrapuntal interest at the same time:

Example 3-50. *Forty Variations* (Version I), Variation 40 (measures 224-225 in published edition).

One significant structural change was made by Beethoven in the Finale, to achieve the same purpose as the change shown earlier in Example 3-9, e.g., to make a modulatory passage less abrupt, by interpolating material (three measures in this case) and thereby lengthening the dominant preparation (Example 3-51). First we see Rudolph's original, and following it, the published version; the four additional measures from 214 through 217 were written out in Beethoven's sketches.

Example 3-51. *Forty Variations*, Variation 40 (Versions I and II), measures 213-218 in published edition.

The climax of the Finale—and of the *Forty Variations*—is the four-voice fugue ending the work, in a tempo marked Allegro moderato assai (♩ = 152). Ninety-six measures long, it is both monothematic and virtually monoharmonic. The subject is the soprano melody of "O Hoffnung," and the countersubject a chromatic eighth-note embellishment of the same (Example 3-52):

Example 3-52. *Forty Variations*, Variation 40 (Fugue), measures 235-238.

The entrances of the four voices are shown in Example 3-53:

Example 3-53. *Forty Variations*, Variation 40 (Fugue), measures 231-248.

The entries of the second and fourth voices a fifth below the first and third voices are certainly unorthodox; although they hint at the dominant, the cadence at measure 238 establishes the tonic again; hence the fugue circles around G major for some thirty measures.

One instance of a problem "corrected" by Beethoven in the autograph but not changed in the published edition concerns the writing of the second entry. In the second phrase (measure 235), Rudolph originally wrote a strict imitation of the subject (Example 3-54):

Example 3-54. *Forty Variations*, Variation 40 (Fugue), [Versions I and II], (measures 231-236 in the published edition).

Beethoven made an X in that measure (235) in the autograph Version II and wrote the letter "E" in the margin; in addition, he entered the note E on the staff for the upbeat eighth note. Nonetheless, the final decision was neither Rudolph's original *F-sharp* nor Beethoven's *E*, but the note *D*.

The material of the fugue, with its nonstop eighth-note motion, punctuated periodically by the distinctive rhythm of the subject, eventually modulates (measure 260) to the dominant, where the eighth-note motion continues against the subject. Changes in registration, voicing, and dynamics are the only elements of contrast. A climactic passage of ascending thirds ends on a fermata (measures 295-298) [Example 3-55]:

Example 3-55. *Forty Variations*, Variation 40 (Fugue), measures 295-298.

This passage is followed by a stretto of eighteen measures, in which brief statements of the principal motive pile up one on top of another (Example 3-56):

Example 3-56. *Forty Variations,* Variation 40 (Fugue), measures 299-301.

With a sustained trill on the dominant, the subject and countersubject are heard; the voices merge into a unison of the dotted rhythms of the ascending scale that accompanies the original theme, and, finally, a quiet recapitulation of the "O Hoffnung" motive ends the work (Example 3-57):

Example 3-57. *Forty Variations,* Variation 40 (Fugue), measures 317-326.

Certain elements characteristic of Beethoven's piano style are represented in the fugue. Rudolph's writing through much of it strongly resembles Beethoven's writing of the piano part in the fugato-style finale of his Sonata for Piano and Cello in D, Opus 102, No. 2, with its interweaving of lines and its scale passages in consecutive thirds and sixths.[17] The passage illustrated in Example 3-

[17]Rudolph's affection for this work, and its influence on his other fugal composition—the variation on Diabelli's waltz theme—is discussed in chapter 4, p. 144ff.

56—a sustained trill under which themes emerge—is similar to passages in the last movements of Beethoven's Sonata in C, Opus 53, and the Piano Trios in B-flat, Opus 11 and Opus 97, among others. The final Beethovenian touch is the unorthodox pedalling in the last measures, blending tonic and dominant harmonies—a technique Beethoven used in Opus 53, Opus 110, and other piano sonatas.

Rudolph's struggle with contrapuntal composition is much in evidence in this fugue, if we can judge from the number of Beethoven's corrections, many of which are numbered in Rudolph's manuscript, and then written out quite fully on the second page of Beethoven's autograph sketches (KRa A 4375). Beethoven was unsparing in his efforts to rid Rudolph's fugue of errors such as faulty voice-leading or parallels; for instance, he dealt with an example of the latter at measure 263 (Example 3-58):

Example 3-58. *Forty Variations*, Variation 40 (Fugue) [Beethoven's sketches], (measures 263-264 in the published edition).

In another passage several measures later, Beethoven wrote out large-scale corrections of parallel fifths and octaves occurring over three measures (Example 3-59):

Example 3-59. *Forty Variations*, Variation 40 (Fugue) [Beethoven's sketches], (measures 276-278 in the published edition).

106

Beethoven considered all the foregoing corrections (and several more) important enough to write them out in his appended sketches, with numbers clearly indicating their points of reference in Rudolph's manuscript. We may conclude our sampling of these with one final passage, where Rudolph's writing contains several examples of problems which he handled inexpertly—dissonant passing tones, poor voice-leading, and clumsy piano writing. Beethoven emended the two measures shown in Example 3-60 in two different sketches, and also made corrections in the margins to ensure Rudolph's understanding of his changes.

Example 3-60. *Forty Variations,* Variation 40 (Fugue) [Beethoven's sketches], (measures 311-312 in the published edition).

The *Forty Variations*—Archduke Rudolph's "masterpiece," as Beethoven termed it—stands as the centerpiece of Rudolph's compositions. Its large-scale conception encompasses an abundance of creative ideas, carried out in a well-crafted, highly imaginative manner.

In the absence of any preliminary sketches, the two autograph versions in Kroměříž offer the only evidence of Rudolph's work on the variations; from their appearance, it seems that the ideas for variations poured out quickly, and substantially in the form in which he put them down. The inspiration to compose on Beethoven's theme seems to have stimulated Rudolph's best and most ingenious efforts.

Beethoven's role in readying the variations for publication is ever-present in the manuscripts, with his meticulous attention to the smallest details. Yet it should be stressed that, for the most part, it is *only* small details that Beethoven fussed over—corrections of minor errors made by the Archduke either in carelessness or ignorance. In the best pedagogical tradition, Beethoven did not impose his own ideas on Rudolph's work excessively, nor did he attempt to recompose Rudolph's work in an attempt to better it. He offered his guidance, corrected what he felt essential, and allowed Rudolph his own voice.

THE WIENER PIANO-FORTE-SCHULE EDITION OF THE FORTY VARIATIONS

The early publication history of the *Forty Variations* is of some interest. A by-product of Steiner's first edition was a truncated version issued by Friedrich Starke in his didactic series of piano works called the *Wiener Piano-Forte-Schule*.[18] On the title page is a list of the "vorzüglichsten Piano-Forte-Spieler und Tonsetzer" represented in the series, including the outstanding composers of piano music of the time—the two Mozarts (father and son), Clementi, Czerny, Dussek, Field, Hummel, Ries, and, of course, Beethoven. Starke, a multifaceted musician who had settled in Vienna early in his

---

[18]Friedrich Starke (1774-1835) pursued careers as a horn player, Kapellmeister, piano teacher, composer, arranger, editor, and publisher during his lifetime. His friendship with Beethoven was of long standing, and Beethoven praised Starke's ability on the horn after the latter played the composer's Horn Sonata, Opus 17.

career, had been in close contact with Beethoven, first as piano teacher to nephew Karl and later as publisher of several of Beethoven's piano compositions in the *Piano-Forte-Schule*.[19] No record exists of any communication between Starke and Archduke Rudolph regarding publication arrangements for the *Forty Variations*, the sole evidence of their relationship being a visiting card of Starke's found among miscellaneous papers in the Kroměříž library. We can infer, however, that it was Beethoven who recommended Rudolph's variations to Starke, since the latter was involved just then with the publication of Beethoven's works in the series. Furthermore, Beethoven was closely connected with Starke's edition of the *Forty Variations* in an editorial capacity, as shall be seen shortly.

The *Piano-Forte-Schule* series version of the *Forty Variations*, as it appeared in 1821, contains twenty-four variations and conspicuously lacks all the longest movements, including the Introduction and most of the Finale, Variation 40.[20] Of the longer variations, only No. 38 (= No. 24 in the *Piano-Forte-Schule*) is included, as the penultimate variation, followed by the Fugue from the end of Variation 40. One significant change was made, aside from the omissions cited: Variation 36, the Adagio in G major (= No. 23 in the *Piano-Forte-Schule*), is abridged to eight measures; the cadenza-like eighth measure leads directly into the G minor variation (No. 38 in the original). In the original *Forty Variations*, the final notes of the cadenza maintained the G major tonality (Example 3-61):

Example 3-61. *Forty Variations*, Variation 36, measure 8.

[19]The "3ᵗᵉ Abtheilung" of the *Wiener Piano-Forte-Schule* appeared in 1821, with a lengthy foreword explaining its lofty educational purpose. Two numbers contained works by Beethoven, including a solo arrangement of the last movement of the Piano Concerto in C Minor, Opus 37 (erroneously listed in the foreword as in "C-dur"), five Bagatelles from Opus 119, and parts of the Piano Sonata Opus 31, No. 2. Another error appears on the title page containing Rudolph's variations: the composer's name is given as "Rudoph [*sic*] E. H. v. Östr."

[20]The complete list of omitted variations is: Variations 7, 8, 9, 17, 18, 21, 22, 24, 26, 27, 28, 29, 30, 37, 39, and all of the Finale (Variation 40) except the Fugue.

In Starke's version, the notes E and B are flatted in order to prepare for the sudden turn to G minor (Example 3-62):

Example 3-62. *Forty Variations* (*Piano-Forte-Schule* edition), Variation 23, measure 8.

In keeping with the didactic purpose of the *Piano-Forte-Schule*, the variations are thoroughly annotated as to the degree of difficulty, the expressive intention, or the specific technical problems found in each one. Some of the annotations are merely descriptive comments, such as that preceding Variation 31 (= No. 18 in the *Piano-Forte-Schule*): "interessirt durch den Bass";[21] others are quite fanciful, as the remarks before Variations 19 and 20 (= Nos. 14 and 15 in the *Piano-Forte-Schule*): "neckend wie eine junge Geliebte, und No. 15, schmeichelnd wie sie."[22] The most elaborate and grandiloquent commentary precedes the Fugue: "Eine künstliche herrliche FUGE über die Haupt-Theile des THEMA's schliesst das Ganze auf eine würdige Weise, und beurkundet auf eine glänzende Art die grosse, wahre Kunstbildung des hohen Verfassers. Das Ganze (welches bei S. A. Steiner u. Comp. in Wien zu haben ist, und hier angewendet werden konnte,) ist eine herliche Gabe, welche die Kunstwelt mit Ehrfurcht empfängt, an der sich Meister und Lehrlinge laben, ein Denkmahl, das auf kräftiger BASIS ruht, und das keine Zeit zerstören wird."[23]

The most significant aspect of the Starke publication is the "bezeichneter Fingersetzung" ("indicated fingering") supplied by Beethoven. Fingerings are fairly unusual in the published piano works of the composer, reserved as a rule for passages of virtuoso demand, such as consecutive thirds or fourths, or places where

[21]"interesting bass line."

[22]"teasing like a young sweetheart, and No. 15, flattering like her."

[23]"An ingenious, wonderful Fugue on the principal parts of the theme brings the whole to a close in a worthy fashion, and confirms in a brilliant manner the great, true artistic competency of its highborn creator. The entire [work], which can be obtained at S.A. Steiner and Co. in Vienna, and which could not be given [fully] here, is a marvelous gift which the art world receives with awe, which masters and pupils enjoy, a monument that rests on a strong base [and] that no [future] epoch will destroy."

Beethoven wanted some special effect, such as in the recitative of the slow movement of the Sonata in A-flat, Opus 110.[24] The *Piano-Forte-Schule* reprinting of the two movements from Beethoven's Sonata in D, Opus 28, also contains annotations and fingerings by the composer, and probably Starke enlisted Beethoven's collaboration to supply the same in the work of his pupil, quite likely as a selling point. The fingerings given in the *Forty Variations* by Beethoven are not numerous and are usually limited to passages in which the division of the music between the two hands presents awkward problems. Most of these passages occur in the Fugue, and Beethoven's fingerings succeed in making the contrapuntal voice-crossings more manageable, as below:

Example 3-63. *Forty Variations* (*Piano-Forte-Schule* edition), Fugue, measures 57-59.

[24]See William S. Newman, "Beethoven's Fingerings as Interpretive Clues," *Journal of Musicology* I, 2 (1982) 171-97.

Plate 25. Beethoven sketches (ink) for corrections in the *Forty Variations*, p. 1.
Facsimile of autograph (Kroměříž, KRa A 4375).

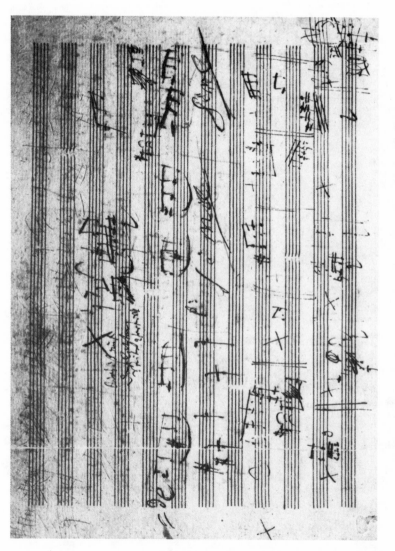

Plate 26. Beethoven sketches (ink) for corrections in the *Forty Variations*, p. 2. Facsimile of autograph (Kroměříž, KRa A 4375).

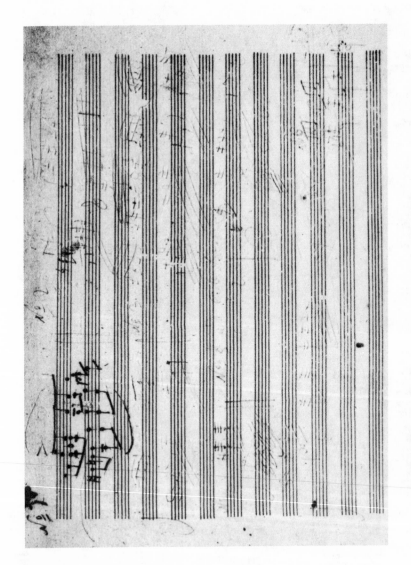

Plate 27. Beethoven sketches (ink and pencil) for corrections in the *Forty Variations*, p. 3. Facsimile of autograph (Kroměříž, KRa A 4375).

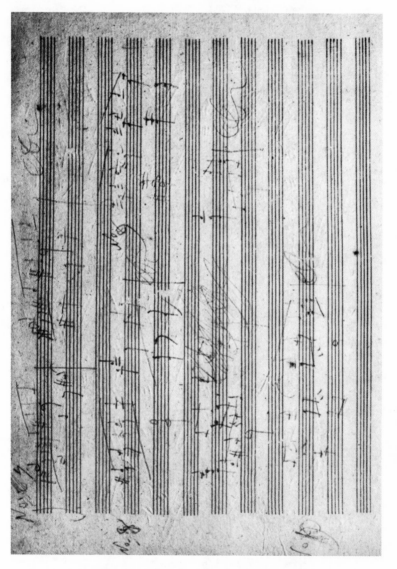

Plate 28. Beethoven sketches (pencil) for corrections in the *Forty Variations*, p. 4. Facsimile of autograph (Kroměříž, KRa A 4375).

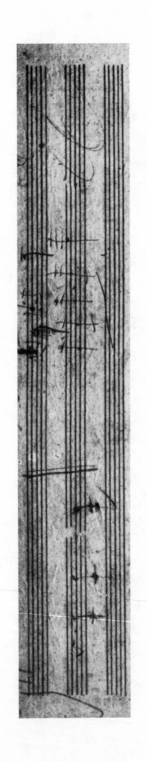

Plate 29. Beethoven sketches (pencil) for corrections in the *Forty Variations*, p. 5. Facsimile of autograph (Kroměříž, KRa A 4375).

Plate 30. Beethoven's suggested title for the *Forty Variations*, p. 6.
Facsimile of autograph (Kroměříž, KRa A 4375).

Plate 31. Beethoven's corrections on the final pages of the manuscript of the *Forty Variations* (Kroměříž, KRa A 4373).

CHAPTER IV

Variations and Other Works for Piano

Archduke Rudolph's accomplishment as a pianist, documented in several contemporary sources, is also reflected in the predominance among his works of music for piano solo, piano duet, or with piano accompaniment. While his physical ailments curtailed his playing (at least in public) in early adulthood, his hundreds of sketches, almost all in piano score, suggests that he composed at the piano, or with the piano in mind.

In his early piano compositions, Rudolph's writing is inconsistent—primitive and sometimes awkward in the earliest works, on occasion asking the impossible. As his composing progressed, his piano writing became more idiomatic, showing more keyboard flair and practical knowledge. Like Beethoven, he eschewed virtuosity as a means of mere display but did not hesitate to make technical demands on the pianist if the course of the music demanded it. In sum, his piano music has a wide range of keyboard styles, from simply accompanied settings of simple themes to the rigorous complexities of contrapuntal writing.

The *Forty Variations* gained the Archduke his greatest recognition as a composer—by Beethoven, by his publisher, and by the public. Other piano compositions, including variation sets that are interesting and skillfully written, have been largely overlooked. In this chapter these works will be examined, and selected examples from them will illustrate Archduke Rudolph's handling of keyboard composition and Beethoven's role in their improvement.

Variations For Piano

Archduke Rudolph's preference for variations began with his earliest compositions and continued throughout his composing career; variation pieces predominate in all his instrumental music, including his sonata works. In general, Rudolph showed himself most comfortable and capable in short, compact structures, especially those found in the traditional variation sets that proliferated in the Classical period. Since most of Rudolph's compositions were written for the instrument he played, variations for piano are numerous. Four of the five piano variation sets are in the key of G, and each was composed at a different period in the Archduke's career.

VARIATIONS IN G (CA. 1809); THEM. CAT. NO. 3

The earliest example of a variations work by the Archduke was, according to the autograph, his very first composition: a set of fourteen variations in G for piano on a theme evidently of his own invention.[1] This work appears to precede the two compositions for czakan (a type of flute), which are dated 1810 (see chapter 5, p. 167ff).

Two autographs of the variations are in Kroměříž (KRa A 4371), both in ink; one is an unfinished draft, the other a fair copy of a final version. The draft goes up to the twelfth variation, which is broken off at the end of page 12; the fair copy, on thirteen pages, is fully edited, with phrasing and expression marks, and consists of fourteen variations and a coda. On a manuscript page preceding the music there is a title written in extremely faded pencil: "Variations/Ier Composition de son A.I. Monseigneur/1'Archiduc Rodolphe d'Autriche."[2] The writing of the bass clef (similar to Beethoven's, but

---

[1] The notational style of two other works (20 Ländler and a keyboard canon on the song "Ach, du lieber Augustin," discussed later in this chapter) points to them as of earlier origin than the variations; accordingly, they are Nos. 1 and 2 in the thematic catalogue. None of these three early works is included in Rudolph's catalogue listing of his own compositions.

[2] The initials "A.I." stand for "Altesse Impériale."

unlike that found in Rudolph's music after 1814) and the misspelling of several words (e.g., "alegretto" and "pollaca") may also be considered evidence of their early origin.

The theme is simple and in a squarely binary form (8+8 measures); the harmony is entirely tonic and dominant; the left hand plays an Alberti bass throughout (Example 4-1):

Example 4-1. *Variations in G,* Theme.

Among the many differences in the fair copy are changes in the order of variations, the entering of expression marks mentioned earlier, and the addition of two new variations and an extended coda in several sections. The convention of varying the theme only slightly in the first few variations and increasing the figural activity gradually is observed by Rudolph. The first three variations maintain the melody, and the broken-chord accompaniment becomes a sixteenth-note scale figure. With the fourth, fifth, and sixth variations (Example 4-2), the sixteenth notes are turned into faster sixteenth-note triplets:

Plate 32. *Variations in G for piano* (Kroměříž, KRa A 4371).

Example 4-2. *Variations in G.*
    2a. Variation 4, measures 1-2.

    2b. Variation 5, measures 1-2.

    2c. Variation 6, measures 1-2.

Other conventions of Classical variations are also present: the traditional character-type variations of a march and a polacca; a fantasy-like slow movement in minor; and a concluding variation and coda in a lively 6/8, returning at the end to the tempo and meter of the theme. The slow variation (Adagio), number twelve in the set, is a fantasy in an improvisatory style, enlarging well beyond the 8 + 8 structure of the preceding variations and modulating into a new key area (B-flat) with new thematic ideas after the double bar. Several measures from this section illustrate Archduke Rudolph's expressive and lyrical extemporization in the new key en route back to G minor (Example 4-3):

Example 4-3. *Variations in G*, Variation 12, measures 20-28.

Noteworthy in this excerpt is the Beethovenian pedal marking in measures 27 and 28, blending the dissonant harmonies of three chords.

In the coda, too, the structure is expanded to include several rhapsodic, cadenza-like passages, an excursion into still another new key (E-flat), and, after more brilliant figuration, a very Beethoven-like conclusion (Example 4-4):

Example 4-4. *Variations in G*, Variation 14, measures 71-89.

If the assumption that the *Variations in G* were composed so close to the start of Archduke Rudolph's composing career is correct (and there is no reason to doubt the accuracy of the title page), his competency in this genre was established very early. The variations reflect both his strengths and his weaknesses, many of which—in either direction—are also evident in variation works he composed much later. The strong points in the variations include tight structure, inventive figuration, and an overall architecture that emphasizes stylistic diversity. The weaknesses are largely those of the student or amateur. In some places Rudolph's piano writing is awkward and unidiomatic; for instance, an attempt to preserve both the theme and the scale pattern of the accompaniment in Variation 3 results in the clumsy passage shown in Example 4-5:

Example 4-5. *Variations in G*, Variation 3, measures 1-4.

Elsewhere the Archduke called for a virtually unplayable octave glissando on the G major scale (Example 4-6):

Example 4-6. *Variations in G*, Variation 10, measure 2.

The majority of Rudolph's failings, however, are of the type that Beethoven painstakingly corrected in later compositions, such as awkward voice leading and poor chord doublings. Beethoven evidently did not look these variations over; it is doubtful that he would have let pass anything so crude as the awkward leap of an augmented fourth (*D-flat* to *G*) in the melody at measures 27-28 in Example 4-3—just one of several similar errors in the variations. On the whole, though, these are minor shortcomings, outweighed by the work's overall level of competence and interest.

(LÄNDLER) VARIATIONS IN G (1814); THEM. CAT. NO. 7

The second variation set for piano solo, chronologically speaking, can securely be assigned to the year 1814, thanks to the dated entry in Archduke Rudolph's catalogue listing of his own compositions. This work is a theme with twelve variations, in three-quarter meter, and is actually a set of *Ländler*-like dances. The autograph is in the Gesellschaft der Musikfreunde (Wgm VII 15418), and there is a manuscript copy in another hand in the Musiksammlung of the Thüringische Landesbibliothek in Weimar, DDR (WRtl Mus V=731).[3]

The entry in the Archduke's catalogue (number 11 of the 17 works listed) includes descriptive information beyond the title of the work: "*Variations*/per il Pianoforte/Original Manuscript und Abschrift in Maroquin gebunden/für die Herzogin von Weimar Marie, Grossfürstin von Russland, Kaiser Alexander des I Schwester componirt im J. 1814."[4] The elegantly bound copy so described was undoubtedly the presentation copy for the dedicatee, the Duchess of Weimar, and is most likely the one now housed in the Thuringian library in Weimar, which is the work of a professional copyist.

Festivities associated with the Congress of Vienna, which took place at the Imperial residence, the Hofburg, from September 1814 through June 1815, were the occasion for the composition of these variations. Housed in the palace as the Congress convened were all the important crowned heads of Europe and their entourages; banquets and balls took place nightly in the two main ballrooms of the Hofburg, the *Grosse Redoutensaal* and the *Kleine Redoutensaal*. The demand for new dance music was heavy; Archduke Rudolph's music catalogue lists dozens of sets of *Ländler* and *Deutsche* composed for specific evenings during that period.

Rudolph's theme and variations could certainly have been functional; the whole work is a series of *Ländler* based on a simple theme whose melody outlines tonic and dominant chords. The structure of the theme itself is the usual binary form of 8 + 8 measures (‖: A :‖ :B :‖); A remains in the tonic and B begins in the dominant and cadences in the tonic. Each of the twelve numbered variations, however, consists

[3] There are also six pages of sketches for the variations in the *Membra disjecta* (KRa A 4433) in Kroměříž.

[4] "Variations/for the Piano/Original manuscript and copy bound in morocco/ composed in the year 1814 for Marie, Duchess of Weimar, Grandduchess of Russia and sister of Emperor Alexander I."

of two 8 + 8 segments (‖: A :‖ :B: ‖: C:‖ :D:‖), in which A and C are alike harmonically, and B is similar to D, thus, in effect, creating twenty-four variations rather than twelve. Unlike the Archduke's other variation sets, these are the harmonic type in structure; the harmonic scheme remains intact (the left hand supplying a waltz-type accompaniment or a variant of it), and the melodic figurations merely furnish embroidery of the tonic-dominant harmonies. There are no changes in meter, naturally, and just one tempo change ("un poco più lento") for the single variation in minor (no. XI). The objective is to produce a continuous dance pattern based on the strong, lilting rhythm of the *Ländler*; the resultant challenge of creating change while adhering to a rigid framework is met by Rudolph with ingenuity. For illustration, the eight-measure introduction, the theme, and the opening measures of four variations (in each case from the first half of the variation) are shown in Example 4-7:

Example 4-7. *(Ländler) Variations in G*, Introduction, Theme and Variations I, IV, VI, and IX.

127

Variation I, measures 1-4.

Variation IV, measures 1-4.

Variation VI, measures 1-4.

Variation XI, measures 1-4.

dolce

VARIATIONS ON "DI TANTI PALPITI" (CA. 1817); THEM. CAT. NO. 9

The third of Archduke Rudolph's variations in the key of G is based on the cavatina "Di tanti palpiti" from Rossini's opera *Tancredi*, which had its first performance in Vienna in December 1816, three years after its Venice premiere. The opera was enormously successful, and the popularity especially of "Di tanti palpiti" is reflected in the outpouring of variation sets and fantasies on the melody by contemporaries of the Archduke, a few dozen of which are recorded in his catalogue.[5] Rudolph wrote enthusiastically to his librarian Baumeister after hearing *Tancredi* at the Baden Theater during the summer of 1817,[6] and he probably began composing his variations on "Di tanti palpiti" shortly thereafter. In the catalogue list of his compositions, these variations are number 16, one of the two entries made in a hand other than Rudolph's during the period 1818-1820.[7] The complete entry reads: "Variations sur un Thème de l'Opera Tancred dédiées à S.A.I. l'Archiduchesse Henriette."[8] In the Gesell-

---

[5] Rudolph's catalogue lists 140 works by Rossini, of which first place is given to numerous editions of *Tancredi*—full scores, piano arrangements, and so on.
[6] Letters in Haus-, Hof- und Staatsarchiv dated 21 July and 30 September 1817.
[7] See Appendix 1 for description of the catalogues.
[8] Archduchess Henriette was the wife of Rudolph's brother, Archduke Karl.

schaft der Musikfreunde are located the two extant manuscripts of the variations; one is an autograph (Wgm VII 15409), the other a professional copy (Wgm Q 15074), which may have been a presentation manuscript for the Archduchess.[9]

In its operatic form, "Di tanti palpiti" is a free da capo aria; the first (A) section, shown in Example 4-8, is eight measures long, with a simple harmonic scheme (I-V-I-V-I) underlying a melody of varied rhythmic ideas:

Example 4-8. Rossini, "Di tanti palpiti" (*Tancredi*), measures 1-8.

There is more harmonic variety in the middle (B) section; its twenty-eight measures modulate to the mediant (B-flat) for four measures, alternate between tonic minor and dominant for several more, and arrive finally at a fermata on the dominant, followed by a short cadenza. The da capo recapitulates the first A section, which is then repeated in an embellished version; a short coda follows in which a new harmony and a new thematic idea are introduced.

In Archduke Rudolph's setting of the theme, the simple form of the ABA—that is, without the extended material in the da capo—is used. The vocal line is given to the right hand, while the orchestral accompaniment is adapted with slight modification to an Alberti bass figure.

The variations follow the traditional structural pattern: in the first seven we find increased rhythmic activity in the figuration, a march variation, and one in minor marked "un poco più lento." Rudolph takes advantage of the hold on the dominant chord in four of the variations to write brief cadenzas similar to the one Rossini composed for the voice at the same place. The eighth variation is in a waltz meter in a slightly faster tempo, preceding a return to the theme. In this coda-like section, Rudolph provides an original and charming touch,

---

[9]The Kroměříž archive contains an unfinished setting of "Di tanti palpiti" for solo clarinet and orchestra, in the key of B-flat (Them. cat. no. U 22). A full set of variations was evidently planned, but the scoring is only roughly sketched.

bringing in the new material from Rossini's da capo and rounding out the structure with it. The melodic line and figuration in the right hand follow Rossini's vocal line closely until the last six measures; there, Rudolph adds a final reference to the original theme, and in the last two measures he uses the same dominant-tonic chords with which he closed the *Forty Variations*. The entire coda is shown in Example 4-9:

Example 4-9. *Variations on "Di tanti palpiti"*, Variation 8 (Coda), measures 65-86.

VARIATIONS ON A THEME BY SPONTINI FOR PIANO DUET (CA. 1816); THEM. CAT. NO. 8

Most of Archduke Rudolph's settings of music for piano duet—either one piano four hands or two pianos—are transcriptions and arrangements of orchestral or chamber music by other composers, which have been described in chapter 2. Of original compositions of this type, the single work he completed is an outstanding example of the Archduke's success with variations; this is a set of ten variations for piano four hands on a theme from Spontini's opera *La Vestale.*[10] An autograph group consisting of three incomplete drafts of the variations, along with a fair copy, are in the Kroměříž archive (KRa A 4393-94);[11] one draft contains a few pencilled corrections in Beethoven's hand. A manuscript copy of the work is in the Gesellschaft der Musikfreunde (Q 11427).

Precise dating of these variations is problematical; one of the three sketches in Kroměříž has certain of the handwriting characteristics associated with Rudolph's early work, e.g., the shape of the bass clefs and spelling of the word "alegretto." In the Archduke's catalogue, however, the entry number for the variations (number 13) and the handwriting of the entry itself ("Duetto a. d. Vestalin von Spontini mit 10 Veränderungen à 4 mains") place the date of composition around 1816.[12] From this contradictory evidence, one may infer that Rudolph conceived the variations and attempted a first draft several years before completing the work, at which time he entered it into his catalogue list. Rudolph received the score of *La Vestale* as a gift from his sister-in-law, Empress Maria Ludovica (third wife of Emperor Franz), on 24 February 1809, according to the information in the catalogue of his music collection listing the works by Spontini in his library. Now in the Gesellschaft der Musikfreunde, this score is

---

[10]Two unfinished compositions for piano duet are in sketch form in Kroměříž: a theme and variations for two pianos (Them. cat. no. U 4) and a set of four marches with trios for two pianos (Them. cat. no. U 5).

[11]In Kroměříž there is also a one-page setting of the theme for clarinet, viola, bassoon, and guitar in the *Membra disjecta* (KRa A 4438).

[12]At this time Rudolph's hands were severely crippled from an arthritic ailment, preventing him from playing the piano and severely distorting his handwriting. In writing the title of the variations ("Duet from *La Vestale* of Spontini with 10 variations, for four hands"), as at other times, Rudolph combines different languages.

handsomely bound in red leather with gold embossing and a gold crest encircling the letter L (for Ludovica).[13]

The theme used by Archduke Rudolph is derived from the cabaletta, ("A te che nel periglio") of a long Duo, "Quanto amistà," from Act I of *La Vestale*, of a spirited, almost martial character. The two vocal melodies are doubled throughout by orchestral instruments, principally clarinets and violins; Rudolph's setting of the theme is based mainly on the orchestral parts. The introduction and the theme, in his setting, are shown in Example 4-10:

Example 4-10. *Variations on a Theme by Spontini*, measures 1-24.

[13]The score may have been a birthday present for Archduke Rudolph, who reached twenty-one on January 8.

133

While Rudolph preserves the basic features of Spontini's writing, including the tonality and the figuration of the accompaniment, his adaptation for purposes of constructing a theme suitable for variations necessitated a few changes. The first eight measures are the same in both Spontini's and Rudolph's versions, but the second section, which in the opera is disproportionately long (43 measures), is abridged by Rudolph to twelve measures, thereby achieving a better balance between the two sections in length. In both the A and B sections the harmonic underpinning consists, again, entirely of tonic and dominant chords; the main attraction of the theme is centered in its rhythmic and melodic buoyancy.

The ten variations follow the same structural pattern familiar in most of Rudolph's variation compositions, relying on varied figuration of increasing rhythmic activity through the first six, and then turning to different character types—a Tempo di Polacca (No. 7), Tempo di Marcia (No. 8), Adagio in minor (No. 9), and finally, an Alegretto [sic] in 6/8 for the final variation and coda. The full expanse of the keyboard is exploited, with the bass part, rather exceptionally here, providing a fair share of melodic interest.

Spontini's harmonic pattern for the theme is retained through most of the early variations; twice (in variations 5 and 7) Rudolph makes changes in the second (B) section to relieve the harmonic repetition. In the Tempo di Polacca, for example, the B section begins in the mediant, then modulates back to the tonic (Example 4-11):

Example 4-11. *Variations on a Theme by Spontini,* Variation 7, measures 9-12 (reduced)

The most adventurous harmonic deviation occurs in the Adagio variation (No. 9), whose first half bears some resemblance to the slow movement of Beethoven's Sonata in A-flat, Opus 26, titled "Marcia Funèbre sulla morte d'un Eroe." Similarities exist in the mournful, dirge-like spirit, slow dotted rhythms, and harmonic procedure (I-III). The example from Beethoven's slow movement (Example 4-12a) is followed by that from Rudolph's (Example 4-12b):

Example 4-12a. Beethoven, *Sonata in A-flat* (Opus 26), 2nd movement, measures 1-8.

Example 4-12b. *Variations on a Theme by Spontini*, Variation 9, measures 1-8.

In the second half of Variation 9 there is a modulation to D-flat (enharmonic C-sharp) and a somewhat abrupt return to the tonic via an augmented-sixth progression. The transition to the final variation, in 6/8, is accomplished imaginatively by repeating two measures from the opening introductory music—a convincing means of unifying the complete set.

The three unfinished drafts in Kroměříž show different stages of Rudolph's work on the variations. The most significant change was made in the Introduction; the musical content was the same, but it consisted of only one measure in one draft, and of two measures in another. In the fair copy, Rudolph finally arrived at the four-measure setting.

The draft containing Beethoven's corrections has the one-measure Introduction, the theme, and most of the third variation (in this draft variation 2 = variation 3 of the fair copy, and variation 3 = variation 4). Judging from the bass clef, this draft was written later than the two others, and from its appearance, some pages have been lost. There are only four corrections by Beethoven, in pencil, treating the most elementary problems: avoidance of parallels, chord voicings, and melodic contour. Two passages marked by Beethoven, both in variation 1, are shown below (Example 4-13):

Example 4-13. *Variations on a Theme by Spontini* (draft version), Variation 1.

4-13a.

4-13b.

In example 4-13a, Beethoven's correction (shown below the system) eliminates the parallel fifths between the soprano and tenor voices; in Example 4-13b (shown above the system), Beethoven varies the melodic fragment *E, D-sharp, F-sharp* in the second of its three repetitions within two measures.

LÄNDLER AND OTHER DANCES

Like so many other Austrian composers of the nineteenth century, Archduke Rudolph was drawn to the *Ländler* or *Deutsche*, those quintessential Austrian dances that found their way into many works of Viennese composers from Haydn and Mozart through Mahler.[14]

[14]Beethoven's compositions in this genre are numerous; in the Kinsky-Halm catalogue, WoO 7-17, there are sets of 6 or 12 dances for orchestra or strings (two violins and bass), variously titled *Menuette, Deutsche Tänze, Ländlerische Tänze,* and *Contretänze.*

Much of this music by Archduke Rudolph's contemporaries was functional, composed for the great balls held in the two Hofburg *Redoutensäle*, especially while the Congress of Vienna convened during the winter of 1814-15. As stated previously, the Archduke's music catalogue lists many such sets of dances, most for orchestra and some for piano, often titled simply *Redouten-Deutsche*, each entry usually accompanied by the specific date of the occasion for which they were composed.

Archduke Rudolph composed several sets of dances, including *20 Ländler* (Them. cat. no. 2), *3 Polonaises* (Them, cat. no. 5), and *3 Ländler* (Them. cat. no. 6), all for piano solo. For piano four hands there is a group of *12 Allemandes* (Them. cat. no. 4A) and the coda of a set of *Deutsche Tänze* (Them. cat. no. 4B). The two last-named works contain basically the same music as two orchestrated sets, one called *Deutsche*, the other *Ländler* (Them. cat. no. 4C). Only the coda is different.[15] There is also a Menuetto and Trio in B (a rare key) for solo piano (Them. cat. no. 14) which, since it exists only in a copy, cannot be dated accurately.

In all these pieces Rudolph follows the traditional pattern common to the *Ländler*; each dance and its trio are binary in structure, both halves eight measures in length. While each dance is in a different tonality, the harmony of the individual dances and trios invariably centers around tonic and dominant chords only, and each dance and its trio are in the same key.

In this genre, the earliest set of dances appears to be the *20 Ländler* for piano. The clef signs in the manuscript are those found in the Archduke's earliest pieces, e.g., his primitive piano arrangements of music by Handel and Gluck (see chapter 2, pp. 59-60 and p. 66), which were probably written before 1809. The *20 Ländler* typify most of Archduke Rudolph's dance pieces—they are extremely simple in design, with waltz-type accompaniments that remain within a very limited range. Variety and interest are sustained by the shape and rhythm of the melodies and continual shifting of tonality from one dance to another (see the thematic catalogue for examples).

Archduke Rudolph's melodic inventiveness is very apparent in the *3 Ländler*, which are of somewhat later origin, to judge by handwriting evidence; some of his melodic ideas here, in fact, have the same

---

[15]It is clear that Archduke Rudolph used these three terms—*Ländler, Deutsche,* and *Allemandes*—interchangeably.

138

immediate appeal as Schubert's dance pieces and often are carried out as expertly. One particularly Schubertian example (the resemblance is in the harmonic progression underlying the melody, from II $^6_3$ to I $^6_4$) is shown in Example 4-14:

Example 4-14. 3 *Ländler* (No. 2), measures 1-9.

The most important of Rudolph's dance sets are the *12 Ländler,* extant in several manuscript copies; with the exception of the coda, all the versions, variously titled *Allemandes, Deutsche,* or *Ländler* (see note 15), are virtually indentical. The settings for piano duet are in the Gesellschaft der Musikfreunde, as *12 Allemandes* (Wgm Q 19886), a manuscript copy, and *Deutsche Tänze* (Wgm VII 29340), an autograph of a coda only, different from the coda in the *12 Allemandes* (the orchestral versions are discussed in chapter 7). An entry for the 12 *Allemandes* in the Archduke's music catalogue list of his works places their composition ca. 1809-10; it is the second entry, before the two czakan compositions with their dates of 1810 (see Chapter 5), and it is likely that Rudolph's entries are in chronological order of composition. Also, the orchestral version in an autograph in Kroměříž is notated in the Archduke's early handwriting, which would confirm their early date of composition.

Typical *Ländler* in their binary structure (8+8) and rather heavily accented waltz accompaniments, the *Allemandes* unfold a variety of rhythmic and melodic ideas, each (dance and trio) in a different tonality. One follows another in a pattern of related keys, usually in a dominant or subdominant relationship (C-F-B-flat-E-flat-A-flat-C-G-D-A-E-A-E-flat); the extensive coda, which almost equals all twelve of the dances in length, begins in C minor and modulates through F,

B-flat, and E-flat before arriving at C and a recapitulation of the first dance.

3 Polonaises are an autograph in the Gesellschaft der Musikfreunde (Wgm VII 15419), on six pages in ink, written out rather crudely, with many measures crossed out. The handwriting and place of entry in Rudolph's catalogue suggest a composition date of ca. 1812. In these dances, the form is more a rounded binary type; each second half is developed so that it is double the length (16 measures) of the first half. The trios are in contrasting keys, and a characteristic polonaise rhythm is carried out in each dance. Unlike the *Ländler*, which were probably written for dancing, the Polonaises do not appear to be functional.

Because the Archduke, as has been noted previously, was most in his element with small forms, these assorted dance pieces, with their compact, simple structures, are successfully realized. The challenge of sustaining interest through melodic invention is met with ease and ingenuity, and the dances, despite their early origin, can be termed among Rudolph's most professional achievements as a composer.

FUGA ON DIABELLI'S WALTZ THEME (CA. 1821); THEM. CAT. NO. 11

When the Viennese composer and music publisher Anton Diabelli conceived the idea of soliciting fifty variations on his own waltz theme from leading Austrian composers, with the purpose of publishing a monument to Austrian musical talent, he approached both Beethoven and his pupil, Archduke Rudolph. While including a member of the Imperial family was undoubtedly both patriotic and politic, it was also an act of recognition of the Archduke's status as a composer. Beethoven, of course, proceeded to create his own personal monument on Diabelli's theme, which Diabelli & Co. published in 1823 as *33 Veränderungen über einen Walzer von Anton Diabelli*, Opus 120. One year later, Diabelli brought out his originally planned project, without a contribution from Beethoven, but including variations by Franz Schubert, the fourteen-year-old Franz Liszt, W.A. Mozart "fils," and, among the many Austrian composers, Archduke Rudolph, whose variation in the form of a fugue (No. 40 in the set) was published under the pseudonymous initials "S.R.D." (Serenissimus Rudolphus Dux).[16]

[16]The history of the whole work and its fifty contributors is described by Heinrich Rietsch in "Ein gemeinsames Werk Österreichischer Komponisten" in *Österreichische Rundschau* III (1905) 438-48.

It may be assumed that Rudolph received a copy of the theme from Diabelli some time in 1819 or 1820.[17] In the miscellaneous sketches in Kroměříž (KRa A 4432), there is a copy, in pencil in Rudolph's hand, of Diabelli's waltz, with all the expression marks that appear in the published theme; on another page there are a few measures of a skeletal sketch for a variation unrelated to the fugue the Archduke finally composed. Otherwise, there are no traces of any preliminary sketches for the fugue extant among Rudolph's manuscripts, and no clue to the exact time of composition.

The subject and countersubject of the Archduke's fugue are drawn from the briefest motivic elements of Diabelli's theme and combined rather ingeniously with another countersubject of Rudolph's invention (Example 4-15):

Example 4-15a. Diabelli: *Waltz Theme,* measures 1-16.

[17]Rietsch gives 1821 as the date of Diabelli's conception, but evidence that Beethoven was making sketches for his variations as early as 1819, as well as the existence of the autograph of Carl Czerny's variation (now in the Österreichische Nationalbibliothek, Ms. 18366) dated May 1819, support the earlier date.

Example 4-15b. *Fuga on Diabelli's Theme*, measures 1-16.

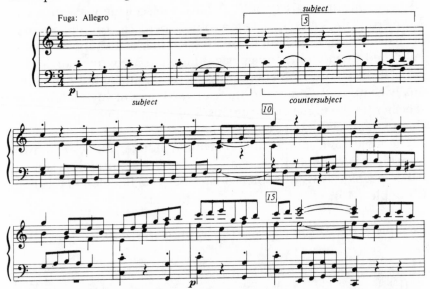

Although the fugue is rather long (136 measures), it is based almost entirely on repeated statements of these three intertwined motives, sometimes heard in inversion, with no contrasting episodes.[18] The repetitiveness of the thematic material is offset by continual, rapid harmonic change; after the first five fugal entries of the subject in measures 1-14, in traditional I-V-I-V-I order, the themes are presented in a series of sequences, with doublings in thirds and sixths, in constant tonicization. The fugue is divided into two halves, arriving at a cadence in E (with a fermata as a dividing point) at measure 76, roughly halfway through, and then followed by canonic entries of the subject, and a series of stretti centering around overlapping tonic and dominant harmonies (Example 4-16):

Example 4-16. *Fuga on Diabelli's Theme*, measures 70-84.

[18]In his description, Rietsch characterized the fugue as composed "*con alcuna licenza, mit einiger Freiheit.*"

Following a deceptive cadence at measure 108, the remaining coda traverses a harmonic route reminiscent of the final measures of the first movement of Beethoven's Piano Sonata in C, Opus 2, No. 3; in both works, the A-flat chord is resolved to I $_4^6$ after a chromatic series of diminished chords (although Rudolph reaches the C major chord from an augmented sixth chord, and Beethoven from a diminished seventh [Example 4-17]):

Example 4-17a. *Fuga on Diabelli's Theme,* measures 107-123 (abridged).

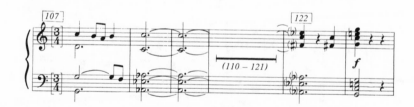

Example 4-17b. Beethoven, *Piano Sonata in C* (Opus 2, No. 3), lst movement, measures 217-232 (abridged).

In the measures leading to the final cadence of his work, Rudolph follows another procedure of Beethoven in the first movement of the same sonata (Example 18):

Example 18a. *Fuga on Diabelli's Theme,* measures 129-134.

Example 18b. Beethoven, *Piano Sonata in C* (Opus 2, No. 3), lst movement, measures 249-252.

The harmonic sequence of IV-V-I is, of course, not unusual; the similarity lies in the spread between the bass notes and the chords.

The most striking characteristic of Archduke Rudolph's style in this fugue in relation to that of Beethoven is in the figuration mentioned earlier, the use of octaves, thirds, and sixths in scale passages—a type of figuration that is ubiquitous throughout the last movement of Beethoven's Sonata for Cello and Piano in D, Opus 102, No. 2. Both sonatas of Opus 102 were particular favorites of Rudolph, and

Beethoven had had manuscript copies made for him.[19] The finale of the D Major Sonata is also a fugue "con alcuna licenza"—that is, an allegro in fugato style, based almost entirely on repetition of the thematic material of subject and countersubject, without contrasting episodes. In Beethoven's work, too, the arrival at a cadence on the mediant is roughly halfway through the movement. It is the style of figuration in the piano part, however—the scale passages with thirds and sixths—that strongly suggests Beethoven's influence on his pupil in the Diabelli fugue,[20] as is illustrated by a comparison of passages from both works (Example 4-19):

Example 4-19a. *Fuga on Diabelli's Theme,* measures 45-63.

[19]In a letter from 1815 (Anderson, *Letters,* p. 520) Beethoven asked Archduke Rudolph to "lend back" the manuscript copy of the sonatas for a few days. Opus 102 was not published until 1817.

[20]This style of figuration can be found in Archduke Rudolph's other fugal composition, the fugue that ends the final variation in his *Forty Variations* (see chapter 3l).

Example 4-19b. Beethoven, *Sonata for Cello and Piano in D*, Opus 102, No. 2, 3rd movement, measures 18-39.

Despite this similarity to Beethoven's compositional style, Rudolph's fugue has original features, particularly in its harmonic aspects. There is a bold use of dissonance, for example, which is a concomitant of the strict voice-leading as the melodic lines cross one another. The development of the fugue is structurally logical notwithstanding the amount of modulation; and above all, it is an interesting composition that artfully uses minimal means.

SMALL WORKS

Among the earliest of small piano works is a canonic setting in G-flat of the melody "Ach, du lieber Augustin" (Them. cat. no. 1); it is only sixteen measures long, but complete, and in the notation of Rudolph's writing ca. before 1809.

A short piece titled *Capriccio* (Them. cat. no. 12) is an example of a well-constructed composition illustrating Archduke Rudolph's capacity for lyrical writing. Although undated, the handwriting suggests it was composed fairly late, after 1820.

The *Capriccio* is scored on two pages, in ink, neatly written with all editing marks, including pedal, and has several pencil corrections in Beethoven's hand (KRa A 4383). In a small ABA form, it is in D-flat with a contrasting middle section in F minor; the tempo marking is Andante and includes a metronome indication of $\downarrow$ = 60. The opening measures (the whole piece consists of seventy-one measures) of the A and B sections are shown in Examples 4-20 and 4-21:

Example 4-20. *Capriccio,* measures 1-7.

Example 4-21. *Capriccio,* measures 26-29.

In the reprise of the A section, a triplet accompaniment is added in the right-hand part beneath the melody, similar to the embellished restatement of the main theme in the slow movement of Beethoven's Piano Sonata in C Minor, Opus 13 ("Pathétique").

Beethoven's corrections in this well-molded little piece are minimal; the most telling one is in the transitional passage linking the B section with the reprise of A, dealing with Rudolph's tendency to weaken melodic or harmonic peaks by anticipation (measure 41) or repetition (measure 43). Beethoven's changes are shown in Example 4-22:

Example 4-22. *Capriccio*, measures 41-43.

In measure 41, Beethoven's correction sustains the C in the melody and the C major harmony through the measure, so that the harmonic change under the *D-flat* in measure 42 coincides with the strong beat, whereas Rudolph's *D-flat* on the last beat of measure 41 weakened the impact of the harmonic change. The change Beethoven made in measure 43 accomplishes two things: by keeping the *D-flat* in the melody (rather than returning to the *C* of measure 41), the importance of *D-flat* as the melodic peak of the phrase is maintained; in addition, a stronger harmony is created with the diminished seventh chord.

A few small corrections were made in the reprise of the A section, one of which is shown in Example 4-23:

Example 4-23. *Capriccio*, measures 48-50.

Aside from making the awkwardly large stretch at measure 50 playable, Beethoven's elimination of *G-flat* in the melody at that place improves the voice-leading and makes the melodic phrase consistent with the original in measures 2-3.

A brief coda, which features a canonic restatement of the theme stripped bare of accompaniment, was corrected in one place by Beethoven (Example 4-24):

Example 4-24. *Capriccio,* measures 59-62.

With the one change of bass notes in measure 60, Beethoven eliminates the doubled third in the chord.

Archduke Rudolph's growth in several areas can be observed as we survey his piano compositions over a span of some thirteen years. In his handling of keyboard technique, for example, the sometimes awkward and careless writing exhibited in his earliest variation works gives way to surer, more fluent writing—difficult, perhaps, as in the Diabelli fugue, but idiomatic. In the later works, variation ideas are more inventive, less wedded to the themes, and harmonies are somewhat more adventuresome.

The extent of Beethoven's role in improving and correcting these works is difficult to assess with absolute certainty, because the visible corrections in this group of manuscripts are rather trivial and small in number. The fact remains, however, that throughout this period Beethoven was giving Rudolph composition lessons steadily, and logic dictates that lesson time was spent at least partially on going over the Archduke's music. We can safely conclude that Rudolph's development was in some measure influenced and shaped by his teacher.

CHAPTER V

Variations for Clarinet
and Other Woodwind Works

The preponderance of compositions for woodwind instruments—
the clarinet in particular—prompted Karl Vetterl, in his description of
Archduke Rudolph's oeuvre, to question whether the Archduke
himself, known to be a pianist, played the clarinet.[1] There is
absolutely no evidence to support this idea; hence, it is more likely
that it was Rudolph's close association with Count Ferdinand de
Troyer that constituted the sole motivation for the many works
Rudolph composed for clarinet. Ferdinand de Troyer and his brother
Franz served as chamberlains in Archduke Rudolph's court retinue
as early as 1809, and undoubtedly the proximity of devoted and
skillful instrumentalists provided a good reason to compose music
for their pleasure and use.

Rudolph's finished compositions for clarinet consist of two large-
scale works: the Sonata in A, published in 1822 with a dedication to
Ferdinand de Troyer, and the Variations in E-flat (on a theme by
Rossini). Other works, left incomplete, include two movements of a
projected three-movement sonata, a single sonata movement, and
two sets of variations—all for clarinet and piano. Almost all of
Rudolph's pieces for various chamber-music ensembles include the
clarinet, often as the principal solo instrument.

[1]Vetterl, "Der musikalische Nachlass," 174.

Two other instruments for which Archduke Rudolph composed were the czakan (a type of flute—see discussion of czakan works later in this chapter) and the basset horn, both apparently played by the Troyers; the czakan works also were dedicated to them, and the basset horn (an instrument in the clarinet family much employed by Mozart) was played chiefly by clarinetists.

The compositions selected for detailed description in this chapter represent music composed both early and late in Archduke Rudolph's career and give evidence of his technical knowledge of the capacities of the clarinet, czakan, and basset horn.

VARIATIONS IN E-FLAT FOR CLARINET AND PIANO (1822); THEM. CAT. NO. 23

The Introduction, Theme, and Variations in E-flat for Clarinet and Piano, on a cavatina ("Sorte! secondami") from Rossini's opera *Zelmira*, is one of the few works by Archduke Rudolph that can be dated with a fair degree of certainty. *Zelmira* was composed in 1821, received its premiere in Naples on 16 February 1822, and was given its first performance in Vienna at the Kärntnerthor Theater in April, 1822, with Rossini himself present. The opera was received enthusiastically, and the instantaneous popularity of Rossini's melodies was widespread among the music-loving Viennese. Since it was Archduke Rudolph's habit to acquire new music as soon as it was published, he undoubtedly obtained a piano-vocal score of *Zelmira* upon its publication in Vienna in 1822.[2]

In several letters to his pupil written from his summer residence at Hetzendorf in July and August of 1823, Beethoven alluded to some new variations by the Archduke:

> So I beg Y.I.H. to be patient a little longer about Y.I.H.'s variations. I think them charming; but all the same I have to examine them more thoroughly.[3]

Two weeks later Beethoven wrote that he expected to see the Archduke in about a week, and added:

[2] Rudolph's music catalogue lists 140 entries of works by Rossini, including piano-vocal scores of 40 operas.
[3] Anderson, *Letters*, 1056 (emended).

I shall bring Y.I.H.'s variations with me. Not many alterations will be necessary, and then it will be a rather nice and pleasant composition for those who enjoy music.[4]

And finally, in a letter from early August:

I have marked a few passages in the variations; orally it will be clearer.[5]

In a footnote to the first letter quoted above, Emily Anderson commented, "Evidently Beethoven had given the Archduke Rudolph another theme on which to compose variations. This second theme has not been identified."[6] The question of which of Rudolph's variations works was meant by Beethoven was the subject of discussion by Paul Nettl,[7] Karl Vetterl,[8] and Gerhard Croll,[9] in their articles about Archduke Rudolph. Both Nettl and Vetterl believed that Beethoven was referring to the variations for basset horn and piano on a Czech folk song, "To jsou koně" (see p. 164-167), which may have been composed close to the same time as the clarinet variations. Croll treats the question only in relation to an unidentified second "Aufgabe," which appears as an entry among Beethoven's works in Rudolph's music catalogue with a date of 1820.[10] From Beethoven's remarks, the variations he is talking about can hardly be those on "To jsou koně," because in the autograph of that work there are extensive pencilled alterations, and many measures are incomplete. Beethoven, however, seems to be referring to a finished work, in which "not many alterations will be necessary," in which he has marked "a few passages"—clearly not a work sketched out only in a rough, preliminary version.

A manuscript that does correspond closely to Beethoven's references is the one containing the Variations in E-flat for Clarinet and Piano on

[4]Anderson, Letters, 1063 (emended).

[5]Ibid., 1079 (emended).

[6]Ibid., 1056. Anderson apparently knew only of the existence of Rudolph's Forty Variations and assumed that these new variations must also have resulted from a theme assigned by Beethoven.

[7]Nettl, "Erinnerungen an Erzherzog Rudolph," 96-97.

[8]Vetterl, "Der musikalische Nachlass," 170.

[9]Croll, "Die Musiksammlung des Erzherzogs Rudolph," 53.

[10]The complete entry reads: "Aufgabe für S.K. Hoheit den Erzherzog Rudolph vor der Abreise. Mödling 11ten September 1820." Whether a new theme was composed for Rudolph by Beethoven, or suggested by him, and whether Rudolph used the "Aufgabe" for a new composition, cannot be determined.

Rossini's theme, which is an autograph manuscript in the Gesellschaft der Musikfreunde (Wgm XI 8244).[11] It bears several emendations in Beethoven's hand; in addition, the watermarks on the paper date it from 1822.[12] All available evidence, then, points to these variations as the subject of Beethoven's letters and establishes their date of composition between April, 1822, when *Zelmira* was first presented in Vienna, and the summer of 1823.

The piano-vocal score that was published by Artaria, taking advantage of the successful performances and audience interest, was arranged by the composer Adalbert Gyrowetz[13] and issued in 1822. Archduke Rudolph's setting of the theme "Sorte! secondami" is identical with Rossini's theme in its piano-vocal arrangement, substituting the clarinet for the voice. Only the key is changed (from D to E-flat) to better suit the B-flat clarinet. The theme is shown in Example 5-1:

Example 5-1. *Variations in E-flat,* Theme, measures 1-40.

[11]A performing edition based on this manuscript, edited by Otto Biba, was published in 1981 by Doblinger Verlag in Vienna as part of their Diletto Musicale series (DM 696). Beethoven's corrections have been incorporated into the edition without further identification.

[12]Robert Winter has identified the two types of paper used in this manuscript, both of which bear watermarks dating from 1822. The paper is identical with that used by Beethoven in the autograph of his Sonata in A-flat, Opus 110, and the sketchbook Artaria 201, also dating from 1822.

[13]Gyrowetz (1763-1850), a prolific Bohemian composer who settled in Vienna and became composer and conductor at the Court Theater, was one of the pallbearers at Beethoven's funeral.

The autograph score in the Gesellschaft der Musikfreunde was prepared with unusual care, bound in green silk with embossed gold edging, and includes a title page in Rudolph's hand: "Cavatina von Rossini/aus der Oper Zelmira (Sorte! secondami)/mit 8 Veränderungen/für das/Piano-forte, mit Begleitung/einer/Clarinette." Detailed expression marks—dynamics, phrasing, pedalling, and metronome numbers—were written in pencil first, then carefully inked over. In the binding process the pages were trimmed, partially excising some of Beethoven's marginal corrections. The music is written out on eight-stave oblong paper, and unlike Rudolph's usually crowded pages that utilize every staff, the three-stave clarinet and piano score is spaced with two unused staves between systems. The uncustomary neatness and completeness of detail suggest that the manuscript was prepared for performance; in all likelihood it was intended for Count Ferdinand de Troyer, the recipient of other woodwind compositions.

In Kroměříž can be found another complete autograph of the score (KRa A 4400). Much of it resembles the manuscript in the Gesellschaft der Musikfreunde in that it is in ink, with the same disposition of measures in each system; but the spacing is crowded, there are dozens of pencilled changes and additions (in Rudolph's hand), and it lacks the detailed finished editing of the Gesellschaft manuscript. This Kroměříž autograph was evidently the preparatory draft for the one in Vienna, which incorporates the pencilled changes.

In addition to the ink manuscript in Kroměříž, there are nineteen pages of very rough, often illegible, pencil sketches (KRa A 4401), most of them relating to the eighth variation, and in the *Membra disjecta* (KRa A 4431-32), several separate sheets of sketches pertaining to the variations can be found. Lastly, there are two copies of the clarinet part alone; one is incomplete, the other written with the same care and neatness of the Gesellschaft autograph, on vertically-scored paper, and evidently for the soloist's use.

These various manuscripts demonstrate Archduke Rudolph's workmanlike and industrious approach to composition. We see the creation of a large-scale piece through its various stages: first, the preliminary pencil sketches, many pages that resemble Beethoven's sketchbooks in the profusion of ideas written down in seeming disorder and relatively illegibly, yet recognizable in their relationship to the work at hand; then the first inked version, already well worked out in details, and despite some cancelled passages, notated with care; and finally, the completed product, to which Beethoven added a few finishing touches.

It is not entirely clear whether or not Beethoven saw the autograph in Kroměříž and made any suggestions about it to Rudolph; the pencilled changes all appear to be in Rudolph's hand only. Beethoven's references to the variations in the letters quoted earlier indicate that his corrections were few and trifling, in which case this work stands as the product of Rudolph's own creative process, and attests to the hard work and professionalism of his methods.

While the Introductions in the two autographs are very different, the theme itself and the variations are substantially alike. The numerous pencil corrections made by the Archduke usually concern figuration—e.g., increasing the rhythmic activity in the accompaniment figure—or improvement of the melodic line. These alterations are sometimes pencilled on the music, sometimes added in the margins. Two such changes are shown in Examples 5-2 and 5-3; in each, the original precedes the changed version.

Example 5-2. *Variations in E-flat* (Kroměříž autograph), Variation 1.

Example 5-3. *Variations in E-flat* (Kroměříž autograph), Variation 3.

The transformation of the Introduction, which Archduke Rudolph first conceived as an elaborate fantasy in a slow tempo, 73 measures long, was thoroughgoing. As in the opening Adagio of the *Forty Variations*, the first version had a second theme and a contrasting section in another tonality; but in the changed version, the Introduction is shortened by about half (42 measures) and is much simpler, remaining in E-flat and without any new thematic material. In the earlier version, the bridge between the Introduction and the Theme consisted of a long, florid cadenza for the clarinet; in the final version, the cadenza was replaced by a simple, two-measure passage in which, surely, the homage paid by the pupil to his teacher could not have escaped Beethoven's keen eye: a quotation (in the piano) of the opening theme from the master's Sonata in E-flat, Opus 81a ("Les Adieux"):[14]

Example 5-4. *Variations in E-flat,* Introduction, measures 41-43.

The structure of this work is similar to that of the *Forty Variations,* beginning with a slow introduction in which the theme for the variations (in this case, the Rossini aria) is used as the basic thematic material. Following the presentation of the theme itself, there are eight variations, among them such standard types as a march and a polacca, and including a contrasting variation in minor. The polacca is the eighth variation, a rondo finale in several sections and of considerable length. Many of the variations are virtuoso in the figuration of the piano part—consecutive thirds and sixths, fast repeated notes, and octave leaps.

Beethoven's emendations number exactly fourteen—not many for a seventy-page manuscript, to be sure—but rather more than the

---

[14]Rudolph refers to the *Lebewohl* motive from "Les Adieux" in another work—his duet, "Ich denke dein" (see chapter 8).

"few" mentioned in his letter. Most of them are the rather minute type of correction Beethoven made throughout the *Forty Variations*— eliminating one or two notes in a chord, for example (or sometimes adding notes to a chord), or slightly emending the melodic line. None of Beethoven's suggestions in this manuscript significantly alters Rudolph's work; rather, they offer refinements. The corrections, with one exception (a one-note change in the clarinet part), are all in the piano part. In addition to notes inserted in the score or entered in the margins, Beethoven occasionally also added the letter names of the notes changed, apparently for amplification. In one case, at the end of the fourth variation, he added a sentence in French: "c'es écrit pur une, mais pas pour doux voix."[15] These rather cryptic words, which do not appear to have any clear relationship with the music that precedes or follows them, may constitute one of the "remarks" that Beethoven intended to explain more fully in Rudolph's presence.

Turning to some examples of specific notations made by Beethoven, we see first changes made in melodic direction. In Example 5-5, the bass line was altered from an imitation of the scale passage in the treble to a figure with more variety, which at the same time removed the parallel fifths created by the upward motion of both lines:

Example 5-5. *Variations in E-flat,* Variation 4, measures 5-6 (piano part only).

Similarly, in Example 5-6, a change in the direction of the bass line brings about contrary rather than parallel motion:

---

[15]"It is written for one, but not for two voices." The spelling is Beethoven's.

Example 5-6. *Variations in E-flat,* Variation 4, measure 33 (piano part only).

In several instances Beethoven's addition of one or two notes to a chord was an apparent attempt to enrich the texture. In one such instance (Example 5-7), although the added notes produced parallel octaves between treble and tenor, Beethoven evidently thought it more important to emphasize the dominant and tonic chords with a richer sound:

Example 5-7. *Variations in E-flat,* Theme, measures 10-11.

In this change Beethoven was actually emending Rossini; in both the orchestral score[16] and in the piano-vocal version of *Zelmira,* the accompanying chords are notated precisely as Archduke Rudolph wrote them.

---

[16]A facsimile edition of Rossini's own original performance score has been published by Garland Press (New York, 1979).

Other Beethoven corrections are concerned with changes in Rudolph's harmonizations. In the following example from the eighth variation (Example 5-8), the clarinet melody is accompanied in the piano part by a dominant seventh chord (measure 29); in the repetition of the melody in the piano part (measure 31), Rudolph had originally changed the harmonization to the II chord (F minor). Beethoven, writing in the margin beneath, changed the right hand chords to make the two melodic segments consistent. In addition, he wrote in a change in the bass notes in measure 30; although the note-head was cut off from the bottom of the page when the manuscript was trimmed for binding, the length of the stem suggests that the G_1 was changed to $E\text{-}flat_2$, undoubtedly to avoid the emphasized dissonance between the G and the $A\text{-}flat$ in the clarinet part, and also to achieve contrary motion between the two parts:

Example 5-8. *Variations in E-flat,* Variation 8, measures 29-32.

Another example of harmonic alteration can be seen in the penultimate measure of the fourth variation, in the group of four sixteenth notes making up the third beat of the measure, which originally repeated the notes of the first beat. Beethoven's change (the right-hand notes are written in the margin below the staff, the left-hand notes in the staff itself) provides more harmonic variety and more propulsion from the third beat to and through the fourth beat (Example 5-9):

Example 5-9. *Variations in E-flat,* Variation 4, measure 39.

One final correction, again from the eighth variation, is shown in Example 5-10. Here, a simplification of the left-hand accompaniment serves to strengthen the dominant by emphasizing the fifth on each beat; at the same time, the reduced motion in the left-hand part does not allow distraction from the chromatic upper line:

Example 5-10. *Variations in E-flat,* Variation 8, measures 66-67 (piano part only).

It can be seen from the six examples illustrated here, representative in both type and in significance of the fourteen in the complete manuscript, that they deal with mere details. One may infer that Beethoven found little to correct and was sincere in his remarks that the variations were "charming" and would be "a delightful and pleasant composition" with a few alterations.

A comparison of Beethoven's corrections in the *Forty Variations* with those in the *Variations in E-flat* leads to the conclusion that in the three years intervening between the composition of the two works, Archduke Rudolph made substantial progress. Admittedly, the *Forty Variations* was a more ambitious work in scope, and in it the Archduke had to cope with the difficulties of fugal composition; still, some of the elementary technical problems that recur throughout the *Forty Variations*, such as awkward voice-leading and poor doubling in chords, are not prevalent in the later work. The manuscript that Rudolph submitted to Beethoven for his approval was thoroughly worked over and polished first, and the faults of the amateurish student are largely absent.

VARIATIONS ON "TO JSOU KONĚ" FOR BASSET HORN AND PIANO (CA. 1822); THEM. CAT. NO. U 28

A work that may be associated with Archduke Rudolph's residency in Czechoslovakia after his appointment as Archbishop is a composition based on a traditional Czech melody, "To jsou koně " ("There are horses"), also known as "Já mám koně" ("I have horses"). A simple folk song akin to a nursery tune, "To jsou koně" originated in the Klattau region of Bohemia and was widely known throughout Moravia as well; it is included in the collection of traditional folk melodies published by K.J. Erben, *České písně a říkadla* (Prague, 1886).[17] This use of a native song is the only example in Archduke Rudolph's oeuvre of any possible regional influence on his music.[18] Although the variations Rudolph composed on "To jsou koně" cannot be dated precisely, there is some evidence that Rudolph worked on them during the early 1820's, at the same time he composed the *Variations in E-flat*; handwriting and sketch methods of

---

[17]The identical melody, with German words of different meaning, was used as a theme for a set of variations for violin and piano by Anton Wranitzky, published in 1793 by Franz Anton Hoffmeister. It is listed in the Hoffmeister catalogue as variations on a canzonetta, "Ich bin lüderlich, du bist lüderlich." Rudolph's acquaintance with the song may conceivably have originated at a different time and in another place.

[18]Several Czech *Singspiele* were among the stage works in Rudolph's music collection.

the two works are similar, and the rhythmic and melodic structures of the polacca themes serving as the finales for both sets of variations are so alike, it is often difficult to distinguish between them.[19] Interestingly, *To jsou kone* is the only example of Archduke Rudolph's work written on paper of Bohemian origin.[20] The melody of the song is shown in Example 5-11:

Example 5-11: "To jsou koně."

In its original conception the *Variations on "To jsou koně"* consists of an Introduction, Theme, and eight variations, the same plan as in the *Variations in E-flat*. In Kroměříž there is a group of autographs (KRa 4509-4513) containing four different draft versions of the score and three versions of the basset horn part (one a copy in another hand), of which none is complete. In addition, there are dozens of pages of rough pencil sketches scattered through the *Membra disjecta*. The extent of the work in its original conception, however, can be adduced because one of the basset horn parts includes almost the entire finale, which begins with an Adagio in 4/4, followed by a lengthy polacca; since none of the four scores continues that far, it appears that some pages have been lost.

The *Variations on "To jsou koně"* were given special attention by the archivists in Kroměříž who originally sorted and catalogued Rudolph's compositions. Dr. Vladimír Helfert (1886-1945), founder of the Music Archives of the Moravian Museum in Brno in 1919, and chief

[19]The confusion is compounded by the lack of clef signs and key signatures, which the Archduke characteristically omitted in his sketches.

[20]The watermark reads WELHARTIETZ IN BÖHMEN. This led Karl Vetterl, and after him Jan Racek, to the conclusion that the use of Czech paper is linked with Rudolph's stay in Moravia after his installation as Archbishop, corroborrating their assertion that the variations stem from the year 1823 and were therefore the work referred to by Beethoven in the letters quoted earlier. However, from Rudolph's letters we know that he spent a good deal of time in Kremsier long before he became Archbishop; further, in view of the large number of compositions he wrote during the early 1820's on paper of Viennese origin, while living in Moravia, this assertion is at best conjectural.

archivist during the 1920's, made a detailed study of the Introduction, comparing and noting the differences among the four manuscript scores.[21] Dr. Helfert stated his belief that, in several places on one manuscript, Beethoven had put in dynamic markings in pencil. This assertion touches on Nettl's theory, accepted by later scholars who wrote about Rudolph's music, that this was the work to which Beethoven alluded so approvingly in his letters of 1823 about the Archduke's new variations.[22] However, of the four autographs of the score of the *Variations on "To jsou koně,"* three do not sustain the slightest resemblance to Beethoven's description of a work in a substantially finished form. One is a four-page draft in pencil (KRa A 4510), rough and incomplete; another, on eight pages, partially in ink and partially in pencil (KRa A 4509), also has many incomplete measures throughout, sometimes lacking the basset horn part, sometimes the piano. This is the draft version that Helfert believed was annotated by Beethoven; there are dozens of pencilled changes of notes, additions in the margins, and dynamic and phrase marks. Their very number lends improbability to Helfert's theory; and while a crescendo or decrescendo sign, or a slur, is too ambiguous to ascribe to any one style of handwriting, there are many specific dynamic signs, such as *sforzandi*, which are assuredly not Beethoven's.[23] The changes in and addition of notes, the writing of words for such indications as crescendo and diminuendo, are all in Rudolph's hand. Along with these facts, the composition breaks off in the middle of the eighth variation.

The fourth of the autograph scores (KRa A 4512) is a fair copy on sixteen pages, in ink; as far as it goes, it is the most complete of the four. At the end of the eighth variation (in this version, a different one from those in the other drafts), a new time signature (4/4) indicates that the final Adagio and polacca variation were probably planned.[24] In some measures the basset horn part is lacking, and there are no expression marks or phrase markings whatsoever. Faint pencil

[21]Helfert's study, on four pages, can be found in KRa A 4513.

[22]See notes 7, 8 and 9 of this chapter.

[23]One need only compare the markings here with those in a Beethoven work from the same period, such as in the facsimile of the autograph of the Piano Sonata in C Minor, Opus 111, to see Beethoven's distinct notational style.

[24]The basset hornist Heinrich Fink, with pianist Richard Laugs, recorded the *Variations on "To jsou koně"* using this score (Musical Heritage Society MHS 1182). In place of the missing finale, Fink substituted a coda of his own composition.

corrections can be seen in a few places, such as a crossed-out note in a chord, but most of these appear to be corrections of handwriting errors rather than attempts to improve the music. After studying this manuscript carefully, I must conclude that it is virtually impossible to ascribe these pencil markings to Beethoven; indeed, where notes are written in, they are clearly in Rudolph's hand. Most telling, though, is the fact that these corrections are completely atypical of the types of alterations Beethoven made in the two works in which there are substantial corrections, namely the *Forty Variations* and the *Variations in E-flat.*

In sum, the *Variations on "To jsou koně"* are evidence of much labor on Archduke Rudolph's part; the existence of four drafts attests to his efforts to revise and improve his work. He may have shown Beethoven the manuscripts as he worked and reworked them, but there is nothing to justify the assumption that Beethoven made any changes in the variations himself, or that the *Variations on "To jsou koně"* rather than the *Variations in E-flat* are the composition Beethoven referred to in his letters.

MUSIC FOR CZAKAN AND PIANO

Because of their early origin, firmly established by dates on the manuscripts, two of Archduke Rudolph's compositions for czakan and piano, composed in 1810, are of special importance to a study of his music.

The czakan (or csákány), also known as a "cane flute," was a recorder-like wooden flute attached to a walking stick, invented around 1807 by one Anton Heberle (dates unknown), a Hungarian composer.[25] Now obsolete, the czakan was in vogue for several years after that in Hungary, Bohemia, and Austria.[26] Archduke Rudolph probably became acquainted with it while the Imperial family was

---

[25]The earliest mention of a czakan was in the *Vereinigte Ofner und Pester Zeitung* of 13 August 1807, advertising some compositions for the instrument by Heberle. There is a czakan in the instrument collection of the Gesellschaft der Musikfreunde, a gift of "Eberle of Pápa." See John S. Weissmann, "Csákány," *The New Grove* (London: Macmillan Publishers, 1980) IV, 82.

[26]Archduke Rudolph's music catalogue lists several works for czakan by different composers, and in his music book catalogue are two method books for czakan.

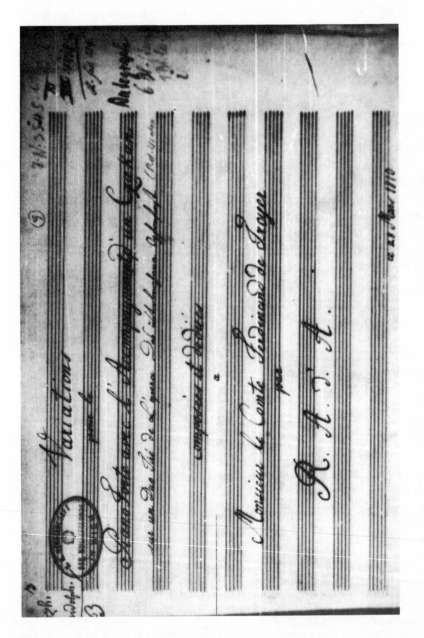

Plate 33. Title page, *Variations for Czakan* (1810) (Vienna, Wgm XI 15414).

living in exile in Ofen (Buda), Hungary, from May 1809 until January 1810. With him were his two chamberlains, Counts Ferdinand and Franz de Troyer (see chapter 1, p. 6), both woodwind players of some proficiency, to whom the two czakan works were dedicated. A set of variations (Them. cat. no. 16), dated 28 March 1810, was dedicated to Ferdinand, for whom the Archduke also composed several clarinet works; a divertissement (Them. cat. no. 17), dated 31 May 1810, was composed for and dedicated to both brothers. In addition to the dated manuscripts, which are both in the Gesellschaft der Musikfreunde, there are two other variation sets in the Kroměříž archive, neither of which is complete.

The czakan is a transposing instrument in A-flat,[27] sounding a major third lower than written, with a compass of approximately three octaves. All of Archduke Rudolph's czakan compositions are in the key of A-flat, with some sections in E-flat.

The dated variations in the Gesellschaft library are an autograph score in ink on eight pages (Wgm XI 15414). The manuscript is written carefully, and the title page, in ornate script, reads: "Variations/ pour le/Piano Forte avec l'Accompagnement d'un Czakan/sur un Duo Tiré de l'Opera das Unterbrochene Opferfest/composées et dediées/à/Monsieur le Comte Ferdinand de Troyer/par R.A. d'A./ce 28 Mars 1810."[28] Two notational peculiarities are consistent with the early date of this work—the bass clef sign[29] and the key signature, with its unconventional placement of the flats:

The jaunty theme of the Duo from the Winter opera is in binary form; like many similarly simple melodies, both halves, in eight-measure segments, cadence in the tonic (Example 5-12):

[27]Weissmann (see note 25) notes the existence of a czakan in A, and Sybil Marcuse, in *Musical Instruments* (New York: Norton, 1975), mentions an instrument in B-flat.

[28]*Das unterbrochene Opferfest*, a comic opera with music by Peter von Winter, had its premiere in 1796 at the Burgtheater, with much success. Beethoven used another theme from the opera ("Kind, willst du ruhig schlafen") for piano variations (WoO 75).

[29]See p. xxi.

Example 5-12. *Variations on "Opferfest" Theme,* measures 1-16.

Rudolph's procedure of dividing the theme between piano and czakan is maintained generally in the eight variations that follow. Changes in figuration, increased rhythmic activity (triplets, thirty-second notes), and such rhythmic devices as syncopation and dotted notes, the means of providing variety common to most variation works of the period, are employed through the first six variations. The opening measures of variations 2, 4, and 8 serve to demonstrate Rudolph's imaginative use of figuration (Examples 5-13, 5-14, and 5-15):

Example 5-13. *Variations on "Opferfest" Theme,* Variation 2, measures 1-2.

Example 5-14. *Variations on "Opferfest" Theme,* Variation 4, measures 1-4.

Example 5-15. *Variations on "Opferfest" Theme,* Variation 8, measures 1-4.

The seventh variation, marked "Minore con espressione," is the traditional slow, lyrical movement; variation eight returns to the tonic major key, with a change in meter (6/8) and tempo (Allegretto) [see example 5-15], followed by a coda in which the theme is restated. The structure of the last two variations—a slow one in minor and a finale in 6/8 in an allegretto tempo—occurs quite frequently in variation movements in chamber works by Beethoven, e.g., the Sonata in A for Violin and Piano, Opus 30, No. 1 (last movement), the two sets of variations for piano trio (in E-flat, Opus 44, and in G, Opus 121a), and the Trio in B-flat for Piano, Clarinet, and Cello, Opus 11 (last movement). The latter work, in fact, might have served as a model for the czakan variations, as there are several similarities between the two works.

Beethoven's theme for the variations movement of the Trio is also from a vocal number in a comic opera,[30] and it resembles the Duo from *Das unterbrochene Opferfest* in its sprightly, energetic melody, binary structure of two eight-measure segments, and harmonic plan. Other similarities include the broken-chord accompaniment to the theme (Example 5-16), a marcia-style variation with dotted rhythms (Example 5-17), and the 6/8 finale (Example 5-18):

Example 5-16. Beethoven, *Trio in B-flat*, Opus 11, 3rd movement, measures 1-4.

[30]The theme is from a Terzett, "Pria ch'io l'impegno," from Joseph Weigl's *L'amor marinaro*, first performed in 1797 at the Wiener Hoftheater.

Example 5-17a. *Variations on "Opferfest" Theme,* Variation 5, measure 1 (piano part).

Example 5-17b. Beethoven, *Trio in B-flat* (Opus 11), 3rd movement, Variation 7, measure 1 (piano part).

Example 5-18a. *Variations on "Opferfest" Theme,* Variation 8, measures 1-4 (piano part).

Example 5-18b. Beethoven, *Trio in B-flat* (Opus 11), 3rd movement, Variation 9, measures 24-27 (piano part).

In both works, a return to duple meter after the 6/8 section closes the movement.

One last example from the czakan variations illustrating inventive use of rhythm is shown in Example 5-19. In this variation (number seven), marked "Minore con espressione," Rudolph employs syncopation through most of the piece, disguising the theme somewhat in the process. Beethoven's use of the same device can be seen in several chamber music works: in the eighth variation of the Variations for Piano, Violin, and Cello, Opus 121a (cited earlier); in the slow movement of the "Archduke" Trio in B-flat, Opus 97; and in Example 5-18b, shown above. One such similarity can be found in yet another Beethoven trio, that of Opus 1, No. 3, whose slow movement is a set of variations. Example 5-19a shows the opening of Variation 7 from Rudolph's "Opferfest" variations, and Example 5-19b shows the Beethoven excerpt:

Example 5-19a. *Variations on "Opferfest" Theme*, Variation 7, measures 1-4.

Example 5-19b. Beethoven, *Trio in C Minor*, Op. 1, No. 3 (2nd movement), Variation 4, measures 1-4.

The second of the two dated works in the Gesellschaft, the *Divertissement* (Wgm Q 17756), is in a copyist's hand, and has a similarly ornate title page: "Divertissement/pour le/Piano Forte/avec l'accompagnement d'un Zakan/Composé et Dedié/aux/Comtes Ferdinand et François de Troyer/par/R.A.d'A./ce 31ᵉʳ Mai 1810." The piano part is on eighteen pages, the czakan part on twelve pages, both in ink.

The *Divertissement* consists of an Introduction in A-flat (Andante), Theme (Allegretto), and six Variations in E-flat, ending with a multi-sectioned coda in A-flat, in which each of its several sections is a characteristic dance type—a Minuet, a Marcia, and a Polacca, each with trio. Simple in all aspects, in keeping with its function as light entertainment music, the technical demands of the *Divertissement* in both parts are minimal, and the range of the czakan line is kept for the most part within the compass of an octave-and-a-half. The simple melody of the theme and the harmonic structure are preserved intact throughout the variations, and small changes in figuration provide the only contrasts. Brief excerpts from the opening measures of the theme (Example 5-20) and two variations (Example 5-21 and 5-22) illustrate the general style of the *Divertissement*:

Example 5-20. *Divertissement*, Theme, measures 1-8.

Example 5-21. *Divertissement,* Variation 3, measures 1-4.

Example 5-22. *Divertissement,* Variation 5, measures 1-4.

The variations and coda are written competently enough but lack the imaginative figural changes Rudolph used in the "Opferfest" Variations. The Introduction, however, is somewhat unusual in its structure; instead of the traditional 8 + 8 measures common to so many of the themes chosen by composers for variations, Rudolph set the melody in phrase units of 3 + 3 + 4 measures.[31] The Introduction is cast in a small ABA form; Example 5-23 shows the A and B sections:

Example 5-23. *Divertissement,* Introduction, measures 1-21.

[31]Mozart used a similarly uneven phrase structure (3 + 3 + 4) in the opening of the Piano Sonata in D, K. 311, among other works.

176

Lending additional interest to the Introduction is the czakan melody at measures 11-13, an unmistakable (and probably intentional) quotation from Mozart's Quintet in A for Clarinet and Strings, K. 581 (1789). The Mozart melody quoted is the second theme of the first movement, as it occurs in the first violin part at measure 42 (Example 5-24):

Example 5-24. Mozart, *Quintet in A for Clarinet and Strings*, 1st movement, measures 42-44.

Of the other two variation works for czakan and piano, both in the Kroměříž archive, one, on a waltz-like theme (Them. cat. no. 18) is an autograph consisting of a complete czakan part (a theme with eight variations and coda), and a piano part, scored separately, that ends with the fifth variation (KRa A 4404).[32] Another version of this work, substantially similar but showing many finishing touches, is in the Gesellschaft der Musikfreunde (Wgm XI 15413), written out by a copyist; it is to this version that the following discussion will refer.

These dance-like variations are simply structured in binary form (8 + 8 measures). The first half is shown in Example 5-25:

Example 5-25. *(Waltz) Variations*, Theme, measures 1-8.

[32]The other unfinished set (Them. cat. no. U 10) also has a complete czakan part, with each of its seven variations and coda titled and carefully edited. The four pages of the piano part extant, however, are only roughly sketched, with many empty measures (KRa A 4403). A final copy of the piano part appears to be lost.

The style of the variations follows Archduke Rudolph's usual pattern, adhering closely to the theme in harmonic structure and relying on imaginative figuration and rhythmic interest for variety. On a technical level, these variations are more complicated than the others we have seen; they are more demanding instrumentally, and in each variation the czakan and piano pursue independent parts with distinctive rhythmic figures, rather than one serving as an accompaniment to the other. In the first variation, for instance (Example 5-26), syncopation in the czakan part is coupled with an even sixteenth-note figure in the piano part, phrased in minute detail:

Example 5-26. *(Waltz) Variations,* Variation 1, measures 1-2.

In the fifth variation, marked "Tempo di Polacca," the dance rhythm is carried out in the piano, coupled with a martial dotted-note figure in the czakan:

Example 5-27. *(Waltz) Variations,* Variation 5, measures 1-2.

The two most interesting variations, however, resemble passages in two of Beethoven's piano sonatas. Not surprisingly, it is the first movement of Beethoven's Sonata, Opus 26—also in A-flat, also in triple meter, and also a theme and variations—that comes to mind when viewing the opening measures of the piano part of the third of Rudolph's variations (Example 5-28):

Example 5-28a. *(Waltz) Variations,* Variation 3, measures 1-3 (piano part).

Example 5-28b. Beethoven, *Piano Sonata in A-flat,* Opus 26, 1st movement, measures 1-3.

The other similarity to a Beethoven piano work is in the Piano Sonata in D Minor, Opus 31, No. 2, in which the slow movement (in B-flat) features a very distinctive bass figure imitating a drum (Example 5-29):

Example 5-29. Beethoven, *Piano Sonata in D Minor*, Opus 31, No. 2, 2nd movement, measures 17-19.

In Rudolph's variations, it is the seventh variation, marked "Adagio— Tempo di Marcia," which has a similar figure in the piano bass part (Example 5-30):

Example 5-30. *(Waltz) Variations*, Variation 7, measures 1-2 (piano part).

The final variation, an Allegro moderato, is followed by a coda of twenty measures; the coda builds climactically to a fermata on a six-four chord and a short, brilliant cadenza for the piano, and it ends with a restatement of the theme in tempo primo. This coda is more elaborate than those seen in other early compositions and more in the style of Archduke Rudolph's later works, in which the codas are often disproportionately long. Here the coda provides an appropriately brilliant ending to the work as a whole.

In all likelihood Archduke Rudolph composed the four czakan compositions around the same period, although only the two in the Gesellschaft are dated. Two clues that support this supposition involve notation—the bass clef sign mentioned earlier, and the spelling of "allegretto," which Rudolph spelled with one "l," just as he did in other early works. Further evidence is that composing for the clarinet took precedence shortly after 1810.

The early origin of the czakan works, verified by the dates on the manuscripts, raises an interesting question about the starting point of

Rudolph's composition studies with Beethoven, which Thayer believed began ca. 1809, following piano study for some five or six years. Thayer's hypothesis was based primarily on the existence of the theoretical extracts that Beethoven copied out for instructional purposes in that year (see chapter 2); it appears unlikely that Thayer ever saw, or was even aware of, any of the Archduke's compositions except the *Forty Variations* and, possibly, the Diabelli variation and the Clarinet Sonata.

The evidence before us in the czakan works, however, attests to a level of skill well beyond that of a beginning student. Rudolph's inventive use of figuration and rhythm, his instrumental knowledge, and his command of formal structures suggest that he had already experienced a fair amount of technical instruction in composition. It is impossible to judge how much Rudolph might have learned earlier in his lessons with Anton Tayber, with whom he probably studied the rudiments of music theory; but even granted that he was a very apt pupil, it is difficult to correlate his expertise in 1810 with the assumption that he had just begun to study composition the year before.

In view of the very high level of the Archduke's piano playing when he first met Beethoven in 1803-04, one may suggest that when Rudolph embarked on his lessons with Beethoven at that time, it was not just to perfect himself as a pianist but also to learn the skills of music composition.

CHAPTER VI

Sonata Compositions

THE CLARINET SONATA IN A (CA. 1812-13): THEM. CAT. NO. 21

Although Archduke Rudolph's preference for small forms is confirmed by their large number among his compositions, he composed two four-movement duo sonatas in traditional Classical style—one for clarinet in A and piano (Them. cat. no. 21) and one for violin and piano (Them. cat. no. 20). Both sonatas, to judge from their entries in Archduke Rudolph's catalogue, were composed approximately at the same time, ca. 1812-13; they are numbers seven and eight in the list of his own compositions following the 1810 czakan variations (the next composition with a dated entry is number eleven, the 1814 variations in G for piano). One other sonata-type composition—a Trio for Clarinet, Cello, and Piano (Them. cat. no. U 19)—also appears to stem from this period but is not listed in the Archduke's catalogue, presumably because he never completed the last movement.[1] Common to all three works is their Classical structure: sonata-form first movements, lyrical slow movements in related keys, scherzo or minuet movements, and fast or moderately fast finales; they all also reveal a stylistic debt to works of Beethoven and Mozart.

---

[1] A modern edition of the first three movements of the Trio was published in 1973 by Musica Rara. See thematic catalogue for details.

The sonatas must have achieved some degree of popularity in the Archduke's circle, since both exist in several manuscript copies. The Clarinet Sonata was published by S.A. Steiner and Co. several years later (early in 1822). In the absence of any correspondence or other written data regarding this publication, one can assume that following the publication by Steiner of the *Forty Variations* in 1819, the firm solicited another work from the Archduke, who then chose the Clarinet Sonata composed earlier. As will be seen, Beethoven had a hand in preparing the sonata for publication and perhaps was also involved in its selection from among Rudolph's works. Like the *Forty Variations,* the sonata came out with the composer's name identified only by the initials "R.E.H." (Rudolph ErzHerzog), and a Roman numeral II on the title page identifies it as Opus 2. The full title page reads: "Sonata/für/Pianoforte und Clarinette/von/R.E.H./II/dem Grafen Ferdinand Troyer/gewidmet/No. 3240/Wien/bei S.A. Steiner und Comp."

The materials relating to the Clarinet Sonata are numerous; they include a print of the Steiner edition and three manuscript copies in the Gesellschaft der Musikfreunde (Wgm XI 3497, Q 17759, Q 17760, Q 17761); another manuscript copy in the Landesbibliothek in Gotha, DDR (GO1 18/1); and a group of autographs in Kroměříž including a complete draft and a fair copy (KRa A 4397) and sixteen pages of additional sketches in the *Membra disjecta* (KRa A 4433).

The appearance of the two drafts in Kroměříž supports the hypothesis that the sonata was originally composed around 1813, then reworked many years later. The first draft is a rough working sketch (32 pages, in ink), missing part of the last movement, eight pages of which can be found in the additional sketches in the *Membra disjecta*. On ten-stave paper, this draft is in the notational style Rudolph used in his other early compositions (e.g., shape of the bass clefs), is strewn with X's denoting changes to be made, and has extensive revisions entered on the unused bottom system of each page; the revisions however, are in Rudolph's later handwriting. It appears, then, that this early draft was revamped at a later date, with expanded or changed ideas written out in the nearest space (the unused bottom staff), most likely in preparation for the publication.

The other autograph is the fair copy (29 pages, in ink) in the Archduke's later handwriting, carefully edited and finished in detail. While there are some differences between it and the earlier draft, the two are substantially alike.

Beethoven's participation in the preparation of the sonata for publication is not visible on either of the two autographs, but it is on one of the three manuscript copies in the Gesellschaft (Wgm Q 17760), which has dozens of small emendations, as well as several written tempo indications, in Beethoven's hand. This manuscript, made from Rudolph's fair copy, is identical with it in every respect and was undoubtedly intended for the engraver; according to a notation in the Gesellschaft card catalogue, the first page is in the hand of Wenzel Schlemmer (Beethoven's favorite copyist until his death in 1823), the rest by one of Schlemmer's students. As usual, Beethoven's corrections are entered in the nearest margins, at the sides or above and below the staff. Some note changes have letter-names above them; most of the trouble spots are indicated with an X and, on occasion, the "-de" of the word "Vide" (the "Vi-" was customarily omitted by Beethoven). The changes were all entered in this manuscript (quite evident from the untidy appearance of each corrected place), and on some pages Beethoven's marginal emendations have inked slash marks through them. A last touch was supplied by the Archduke, who added metronome numbers for each movement.

Archduke Rudolph's choice of the A clarinet for the sonata deserves comment, since the B-flat clarinet was the preferred instrument at that time, and solo compositions for the A clarinet were rare. The two notable exceptions were Mozart's Quintet for Clarinet and Strings (K. 581) and Clarinet Concerto (K. 622), both in the key of A; Rudolph, in fact, turned to the Quintet as a model, as will be shown later. While both the A and B-flat clarinets had only five or six keys as a rule, there is evidence that, during this period of experimentation with the instrument, craftsmen often added keys to improve the capacity and flexibility of the clarinet. Such was the case with the basset clarinet owned by the famous Anton Stadler (1753-1812), for whom Mozart composed the two clarinet works,[2] and since the solo part in Rudolph's sonata encompasses a similar range as that in the Quintet, it is likely that Ferdinand de Troyer's clarinet was similarly

[2]See Pamela Weston, "Anton Stadler," in *The New Grove*, XVIII, 46: Nicholas Shackleton, "Clarinet," *ibid.*, IV, 440; and F. Geoffrey Rendall, *The Clarinet* (London: Williams and Norgate Ltd., 1954) 74-98.

outfitted.[3] The compass of the clarinet part in the sonata extends from E_1 (sounding C-$sharp_1$) to B^3 (sounding G-$sharp^3$), but most of it lies comfortably in a middle range, where the clarinet is most expressive.[4]

Stylistically, the sonata is typical of Classical tradition, conforming structurally and harmonically to countless sonata-type works of the early nineteenth century. There is a first-movement Allegro in sonata form, followed by a Menuetto and Trio, an Adagio, and, for the fourth movement, a theme and variations; the sonata's structure differs from that of Mozart's Quintet only in the ordering of the second and third movements. The large scope of the sonata posed some problems for the Archduke, but at the same time he demonstrates that he had absorbed the essentials of the sonata cycle.

The most problematical movement is the first, with its sprawling sonata form. It has often been noted in this study that Rudolph was most comfortable with small, compact forms, and the length and architecture of a conventional sonata-form movement put some strain on his creative ingenuity. With the exposition repeat, the movement is close to 400 measures long but lacks the melodic and harmonic interest needed to sustain its length. The main themes are discursive, tending to meander somewhat shapelessly, often disjunct, and dwelling monotonously on tonic and dominant harmonies. This repetitiveness can be observed in the opening material of the movement, which after thirty-two measures is still in the tonic (Example 6-1):

Example 6-1. *Clarinet Sonata*, 1st movement, measures 1-32 (edition published in 1973 by Musica Rara (London, W. 1).

[3]One can only speculate about the exact instrument for which Rudolph composed the sonata, since it is unspecified in the first draft (the fair copy has "Clarinet in A" indicated on the solo part and the score). Troyer played the basset horn and the czakan in addition to the clarinet, and it is not unlikely that he owned a basset clarinet similar to Stadler's.

[4]If the Archduke needed technical instruction on composing for the clarinet, it was readily available in his library; his catalogue of music books lists at least three important clarinet tutors: J.G.H. Backofen's *Anweisung zur Klarinette nebst einer kurzen Abhandlung über das Basset-Horn* (1805); S.(?) Koch, *Tonleiter für die Clarinette* (18-?); and J.F. Fröhlich, *Vollständige Practische Musikschule* (1810).

One of the many small revisions made by Rudolph in the first draft concerned the final three notes of the opening phrase; in his original conception, the melody ended on the leading tone, robbing the melodic peak of much of its domination as the high point of the opening phrase (Example 6-2):

Example 6-2. *Clarinet Sonata* (first draft), 1st movement, measures 1-3.

The tonal plan is conventional, moving from tonic to dominant for the second theme; here again the melody is rather bumpy and disjunct, and the accompaniment in the piano is static (Example 6-3):

Example 6-3. *Clarinet Sonata*, 1st movement, measures 49-56.

The development section centers around a rhythmic motive consisting of three eighth notes functioning as an upbeat, hints of which can be found in the opening theme (last three eighth notes in measures 3, 11, and 12, for example), but which becomes prominent in the clarinet part as a closing theme toward the end of the movement (Example 6-4):

Example 6-4. *Clarinet Sonata,* 1st movement, measures 80-84 (clarinet part only).

Modulation in the development section takes place at a leisurely pace; Rudolph's tendency is to stay in a new tonality a little too long to sustain interest, particularly since the melodic material is thin. Two of the main changes in the tonality are accompanied by changes of key signature—one to F-sharp major (originally notated as G-flat in the first draft), the other to B-flat, before returning to the tonic. The transition to the recapitulation is achieved by a device Beethoven often used for dramatic effect—a ritardando to a fermata, followed by a return to tempo (although Beethoven liked to use this procedure before a coda). Rudolph's handling of this idea is seen in Example 6-5:

Example 6-5. *Clarinet Sonata,* 1st movement, measures 152-158.

189

This passage, too, underwent a change from the first draft to the final version; originally the Archduke had written an additional eight measures following measure 153 which modulated through several diminished seventh chords before arriving at the tonic in measure 156 (Example 6-6):

Example 6-6. *Clarinet Sonata* (first draft), 1st movement.

The pruning in this passage, eliminating repeated harmonies, effectively tightened the structure; the alternative passage Rudolph composed for the transition gives more dramatic emphasis to the return of the main theme. The rewritten passage is highly suggestive of Beethoven's methods; although there is no written indication in the first draft of his direct involvement, he may well have suggested the change (or something like it) to Rudolph.

The discursiveness of the first movement is reinforced by the length of the recapitulation, which, in a stereotype of sonata form, restates the entire material of the exposition, remaining in the tonic. A short coda, based on the closing theme of the exposition, ends the movement.

In the Menuetto movement which follows (in the key of E), the melodic character is alternately smooth and choppy, with Rudolph's favorite dotted rhythms lending a martial air (Example 6-7):

Example 6-7. *Clarinet Sonata*, 2nd movement, measures 1-16.

If the triadic descent of the melody in the clarinet part sounds somewhat disjunct, it is offset by the smooth lyricism of the melody in measures 9 to 16, which must be counted as one of the Archduke's loveliest settings of melody and accompaniment.

Rudolph's original concept for the Trio in the first draft was scrapped in favor of a completely different idea. He did not abandon it entirely, however—it turns up as one of the variations in the fourth movement. The revised Trio centers around a rhythmic figure that suggests a polonaise (Example 6-8):

Example 6-8. *Clarinet Sonata,* 2nd movement, measures 84-88.

Archduke Rudolph encountered no problems in handling the formal structures of the third and fourth movements; the brief, lyrical slow movement is joined to the theme and variations. In the slow movement (Adagio) in A minor, Rudolph demonstrates a gift for expressive melodic writing of long breadth, a characteristic not always present in his music. The opening measures are shown in Example 6-9:

192

Example 6-9. *Clarinet Sonata,* 3rd movement, measures 1-10.

Among the memorable features of this opening are the sharing of the theme between the piano and the clarinet; the color achieved by the Neapolitan chord in measure 6; and the rhythmic interest, especially effective in measure 8, as the triplets in the clarinet part unfold against the even rhythms of the accompaniment.

Following brief development with a modulation to C, the opening material returns, is repeated in A major, and arrives (again with a ritardando to a fermata) at the opening theme of the finale. The structure here, as well as some of the musical content, seems to be modeled on Beethoven's Sonata in A for Cello and Piano, Opus 69 (in this sonata, too, the scherzo and slow movement are reversed from the traditional order). We have seen in other works of Rudolph's that there is often some influence—or inspiration, perhaps—derived from a composition of Beethoven's in the same key; the relationship between these two works in A appears to bear this out. In both sonatas, the brief, lyrical slow movement pauses on the dominant chord, followed by the presentation of the opening theme of the fourth movement by the solo instrument, which is accompanied by repeated eighth-note chords in the bass of the piano. A comparison of the two passages can be seen in Examples 6-10 and 6-11:

Example 6-10. *Clarinet Sonata*, 3rd and 4th movements, measures 43-52.

Example 6-11. Beethoven, *Sonata in A for Cello and Piano* (Opus 69), 3rd and 4th movements, measures 17-25.

Rudolph's theme (marked "Alegretto" in the first draft) is squarely structured; an antecedent of eight measures cadences on the mediant (see Example 6-10, measure 52), and a consequent of the same length starts off on the dominant. Both halves of the theme are marked with repeat signs. (In the fair copy and the printed edition, the nine variations [each with repeat signs] are not numbered or identified as variations, as they are in the first draft.)

Unlike Rudolph's usual procedure in variation sets, in which the first few variations gradually build up in rhythmic activity and figurative complexity, these variations, after the first, feature markedly contrasting rhythms and tempos. At the same time, there are some of the standard character types—a march, an Adagio in minor as the penultimate variation, and then an Allegretto in 6/8 in the original key. Example 6-12 shows a sampling of some of the diverse ideas used by the Archduke in the variations:

Example 6-12. *Clarinet Sonata*, 4th movement, variations 3, 5, and 8.

Variation 3, measures 1-3.

Variation 5, measures 1-4.

Variation 8, measures 1-4.

Variation 7 had originally been planned in the first draft as the Trio section of the Menuetto. In 3/4 meter, this variation represents Archduke Rudolph's favorite dance type, the polacca, which is present in almost every variation set he wrote; the second half of variation 7 has a strong polonaise rhythm (Example 6-13):

Example 6-13. *Clarinet Sonata,* 4th movement, variation 7, measures 9-16.

The Archduke's familiarity with Mozart's Clarinet Quintet reveals itself clearly in the first variation, in which Rudolph patterns the writing of the clarinet part, with its distinctive leaps and rhythm, directly after the first variation in the fourth movement of the Quintet.[5] In both works, this occurs in the second half of the variation, where the harmonic structure is similar (Example 6-14):

Example 6-14a. *Clarinet Sonata,* 4th movement, measures 69-76 (clarinet part).

[5]Rudolph's intimate acquaintance with the Clarinet Quintet was noted earlier in the discussion of the Divertissement for Czakan and Piano (see chapter 5, p. 178).

Example 6-14b. Mozart, *Quintet for Clarinet and Strings* (K. 581), 4th movement, measures 25-32 (clarinet part).

In the coda there is an allusion to Beethoven's music that seems to be another instance of homage from pupil to teacher, an example of which we have already noted in the Variations for Clarinet and Piano on a theme by Rossini (chapter 5, p. 159). At measure 260 of the finale, an unexpected modulation to the key of E-flat accompanies a passage whose figuration vividly recalls the finales of two piano works of Beethoven—both in E-flat, and both dedicated to the Archduke—the Sonata Opus 81a ("Les Adieux") and the "Emperor" Concerto, Opus 73. Examples 6-15 and 6-16 illustrate the passages under discussion:

Example 6-15. *Clarinet Sonata,* 4th movement, measures 255-261.

Example 6-16a. Beethoven, *Piano Sonata in E-flat* (Opus 81a), 3rd movement, measure 39.

Example 6-16b. Beethoven, *Piano Concerto No. 5 in E-flat* (Opus 73), 3rd movement, measure 144.

Although the two Beethoven passages quoted are in different keys, they are both heard, somewhat varied, in E-flat also during the course of the movement. The resemblance in Rudolph's score at measure 260—the 6/8 meter, and the arpeggiated figuration, first in sixteenth notes and then in triplets—seems too pointed to be mere coincidence.

We come now to Beethoven's corrections, numbering approximately three dozen, all (with one exception) in the piano part. None of them calls for a major change, since, as noted earlier, the manuscript copy with Beethoven's emendations was evidently a final one prepared for the publisher, and probably incorporated important suggestions by Beethoven made at an earlier stage. Most of Beethoven's indications deal with the same small details characteristic of his editing of the *Forty Variations*—problems concerning parallels, smoother voice leading, and note doubling in chords. Others are concerned with creating more rhythmic activity, with the spelling of notes in chords, and, in a few cases, with a harmonic change in the accompaniment. A few selected examples, representative of these various types of corrections, will serve to illustrate Beethoven's meticulous attention to these details in readying Rudolph's work for the public eye.

The largest number of changes deals with parallels, often somewhat hidden because of the thick textures of the piano writing, but not too obscure for Beethoven to ferret out. The next three examples (6-17, 6-18, and 6-19) show brief excerpts which Beethoven corrected in the margins.

Example 6-17. *Clarinet Sonata*, 1st movement, measures 208-209.

Example 6-18. *Clarinet Sonata*, 3rd movement, measure 12.

Example 6-19. *Clarinet Sonata*, 4th movement, measure 97.

In all three examples, the change accomplishes the elimination of the parallels and, in Example 6-17, gives stronger definition to the downbeat by providing contrary motion in the bass line.

Beethoven's change of harmonization in the accompaniment occurs in two places in the score. In the first (Example 6-20), from the Menuetto, Rudolph originally ended the first section of the Menuetto on a dominant chord, against a half-note appoggiatura in the clarinet part—a dissonant clash that Beethoven eliminated by putting the appoggiatura on an inverted tonic (I $^6_4$) chord:

Example 6-20. *Clarinet Sonata*, 2nd movement, measures 15-16.

The other harmonic change made by Beethoven takes place in a repeated phrase toward the end of the slow movement. Beethoven not only altered the harmony the first time the phrase is heard, but in the repetition made the alteration even more pointed:

Example 6-21. *Clarinet Sonata*, 3rd movement, measures 33-36.

Beethoven's subtle coloring of the harmony on the second half-beat in measure 34 with an *F-natural* is further stressed in the repetition in measure 36, placing *F* on the beat (doubling it in the right-hand chord) and changing the figuration.

In two transitional passages from different movements Rudolph misspelled the diminished seventh chord just preceding an *E* chord, which Beethoven changed with a *D-sharp* instead of *E-flat* (Example 6-22):

Example 6-22a. *Clarinet Sonata,* 1st movement, measure 144.

Example 6-22b. *Clarinet Sonata,* 3rd movement, measure 21.

Beethoven's suggested changes regarding rhythm usually attempt to maintain a forward drive; for instance, in the opening measures of the first movement of the sonata, as originally written by Archduke Rudolph, the rhythmic motion comes to a halt at the conclusion of the first phrase (Example 6-23):

Example 6-23. *Clarinet Sonata,* 1st movement, measures 1-4.

In the many repetitions of this phrase throughout the first movement, Beethoven filled the rhythmic gap on the third beat of the fourth measure with an additional note or chord.

The only emendation of the clarinet part was made in the "Tempo di marcia" variation (Variation 6) of the last movement. In a brief melodic segment (repeated a third lower four measures later), Beethoven made a chromatic alteration in the triadic shape of the clarinet phrase (Example 6-24):

Example 6-24. *Clarinet Sonata,* 4th movement, measures 149-150.

The piano part in the march variation was also changed by Beethoven; in measures 158 and 160 (Example 6-25), the voice-leading in the sixteenth-note line is awkwardly resolved with a leap to the chords in measures 159 and 161. Beethoven's alteration smooths out the voice-leading, provides more contrary motion, and also makes the V chord at measure 159 stronger by eliminating *G-sharp* on the last quarter-note beat of measure 158:

Example 6-25. *Clarinet Sonata,* 4th movement, measures 157-160.

Several features of the Clarinet Sonata place it on a high level among Archduke Rudolph's works and make understandable its selection—in 1822 and again in 1973—as a publishable composition.

In many of Rudolph's duo works, e.g., the sets of variations for clarinet, czakan, and basset-horn with piano accompaniment, the piano part tends to dominate the partnership; in this sonata, however, the Archduke's careful writing of both instrumental parts prevents the clarinet part from being overshadowed. The clarinet writing, while not virtuosic, is particularly idiomatic, taking advantage of the agility and expressive qualities of the instrument.

The first movement is very long, and that, coupled with its somewhat uninspired melodic ideas, makes it the weakest of the four movements. In compensation, the other three movements provide interest and vitality; the variations, in fact, are among Rudolph's most inventive.

Archduke Rudolph's sonata can be regarded as a useful addition to the rather limited repertoire of sonata works for clarinet and piano.

VIOLIN SONATA IN F MINOR (CA. 1812-13): THEM. CAT. NO. 20

Archduke Rudolph composed only two works for violin and piano duo: a set of variations in F (one of his earliest compositions; see chapter 7, pp. 225-229) and the Sonata in F Minor. As noted before, from the placement of their entries in Rudolph's catalogue (nos. 7 and 8, respectively), the violin and clarinet sonatas may be presumed to have been composed around the same time, ca. 1812-13; indeed, stylistic similarities bear this out.

Rudolph's apparent lack of interest in composing for the violin (compared with the large number of woodwind works in his oeuvre) can be attributed, perhaps, to the absence of a ready performer of artistic skill on that instrument in his household retinue. There was no violinist who enjoyed the privileged relationship of musical chamberlain to Rudolph such as that of Ferdinand de Troyer and his brother Franz, who played a variety of woodwind instruments.[6] In 1812, however, the Archduke came into contact with the renowned French violinist Pierre Rode (1774-1830), who was visiting Vienna at that time. Rode and Archduke Rudolph joined forces to give the first performance of Beethoven's Sonata for Piano and Violin in G, Opus 96, dedicated to Rudolph; two performances took place at Prince Lobkowitz's palace on the evenings of 29 December 1812 and 7 January 1813 (see chapter 1, pp. 29-30). The opportunity to play with such a highly esteemed artist may have provided the impetus for Rudolph to compose a violin sonata of his own.

The extant manuscripts (several were made by various copyists, both score and parts) indicate that the Archduke worked industriously to revise and improve the sonata after writing a first draft. The autograph of a first draft is in Kroměříž (KRa A 4405 and A 4407);[7] some pages from the third movement are missing. Three manuscript copies, each in a different hand, are in the Gesellschaft der Musik-freunde (Wgm Q 17754, Q 17757, and Q 17758), and another copy, of the piano part only, can be found in the Musiksammlung of the Landesbibliothek in Gotha, DDR (GO1 Mus. pag. 14 d/7). All four

---

[6]Among the sixty-six household servants in Kremsier named in Rudolph's will to receive pensions, there were eight *Kammermusiker*, all with Czech names.

[7]The archivists in Kroměříž did not recognize the relationship between the slow movement and the other three movements of the sonata, and they therefore catalogued it as a separate composition.

copies contain careless errors by the copyists, such as wrong notes, omitted slurs and dynamic indications, and the like.

Like its counterpart for clarinet, the violin sonata is in a traditional four-movement structure: a fast first movement (Allegro) in sonata form, lyrical slow movement (Adagio), Menuetto, and fast finale (Allegro assai quasi presto). The first and last movements are both in F minor, framing inner movements in related tonalities—D-flat for the slow movement and B-flat for the Menuetto, which has two trios.

The general procedures involved in sonata composition are followed by Archduke Rudolph, differing very little from those seen in the clarinet sonata. A study of the violin sonata provides little insight into Rudolph's craft as a sonata composer, but there are several details of interest.

The extended sonata form of the first movement relies basically on a single thematic idea—a motive derived from the main theme of the first movement of Mozart's Quartet for Piano and Strings in G Minor, K. 478. Mozart's quartet, it will be remembered, was transcribed by Archduke Rudolph at one time (see chapter 2, p. 60). The opening measures of both works are shown in Example 6-26:

Example 6-26a. *Violin Sonata*, 1st movement, measures 1-4.

Example 6-26b. Mozart, *Piano Quartet in G Minor* (K. 478), 1st movement, measures 1-4.

The second theme of the first movement of the sonata, in the relative major (A-flat), is rhythmically identical with the first theme, contrasting only in tonality and dynamics (Example 6-27):

Example 6-27. *Violin Sonata,* 1st movement, measures 41-44.

This pronounced rhythmic motive permeating the entire first movement (358 measures with the repeat of the exposition) is varied only by the kind of melodic inversion heard in the second theme. In the first draft, Rudolph imitated Mozart's opening melody more exactly during the closing portion of the exposition (Example 6-28):

Example 6-28. *Violin Sonata* (first draft), 1st movement, measures 101-102.

Such direct references to Mozart were lessened in the final version.

The first movement not only lacks variety in its melodic ideas; harmonic interest is also largely absent, and there are long passages of alternating tonic-dominant harmonies seemingly without direction. What helps carry the movement, though, is the energetic sixteenth-note figuration accompanying the second theme (see Example 6-27), which plays a large part in the writing for both instruments and provides forward motor drive.

The slow movement, an Adagio in song form with a contrasting middle section in minor, is lyrical and well-shaped, its three sections nicely balanced in length. The theme is introduced by the piano, then repeated by the violin. In the reprise, Rudolph embellishes the accompaniment with a triplet figure, and offers a harmonic surprise in the coda, with a brief excursion into the remote key area of A major.

A strange feature of the Menuetto is its ambiguous tonality; although the key signature indicates B-flat, the first section begins and ends in F (Example 6-29); not until the final cadence of the Menuetto does one feel that B-flat has been established.

Example 6-29. *Violin Sonata,* 3rd movement, measures 1-15.

The first draft accentuates the tonal ambiguity of this movement—the key signature has one flat, not two.

One other peculiarity of the Menuetto is the phrase structure. The traditional even, compact sections of Classical dance movements are replaced by two odd-numbered, unbalanced halves; the A section is 15 measures, the B section 38, producing a rather lopsided, meandering minuet. The two Trios are more conventional in length, and each provides an interesting element. Trio I, in B-flat minor, is imitative in style; in the first half, the violin follows the piano treble; in the second half, the violin leads off, followed by the piano bass in octaves (Example 6-30):

Example 6-30: *Violin Sonata*, 3rd movement, measures 64-68 and 72-76.

Trio II is in a somewhat remote key (D major) and very similar to the Menuetto movement of the clarinet sonata in its themes and its rhythmic aspects, such as dotted-rhythm scale figures.

The finale, as in the first movement, is a long sonata-form piece, without a repeat of the exposition; also like the first movement, the rapid figuration, coupled with the indicated presto tempo, propels the movement along despite its length. There is more contrast between the first and second themes in this movement; the latter, in the relative major in the exposition and in the parallel major in the recapitulation, is lyrical and well-shaped. Both themes are shown in Example 6-31:

Example 6-31. *Violin Sonata,* 4th movement, measures 1-4 and 52-55.

On the whole, the violin sonata is well-crafted, but the problems of dealing with large-scale formal structures are not handled in an interesting enough fashion to sustain the length of the work. The imaginative ideas that Archduke Rudolph displays in short forms seem to elude him in large ones. To his credit, however, one must note that the violin part is well-written for the instrument, thoroughly

210

idiomatic, and allowing the performer to display technical brilliance. Only on a few occasions does Rudolph place the solo part on the lower strings, where it is covered by the piano part.

In conclusion, the two sonatas Rudolph composed early in his career, though written competently, are not the most successful of his works. The composer himself apparently abandoned further attempts at sonata composition after this time and turned to the genre which most suited his creative ideas—variations.

CHAPTER VII

Other Music for Instrumental Ensembles

Archduke Rudolph's compositions for chamber ensembles were limited for the most part to duos—piano with either a woodwind or violin. His only trio (for clarinet, cello, and piano: Them. cat. no. U 19) and one sextet (Them. cat. no. U 23) were left incomplete, and although there are a few pages of sketches for string quartet, no work in that genre was composed.

Rudolph was drawn to quartet composition, but of a highly unusual kind: prominent among his works are several for a quartet consisting of B-flat clarinet, viola, bassoon, and guitar. Although the guitar was fairly popular at the time, there is no known precedent for such an instrumental combination. The fact that Archduke Rudolph composed no fewer than seven works for this instrumental quartet (of which two were completed) indicates that such a group was available to him, perhaps in his own household, or possibly among musical friends in Vienna.[1]

These seven compositions are all in the key of B-flat, with the exception of one piece (and an occasional movement in the B-flat

[1]The guitarist may have been Mauro Giuliani (1781-1829), Italian guitarist, cellist, and composer, who settled in Vienna in 1806. He was among the players in the orchestra at two benefit concerts in December 1813 at which Beethoven conducted his Symphony No. 7 and *Wellington's Victory*.

works) in E-flat; to judge from the handwriting in the manuscripts, entries in Archduke Rudolph's catalogue, and the close relationship of certain compositional elements in the music, all these works were composed around 1811-12.[2] Two of them—a *Serenade* in six movements (Them. cat. no. 22) and a set of variations on a song, "Vous me quittez pour aller à la gloire" (Them. cat. no. 19), are in the Gesellschaft der Musikfreunde; both are manuscript copies.[3] The remaining works, all autographs, are in Kroměříž. The two works in the Gesellschaft are complete; those in Kroměříž are unfinished, or fragments of varying lengths, some utilizing the same themes. No instruments are specified on the Kroměříž manuscripts, but the clef signs, as well as the instrumental writing, leave no doubt as to their instrumentation. The quartet compositions are as follows:

In the Gesellschaft der Musikfreunde:

Serenade pour Clarinette, Viole, Fagotte, et Guitarre, Them. cat. no. 22 (copyist's score); Wgm Q 17762.

Variations sur la Romance: "Vous me quittez pour aller à la gloire"[4] *pour une Clarinette, Viole, Fagotte, et Guitarre,* Them. cat. no. 19 (copyist's score); Wgm XI 15421.

In Kroměříž:

Variations in B-flat, Them. cat. no. U 11 (KRa A 4412). Autograph. The theme is identical with that of the fourth movement of the *Serenade.* Unfinished, 8 pp.

Variations (Andante) in B-flat, Them. cat. no. U 12 (KRa A 4413). Autograph. Unfinished, 4 pp.

Variations in B-flat, Them. cat. no. U 13 (KRa A 4414). Autograph. Unfinished, 16 pp.

Variations in B-flat, Them. cat. no. U 14 (KRa A 4417). Autograph. Unfinished, 4 pp.

Composition in E-flat, Them. cat. no. U 15 (KRa A 4433-38). Autograph. Unfinished, 4 pp.

---

[2]A watermark on one manuscript in the Gesellschaft der Musikfreunde (Wgm XI 15421) dates the paper from before 1812. The *Serenade* is entry no. 9 in Rudolph's catalogue, following the two sonatas.

[3]The Gesellschaft der Musikfreunde card catalogue erroneously identifies the variations as an autograph.

[4]The title on the first page of the Gesellschaft manuscript, in the Archduke's handwriting, has the word "guerre" instead of "gloire." The title is given correctly in Rudolph's catalogue entry.

In Kroměříž there are also two unfinished drafts (4 pp. and 8 pp.) of variations on "Vous me quittez pour aller à la gloire" (see Them. cat. no. 19). Other fragments in the *Membra disjecta* include a setting (in B-flat) of the theme from Spontini's *La Vestale* on which Rudolph composed variations in A for piano four hands (see chapter 4) and a one-page transcription of the Minuet from Beethoven's Septet, Opus 20 (see chapter 2).

Although the word "unfinished" is used in the preceding list to describe these various fragments, and despite the fact that in some cases the instrumental parts were truly only partially sketched out, several of the manuscripts were written neatly in fair copies, carefully edited, and are incomplete because of lost pages. One draft of the variations belonging to Them. cat. no. 19, for example, lacks only a final phrase of eighteen measures; another (Them. cat. no. U 14) is missing two pages in the middle. The explanation for these missing pages may lie in the amount of handling in the processes of sorting, examining, cataloguing, and re-cataloguing that the Kroměříž collection has undergone in the century and a half since the Archduke's death. Several misplaced pages from various works of Rudolph's can be found in the miscellaneous sketch collections in Kroměříž, but others seem to be permanently lost.

The sonority produced by this group of four instruments, despite the dissimilarity in their timbres, is very homogeneous.[5] In his writing for the ensemble, Rudolph demonstrates a knowledge of the idiomatic characteristics of the four instruments—e.g., the soloistic virtuosity of the clarinet, which is the chief melodic instrument; the cohesive harmonic function of the viola; the fundamental bass line of the bassoon; and the accompaniment of the guitar, which is sometimes strummed and at other times figured in an Alberti bass fashion, but is never used soloistically. In some variations, the viola and bassoon have solo turns—some, for the bassoon in particular, technically demanding.

Among the characteristics shared by this group of compositions, in addition to the tonality, are: simple binary forms, with the first half structured in an eight-measure segment; duple meter; and the practice of beginning the theme with an upbeat.

---

[5]The *Serenade* can be heard on a Telefunken recording (Tel. 6.42171) in a performance by the Consortium Classicum.

THE SERENADE (THEM. CAT. NO. 22)

The *Serenade,* typical of its genre, is characterized by a spirit of lightheartedness. It consists of six contrasting movements, four of which are standard dance types; the order of the six movements is: (1) Tempo di marcia; (2) [Allegretto]; (3) *Ländler;* (4) Variations (Allegro non troppo); (5) Adagio—Alla Polacca; (6) Marcia. The guitar part is notated in the treble clef with one sharp in the key signature, sounding a major sixth lower than written (the player is instructed to use a "capo d'astra in la terza posizione").[6] All the expression indications, as well as the titles, are in Italian. The arrangement of the six movements is designed to provide maximum contrast, with the two march movements framing movements of varied tempos and moods, and one movement (the *Ländler*) in a different tonality, E-flat (all the others are in B-flat). Rudolph's interest in and success with variations are exemplified here, too; the centerpiece of the *Serenade,* the fourth movement, has a sprightly theme with four variations that make virtuoso demands on the players. The Archduke's penchant for dotted rhythms and the martial spirit that accompanies them are in evidence here also. For illustration, the theme and a sampling of the variations are shown in Examples 7-1 through 7-5:

Example 7-1. *Serenade,* 4th movement, measures 1-8.

* sounds a major sixth lower

---

[6]The "capo d'astra," a corruption of the Italian "capo tasto," was a device placed on the strings to raise the pitch to another tonality.

The clarinet is featured in the first variation in a virtually non-stop figuration of fast running notes, including a cadenza; the opening measures are shown in Example 7-2:

Example 7-2. *Serenade.* 4th movement, Variation 1, measures 1-4.

In the second variation the viola and bassoon share the theme, reverting back to dotted rhythms (Example 7-3), and Variation 3 contrasts with a legato, even-note motion (Example 7-4):

Example 7-3. *Serenade*, 4th movement, Variation 2, measures 1-4.

Example 7-4. *Serenade*, 4th movement, Variation 3, measures 1-4.

The final variation features a brilliant bassoon solo that demands considerable technical skill. Like the solo for clarinet in the first variation, it proceeds almost nonstop with scarcely an opportunity to breathe (Example 7-5):

Example 7-5. *Serenade*, 4th movement, Variation 4, measures 1-4.

A short coda ends the movement. Throughout, the guitar provides an accompaniment of either strummed chords or arpeggiations.

218

This variation movement has a counterpart in Kroměříž, as noted earlier, but only the theme is the same. In the Kroměříž piece (Them. cat. no. U 11) there are five variations; in several, one or more parts are left bare. The variation ideas are less inventive than in the *Serenade*, tending to cling more literally to the basic theme. On the final page of this version are the opening measures of the second movement of the *Serenade*, suggesting that the Kroměříž manuscript served as a draft for the final version. Other than these variations, there are no extant autograph sketches for the other movements of the *Serenade*.

VARIATIONS ON "VOUS ME QUITTEZ..." (THEM. CAT. NO. 19)

These variations on a "Romance" are probably of earlier origin than the *Serenade*, that is, ca. 1810-11; the entry for them in Archduke Rudolph's catalogue is number 5, following the two 1810 compositions for czakan.

Both drafts of the variations in Kroměříž are incomplete. One is on four pages, very roughly sketched; the other is more fully outlined and was apparently once complete, since its final pages are intact. It lacks the two folios that would comprise the end of the first and most of the second variation. This later draft is in ink, with most of the viola part originally left bare, and filled in (in faded brown ink) in another hand—the same handwriting as that in the Gesellschaft copy (Wgm XI 15421). A comparison of this draft with the Gesellschaft manuscript reveals that considerable revisions were made in the latter.

The theme for the variations is taken from a song, "Les Adieux,"[7] of which the words "Vous me quittez pour aller à la gloire" make up the first line. In Rudolph's adaptation the eight measures of the song are used, preceded by an introductory dominant chord with a fermata, and followed by his own quasi-coda cadence of four measures (Example 7-6):

[7]The popularity of this song is attested by its inclusion in at least three different volumes of collected French romances of the early nineteenth century, some with guitar accompaniment, some with piano or harp, dating from 1800-1820; the three volumes are in the collection of the music division of the New York Public Library at Lincoln Center. The text of the song is by the Comte de Ségur; the music is anonymous.

Example 7-6. *Variations on "Vous me quittez...," measures 1-12.*

Clar.

Vla.

Bsn.

Guit.*

* sounds a major ninth lower

Each of the variations, which are not numbered, follows in a similar pattern after the fermata.

It will be noted that the guitar part in this work, as well as in most of the others, is written in the key of C—a somewhat mystifying notation, since the guitar is not a transposing instrument, and normally sounds an octave lower than the written pitch. The guitar part in these manuscripts is notated to sound a major ninth lower than written; in the absence of any instructions to the player such as those found in the *Serenade*, one may assume that scordatura was called for in order to provide the proper tonality for the guitar part.

While the guitar supplies its arpeggiated harmonic support, the other three instruments exchange solo turns with variants of the theme, along with variants of the sixteenth-note accompanying figure. In the first variation (Example 7-7), the clarinet elaborates the harmonic outline of the theme, the bassoon parodies it with a syncopated figure, and the viola fills in the harmony with still another rhythmic variant:

Example 7-7. *Variations on "Vous me quittez . . . ,"* Variation 1, measures 14-17.

* sounds a major ninth lower

The final variation turns to 6/8 meter, continuing the elaboration of tonic-dominant harmonies with figuration for another twenty-four measures, ending with a return to the opening twelve measures (slightly varied) and a final cadence.

VARIATIONS FOR VIOLIN, FLUTE, CLARINET, VIOLA, CELLO AND PIANO (THEM. CAT. NO. U 23)

For another medium, Archduke Rudolph composed a work which is among those which seem to lack some pages. This is a set of variations for a sextet consisting of violin, flute, clarinet in A, viola, cello, and piano, special because the theme, and each variation, is conceived as a solo for one of the instruments accompanied by the piano, with one variation reserved for piano solo. The keyboard part specifies "Forte Piano" on the first page of the manuscript—a unique indication among the Archduke's keyboard works—although at the fourth variation, for piano alone, the heading reads "Piano Forte."

Rudolph handles the structure and content of these variations with maturity and ease. This is clearly a late work, evident from the style, as well as the appearance of the manuscript, which is in Rudolph's mature handwriting. The music is neatly written and provided with all sorts of details relating to phrasing and dynamics. Although it breaks off abruptly at the end of the eighth page, leaving the cello solo variation (the fifth and probably final one) unfinished, it gives every appearance of having once been a completed work.

The theme, in A minor, recalls Mozart's *Rondo in A Minor,* K. 511, for piano, particularly in its use of 6/8 meter and the chromaticism in the melody, giving it a poignant quality. It is not without significance that there are only two works in a minor key in Archduke Rudolph's total oeuvre (the other being the Violin Sonata in F Minor), and both were influenced by works of Mozart.

The construction of the theme—two repeated sections with a coda—is somewhat unusual for Rudolph:[8]

‖: A :‖	‖: B :‖	Coda
8 measures	10 measures	6 measures

Although no tempo is indicated, the theme lends itself to a gentle flow, similar to the Andante of Mozart's Rondo. The theme is shown in its entirety in Example 7-8:

Example 7-8. *Variations for Violin, Flute, Clarinet, Viola, Cello, and Piano,* measures 1-24.

----

[8]Rudolph ordinarily did not write a coda in his binary forms.

Each variation has its own character, emphasized by changes in meter; for example, the clarinet variation is in 9/8 and in a pastoral style. Rudolph achieves unity in the set by keeping the coda ending of the theme in the piano alone following each variation.

VARIATIONS IN F FOR VIOLIN AND PIANO (THEM. CAT. NO. 15)

A set of variations for violin and piano on a theme by Prince Louis Ferdinand of Prussia,[9] one of Archduke Rudolph's two compositions for that instrumental duo (the Sonata in F Minor has been described in chapter 6), is one of his earliest works, according to his catalogue listing of his own compositions, where it is the first entry. It therefore presumably dates from ca. 1809-10, preceding the two czakan pieces from 1810. The theme for the variations is from Louis Ferdinand's Quartet for Piano, Violin, Viola, and Cello in F Minor, Opus 6— specifically, the first Trio from the third movement Menuetto, which is in F major.

There are two differing versions of this work: Version A survives in an autograph in the Gesellschaft der Musikfreunde (Wgm XI 15410);[10] Version B appears in three manuscript copies, also in the Gesellschaft der Musikfreunde, to be discussed later.

The handwriting of Version A conforms to other early works of Rudolph, ca. 1810—not only in the writing of clef signs and tempo

[9]This talented royal composer ranked highly in Rudolph's music collection; among the composers under the letter L, Louis Ferdinand was accorded first place, and all sixteen of his published compositions were in the collection.

[10]The card catalogue of the Gesellschaft mistakenly lists these as *Variations für Clavier und Clarinette*, owing to an identification error on the first page, which is not in Rudolph's hand.

indications, but also in the generally messy writing of the notes and the careless alignment of the violin and piano parts. As the work progresses (it is 39 pages long), the writing becomes less and less legible. The style of the variations is exuberant and extravagantly virtuosic, particularly in the writing of the dominating piano part, although the violin part has its share of difficulty at times.

The graceful, sedate theme by Louis Ferdinand is stated at the outset much as it appears in his Quartet. In that work, the theme is a rounded binary form, with a first section of eight measures repeated, and a second section of thirty-six measures; Rudolph's only change is to abridge the theme by eliminating several bars, but otherwise Louis Ferdinand's harmony and basic setting of the melody are retained (Example 7-9):

Example 7-9. *Variations in F for Violin and Piano*, measures 1-28.

The Menuetto theme lends itself to other dance styles, and several variations have the rhythmic character of the polonaise. Other standard character types, favorites of Rudolph's, include march variations, a canonic variation, and one in minor. There are thirteen variations all told, the final one of which is an extended, multisectional conclusion, with numerous changes in meter, tempo and tonality, and several cadenza-like sections.

Among the technical difficulties in the piano part are fast passages with consecutive thirds and sixths (in both hands), rapid repeated notes, and incessant runs that cover the keyboard—figuration that would daunt the best-equipped technicians.

Version B of these variations, on the same theme, can be found n three nearly identical manuscript copies in the Gesellschaft der Musikfreunde (Wgm Q 17755, Q 17763, and Q 17764); it differs greatly from the autograph version. Although there is no autograph evidence to determine whether this set is a later revision of his early work (perhaps because that one proved unplayable?), the style of composition shows a different approach, one that is more refined and controlled, eminently more playable, and better balanced between violin and piano—in sum, more in conformity with Rudolph's mature style. While Version B has seven variations instead of thirteen, some general similarities exist between the two pieces; four variations begin in the same way, and the finale of Version B is also multisectional, and so extensive that the two versions are about equal in overall length. The later set also has several piano cadenzas, and in both sets there is a return to the theme to conclude the finale.

In the setting of the theme itself, Archduke Rudolph made some improvements in Version B; for example, he provided more textural variety by giving the piano the theme in the first eight measures, and the violin the theme in the repeat. He also changed the register of the accompaniment and colored the harmony in the second measure with a passing *F-sharp* (Example 7-10):

Example 7-10. *Variations in F for Violin and Piano* (Version B), measures 1-4.

A similar change in registration was made later in the theme, along with a more active and interesting transition back to its A section:

Example 7-11. *Variations in F for Violin and Piano* (Version B), measures 13-20.

One example of Rudolph's changes in figuration between the two settings of the variations will illustrate the moderation of the technical demands of the piano part in the second version. Example 7-12 shows the opening measures of Variation 5 in version A and the corresponding measures in Variation 4 of version B:

Example 7-12a. *Variations in F for Violin and Piano* (Version A), Variation 5, measures 1-2.

Example 7-12b. *Variations in F for Violin and Piano* (Version B), Variation 4, measures 1-2.

ORCHESTRAL LÄNDLER (THEM. CAT. NO. 4C)

The discussion in chapter 4 of Archduke Rudolph's dance compositions for piano—*Ländler, Deutsche,* and *Allemandes*—suggested that the Archduke composed at least some of them for functions at the Imperial palace, the Hofburg, where balls were given regularly in the *Redoutensäle*. This supposition is supported by the existence of a set of orchestral parts for the *12 Ländler* for orchestra made by a professional copyist; in fact, some of the parts are in multiple copies (three for the violino primo, two for the basso). This set contains basically the same music as the *12 Allemandes* for piano four hands (Them. cat. no. 4A), with the exception of the coda. The following outline may help clarify the confusion concerning the location, contents, and titles of the various sources for this work:

In Kroměříž:
1. *12 Ländler* for orchestra, with trios and coda; autograph score (KRa A 4418).
In the Gesellschaft der Musikfreunde:
2. *12 Ländler* for orchestra, with trios; copyist's score (Wgm XV 15423).[11] Same music as No. 1 above.
3. *12 Deutsche* for orchestra, with trios and coda; copyist's parts (Wgm XV 9547). Same music as No. 1 above.
4. *Deutsche Tänze* for piano four hands, coda only; autograph (Wgm VII 29340). Same music as coda of No. 1 above.
5. *12 Allemandes* for piano four hands, with trios and coda; copy (Wgm Q 19886). Same music as No. 1 above, except for coda.

Why Archduke Rudolph composed a different coda for the four-hand *Allemandes*, and when he composed it, cannot be established, since the date of the copy is unknown. One may assume that Rudolph's setting of the dances for four hands preceded the orchestrated version; the catalogue entry for his compositions, number two in the list, reads simply:

12 Allemandes avec Trios et Coda p. Pf. à 4 mains
—detti à grand Orchestre

One fact seems certain: the *Allemandes* and their orchestral version, the *Ländler*, are of very early origin, ca. 1809-10.

The "grand orchestre" consists of: 2 piccolos, 2 flutes, 2 oboes, 2 clarinets, 2 bassoons; 2 horns, 2 trumpets, and timpani; first and second violins, and bass.[12] The instrumentation differs for the various dances, as does the key structure.

In making the orchestral arrangement, Rudolph was rather conventional. The treble melodies are simple and shared by the high woodwinds and the violins, sometimes played in unison; their limited range rarely requires the violins to play above third position.

---

[11]This copy is erroneously identified in the Gesellschaft card catalogue as an autograph.
[12]In the Kroměříž version, Rudolph originally wrote three violin parts. The use of two violin parts and bass follows the standard orchestration also found in Beethoven's orchestral dances (WoO 7-WoO 15), for example.

The brass and timpani are restricted primarily to rhythmic reinforcement of the beat.

The most interesting facet of the orchestral *Ländler* concerns changes that were added to the Kroměříž version, which was obviously the original setting, because these changes are in the hand of the same copyist who wrote out the Gesellschaft manuscript and are entered on empty staves beneath Rudolph's scoring. Most of the revisions are in the trumpet and piccolo parts, with a few in the horn parts. These all consist of slight changes in chord positions, and usually they simplify Rudolph's scoring. Some melodic changes were also made, mainly to redistribute the melodic phrases among the treble instruments. In a few instances the actual shape of the melody was altered; one such revision is illustrated in Example 7-13:

Example 7-13. *12 Ländler*, No. 1, measures 1-8.

None of the melodic revisions is any more significant than the one shown here.

It is conceivable that Rudolph composed the *Allemandes* quite early and revised (as he did with the Clarinet Sonata) and orchestrated them at a later date—perhaps for a ball at the Hofburg at the time of the Congress of Vienna. The question of who suggested the actual changes (was it Rudolph himself, looking over his earlier work with a new eye, or did Beethoven have a hand in it?) must, in the absence of any pertinent evidence, remain moot.

Plate 34. Sketch with doodles (Kroměříž, KRa A 4433-38).

CHAPTER VIII

Compositions for Voice

Although Archduke Rudolph composed comparatively little vocal music, the few works he completed demonstrate his ability to write effectively for the voice. The finished vocal compositions, all autographs in the Kroměříž archive, consist of three solo songs ("La partenza," "Je vous salue," and "Wenn in des Abends letztem Scheine") and a four-part song ("Lieber Beethoven, ich danke"). The three solo songs have piano accompaniments; "Lieber Beethoven" is an unaccompanied four-part canon.

In addition, Rudolph left many unfinished and fragmentary songs of varying lengths, all in manuscript in Kroměříž. One of these, to be discussed later, is a duet with piano accompaniment, "Ich denke dein," which although incomplete in the accompaniment, is otherwise fully sketched out. Among the fragments are sections of sacred choral works, including a Requiem and a Te Deum. In one of the miscellaneous sketch collections (KRa A 4432) can be found four songs in which either the melody or the accompaniment is incomplete. One other work, of very early origin, has the appearance of either a secular cantata or a stage work, with several voice parts indicated either by initials or by abbreviations for names (KRa A 4425); owing to the illegibility of Rudolph's script, however, the text is virtually undecipherable. None of the songs bears a date, but handwriting and other evidence show that the dates of composition range from ca. 1808-09 to ca. 1820.

233

LA PARTENZA (THEM. CAT. NO. 26)

Of primary interest among Rudolph's vocal works is his setting of "La partenza" for bass voice and piano, because the autograph in Kroměříž was corrected in detail by Beethoven. There are two other manuscripts of "La partenza" in the Gesellschaft der Musikfreunde; one is also an autograph (Wgm VI 42159) and the other a copy in another hand (Wgm VI 15408).

The text of "La partenza" is a canzonetta by Pietro Metastasio (1698-1782) which was popular among composers, among them Mozart and Beethoven.[1] Kinsky notes settings by Graun, Kirnberger, Reichardt, Rust, and Salieri, and others were made by Metastasio himself and several Italian composers as well.[2]

"La partenza" has seven stanzas, five of them ending with the two-line refrain, "E tu, chi sa se mai,/Ti sovverai di me!" Metastasio altered the refrain in the last two verses slightly. Following the form of the canzonetta, Rudolph set the poem in strophic style; the vocal line and accompaniment are almost identical in all but the seventh, and final, stanza. The accompaniment in both autographs is omitted entirely in verses two through six; in the Gesellschaft copy, however, the accompaniment—unchanged—is written out in full for each verse and may, therefore, have been a copy intended for use in performance.

The Kroměříž autograph consists of eight pages in ink and two separate pages of a pencil sketch of the piano introduction and the first verse. At the beginning the tempo indication *Andante* is in ink, and a pencil addition reads " ♩ =80, Metronome de Mälzl." Beethoven's numerous corrections are also in pencil. On the final page, the theme of Beethoven's "O Hoffnung" is written out on two empty staves, in Rudolph's hand.[3] None of the manuscripts is dated, but the catalogue entry for "La partenza" among the Archduke's own compositions (No. 12) is in the contorted, slanted handwriting which reflected his bout with a crippling arthritic condition around 1816-17.

In setting the text to music, Rudolph adopted an essentially syllabic

[1] Mozart's setting, a "Notturno" for three voices and three basset horns (K. 436) was composed in 1783; Beethoven's setting (WoO 124) dates from 1797-98.

[2] Kinsky-Halm, *Das Werk Beethovens*, 586.

[3] Although Rudolph's writing of "La partenza" and "O Hoffnung" here are fundamentally similar, some small notational differences indicate they were not written down at the same time.

approach. The dactylic meter of the poem ("Ecco quel fiero istante!/ Nice, mia Nice, addio") is anticipated in the four measures of the piano introduction and then carried out in the opening vocal line (Example 8-1):

Example 8-1. "La partenza" (Gesellschaft autograph), measures 1-32.

The harmonic structure of this first stanza—the conclusion of the first phrase in the tonic (measure 12) and the continuation in the dominant (measure 15)—constitutes the sole similarity of Archduke Rudolph's setting to Beethoven's; in all other respects the two songs differ.[4] The harmonic structure common to both settings was, of course, standard in song literature of the period.

En route to the return to the tonic a harmonic digression (measures 21-23) serves to color the bland harmonic scheme of the whole. The descent of the vocal line to A_1 (measure 24) is balanced by the

---

[4]Beethoven's setting is of the first stanza only, in the key of A, 2/4 meter, for high voice.

ascending passage repeating the last line of the refrain, which reaches C^1. The piano postlude, in contrast with the somewhat static piano introduction, flows smoothly over a two-octave range (measures 25-32).

In the final verse several changes emphasize textual differences in the refrain, which now begins "Pensa—ah, chi sa se mai." Two additional measures are interpolated before the dominant seventh chord (which Rudolph first spelled as an augmented sixth chord; see Examples 8-7 and 8-12):

Example 8-2. "La partenza," Verse 7, measures 189-91.

The piano postlude begins almost identically as in the earlier verses (the last three eighth notes of the second measure are changed), breaks off after the second measure to accompany a repeat of the refrain, and then completes the remainder of the postlude (Example 8-3):

Example 8-3. "La partenza," measures 199-206.

In the Kroměříž autograph, Beethoven's corrections can be found in each verse; most of them are concerned with problems of text-setting such as elision of words and the lengthening and shortening of note values. An illustration of the latter is shown in four brief examples from the first verse (Example 8-4, a-d):

Example 8-4. "La partenza"

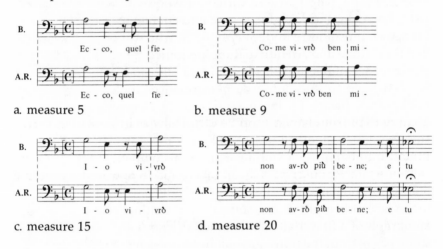

a. measure 5   b. measure 9

c. measure 15   d. measure 20

In the first three examples (8-4 a, b, c), the change in note values—eighth notes instead of quarter notes on the last beat of each measure—breaks up the rather square-cut rhythm with its metrical emphasis on the beat. In Example 8-4 d, on the other hand, Beethoven gives longer value to the last syllable of "bene" rather than cutting if off with an eighth note.

In other verses Beethoven deletes unnecessary notes in those places that occur so often in the Italian language when syllables are elided (Example 8-5, a and b):

Example 8-5. "La partenza"

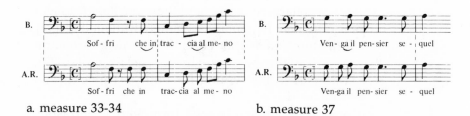

a. measure 33-34   b. measure 37

In some cases note values were changed and notes added:

Example 8-6. "La partenza," measures 127-32.

In each case, Beethoven's alterations succeed in underscoring the mellifluous and smoothly flowing qualities of Italian as well as in avoiding metrical stress on the strong beats.

In the final verse there are several corrections of the kind shown in the foregoing examples, and some changes of a more substantial nature. In the first of these, Beethoven altered both the vocal line and the accompaniment (Example 8-7):

Example 8-7. "La partenza," measures 189-91.

239

The harmonic alteration is evidently an attempt to provide variety and makes more logical the voice-leading in the bass, descending from *C* to *A-flat* rather than *C* to *B-flat* and back to *C*. The change in the vocal line is necessitated by the harmonic change.

In the second case, Beethoven's revisions are entered on a staff added by him beneath the score; they constitute a significant change in the final, climactic measures of the song:

Example 8-8. "La partenza," measures 203-206.

The fermata placed on the two highest notes adds emphasis and, more importantly, rhythmic variety, to the final phrase, differentiating it from the endings of the previous verses.

One final correction was made by Beethoven in the piano postlude, at measure 207 (Example 8-9):

Example 8-9. "La partenza," measures 206-209.

The finality and potency of the cadence is achieved far more effectively by reserving the dominant chord for the penultimate measure, instead of its anticipatory appearance in measure 207.

The two pages of Rudolph's pencil sketches accompanying the Kroměříž autograph, of the first verse only, are on a separate sheet (two sides); the piano accompaniment is roughly sketched in some measures, often in a compositional shorthand, with chords representing the figuration that was written out in the final version. There are several differences between the sketch and the finished autograph, such as the changes made in the four-measure introduction (Example 8-10):

Example 8-10. "La partenza" (pencil sketch), measures 1-4.

Only the rhythmic motive of the first two measures (♩ ♩ ♪ ♪ | ♩ ♩) is maintained in the finished version; the descending third of the voice part thus has a fresh sound (cf. Example 8-1).

Curiously enough, the vocal part in this sketch is notated with all Beethoven's corrections incorporated, whereas the piano part underwent many revisions before its final version, indicating possibly that another sketch existed in which final changes were made in both parts.

At the end of the pencil sketch Rudolph tried out several different ideas for the piano postlude before arriving at the final version in measures 28-32 (Example 8-1). The notation is not always clear enough to decipher with certainty, but it appears to read as follows (Example 8-11):

Example 8-11. "La partenza" (pencil sketch), page 2.

Rudolph's final choice of figuration in the third measure, which maintains eighth-note movement in the right hand rather than sixteenths, preserves the basic rhythmic scheme of the song. The same problem that was solved by Beethoven in measure 207 (Example 8-9) is considered here—whether the dominant should appear before the penultimate measure and anticipate the cadence— and the same solution was determined.

Both manuscripts of "La partenza" in the Gesellschaft der Musik-freunde, as mentioned earlier, incorporate Beethoven's corrections. Although the two copies are catalogued in the Gesellschaft as

242

autographs, one (Wgm VI 15408) is clearly not in Rudolph's hand.[5] This is the only manuscript in which the accompaniment is written out for all verses.

The autograph in the Gesellschaft (Wgm VI 42159), with Beethoven's corrections incorporated, differs only slightly from the one in Kroměříž. The most significant change is of the chord in measure 21 under the word "tu!" which, it was noted on p. 237, Rudolph originally spelled with *F-sharp* instead of *G-flat* (Example 8-12):

Example 8-12. "La partenza" (Kroměříž autograph), measure 21.

In the empty staff beneath this measure two chords are written, but so faintly that the upper note cannot be discerned clearly. Similarly, in the last verse, at the words "Pensa, pensa" (measure 189), some chords are notated in the margin. The music at measure 189 is heavily smudged, and the chords in the margin may have been intended just for clarification. They may well be in Beethoven's hand, but this is not certain.

WENN IN DES ABENDS LETZTEM SCHEINE (THEM. CAT. NO. 24)

Archduke Rudolph's *Lied* whose first line is "Wenn in des Abends letztem Scheine" is a setting of the first two stanzas of the poem "Lied aus der Ferne" by Friedrich von Matthisson (1761-1831).[6] The autograph in Kroměříž consists of five pages—four contain the music, with the text, and on a fifth page the text of the poem is printed out with many misreadings of the words.[7] The first page of the song is

[5]There is little similarity to Rudolph's writing style either in the notation itself, in the writing of the text, or in certain spellings (e.g., the name Mälzl, which is written as "Mältzl" in this copy).

[6]Schubert set the "Lied aus der Ferne" (D. 107) in 1814; it was not published until 1894.

[7]This page, probably written out by one of the archivists in Kroměříž, was possibly an attempt to make Rudolph's illegible rendering of the text beneath the music coherent. The illegibility also no doubt accounts for the song being listed as a fragment in the Brno card catalogue.

notated neatly, but the remaining three become progressively careless; several measures are crossed out and new ones substituted, but the song is complete. The writing of the clef signs and the placement of the accidentals in the key signature (the key is E-flat) establish an early date for this song, ca. 1809-10.

The form of Rudolph's setting follows the form of the poem, coming to a cadence at the close of the first strophe, and repeating the opening three measures of the vocal melody for the second.

The text is one of serenity, dealing with aspects of twilight and evening, and the tranquil moods and feelings associated therewith. Rudolph's setting of the piano introduction captures these moods with the slow, rippling triplets in the right-hand part (Example 8-13):

Example 8-13. "Wenn in des Abends," measures 1-5.

The triplet figure accompanies the vocal line, which unfolds calmly and smoothly in longer note values (Example 8-14):

Example 8-14. "Wenn in des Abends," measures 11-20.

The first verse remains, by and large, in E-flat; the second ("Wenn in des Mondes Dämmerlichte . . .") begins identically to the first, continues with some variation in the melody, and arrives at a cadence in E-flat (Example 8-15, measure 41). In the last three lines, a harmonic progression establishes the tonality of E for three measures (measures 46-48) before returning, by way of a second dominant, to E-flat minor and finally the tonic (measures 48-50). In Example 8-15, showing the passage just cited, omitted accidentals have been added above the notes.

Example 8-15. "Wenn in des Abends," measures 40-58.

Archduke Rudolph's handling of the harmonic procedures in this setting reveals a degree of sophistication not usually found in his compositions, particularly those from his early years. The modulation to and away from the harmonic area of the Neapolitan, spelled with *E* and *B* instead of *F-flat* and *C-flat,* in measures 42 to 50 (aside from the probable error in measure 43 of *E-natural* in the voice part and *E-flat* in the piano) is unusual in the song literature of the period and highly effective in its expressive character as the climax of the song.[8] The

---

[8]Schubert employs a similar harmonic relationship in two well-known songs from *Winterreise,* "Irrlicht" and "Einsamkeit," although in the latter the lowered supertonic is used more as a passing harmony.

piano introduction, which meanders with little harmonic variation for ten measures, seems rather overlong in the context of the tight structure of the song itself, although it certainly establishes the mood. But on the whole, the song is well-crafted technically in the way melody and accompaniment fit together, in the smoothness of the vocal writing, in the way the music reflects the text, and in the poignancy of its expression.

JE VOUS SALUE, O LIEUX CHARMANTS (THEM. CAT. NO. 25)

The remaining solo song in Kroměříž, a setting of a poem by J. de Florian,[9] is "Je vous salue, o lieux charmants" (KRa A 4423). It is interesting to note that Rudolph composed two entirely different versions of the poem, with several sketches for each that vary in significant details and show the composer struggling to find the appropriate setting. There are twelve pages of manuscript altogether; one version is in the key of A major, in 3/4 meter (two pages); the other is in F major, in duple (4/4) meter (ten pages). The version in A has one sketch in which the vocal part is complete, and the accompaniment in a skeletal shorthand; the second page contains both parts completed, in a careless handwriting. The handwriting, clef signs, and other notational signs place the date of composition around 1816, the same time as "La partenza." The piano introduction and the opening vocal phrase are shown in Example 8-16:

Example 8-16. "Je vous salue," measures 1-16.

[No tempo given]

[5]

---

[9]Several romances by Boieldieu were composed on texts by Florian.

The text-setting reveals some disregard for the natural accentuation of the French language, i.e., letting the word "de" fall on a strong beat and stretching the second syllable of "avec" by placing it on a note of long value.

Judging from the number of sketches of the version in F, it appears that Archduke Rudolph spent considerable time working on it. There are four sketches, all more or less complete, with identical vocal lines but different endings in the accompaniments. In two of these sketches, Rudolph set down the introduction and first verse complete and then wrote out just the vocal line and text of the other four strophes. One of the two is a fair copy (two pages) with phrasing, tempo, and dynamic markings included.[10] The same awkward handling of the text is apparent—even more awkward, perhaps, because of the duple meter. As in the setting shown in Example 8-16, Rudolph takes advantage of the word 'tristesse" to do a little word painting by turning briefly to minor. Example 8-17, from the fair copy of the version in F major, shows the piano introduction and the first verse.

Example 8-17. "Je vous salue" (F major version), measures 1-22.

[10]One mysterious feature of this sketch is that while the writing of the notes and text appear to be in Rudolph's hand, the other notational symbols—clefs, time signature, and the like—were not made by him.

The fact that Rudolph concentrated most of his efforts on the version in F seems to indicate his preference for this setting, although the nostalgic sentiments of the text (see Appendix 2, p. 311) appear better reflected in the setting in A. The version in F has a rather martial character, owing to the duple meter and the use of dotted rhythms, that is much less compatible with the text of the poem.

Two pages of the sketches show a varied treatment of the vocal part. Both of these manuscripts are notated very carelessly and are replete with crossed-out measures, ink blots, and doodles in the margins. Example 8-18 shows Rudolph's setting of the final verse, and Example 8-19 is still another version of the song's opening:

Example 8-18. "Je vous salue" (sketch in F)

Example 8-19. "Je vous salue" (other sketch in F)

ICH DENKE DEIN (THEM. CAT. NO. U 32)

Although unfinished, the duet, "Ich denke dein" is of more than ordinary interest because of a twofold association with works of Beethoven. The text of "Ich denke dein" is the poem "Andenken" by Friedrich von Matthisson, which Beethoven set to music in 1809 (WoO 136).[11] Archduke Rudolph's setting of the same poem is linked

---

[11]"Andenken" was published by Breitkopf & Härtel that year. The text of the poem can be found in Appendix 2, p. 312.

not with the Beethoven song but with the latter's piano sonata Opus 81a, "Les Adieux," composed for the Archduke in 1809-10 on the occasion of the Imperial family's departure from (and subsequent return to) Vienna at the time of the French invasion of Austria. The notation of Rudolph's manuscripts of his setting of "Ich denke dein" places its date of composition at a later time, ca. 1815-16. In setting the poem, Rudolph refers directly to the opening horn call motive of the Beethoven sonata, using it throughout as a sort of motto: [12]

Example 8-20. Beethoven, Piano Sonata Opus 81a ("Les Adieux"), 1st movement, measures 1-2.

Example 8-21 shows the piano introduction and opening vocal parts of "Ich denke dein," with its quote (in a different key) from "Les Adieux," in measures six and seven:

Example 8-21. Archduke Rudolph, "Ich denke dein," measures 1-8.

[12]The question of whether Beethoven could have derived the opening "Lebewohl" motive from Rudolph's song, rather than vice versa, is raised by both Vetterl, "Der musikalische Nachlass," and Racek, "Beethoven's Beziehungen;" both writers conclude this is unlikely.

Two settings of the song are extant, one in the key of B-flat, shown above, and another in F; the vocal lines and the sketchily-written accompaniments, however, are alike. Most of the accompaniment is omitted entirely in both versions, but all four verses of the text are written out, suggesting that the song was completed and that this manuscript was an interim working copy, with much of the notation in Rudolph's "shorthand," i.e., chords representing figuration. The musical style, with its three-note upbeat and Alberti bass accompaniment, is very similar to that of "Je vous salue."

The manuscript of one other vocal duet with piano, titled "Adieu ma douce amie," is in the Kroměříž archive; this song, set to words by A. de Coupigny,[13] appears to be a copy of a work by someone else.

LIEBER BEETHOVEN, ICH DANKE (THEM. CAT. NO. 27)

The final finished song in the archive is something of a novelty—a four-voice musical "thank you" to Beethoven in answer to the latter's New Year's greeting of 1820 in the form of a four-part canon (Example 8-22):

Example 8-22. Beethoven, "Alles Gute! Alles Schöne!" (WoO 179), measures 1-10.

Rudolph's answering canon, to the words "Lieber Beethoven, ich danke für Ihre Wünsche zum neuen Jahre und nehmen Sie auch meine mit Nachsicht an" (KRa A 4376), is patterned after Beethoven's model, beginning homophonically with all four voices, and then continuing canonically[14] (Example 8-23):

[13]Poems by Coupigny were set to music by Boieldieu and Cherubini, among others.

[14]Rudolph's rendering of Beethoven's name in the song, accentuating the second syllable (Beet-ho-ven), was in conformity with 19th-century Viennese pronunciation. See Paul Nettl, *Beethoven Handbook* (New York: Frederick Ungar, 1967) 150-151.

Example 8-23. Archduke Rudolph, "Lieber Beethoven."[15]

[15]Nettl, "Erinnerungen an Erzherzog Rudolph," reproduced the entire song (pp. 98-99). In measures 2 and 36 he transcribed the top note of the chord as G instead of an F, which I believe to be an error.

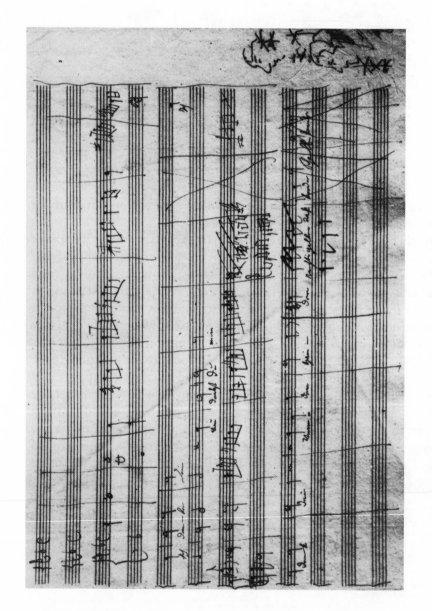

Plate 35. Page from "Ich denke dein" (Kroměříž, KRa A 4424).

The weaknesses of this setting are readily apparent; the monotony of the tonic-dominant harmonies, four-square rhythm, and non-poetic text all contribute to a rather uninspired composition. It should be remembered, however, that simple harmonic schemes and repetitive rhythms are characteristic of many vocal canons, Beethoven's included. In his article, Nettl concluded with the words, "Der Erzherzog tat recht daran, wenn er Beethoven um Nachsicht bat."[16] It seems unfair, however, to regard this canon as other than a private communication, in a friendly and humorous vein, between pupil and teacher. Certainly it is not representative of Rudolph's skills as a song composer.

One last work, characterized in the archive catalogue as a "Duetto" between "Robert and Amorone," was mentioned at the beginning of this chapter as problematic because of its illegible text; in addition, the music is very disjointed, with the tonality, meter, and number of voices varying on many of the eight pages of the manuscript. The text, in German, is squeezed in in such a small script that only a few isolated words can be deciphered. Despite its identification as a Duetto in the Brno card catalogue, it is clearly not for two voices only; on one page, abbreviations for five voices next to the staves can be

---

[16]Nettl, "Erinnerungen an Erzherzog Rudolph," 98.

discerned. According to the writing of the clef signs and key signatures, as well as the primitive-looking notation, this piece dates from before 1809.

SACRED CHORAL WORKS

The last group of vocal works in the Kroměříž archive contains unfinished sketches of sacred choral compositions: parts of a Requiem mass, a Te Deum, and the antiphons Salve Regina and Regina Caeli. Some of these are fragments of only one or two pages in length; although ambitious in scope, none is long enough to warrant detailed discussion. They are of interest to us primarily because they represent the sole link between Archduke Rudolph's ecclesiastic and composing careers. Some appear to have been written at the very start of Rudolph's composing years, and others date from his maturity.

The largest group of sketches is for different sections of the Requiem, most of them for four-part chorus and four solo voices (Them. cat. no. U 30): these include parts of the texts of "Requiem aeternam," "Kyrie eleison," and "Quam olim Abrahae," all in ink, on twenty-six pages (KRa A 4426). This group, along with a two-page fragment of a Te Deum (Them. cat. no. U 31) are in the Archduke's early notation. Other fragments, in Rudolph's mature hand, include partial settings of the text "Lux aeterna" (Them. cat. no. U 35),[17] Regina Caeli (Them. cat. no. U 34) and Salve Regina (Them. cat. no. U 35) [KRa A 4426 and 4427].

The first section of the Requiem, "Requiem aeternam," has an introduction of thirteen measures, notated on two staves, following which the accompaniment is omitted. The opening vocal phrase is set homophonically, but the prevailing vocal treatment in most of the Requiem is polyphonic, often strictly imitative. The entire text of "Requiem aeternam" is set, alternating between chorus and soloists. In the "Kyrie" which follows, three pages are a setting for four voices, and eight pages, seven of them textless, continue the "Kyrie" for eight voices, presumably four solo and four choral, with many measures

[17]There is also a pencil sketch on one page of the opening of "Libera me," which lacks clef signs and is barely legible.

crossed out. The openings of both sections are shown in Examples 8-24 and 8-25:

Example 8-24. "Requiem aeternam," measures 1-8.

Example 8-25. "Kyrie eleison," measures 1-4.

The third fragment belonging to the Requiem is a setting of one phrase from the Offertorium, "Quam olim Abrahae promisisti et semini ejus." It is in ink, on eight twelve-stave pages; although only four voice parts are notated, all twelve staves have bar-lines drawn through them, as if Rudolph intended writing more vocal parts. The first four measures are shown in Example 8-26.

Example 8-26. "Quam olim Abrahae," measures 1-4.

The "Lux aeterna," also from the Requiem, is a setting of one phrase of text ("Lux aeterna luceat eis, Domine: cum sanctis tuis in aeternam, quia pius est"); it is noteworthy because of its resemblance to a passage with the same text from Mozart's *Requiem* (Examples 8-27 and 8-28), both of them patterned after Gregorian melodies:

Example 8-27: Mozart, *Requiem*, Agnus Dei, measures 54-56.

Example 8-28. Archduke Rudolph, "Lux aeterna," measures 1-6.

This is another example of several we have seen that reveal Archduke Rudolph's thorough familiarity with Mozart's music and its influence on his own compositions (see chapter 2, pp. 60-61); among Rudolph's piano transcriptions are two settings of the fugue from the Kyrie of Mozart's *Requiem*.

There are eight pages of pencilled sketches for the Regina Caeli for four voice parts (on two staves) and instrumental lines, without clef signs, on the staves above and below. The homophonic setting of the opening measures is shown in Example 8-29:

Example 8-29. *Regina Caeli*, measures 1-4.

Like the "Libera me" fragment, the setting of the opening of Salve Regina is on one page only, roughly sketched in pencil and barely legible; only eight measures are complete for all four voices. This sketch appears on the final page of an unfinished Sonata for Clarinet in B-flat (Them. cat. no. U 25), which suggests its composition dates from around the same time, ca. 1822.

259

Finally, there is the Te Deum fragment, Archduke Rudolph's most ambitious attempt at choral writing; its two surviving pages (a fair copy in ink, carefully notated and edited) indicate that more of it once existed. The work is scored for three four-voice choirs (coincidentally, the same forces Berlioz employed in his Te Deum, Opus 22) and two unspecified instruments, one treble and one bass. The opening measures, for all the voices in unison, are an energetic and forceful setting of the text "Te Deum Laudamus, te Dominum confitemur" (Example 8-30):

Example 8-30. Te Deum, measures 1-2.

Te De - um, lau-da - mus, Te Do mi-num con-fi- te - mur

An assessment of these sacred choral fragments must take into account that they were all left incomplete, or discarded, presumably because Rudolph himself found them wanting or could not proceed satisfactorily to their conclusion. Elementary problems of composition abound in the early works—awkward leaps, voice-crossings (unidiomatic in this period), parallels, poor doublings in chords, and abrupt endings of melodic phrases. The association of these choral fragments with Rudolph's youth suggests that his theoretical studies with Beethoven ca. 1809 of extracts from the teaching of Fux, Albrechtsberger, and others may have generated an interest in polyphonic vocal composition.

Our evaluation of Rudolph's skill in composing for voice, however, cannot be based on these fragments, but rather on those few but well-crafted songs which better exemplify his abilities in that genre. The Archduke's handling of the relatively brief, compact song structure is for the most part expert; there is little of the overlaboring of material that sometimes impairs the larger structures of some of his instrumental compositions. In one song—"Wenn in des Abends letztem Scheine"—Rudolph's musical setting exhibits sensitivity to the substance of the text. In the harmonic area, the songs are rather conventional; but in both "Wenn in des Abends letztem Scheine" and "La partenza," Rudolph utilizes modulations and remote key areas for expressive purposes that are somewhat unusual.

In sum, while vocal music does not occupy a large place in Archduke Rudolph's oeuvre—probably because instrumental music interested him more than song—the vocal works he composed reveal technical skill as well as a feeling for the genre.

Plate 36. Archduke Rudolph memorial monument, Bad Ischl, Austria.

CHAPTER IX

Conclusion

The prime aim of the foregoing study has been to illuminate the life and work of a gifted amateur composer—an amateur in the true sense of the word, because love of music permeated the whole fabric of Archduke Rudolph's existence. By fortunate circumstance, the Archduke had the unique privilege of being the only composition student of Ludwig van Beethoven. In the course of this study, we have attempted to provide an answer to a hitherto unasked question: is the music of Archduke Rudolph distinguished by artistic quality on a level that justifies such a study?

As a composer, Archduke Rudolph was fully au courant with the music of his time. He was drawn primarily to instrumental music, wrote in forms that were currently prevalent, especially variation works, and composed mainly for the most popular instrument of the nineteenth century, the piano. There are occasional flashes of originality, which have been pointed out in the chapters devoted to his music, but fundamentally Rudolph used the musical vocabulary of the period and floated comfortably in the mainstream.

While the quality of Archduke Rudolph's oeuvre is uneven, many works composed both early and late in his career exhibit considerable skill. Among the variation sets, in particular, we have commented on several of which the structures and figuration are as inventive and effective as those of his better known *Kleinmeister* contemporaries.

263

Perhaps the most compelling answer to the question posed above is provided by Beethoven's role in overseeing Archduke Rudolph's creative output. Beethoven's interest in Rudolph as a composition student could perhaps be regarded merely as attributable to the debt he owed to the Archduke's patronage; however, the amount of time and attention Beethoven lavished on Rudolph, the meticulous critical corrections to refine Rudolph's work, Beethoven's comments to others praising Rudolph's talent, and his actions on behalf of publication of Rudolph's music—all these suggest that Beethoven had faith in the ability of his student. It is pertinent, perhaps, to reiterate the concluding statement made in the Introduction: Rudolph was not a composer of major consequence, but his talent and industry succeeded in producing a small but well-crafted body of music.

The second major aim of this study has been to shed light on Beethoven as a teacher of composition. Through Beethoven's corrections on Rudolph's manuscripts, we have been privy to some basic aspects of his thought on such fundamentals as rhythm, melody, and harmonic syntax. More revealing, even, is Beethoven's perception of his pedagogical role—the things he did not attempt to do as the Archduke's teacher. From all we know of Beethoven's character—the stubbornly independent artist whose individuality is one of his strongest traits—we would expect to find the imprint of his style much more in evidence in Rudolph's work. Beethoven, however, followed the wisest educational course—he corrected obvious mistakes, gave suggestions for improvement, but he did not impose his own personality as a composer on Rudolph; thus as he shone as an artist, so he shone as a teacher, permitting his pupil to develop his own esthetic identity, and serving as the catalyst for a significant output of a minor but not unimportant composer.

Bibliography

Albrecht, Otto. "Beethoven Autographs in the United States," *Beiträge zur Beethoven-Bibliographie*, ed. Kurt Dorfmüller. Munich: Henle, 1978.

Allgemeine musikalische Zeitung III (January 1820) 33-41; XLVII (June 1820) 369-73; and passim.

[Beethoven]. *Beethovens sämtliche Briefe*, 2nd ed., 5 vols., ed. A.C. Kalischer and Theodor Frimmel. Leipzig: Schuster & Loeffler, 1908-11.

[Beethoven]. *The Letters of Beethoven*, 3 vols., trans. and ed. Emily Anderson. New York: St. Martin's Press, 1961.

[Beethoven]. *New Beethoven Letters*, trans. and annotated Donald W. MacArdle and Ludwig Misch. Norman, Oklahoma: University of Oklahoma Press, 1957.

Beethoven Abstracts, ed. Donald W. MacArdle. Detroit: Information Coordinators, Inc., 1973.

Beethoven-Forschung, ed. Theodor Frimmel. Vienna: Kommissionsverlag G. Gerold & Co., 1911-25.

Beethoven Studies, ed. Alan Tyson. New York: Norton, 1973.

Beethoven Studies 2, ed. Alan Tyson. London: Oxford University Press, 1977.

Beethoven Studies 3, ed. Alan Tyson. Cambridge: Cambridge University Press, 1982.

Boettcher, Hans. *Beethoven als Liederkomponist*. Augsburg, 1928.

Croll, Gerhard. "Die Musiksammlung des Erzherzogs Rudolph," *Beethoven-Studien* (1970) 51-55.

_____. "Zu Mozarts Larghetto und Allegro Es-dur für 2 Klaviere KV deest," *Mozart Jahrbuch* (1964) 28.

Deutsch, Otto Erich. *Schubert: Memoirs by His Friends*. London: Black, 1968.

Federhofer-Königs, Renate. "Rudolph, Johann Joseph Rainer, Erzherzog von Österreich," *Musik in Geschichte und Gegenwart*, ed. Friedrich Blume. Kassel: Bärenreiter (1963) XI, 1058-1062.

Frimmel, Theodor. *Beethoven-Handbuch*, 2 vols. Leipzig: Breitkopf & Härtel, 1926.

Kinsky, Georg and Hans Halm. *Das Werk Beethovens: Thematisch-Bibliographisches Verzeichnis seiner sämtlichen vollendeten Kompositionen*. Munich: G. Henle, 1955.

Kohler, Karl-Heinz and Grita Herre, eds. *Ludwig van Beethovens Konversationshefte*. Leipzig: VEB Deutscher Verlag für Musik, 1968-1983 (Vols. 1-8).

Kramer, Richard. "Notes to Beethoven's Education," *Journal of the American Musicological Society* XXVIII, No. 1 (1975) 72-101.

MacArdle, Donald W. "Beethoven and the Archduke Rudolph," *Beethoven Jahrbuch* (1959-60) 36-58.

Macartney, C.A. *The Habsburg Empire 1790-1918*. New York: MacMillan, 1969.

McGuigan, Dorothy Gies. *The Habsburgs*. Garden City, New York: Doubleday, 1966.

Mann, Alfred. "Beethoven's Contrapuntal Studies with Haydn," *Musical Quarterly* LVI (1970) 711-26.

Marek, George. *Beethoven: Biography of a Genius*. New York: Thomas Y. Crowell, 1972.

Marx, A.B. *Ludwig van Beethoven: Leben und Schaffen*, 2 vols. Berlin: Janke, 1908.

Nettl, Paul. *Beethoven Handbook*. New York: Frederick Ungar, 1967.

_____. "Erinnerungen an Erzherzog Rudolph, den Freund und Schüler Beethovens," *Zeitschrift für Musikwissenschaft* IV (1921-22) 95-99.

Newman, William. "Beethoven's Fingerings as Interpretive Clues," *Journal of Musicology* I, 2 (1982) 171-97.

Nottebohm, Gustav. *Beethoveniana*. New York: Johnson Reprint [of 1872 ed.] 1970, 154-203.

_____. *Beethoven's Studien*, vol. I: *Beethoven's Unterricht bei J. Haydn, Albrechtsberger und Salieri*. Leipzig & Winterthur: Rieter-Biedermann, 1873.

Novotny, Alexander. "Kardinal Erzherzog Rudolph (1788-1831) und seiner Bedeutung für Wien," *Wiener Geschichtsblätter* IV (1961), 341-47.

Racek, Jan. "Beethovens Beziehungen zur Mährischen Musikkultur im 18. und 19. Jahrhundert," *Beethoven Jahrbuch* (1977) 377-93.

Reichardt, Johann Friedrich. *Vertraute Briefe geschrieben auf einer Reise nach Wien und den Österreichischen Staaten zu Ende das Jahre 1808 und zu Anfang 1809*. Amsterdam, 1810.

Rendall, F. Geoffrey. *The Clarinet*. London: Williams and Norgate, 1954.

Rietsch, Heinrich. "Ein gemeinsames Werk Österreichischer Komponisten," *Österreichische Rundschau* III (1905) 438-48.

Schindler, Anton. *Beethoven As I Knew Him*, ed. Donald W. MacArdle, trans. Constance S. Jolly. New York: Norton, 1972.

_____. *Biographie von Ludwig van Beethoven*. Münster: Aschendorff, 1840.

Schünemann, Georg. "Beethovens Studien zur Instrumentation," *Beethoven-Jahrbuch* VIII (1938) 146-61.

Seyfried, Ignaz Ritter von. *Ludwig van Beethovens Studien im General-Basse, Contrapuncte, und in der Compositionslehre.* Vienna: T. Haslinger, 1832.

Solomon, Maynard. *Beethoven*. New York: Schirmer Books, 1977.

_____. "The Dreams of Beethoven," *American Imago* XXXII (1975) 113-44.

Sonntägsblätter IV (1845) 385-89, 417-19.

Taylor, A.J.P. *The Habsburg Monarchy 1809-1918*. New York: Harper, 1965.

Thayer, Alexander Wheelock. *Ludwig van Beethovens Leben*, 3 vols. Berlin: Schneider, 1866; Weber, 1872, 1879; 2nd ed. ed. and enl. Hermann Deiters and Hugo Riemann, 5 vols. Leipzig: Breitkopf & Härtel, 1901-11.

Thayer's Life of Beethoven, rev. and ed. Elliot Forbes. Princeton: Princeton University Press, 1970.

Thieme, Ulrich and Felix Becker. *Allgemeines Lexikon der Bildenden Künstler von der Antike bis zur Gegenwart, unter Mitwirkung von etwa 400 Fachgelehrten des In- und Auslandes*, 37 vols. Leipzig: Seeman, 1907-50.

Thomas Attwoods Theorie- und Kompositionsstudien bei Mozart, ed. Erich Herzmann *et al.* Kassel: Bärenreiter, 1965.

Tiedge, Christoph August. *Urania: über Gott, Unsterblichkeit und Freiheit, ein lyrisch-didactisches Gedicht in sechs Gesängen . . .* Halle: Renger, 1801.

Vetterl, Karl. "Der musikalische Nachlass des Erzherzogs Rudolf im erzbischöflichen Archiv zu Kremsier," *Zeitschrift für Musikwissenschaft* IX (1926-27) 168-79.

Volkmann, Hans. *Beethoven in seinen Beziehungen zu Dresden*. Dresden, 1942.

Wegeler, Franz and Ferdinand Ries. *Biographische Notizen über Ludwig van Beethoven*. Coblenz, 1838.

Wurzbach, Constantin von. *Biographisches Lexikon der Kaiserthums Österreich 1750-1850*. Vienna, 1856-91.

Plate 37. Archduke Rudolph commemorative silver medal struck in 1820.

Archduke Rudolph's Music Catalogues

The many references to Archduke Rudolph's music catalogues in the preceding chapters of this study have touched upon different aspects of their value and interest. As far as his own compositions are concerned, Archduke Rudolph's inclusion in one catalogue (the *Musikalien-Register*, (No. 9 on list, p. 270) of a page devoted to a chronological listing of his own works is extremely important; although it does not include all his compositions, it offers vital dating information that is otherwise lacking. In chapter 1 we have seen how many allusions to the catalogues and to the Archduke's music collection appear in his correspondence.

The history of Archduke Rudolph's catalogues is inextricably bound up with the history of his music collection. This history begins early: from information provided by the Archduke himself in his first catalogue (No. 1 on list), he was a mere thirteen years old, in 1801, when he started to collect music. In 1806 he began systematically to catalogue all the works he owned, which by then represented the oeuvre of over 250 composers, in his own hand, in large registers of his own devising. The cataloguing became a necessity, the means of maintaining order in a collection which was to reach vast proportions over a period of thirty years. As the collection expanded, new catalogues were begun, many of them devoted to specialized genres; by 1817, there were ten catalogues in all. One catalogue (No. 10) contained a running account year by year of the number of scores and composers in the Archduke's collection; we learn from it that by July 1819—the last date entered—the number of composers represented was over 1,200, and the number of individual works or collective volumes over 7000. By the time of Rudolph's death, in 1831, the number of composers in the collection had doubled, to over 2400. In addition to collecting music, Archduke Rudolph acquired theoretical works, histories and dictionaries of music, treatises, method books, and journals related to music.

The ten catalogues will be described below, following a numbered list of their titles, locations, and library sigla.

LIST OF CATALOGUES

In Kroměříž, Czechoslovakia (Státní Zámek)

1. *Register über die Musikalien-Sammlung welche von Seiner kön. Hoheit dem Erzherzoge Rudolph in dreyzehnten Jahr ihres Alters in Jahre 1801 angefangen und worüber gegenwärtiges Register im Julien 1806 entworfen wurde.*
   130 p., 9″ × 14″ Siglum: KRa A 4449.
2. *Alphabetisches Register über Beethoven's Werke.*
   6 p., 10″ × 15″ Siglum: KRa A 4443.
3. *Musik-Stücke für Klavier und Harpfe, oder 2 Pianoforte.*
   9 p., 14½″ × 19½″ Siglum: KRa A 4445.
4. *Klavier-Stücke auf drey, vier, und fünf Hände.*
   22 p., 14½″ × 19½″ Siglum: KRA A 4444.
5. *Partituren und Klavierauszüge in alphabetischer Ordnung.*
   30 p., 14½″ × 19½″ Siglum: KRa A 4446.
6. *Sammlungen von Musikstücken.*
   55 p., 14½″ × 19½″ Siglum: KRa A 4448.
7. *Verteiler.*
   11 p., 14¾″ × 9¾″ Siglum: KRa A 4442.
8. *Verzeichnis der Seiner Kais. Hoheit den Erzherzog Rudolph zuständigen Bücher, Kupferstiche, und Landkarten.*
   19 p., 18½″ × 24″ Siglum: KRa Ž/bl.

Gesellschaft der Musikfreunde (Vienna, Austria)

9. *Musikalien-Register.*
   410 p. (in two boxes: A-K, L-Z), 9½″ × 12″ Siglum: Wgm 1268/33.
10. *Alphabetisches Verzeichnis des Musik-Compositoren.*
    55 p., 9½″ × 12″

Compositoren: 26 p.
Sammlungen von Musikstücken: 6 p.
Von der Musik handelnde Bücher: 19 p.
Siglum: Wgm 1268/33.

All ten catalogues were designed and executed by Archduke Rudolph himself with painstaking care; some have small artistic touches, such as decorations or red lettering on the title pages. The entries are almost entirely written by Rudolph, except for those from one brief period ca. 1818-19, when he assumed the Archbishopric of Olmütz, and from the last four years of his life.

In the early years Rudolph's musical library was housed in his apartments at the Imperial palace, the Hofburg, in Vienna, and presumably it was moved to Kremsier when he became Archbishop. Although he was frequently away from Kremsier for short periods of time—on church business, in Vienna, or more frequently at Baden for the curative baths, it was in Kremsier that he studied music, composed, and continued to add to and catalogue his collection.

Three years after Rudolph's death in 1831, the entire collection—music and books—was shipped to the Gesellschaft der Musikfreunde in Vienna, to which Rudolph, as its first Protector, had bequeathed it. The two largest and most comprehensive catalogues—Nos. 9 and 10—accompanied the collection; the other eight catalogues (plus a fragment of one now lost, containing only composers starting with the letter L [KRa A 4447]), remained behind in Kremsier, along with most of the Archduke's compositions.

In the following description, the basic facts about each catalogue, and points of special interest, will be given.

The first catalogue on the list in Kroměříž (No. 1) is the one started in 1806, when Archduke Rudolph was eighteen (fig. 1, p. 272); the cataloguing method used in this "register" is characteristically precise and efficient: the first two pages, divided into alphabetical columns, list the names of composers, with a number indicating the column in the succeeding pages where the works of that composer are located. These are followed by 128 pages of listings of composers, in alphabetical order; each page is divided in long, narrow columns (usually four or five per page), headed by the individual composer's name, or a music collection of some sort (e.g., "Musikalische Arabesken," "Märsche," or "Tänze"). The columns are numbered in

271

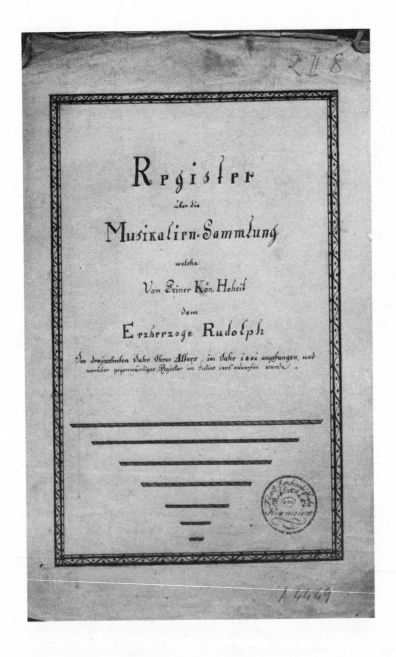

Figure 1. *Register über die Musikalien-Sammlung,* cover.
(Kroměříž, KRa A 4449).

order under an umbrella letter; for example, there are seven pages under the letter W, with thirty-five columns, each with a number pencilled in above the column heading the composer's name. In fig. 2 (p. 274), the first page of listings under B is shown for illustration. It is interesting to note that when this catalogue was inaugurated, Beethoven was not accorded the place of most importance at the start of the B listing, as he was in the later catalogue, the *Musikalien-Register*.

Most of the entries have some details of identification—opus number, date, place of publication, or name of dedicatee; for example, the seventh entry under C.P.E. Bach in fig. 2, the oratorio *Die Israeliten in der Wüste*, shows the place of publication (Hamburg), the date (1775), and the additional information that it is a bound score ("Part. geb[unden]"). This kind of detail is given more consistently and more fully in the *Musikalien-Register*, whose format and conception are almost identical with that of the earlier register.

As each new work, or re-issue of an older work, was acquired by the Archduke, he entered it into the catalogue; hence there is a fairly accurate chronological order to the entries. The original spacing Rudolph planned out provided a good deal of room for future entries, but for some composers, this quickly proved insufficient, and additional space was "borrowed" in unused columns further ahead. In such cases, the user was directed to a continuation under the same letter, with the words "siehe Spalte ____."

The slash through each composer's name is explained by the fact that this catalogue was in use only through ca. 1810, when its contents were transferred to the *Musikalien-Register*. The 1810 date is confirmed by the Beethoven listings, which included 121 entries before the discontinuation; two of the last three entries are for the "Lied aus der Ferne" (WoO 137), published in February 1810, and a manuscript of a *Marcia*, undoubtedly the manuscript of the *Marsch für Militärmusik* (WoO 19), which Beethoven sent to Rudolph at his request in the summer of 1810. From the physical appearance of this catalogue, with its dog-eared, thin page edges, it was heavily used.

An unusual item in this catalogue is a thematic index—unique in the Archduke's catalogues—of seventeen of Mozart's piano concertos (fig. 3, p. 275). This thematic index—and the whole layout of the first Mozart page shown in the illustration—reflect Rudolph's veneration for Mozart, which has been commented on several times in connection with the composer's direct influence on some of Rudolph's own works.

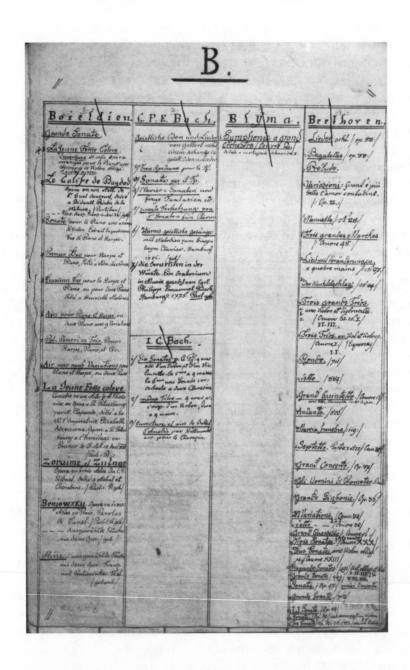

Figure 2. *Register über die Musikalien-Sammlung,* "B" page.
(Kroměříž, KRa A 4449).

Figure 3. *Register über die Musikalien-Sammlung*, Mozart page.
(Kroměříž, KRa A 4449).

Of the specialized catalogues in Kroměříž, one is devoted exclusively to Beethoven's music (No. 2 on list). Its five pages of entries list Beethoven's works alphabetically, either by title or by genre (fig. 4 and 5, p. 277 and 278). This catalogue is actually an index to the Beethoven listings in the *Musikalien-Register*; the numbers following each entry refer to their placement in the large catalogue, and thus many of them lack the details accompanying each entry in the *Musikalien-Register*. This catalogue was evidently discontinued after 1817; among its final listings is one for the Symphony No. 8, published in that year. A point of interest is the inclusion of each arrangement and transcription in the collection; for example, in the second column, under *Sinfonien* (fig. 5), there is the Symphony No. 7 ("VIIeme grande Sinfonie aus A dur"), and beneath it, seven arrangements—for piano four hands, for trio, for quintet, and so on.

Catalogue No. 3, containing music for piano and harp, or two pianos, consists mainly of orchestral or chamber music works transcribed for two pianos; only two compositions actually composed for piano and harp are listed. This catalogue is also cross-indexed to the *Musikalien-Register*—not only by numbers for each entry but also by "Spalte" numbers for each composer (fig. 6). The large number of arrangements for two pianos of chamber music pieces by Prince Louis Ferdinand of Prussia is noteworthy; Rudolph's fondness for his music is borne out by Louis Ferdinand's first-place position in the *Musikalien-Register* under the L's, and several letters to his librarian requesting that certain of Louis Ferdinand's compositions be sent to him while he was away.

The register of music for three, four, and five hands (No. 4 on list) is somewhat larger than the preceding, and somewhat inaccurately titled. There are all of four works for piano three hands, and two for piano five hands listed on the first page (fig. 7); the remaining twenty-one pages contain music for the conventional four hands, most of them arrangements. Again, the numbers following individual works are keyed to column numbers in the *Musikalien-Register*.

The catalogue of *Partituren und Klavierauszüge* (No. 5 on list) is quite extensive; an inside page (fig. 8) lists more than 450 volumes of opera, cantata, and ballet scores in Rudolph's collection as of April 1816. The works in this catalogue, listed alphabetically by title, are mostly operas and oratorios. One page of entries under the letter A is shown (fig. 9, p. 282); under Handel's *Alexander's Fest*, for example, the three entries are listed with precise identification: a manuscript

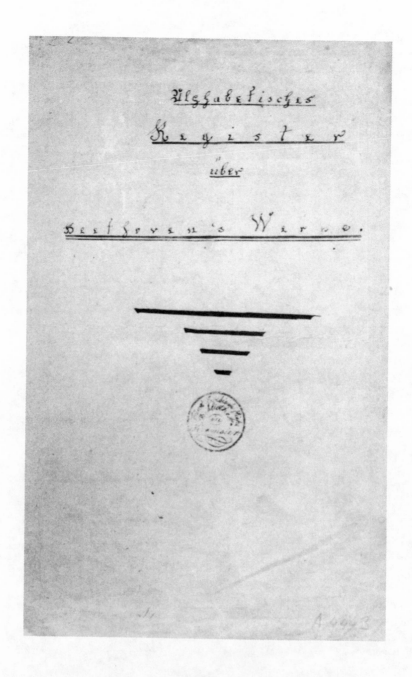

Figure 4. *Alphabetisches Register über Beethoven's Werke*, cover. (Kroměříž, KRa 4443).

277

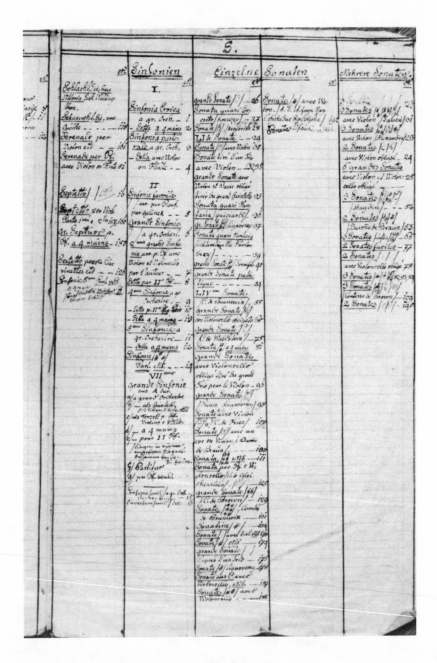

Figure 5. *Alphabetisches Register über Beethoven's Werke, "S" page.*
(Kroměříž , KRa A 4443).

278

Figure 6. *Musik-Stücke für Klavier und Harpfe . . .*, "L" page.
(Kroměříž, KRa A 4445).

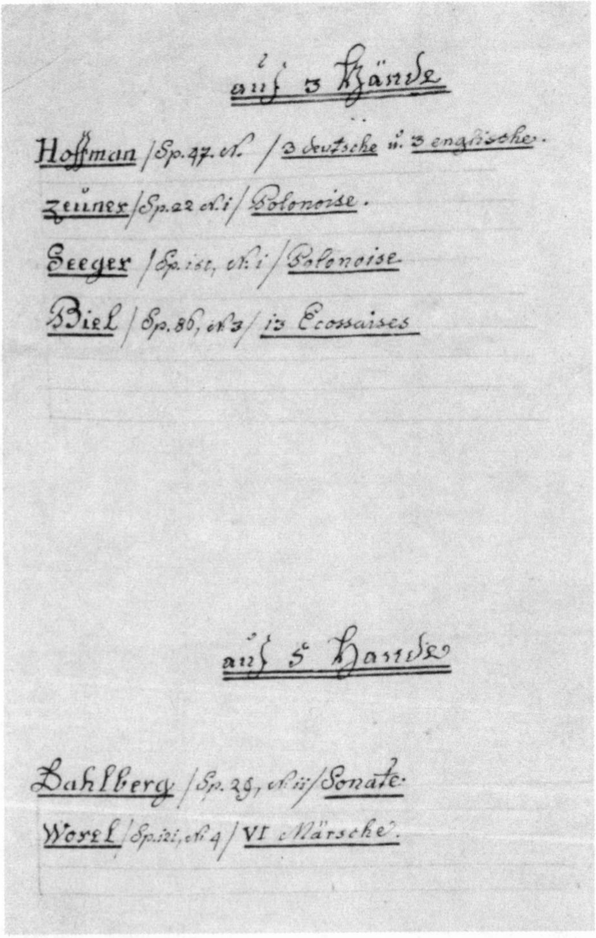

auf 3 Hände

Hoffman / Op. 47. N. / 3 deutsche u. 3 englische.

Zeüner / Op. 22 N. 1 / Polonoise.

Seeger / Op. 181, N. 1 / Polonoise

Biel / Op. 86, N. 3 / 12 Ecossaises

auf 5 Hände

Dahlberg / Op. 29, N. 11 / Sonate.

Worel / Op. 121, N. 4 / VI Märsche.

Figure 7. *Klavier-Stücke auf drey, vier, und fünf Hände,* page 2. (Kroměříž , KRa A 4444).

Figure 8. *Partituren und Klavierauszüge...*, inner page.
(Kroměříž , KRa 4446).

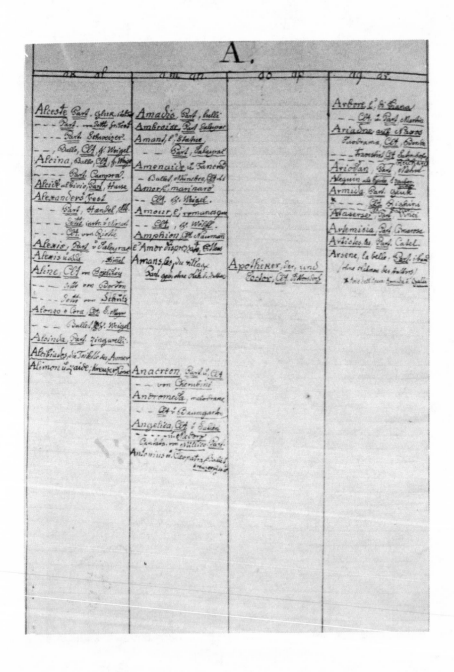

Figure 9. *Partituren und Klavierauszüge,* "A" page.
(Kroměříž, KRa 4446).

282

score; a score with instrumentation by Mozart; and a piano score (*Clavier-auszug*, abbreviated CLA) by Riotte.

The largest catalogue in Kroměříž, the *Sammlungen von Musik-stücken* (No. 6 on list), is a handsome volume bound in blue leather with gold tooling. This register is devoted to music in collective volumes, in which every individual piece in every volume is listed by title. The neatness and detail with which this catalogue is written, reflecting hours of painstaking work, are quite extraordinary. The catalogue begins with four pages of an "Alphabetisches Register" giving the titles of the various volumes, e.g., *Musikalisches Wochenblatt, Le Claveciniste, Pot-Pourri, National Melodies, Choral-Gesänge, Monath-Früchte, Sammlung neuer deutscher Kriegslieder*, to name a few; these are followed by page and column numbers, in which the individual pieces are listed under the volume titles. A typical catalogue page, with a volume listing forty-six settings of the poem "In questa Tomba oscura," is shown for illustration in fig. 10, p. 284. (The number following each name is the page number in the volume.)

The final music catalogue in Kroměříž (No. 7 on list), a so-called *Verteiler*, or "distributor," is an index to the shelf location of the works in the Archduke's library. The page showing the contents under the letters A.B. (fig. 11) illustrates the method of indicating the shelf arrangement in the catalogue. The last Beethoven numbers are for works published ca. 1817-18, (e.g., the Piano Sonata in A, Opus 101, and the song "Resignation" (WoO 149), suggesting that this catalogue too was discontinued at that time.

One last catalogue (No. 8 on list), while not a music catalogue, should be mentioned here because it includes music books and reflects Rudolph's wide-ranging collecting interests as well as his art-work. In this catalogue are listed such diverse subjects in the Archduke's library as histories, jurisprudence, theology, philosophy, mathematics, and different branches of science, along with maps and engravings. Instead of writing entries, Archduke Rudolph designed and painted each page to look like a book-case standing on a parquet floor and painted in the entries in the form of book titles. The page containing music books is shown in fig. 12 (p. 286), with the titles painted in on the "shelves" according to their size ("in 8ᵛᵒ," "in 4ᵛᵒ," and so on). The crowding of names makes them difficult to read, but one can distinguish several standard treatises in music, by Türk, Choron, Kirnberger, and others. Fig. 13 (p. 287) shows another page from this catalogue, which in like manner depicts copper engravings

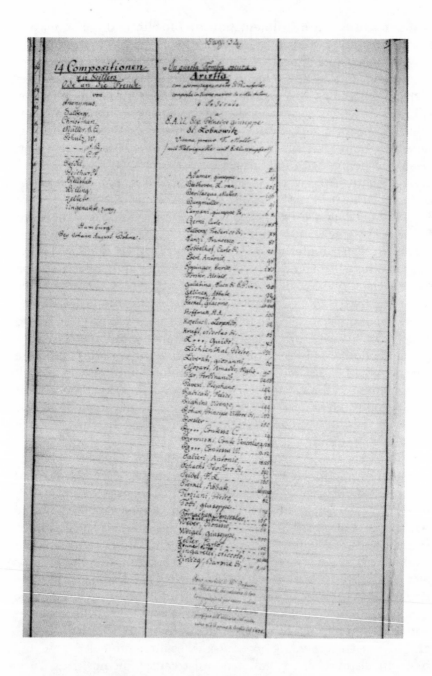

Figure 10. *Sammlungen von Musikstücken*, page 34.
(Kroměříž, KRa A 4448).

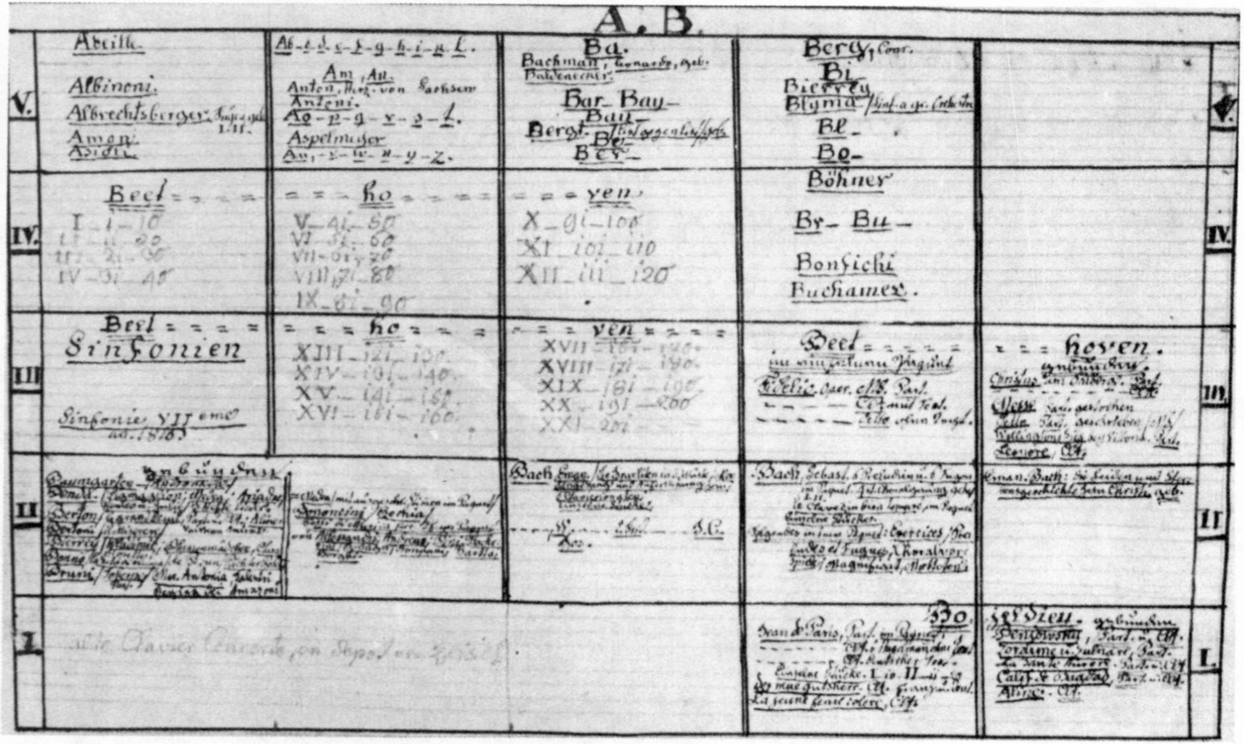

Figure 11. *Verteiler,* "A. B." page. (Kroměříž, KRa A 4442).

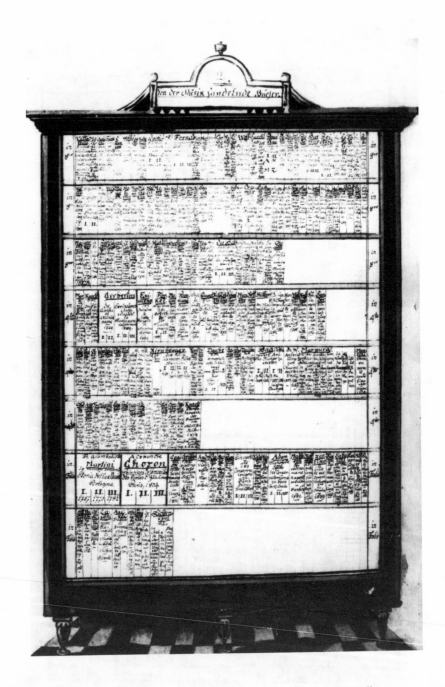

Figure 12. *Verzeichnis der . . . Bücher, Kupferstiche, und Landkarten,*
page of music books. (Kroměříž, KRa Ž/bl).

286

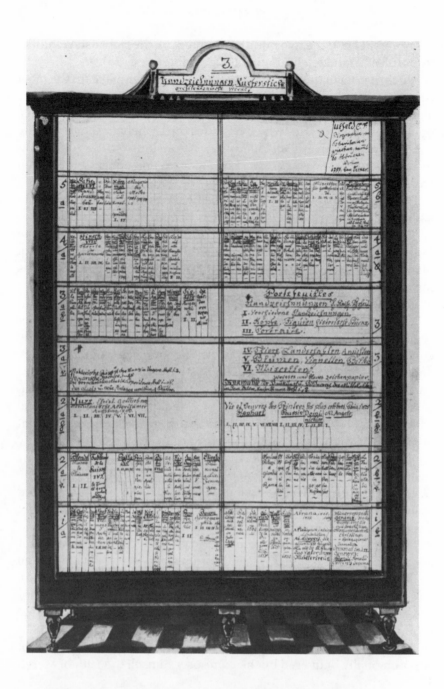

Figure 13. *Verzeichnis der . . . Bücher, Kupferstiche, und Landkarten,*
page of Kupferstiche. (Kroměříž, KRa Ž/bl).

287

("Kupferstiche"); the two middle "shelves" on the right list Archduke Rudolph's "Handzeichnungen" (see chapter 1, p. 35).

We turn now to the two catalogues that together make up the most comprehensive registers of Archduke Rudolph's collection of music and music books—the *Musikalien-Register* (No. 9) in two boxes, and a bound volume (No. 10), which includes the alphabetical index to the composers listed in the *Musikalien-Register*, an index to the volumes in the *Sammlungen von Musikstücken*, and seventeen closely-written pages containing a detailed listing of music books.

The 400-odd pages of the *Musikalien-Register* contain the complete list of music in Archduke Rudolph's collection up to ca. 1830 and supersede the register in Kroměříž (No. 1) described earlier; the *Musikalien-Register* is unbound, with odd-numbered gatherings of several sheets sewn together. Like all the other catalogues, this was mostly the product of Rudolph's own handiwork, up until ca. 1826, after which the entries are in other handwritings.

The format of the *Musikalien-Register* follows that of the earlier register in Kroměříž; each page is divided into six columns, with the composer's name at the head. For each composer, operas, masses, and other large-scale vocal works are listed first; symphonies follow, and then a column titled "In den Sammlungen," with numbers keyed to the *Sammlungen* catalogue (No. 6). Finally there is a numerical listing, item by item, of each publication, manuscript, or reprint edition as it came into Archduke Rudolph's possession. For many composers—Beethoven, for example—the number of new additions over the years outgrew the planned space by the hundreds; hence the Beethoven listings, which number 336 individually, are distributed over twelve additional pages among the B's (fig. 14 shows the first Beethoven page, and fig. 15 [p. 290] a later one).

The detailed information given for each work includes the publisher and plate number (where present); often a date is also given, as well as the exact wording of dedications on title pages. In some instances, Archduke Rudolph adds personal comments, such as those under the entry for the manuscript of the *Missa Solemnis* (fig. 14): "Dieses schön geschriebene MS, ist von dem Tondichter dem 19ᵗ März 1823 selbst über-geben worden" ("This beautifully written manuscript was personally delivered by the composer himself the 19th of March 1823").

Also included on a separate page in the *Musikalien-Register* is the listing of Archduke Rudolph's own works, to which many references

Figure 14. *Musikalien-Register*, first Beethoven page.
(Vienna, Wgm 1268/33).

289

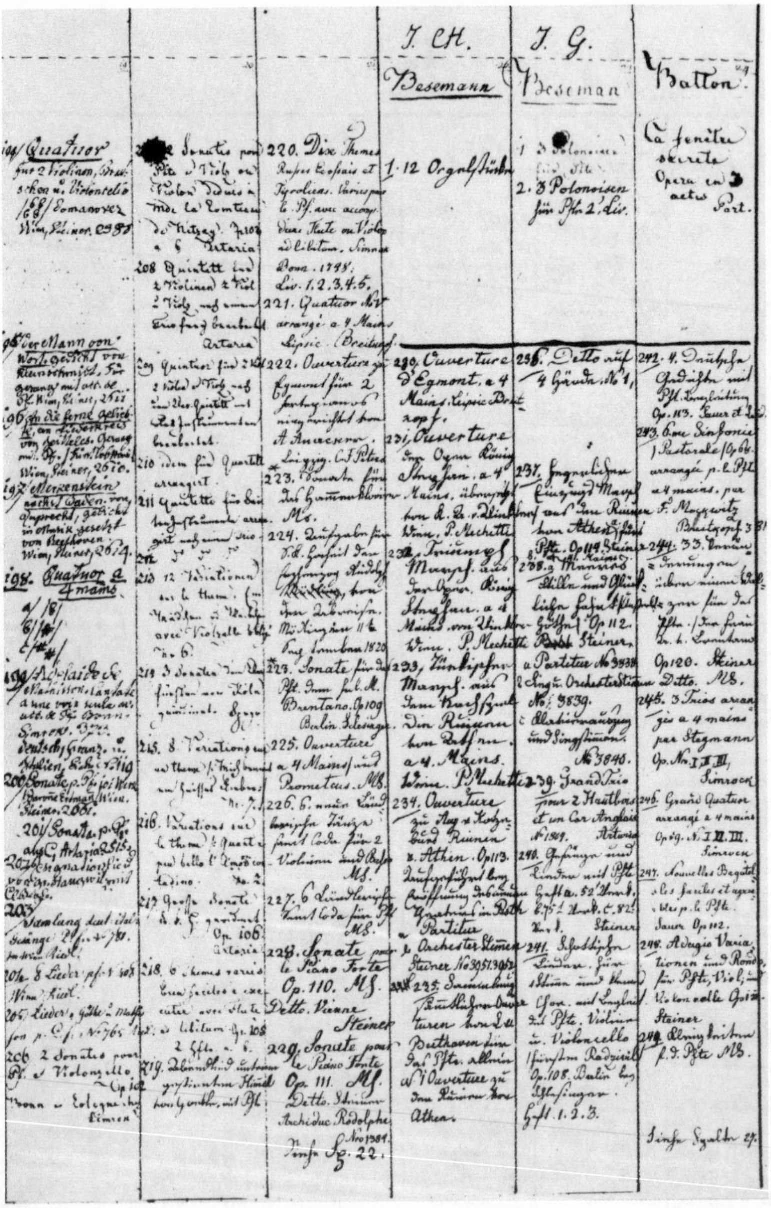

Figure 15. *Musikalien-Register*, later Beethoven page.
(Vienna, Wgm 1268/33).

have been made in previous chapters (fig. 16, p. 292). The compositions listed range in date from ca. 1809 to 1822. The discussion of the various handwritings shown on this page can be found in the Introduction, p. xxi-xxii.

To conclude our survey, three illustrations of pages from the bound catalogue (No. 10) are shown. The first illustration (fig. 17) is page two of the *Alphabetisches-Verzeichnis,* one of several pages in various catalogues on which Rudolph inscribed a poem or epigram about music.

Figures 18 and 19 (p. 294 and 295) show two pages from the book catalogue; first we see the opening page, which is well-spaced, carefully listing the particulars for each entry under headings of "in folio," "in quarto," or "in octavo." Rudolph's collecting expertise is demonstrated in his remarks under certain items, e.g., a 1791 edition of Leopold Mozart's *Violinschule* ("*selten*")—he owned at least five different editions—and a manuscript of Fux's *Singfundament* ("*sehr selten*").

The later page (fig. 19) is crammed with names and titles, making most of them difficult to decipher. The variety of books (over 1000 titles) is staggering; histories, theoretical works, dictionaries and encyclopedias, method books and tutors for voice and every conceivable instrument (including the serpent and the flageolet) can be found in their original languages, for example, Russian, Greek, Latin, and English.

Archduke Rudolph was a true collector; his passion was music, and he had the means, and found the time, to indulge that passion to the full. His collection, in which he methodically acquired virtually every publication or manuscript that was available, is a reflection both of his own musical interests and the taste of his time.

His music catalogues are the indispensable tool for studying an enormous corpus of music and books for a variety of scholarly purposes. Because the collection is, for the most part, intact at the Gesellschaft der Musikfreunde, the *Musikalien-Register* and the accompanying bound catalogue provide a practical and efficient index to the various works and their composers, both well-known and obscure. The accuracy and completeness of detail in each entry supply an invaluable aid in the dating and authentication of published editions and manuscripts. As a chronicle of what was available from publishers and copyists, as a dating instrument, in furnishing plate

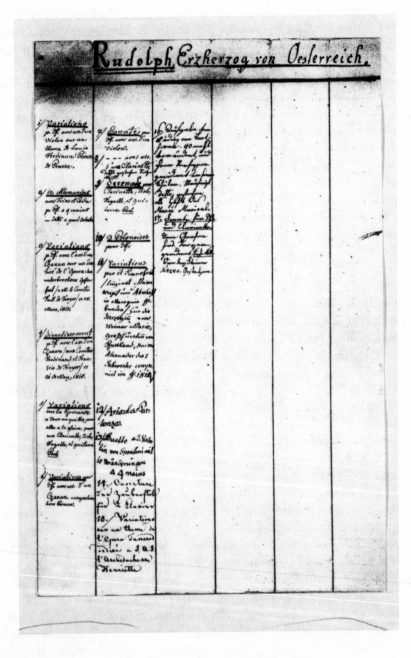

Figure 16. *Musikalien-Register*, Archduke Rudolph's compositions.
(Vienna, Wgm 1268/33).

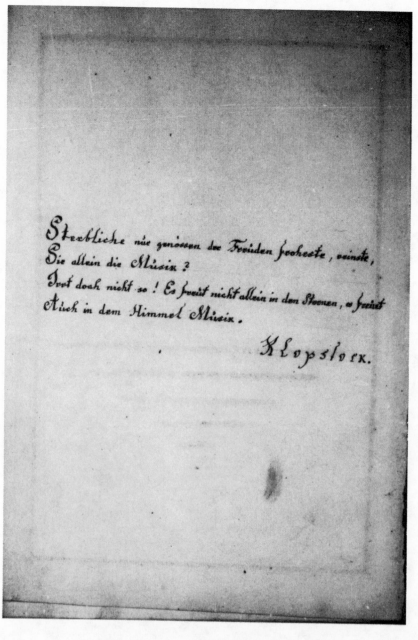

Figure 17. *Alphabetisches Verzeichnis . . .* page 2.
(Vienna, Wgm 1268/33).

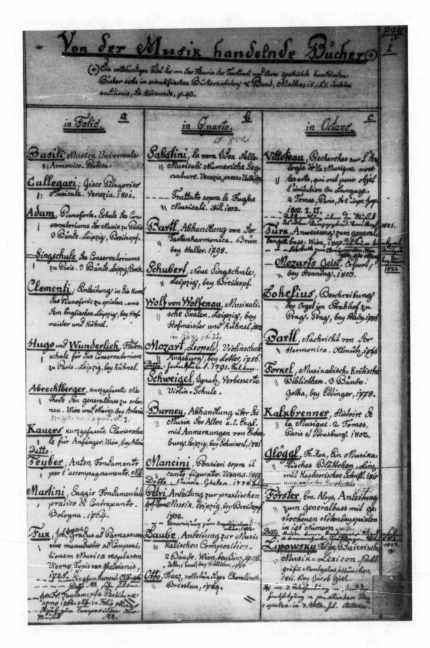

Figure 18. *Alphabetisches Register* . . . Von der Musik handelnde Bücher, page 1.
(Vienna, Wgm 1268/33).

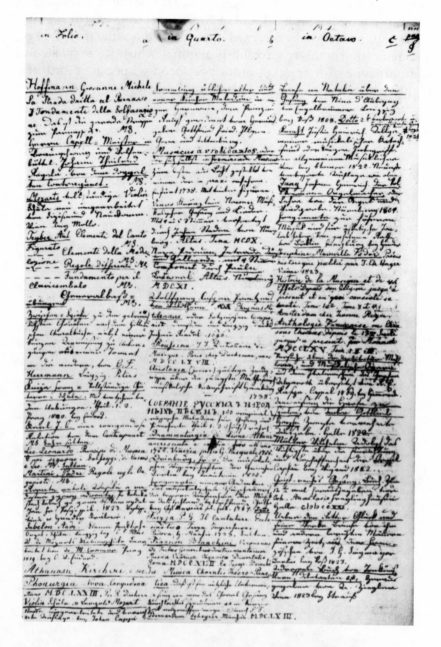

Figure 19. *Alphabetisches Register* ... Von der Musik handelnde Bücher, later page. (Vienna, Wgm 1268/33).

numbers for lost works, and for many other reasons, the catalogues constitute a bibliographical tool of the utmost importance.

Last but not least, the ten catalogues are a monument to the zeal and dedication of this remarkable individual, whose joy in music and compulsiveness in creating order produced a special record of a highly personal and special collection.

Original Texts for Translated Material and Vocal Music

Unless otherwise noted, all German texts for the passages quoted from Beethoven's letters are taken from *Beethovens sämtliche Briefe*, 2nd ed., 5 vols., ed. A.C. Kalischer and Theodor Frimmel (Leipzig: Schuster and Loeffler, 1908-11). The reference for each text will be abbreviated KAL, followed by the volume and page number. The original spelling and punctuation in Archduke Rudolph's and Beethoven's letters have been preserved.

CHAPTER I

Footnote number

21. Ich gehe heute Abends in "Johann von Paris," der zum ersten Mahle aufgeführt wird.

22. Den "Johann von Paris" haben sie hier recht gut aufgeführt gestern Nacht.

23. Gestern sahen wir die "Aline" recht gut aufführen.

24. Mich freut es das Md. Grünbaum ihren Beifall gefunden, und er macht mich recht neugierig sie selbst einmahl zu hören.

25. Heute werden Sie wohl im Theater gewesen sein, und ich erwarte mir die Beschreibung von der Aufführung des "Sargino" durch Dll. Teyber.

26. Mit Vergnügen habe ich . . . Ihren Brief empfangen, und daraus erfahren, dass es Ihnen wieder besser geht, und Sie unterdessen vieleicht schon im "Don Giovanni" waren.

27. Haben Sie die Catalani gehört, und wie gefällt sie Ihnen, man sagt sie würde auch hier singen.

28. . . . der Sie gewiss unterhalten wird, er hat mir auch recht gut gefallen.

29. Bitte zurück der Dichterin meinen Dank dafür abzustatten und sie zu versichern dass ich dieses neue Werk mit vielen Vergnügen gelesen zugleich auch den Wunsch geäussert es möchte bald mit neuer der Dichtung würdigen Musik aufgeführt werden.

30. Das übrige bliebene Geld verwenden Sie zu einem beliebigen wolthätigen Zweck. Das Cronographickum hat mir recht gut gefallen um so mehr als ich den Inhalt von ganzen Seele wünsche.

31. Da ich Ihre Thermometerliebhaberei kenne, so schreibe ich, dass die Hitze denselben im Schatten bis 29 Grade getrieben.

32. Der Kardinal, der mir recht viel an Sie aufträgt, befindet sich viel besser als die vorigen Jahre.

33. Gestern hat der Kardinal den neuen Brünner Bischof Stuffler zum Bischof geweiht, wozu auch von allen Gegenden sich Menschen versammelt haben . . . Auch der Bischof Kollowrat ist dazu gekommen, in dessen Begleitung der Domherr Souppé, der Sie grüssen lässt.

34. Ich kann mir leicht vorstellen dass der unerwartete Besuch des Erzbischofs von Lemberg Ihnen viel Vergnügen gemacht hat, auch mich wird es freuen diesen schätzenswehrten Mann wieder zu sehen.

35. Liebster Baumeister! Ich hätte schon früher geschrieben, wenn ich nicht, nach vollendeten 40 Tägen, denn 27 October, in der früh, von meinen Nervenzustanden, angefallen worden wäre; doch muss ich denn Allerhöchsten meinen Dank abstatten, weil er mich, dieses mahl, fiel leichter befreyte. Denn, nach zwey Anfälle, welche in sich schon schwächer als sonst waren, schlief ich recht viel, der Kopf war nicht so betäubt, die Krämpfe viel schwächer, und heute erschien ich schon wieder bei der Tafel. Ich hoffe also, mit der Hülfe Gottes, wenigstens wieder auf 40 Täge befreyt zu seyn.

36. Sie wissen wie ich stets gedacht, also können Sie sich leicht vorstellen wie sehr der Friede mich freute, aber ganz zufrieden

werde ich erst dann seyn, wenn ich Sie werde mündlich versichern können wie sehr ich stets seyn werde Ihr dankbarer Zögling.

37. So leid es mir war, aus Ihrem letzten Briefe zu erfahren, dass Sie das Landleben geendet und der neue Aufenthalt in der Stadt, Ihnen nicht gleich gut angeschlagen, so hoffe ich doch, dass Sie jetzt schon ganz sich werden wieder daran gewöhnt haben, um so mehr, als ich glaube dass Sie an diesen Tagen nicht viel davon genossen hätten, denn die vorigen waren über die Maasen heitz, und seit Gestern Abend, regnet es hier fast immer fort. Ich befinde mich seit meinem letzten Wieneraufenthalt recht gut, und war auch im Theater, wo ich die Bekantschaft eines sehr guten Schauspielers aus dem Josephstädter Theater gemacht, nehmlich des Herren Raymund, der einer der besseren Komiker ist, die ich in diesem Fache gesehen . . . Ich habe heute früh mit dem 25ten Bade meine Kur vollendet und wünsche nur, mit der Hülfe Gottes, den zukünftigen Winter, so zufrieden mit dem Erfolge derselben, zuzubringen, als wie denn verflossenen. Ich denke den 4ten September nach Wien zu kommen, und hoffe Sie dort ganz wohl anzutreffen, da ich Sie schon das letzte Mahl, zu meiner grossen Freude, um so viel besser verlassen habe; daselbst werde ich ein paar Täge bleiben, um Sie aufs neuen, mündlich zu versichern, wie sehr ich stets bin

Ihr ergebenster Schüler, Erzherzog Rudolph

Machen Sie Ihren Kindern meine Empfehlungen, und ich hoffe die Landluft wird Ihnen auch recht gut anschlagen. Meine Brüder und Kammerherren fragen mich immer um Ihre Gesundheit und lassen sich Ihnen empfehlen.

38. Wie oft habe ich während der ausserordentlichen Hitze, die uns diese fünf Tage hindurch plagte, an meinen guten Baumeister gedacht, da ich wusste, wie sehr Sie dabei leiden, doch wird es Ihnen jetzt, da es wieder kühler ist, um so besser gehen, wenn Gott mein eifriges Gebet erhörte.

40. Ich bitte Sie mir die *Trios* von Prinzen Louis Ferdinand von Preussen zu überschicken . . . Ich glaube es werden 3 oder 5 Trios seyn.

41. Ich bitte Sie schikken Sie mir bey nächster Gelegenheit das Quartet von Prinzen Louis Ferdinand von Preussen, das dem Rode dedicirt ist, samt denn Stimmen, und die Werke von Domenico Scarlatti, indessen blos die blau gebundenen.

42. Ich bitte schikken Sie mir von Hummel die Variationen auf den Marsch aus dem *Aschenbrödel*, von Beethoven die 3 Sonaten die dem Salieri dedicirt sind. Von den Kunstwerken in strengen Stil, die 2

Hefte wo die Fugen und Sonaten von Händel sind. Die Antologie Musicale, alle Hefte. Und den Volkommenen Kapellmeister von Mattheson.

43. Ich danke für die überschickten Musikalien, sie waren alle richtig, bis auf ein Stück von *Jomelli*, wo ich um eine *Missa* in *manuscript* gebeten, und ein gedrücktes *Miserere* bekommen habe. Ich schikke Ihnen mehrere Stücke, die ich nicht mehr brauche, zurück, und bitte dieselben bey Gelegenheit einzulegen. Auch bitte ich Sie, wenn es Ihre Gesundheit erlaubt, mir die hierbey aufgeschriebenen Stücke... heraus zuschikken, und auch den Katalog von den Stücken auf 4 Hände, der mir izt recht nothwendig ist.

47. Machen Sie meine Neujahrswünsche dem Dobenz, Parkar, Zeiler, Lany, Teyber, Beethoven, dem ich für die mir überschickte Fantasie danke, welche mir sehr gefallen hat.

53. Ich habe einigemal bemerkt, dass eben, wenn ich andern etwas widme, und er dies Werk liebt, ein kleines Leidwesen sich seiner bemächtigt, diese Trios hat er sehr lieb gewonnen, es würde ihn daher wohl wieder schmerzen, wenn die Zuschrift an jemand andern ist, ist es aber geschehen, so ist nichts mehr zu machen.
    (KAL I, 274)

54. Ich überschicke hier die Zueignung des Trios an I.K.H. auf diesem steht es, aber alle Werke, worauf es nicht auch angezeigt ist und die nur einigen Werth haben, sind I.K.H. zugedacht.
    (KAL III, 64)

56. (Letter from May 1822 to Schlesinger not available in German.) Letter of July 1823: Da E.K.H. schienen Vergnügen zu finden an der Sonate in C moll, so glaubt ich mir nicht zu viel herauszunehmen, wenn ich Sie mit der Dedication an Höchstdieselben überraschte.
    (KAL IV, 282)

58. Der Tag wo ein Hochamt von mir zu den Feierlichkeiten für I.K.H. soll aufgeführt werden, wird für mich der schönste meines Lebens sein, und Gott wird mich erleuchten, dass meine schwachen Kräfte zur Verherrlichung dieses Feierlichen Tages beitragen—
    (KAL IV, 3)

60. Meinen grössten Dank für Ihr Geschenk—
    (KAL II, 212)

61. So muss ich jetzt dafür alle Tage 2 Stunden Lekzion geben bei Sr. Kaiser. Hoheit dem Erzherzog Rudolph, dies nimt mich so her, dass ich beinahe zu allem andern unfähig bin, u. dabei kann ich nicht

leben von dem, was ich einzunehmen habe, wozu mir meine Feder helfen kann.
(KAL V, 77)

62. Geht man nicht, ein *crimen legis majestatis* meine Zulage besteht darin, dass ich den elenden Gehalt noch mit einem *Stempel* erheben muss.
(KAL IV, 238)

63. Möchte Ihr Aufenthalt in dieser gefunden und schönen Gegend gleiche Wirkung auf Ihren Zustand hervorbringen, so wäre mein Zweck, den ich durch Sorge für Ihre Wohnung beabsichtigt, gänzlich erfüllt.

64. Ich nahm die Wohnung indem ich dachte, dass E.K. Hoheit mir einen kleinen Theil erstatten würden, ohne dieses hätte ich Sie nicht genommen.
(Gustav Nottebohm, *Zweite Beethoveniana* [Leipzig: J. Rieter-Biedermann, 1887] 346)

67. (Autograph in private hands.)

68. Ich ersuche höflichst mir die 2 Trios für das Klavier mit Violin und Violonschell von meiner Composition nur auf heute zu leihen ... wenn mir recht ist, haben S. Kaiser. Hoheit solche geschrieben in ihrer Bibliothek.
(KAL II, 82)

69. Ich ersuche euer Wohlgebohrn mir die Stimmen von der Sinfonie in A sowie auch meine Partitur zu schicken; Seine Kaiserliche Hoheit können immer wieder dies M. haben.
(KAL II, 133)

70. Ich war in Wien, um aus der Bibliothek I.K.H. das mir Tauglichste auszusuchen.
(KAL IV, 27)

72. Es wurde auch schön sein, wenn I.K. Hoheit mir die letzte Sonata im Manuscript zurücksendeten.
(KAL II, 195)

73. Ich bitte die Gnade zu haben, mir die Sonata in E moll zukommen zu lassen; da ich sie der Korrectur halben bedarf.
(KAL II, 272)

74. Wenn Sie das Manuscript der Sonata für's Klavier nicht mehr benöthigt sind, bitte ich sie mir selbes zu Borgen, da der Erzherzog Rudolf solches früher von mir hatte, und nun wieder wünschte zu haben.

(Max Unger, *Ludwig van Beethoven und seine Verleger S.A. Steiner und Tobias Haslinger in Wien, Ad. Mart. Schlesinger in Berlin* [Berlin und Wien: Schlesingersche Buch- und Musikhandlung, 1921] 41)

77. Meine gehorsamste Bitte besteht darin, dass I.K.H. die Gnade hätten, nur ein Wort an den vormaligen rector magnificus der Universität durch den Baron Schweiger gelangen zu lassen, wo ich gewiss diesen Saal erhalten würd.
(KAL II, 153)

80. Sie sind so gnädig mit mir, wie ich es auf keine weise je verdienen kann—ich statte I.K.H. meinen Unterthänigsten Dank ab für Ihre Gnädige Verwendung wegen meiner Angelegenheit in Prag.
(KAL II, 258)

82. Sr. Kais. Hoheit, Eminenz u. Kardinal, die mich als Freund und nicht als Diener behandeln, würden ungesäumt ein Zeugnis ausstellen sowohl über meine Moralität.
(KAL IV, 43)

83. Mein Verhältnis zu Sr. Kaiser. Hoheit dem Erzbischof von Ollmütz mich von Selbem auch noch manches erfreuliche hoffen lässt.
(KAL IV, 82)

84. den schwachen Cardinal
(KAL IV, 103)

85. Auch glaube ich ist die aufscheinende Kargheit [nicht seine Schuld].
(KAL IV, 148)

86. Durch meine unglückliche Verbindung mit diesem Erzherzog bin ich benahe an den Bettlestab gebracht.
(Thayer, *Ludwig van Beethovens Leben*, IV, 94)

88. Du siehst mein lieber guter Gleichenstein aus Beigefügtem wie ehrenvoll nun mein Hierbleiben für mich geworden—der Titel als Kaiser. Kapellmeister kömmt auch nach.
(KAL I, 256)

89. Mein gnädigster Herr Erzbischof u. Kardinal hat noch nicht Geld genug, seinem ersten Kapellmeister gehörig das Seinige zukommen zu lassen.
(Leopold Schmidt, *Beethoven-Briefe an Nicolaus Simrock, F.C. Wegeler, Eleonore v. Breuning und Ferd. Ries* [Berlin: N. Simrock, 1909] 23)

90. Der Erzherzog Rudolph wird nun endlich seine vorige Bestimmung als Erzbischof von Olmütz antreten—aber noch sehr lange kann es anstehen, bis ich Verbesserung erhalte.

(*Beethoven-Jahrbuch,* ed. Theodor Frimmel [Munich and Leipzig, 1909] II, 184)

91. Ich habe schon seit einigen Tägen Kopfweh, doch heute im höchstens Grade, ich hoffe es wird jedoch sich bis Morgen bessern, und dann werde ich sicher Sr. Kaiserl. Hoheit Abends aufwarten.
(KAL I, 340)

92. Krank von Baden hierher kommend war ich verhindert meinen Wünschen gemäss, mich zu I.K.H. zu begeben . . . Morgen werde ich Vormittags das Vergnügen haben, meine Aufwartung zu machen.
(KAL V, 76)

93. Ich bin schon seit Sonntag nicht wohl, zwar mehr geistig als körperlich, ich bitte tausendmal um Verzeihung, wenn ich mich nicht früher entschuldigt.
(KAL II, 105)

94. Noch erschöpft von Strapatzen, Verdruss, Vergnügen und Freude alles auf einmal durch einander, werde die Ehre haben, I.K.H. in einigen Tägen aufzuwarten.
(KAL II, 212)

95. Ich bitte um Nachsicht für mein langes Ausbleiben, es ist trotz meinem gesunden aussehen wirklich Krankheit, Abspannung der Nerven.
(KAL III, 136)

96. Ich wollte schon Morgen in die Stadt eilen, um I.K.H. aufzuwarten, allein es war kein Wagen zu erhalten.
(KAL IV, 97)

97. Wie traurig bin ich, dass mich die Gelbsucht u.—da ich unterliege, verhindert, sogleich zu I.K.H. zu eilen.
(KAL IV, 115)

98. Ich kann wenigstens 3 Mahl in der Woche das Glück haben, I.K.H. wieder aufwarten zu können.
(KAL III, 119)

102. Ich bin immer in ängstlicher Besorgniss, wenn ich nicht so eifrig, nicht so oft, wie ich es wünsche, von I.K.H. sein kann. Es ist gewiss wahrheit, wenn ich sage, dass ich dabei sehr viel leide.
(KAL II, 8)

103. Meine heissesten Wünsche fangen mit dem neuen Jahre für das wohl I.K.H. an. Zwar haben Sie bei mir weder Anfang noch Ende;

ʼ denn alle Tage hege ich dieselben wünsche für I.K.H. Darf ich noch einen Wünsche für mich selbst hinzusetzen, so lassen I.K.H. mich in Ihrer Gnade und Huld täglich wachsen und zunehmen. Stets wird der Meister trachten, der Gnade seines erhabenen Meisters und Schülers nicht unwürdig zu sein.
(KAL III, 80)

104. Übrigens bitte ich I.K.H. manchen Nachrichten über mich kein Gehör zu verleihen; ich habe schon manches hier vernommen, welches man Geklatsche nennen kann, und womit man sagen I.K.H. glaubt dienen zu können. Wenn I.K.H. mich einen Ihrer werthen Gegenstände nennen, so kann ich zuversichtlich sagen, dass I.K.H. einer der mir wertheften Gegenständte in Universum sind... Gott erhalte I.K.H. zum Besten der Menschheit und besonders Ihrer Verehrer gänzlich gesund.
(KAL IV, 94)

105. einen liebenswürdigen talentvollen Prinzen
(Ludwig Nohl, *Neue Briefe Beethovens* [Stuttgart's Cotta'schen, 1867] 16)

106. Etwas kleineres als unsere Grossen gibt's nicht, doch nehme ich die Erzherzoge davon aus.
(KAL I, 328)

107. Denn Musik versteht er, und er lebt und webt darin. Mir tut es wirklich um sein Talent leid, dass ich nicht mehr soviel an ihm Theil nehmen kann als früher.
(Postscript): Um Erlaubnis der Dedikation brauchen Sie nicht einzukommen, er wird und soll überrascht werden.
(KAL V, 50)

108. Der Erzbischof Kardinal ist hier, ich gehe alle Woche 2 Mal zu ihn, von Grossmuth und Geld ist zwar nichts zu hoffen, allein ich bin doch auf einem so guten vertrauten Fuss mit ihm, dass es mir äusserst wehe thun würde, ihm nicht etwas angenehmes zu erzeigen, auch glaube ich ist die anscheinende Kargheit nicht keine Schuld.
(KAL IV, 148)

109. Wenn nur auch ich fähig wäre, etwas Ihrer wehrtes zuwege zu bringen.

110. Der Erzherzog, der sehr zufrieden war, äusserte nun, er wolle uns auch etwas spielen, und wenn wir die schwere Orchester-Partie übernehmen wollen, so werde er uns ein Mozartsches Konzert in

B-dur vorspielen. Wir waren sogleich bereit, und der Erzherzog spielte trefflich.
(*Schubert: Die Erinnerungen seiner Freunde*, ed. O.E. Deutsch [Leipzig: Breitkopf und Härtel, 1957]

111. Nach dem Diner bei Fürst Lobkowitz . . . ein grosses Konzert, in welchem der Erzherzog Rudolph, Bruder des Kaisers, mehrere der schwersten Sachen von Prinzen Louis Ferdinand und von Beethoven auf dem Fortepiano mit vieler Fertigkeit, Präzision und Zartheit spielte. Dabei ist der Erzherzog so anspruchlos und bescheiden in seinem ganzen Wesen, und so zwanglos, dass es einem bald recht wohl in seiner Nähe wird.

112. In einem grossen Konzert beim Fürsten Lobkowitz haben wir wieder das in einem Fürsten so seltne, ausgezeichnete Talent des Erzherzogs Rudolph bewundert. Die schwersten Konzerte von Beethoven und Sonaten von Prinz Louis Ferdinand spielte der Erzherzog mit grosser Besonnenheit, Ruhe, und Genaugkeit.

113. Bei dem Fürsten von Lobkowitz währen die schönen Quartetten und die Abendkonzerte für den Erzherzog Rudolph noch immer fort . . . Seidler selbst zeichnet sich bei jedem Konzert durch eigene Konzertsätze und durch seine vortreffliche Art aus, dem Erzherzoge die schweren Beethovenschen und Louis Ferdinandschen Trio's zu begleiten.

114. Morgen in der frühesten Frühe wird der Kopist an dem letzten Stück anfangen können, da ich selbst unterdessen noch an mehreren anderen Werken schreibe, so hab er um der blossen Pünktlichkeit willen mich nicht so sehr mit dem letzten Stücke beeilt, um so mehr, da ich dieses mit mehr Überlegung in Hinsicht des Spiels von Rode schreiben muste; wir haben in unsern Finales gern rauschendere Passagen, doch sagt dieses R. nicht zu und—schenirte mich doch etwas—
(KAL II, 107)

115. Lieber Beethoven
Übermorgen Donnerstags ist um ½ 6 Uhr Abends wieder Musik bey dem Fürsten Lobkowitz, und ich soll daselbst die Sonata mit dem Rode wiederholen. Wenn es Ihre Gesundheit und Geschäfte erlauben, so wünschte ich Sie Morgen bey mir zu sehen, um die Sonate zu überspielen.

116. Der grosse Violinspieler Hr. *Rode* hat dieser Tage eine neues Duett für Pianoforte und Violin mit Sr. K. Hoheit dem Erzherzog *Rudolph* bei Sr. Durchl. dem Fürsten *Lobkowitz* gespielt. Das Ganze wurde

gut vorgetragen, doch müssen wir bemerken, dass der Clavier-Part weit vorzüglicher, dem Geiste des Stücks mehr anpassend, und mit mehr Seele vorgetragen ward, als jener der Violine.

117. [Ich] während meiner dreimonatlichen Krankheit zubrachte zu meinem grossen Leidwesen beraubten mich diese gichtischen Schmerzen lange Zeit des Gebrauches meine Hände, und eben dadurch meines grössten Vergnügens, des Klavierspielens.

118. Ich bemühe mich, sie recht zu üben, um der Kunst des Kompositeurs die der Verleger, durch die wahrhaft schöne Auflage seinen verdienten Tribut zollte, auch jenen das Spielens beizurücken.

122. Daher bitte ich E.K.H. gnädigst sich noch zu gedulden mit den Var. . . . Fahrer E.K.H. nur fort, besonders sich zu üben, gleich am Klavier ihre Einfälle flüchtig kurz niederzuschreiben, hiezu gehört ein kleines Tischchen an's Klavier. Durch dergleichen wird die Phantasie nicht allein gestärkt, sondern man lernt auch die entlegensten Ideen augenblicklich festhalten, ohne Klavier zu schreiben ist ebenfalls nöthig, u. manchmal eine einfache Melodie choral mit einfachen u. wieder mit verscheidenen Figuren nach den Kontrapunkten und auch darüber hinaus durchführen, wird E.K.H. sicher kein Kopfweh verursachen, ja eher, wenn man sich so selbst mitten in der Kunst erblickt, ein grosses Vergnügen.
(KAL IV, 279)

123. Die Fortschritte in den Ausarbeitungen E.K.H. habe ich wohl bemerkt, nur aber auch leider, dass Missverständnisse hiebey obwalten; das Beste ist vor der Hand bezifferte Bässe von guten Komponisten in 4 Stimmen aus zu ziehen, und manchmal einen 4 Stimmigen Gesang zu komponieren, bis ich wieder das Glück habe, in der Nähe von E.K.H. zu seyn, auch 4 Stimmigen für das Klavier zu schreiben, kann guten Erfolg haben, obschon es gerade hiefür schwerer, da man das übersteigen oder herabsteigen der Stimmen nicht so natürlich als beym Gesang, bewerkstelligen kann.

124. Dem Wiener Musikverein, dessen Protector ich bin, meine sämtlichen musikalischen Sammlungen, wozu auch die musikalische Bibliothek gehört, wie sie in dem Musikalienzimmer zu Kremsier aufgestellt ist.

125. ein Stück französische schwarzer Kreide

126. Gestern habe ich das erste Mahl wieder angefangen zu zeichnen welches noch so ziemlich vorwärts gegangen ist.

127. das Portrait der Kaiserin Louise, so ich selbst gemalt habe.

129. Mehr kann ich nicht vor lauten Müdigkeit von Spazierfahren, Etiquetten, Stiegensteigen und Kleiderwechseln nicht schreiben.

130. Wenn ich etwas vollendet habe, bis jetzt hatte ich noch keinen Augenblick Zeit dazu, es Ihnen zur Ausstellung der Fehler, und meiner Belehrung übersenden.

132. Rücksichtlich der Händelschen Werke für S. Kaiserliche Hoheit Erzherzog Rudolph kann ich bis jetzt noch nichts gewiss sagen. Ich werde aber in wenig Tagen an ihn schreiben und darauf aufmerksam machen.

   (Thayer, *Ludwig van Beethovens Leben*, V, 460)

CHAPTER II

3. Auszüge aus den theoretischen Werken von C.P.E. Bach, Türk, Kirnberger, Fux und Albrechtsberger zu machen, und die ausgewählten Stellen der Reihenfolge nach abzuschreiben um sie später bei dem Unterricht des Erzherzogs Rudolph zu verwenden.

   (Thayer, *Ludwig van Beethovens Leben*, III, 79)

8. Ich unterrichte Jemanden eben im Contrapunct, und mein eigenes Manuscript hierüber habe ich unter meinem Wust von Papieren noch nicht herausfinden können.

   (Seyfried, *Ludwig van Beethovens Studien*, Anhang, 14)

11. Wofür uns die Alten zwar doppelt dienen, indem meistens reeler Kunstwerth (Genie hat doch nur unter ihnen der *deutsche Händel* u. *Seb. Bach* gehabt).
   KAL IV, 27)

16. N.B. Die verlangte Pferde-Musik wird mit dem schnellsten Galop bey Euer Kaiserl. Hoheit anlangen.
   (KAL II, 212)

CHAPTER III

6. Und diesem ist es nur zuzuschreiben, dass ich nicht schon selbst bein I.K.H. gewesen, noch dass ich Auskunft gegeben habe über die meisterhaften Variationen meines hochverehrten erhabenen Schülers und Musen-Günstlings. Meinen Dank für diese Überraschung und Gnade, womit ich beehrt bin worden, wage ich weder mündlich noch schriftlich auszudrücken. In einigen Tägen hoffe ich das mir gesendete Meisterstück von I.K.H. selbst zu hören und nichts kann

mir erfreulicher sein, als dazu beizutragen, dass I.K.H. den schon bereiteten Platz für Hochdieselbe auf dem Parnasse baldigst einnehmen.

(KAL IV, 1)

7. Eben Gestern wollte ich die Variationen überbringen, sie dürften wohl kühn an das Tageslicht treten.

(KAL IV, 22)

8. (Autograph in Institute of Science, Leningrad, U.S.S.R.)

9. Meinem erhabnen Musik-Zögling, selbst nun schon mitstreiter um die Lorbeeren des Ruhmes, darf Einseitigkeit nicht Vorwurf werden . . . Hier 3 Gedichte, woraus sich I.K.H. vielleicht eines aussuchen könnten, in Musik zu setzen. Die Oesterreicher wissen es nun schon, dass *Apollos Geist* im Kaiserlichen Stamm neu aufgewacht. Ich erhalte überall Bitten, etwas zu erhalten . . .

(KAL IV, 27)

10. Was das Meisterwerk der Variationen I.K.H. betrifft, so glaube, dass selbe unter folgenden Titel könnten herausgegeben werden, nemlich: Thema oder Aufgabe/gesetzt von L. v. Beeth./vierzigmal verändert/ u. seinem Lehrer gewidmet/ von den durchlauchtigsten Verfasser. Der Anfragen deswegen sind so viele u. am Ende kommt dieses ehrenvolle Werk durch verstümmelte Abschriften doch in die Welt . . . also in Gottes Namen bei so vielen Weihen, die I.K.H. jetzt erhalten u. bekannt werden, werde denn auch die Weihung Apolls (oder christlicher Caeciliens) bekannt, zwar könnte I.K.H. vielleicht mich der Titelkeit beschuldigen; ich kann aber versichern, dass in dem zwar diese Widmung meinem Herzen theuer ist u. ich wirklich stolz darauf bin, diese allein gewiss nicht mein Endzweck hierbey ist . . . Es fragt sich nun ob Ihro K.H. mit dem Titel zufrieden sind? Ob sie herausgegeben werden sollen, darüber dachte ich, sollten I.K.H. gäntzlich die Augen zudrücken.

(KAL IV, 29)

11. Dem Ehrenwerthen Tobiasserl habe ich von Var. des Erzherzogs gesprochen, ich habe Sie dazu vorgeschlagen, da ich nicht glaube dass Sie Verlust dabei haben werden, u. es immer Ehrenvoll ist von einem solchen principe Professore etwas zu stechen.

(KAL IV, 37)

12. Steiner hat schon die Var. von I.K.H., er wird sich selbst bedanken bey ihnen, hiebey fällt mir ein, dass Kaiser Joseph unter dem Namen eines Grafen v. Falkenstein reiste, des Titels halber—

(*Beethoven-Forschung*, ed. Theodor Frimmel [Wien: Kommissions-verlag G. Gerold & Co., 1913] IV, 114-15)

CHAPTER V

3. Daher bitte ich E.K.H. gnädigst sich noch zu gedulden mit den Var. von höchstenselben welche mir allerliebst zu seyn scheinen, aber doch noch eine genaure Durchsicht von mir erfordern.
   (KAL IV, 281)

4. Die Variat. von E.K.H. werde ich mitbringen. Es wird nicht viel dürfen geändert werden, u. so wird es ein recht hübsches, angenehmes Werk für Musikgeniessende werden.
   (KAL IV, 289)

5. In den Variationen ist einiges angezeigt, mündlich wird es deutlicher—
   (KAL IV, 317)

CHAPTER VIII

(Note: the texts are given as they appear in Archduke Rudolph's settings. In a few instances, where his handwriting is indecipherable, the closest reading possible is given.)

"La partenza"

Ecco quel fiero istante!
Nice, mia Nice, addio.
Come vivrò, ben mio,
Così lontan da te?
Io vivrò sempre in pene,
Io non avvrò più bene;
E tu, chi sa se mai
Ti sovverai di me!

Soffri, che in traccia almeno
Di mia perduta pace
Venga il pensier seguace
Sull' orme del tuo piè.
Sempre nel tuo cammino,
Sempre m'avrai vicino;
E tu, chi sa se mai
Ti sovverai di me!

Io fra remote sponde
Mesto volgendo i passi,
Andrò chiedendo ai sassi,
La ninfa mia dov' è?
  Dall' una all' altra aurora
Te andrò chiamando ognora;
E tu, chi sa se mai
Ti sovverai di me!

Io rivedrò sovente
Le amene piagge, O Nice,
Dove vivea felice,
Quando vivea con te,
  A me saran tormento
Cento memorie e cento;
E tu, chi sa se mai
Ti sovverai di me!

Ecco, dirò, quel fonte,
Dove avampò di sdegno,
Ma poi di pace in pegno
La bella man mi diè.
  Qui si vivea di speme;
Là si languina insieme:
E tu, chi sa se mai
Ti sovverai di me!

Quanti vedrai giungendo
Al nuovo tuo soggiorno,
Quanti venirti intorno,
A offrirti amore e fe?
  Oh Dio! Chi sa fra tanti
Teneri omaggi e pianti,
Oh Dio! chi sa se mai
Ti sovverai di me!

Pensa qual dolce strale,
Cara, mi lasci in seno:
Pensa che amò Fileno
Senza sperar mercè,
  Pensa mia vita, a questo
Barbara addio funesto;
Pensa, pensa, A chi sa se mai
Ti sovverai di me!

"Wenn in des Abends letztem Scheine"
(*Lied aus der Ferne*)

Wenn in des Abends letztem Scheine
dir eine lächelnde Gestalt,
Am Rasensitz im Eichenhaine,
mit Wink und Gruss vorüberwallt;
das ist des Freundes treuer Geist,
der Freud' und Frieden dir verheisst.

Wenn in des Mondes Dämmerlichte
sich deiner Liebe Traum verschönt,
durch Cytisus und Weymuthsfichte
melodisches Gesäusel tönt,
und Ahndung dir den Busen hebt;
das ist mein Geist, der dich umschwebt.

"Je vous salue"

Je vous salue, o lieux charmants
Quittez avec tant de tristesse
Lieux chéris où de ma tendresse
Je vois partout les monuments.

Lorsqu' une sévère defense
M'enilade [*sic*] ce beaux séjour
J'en partis avec mon amour,
Et j'y laissai mon espérence.

J'ai retrouvé dans d'autres lieux
Des eaux, des fleurs et des feuillage (de l'ombrage;)
Mais ces fleurs, ces eaux de feuillage
N'a voient point de charme à mes yeux.

On n'est bien que dans sa patrie,
C'est là que plaisent les ruisseaux,
C'est là que les arbres plus beaux
Donnent une ombre plus chère.

Qu'il est doux de finir ses jours
Aux lieux on commence la vie

(Remainder of final verse illegible.)

"Ich denke dein"

Ich denke dein
wenn durch den Hain
der Nachtigallen
Akkorde schallen!
Wann denkst du mein?

Ich denke dein
im Dämmerschein
der Abendhelle
am Schattenquelle!
Wo denkst du mein?

Ich denke dein
mit süsser Pein
mit bangem Sehnen
und heissen Tränen!
Wie denkst du mein?

O denke mein,
bis zum Verein
auf besserm Sterne!
In jeder Ferne
denk' ich nur dein!

APPENDIX 3

Thematic Catalogue of the Compositions of Archduke Rudolph

The thematic catalogue is in three parts. Section I lists Archduke Rudolph's finished compositions by genre, with the works in each genre in approximate chronological order of their composition. Section II lists all his unfinished works, also by genre and in approximate chronological order of composition; in this section each entry is preceded by the letter U. Section III contains Archduke Rudolph's copies and transcriptions of works by other composers, listed alphabetically; each entry in this section is preceded by the letter T.

LIBRARY SIGLA

Austria
Wgm   Vienna: Gesellschaft der Musikfreunde
Wn   Vienna: Österreichische Nationalibibliothek, Musiksammlung

Czechoslovakia
KRa   Kroměříž: Státní Zámek, Hudební Archív

313

Germany
GO1   Gotha, DDR: Landesbibliothek
WRt1   Weimar, DDR: Thüringische Landesbibliothek, Musiksammlung

I. FINISHED WORKS

Compositions for Piano

1 CANONE ALL' OTTAVA

Date: Before 1809?
Autograph: KRa (A 4377). 1 page, ink. Across top of the page, in pencil, in
                Latin script: *Rudolph E.*

2 TWENTY LÄNDLER

12.

13.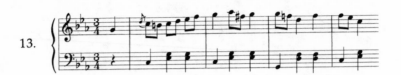

14.

15.

16.

17.

18.

19.

20.

Date: Before 1809?
Autograph: KRa (A 4379). 10 pages, ink.

3 VARIATIONS IN G MAJOR

Allegretto

Date: Ca. 1809.
Autograph: KRa (A 4371). 25 pages, ink.
               (a) Draft: Theme and 12 variations, unfinished, 12 pages.
               (b) Fair copy: Theme and 14 variations with coda, 13 pages.
               Title in pencil on p. 13: *Ier Composition de son A.I. Monseigneur l'Archiduc Rodolphe d'Autriche.*

4A TWELVE ALLEMANDES [FOR PIANO FOUR HANDS]

1.

2.

3.

Date: Ca. 1809-10.

Ms. copy: *Wgm* (Q 19886). 44 pages, ink.

4B DEUTSCHE TÄNZE [FOR PIANO FOUR HANDS]: Coda

Date: Ca. 1809-10.

Autograph: *Wgm* (VII 29340). 6 pages, ink.

4C TWELVE LÄNDLER [FOR ORCHESTRA]

Date: Ca. 1809-10.

Autograph: *KRa* (A 4418). 52 pages, ink. The music of the *Ländler* is identical with 4A above. The music of the coda is identical with 4B above. Scored for: piccolo, flute, 2 oboes, 2 clarinets, 2 bassoons, 2 horns, 2 trumpets, violins 1, 2, and 3, bass, and timpani. Scoring differs for each *Ländler*.

Ms. copies: *Wgm* (XV 15423) ["12 Ländler mit Trio"]. 24 pages, ink. Lacks a coda. Erroneously catalogued as an autograph. *Wgm* (XV 9547) ["12 Deutsche Tänze mit Coda"]. 209 pages, ink. Orchestral parts: 2 piccolos, 2 flutes, 2 oboes, 2 clarinets, 2 bassoons, 2 horns, 2 trumpets, violins 1 and 2, bass, and timpani. The coda is identical with 4B above.

5 THREE POLONAISES

Date: Ca. 1812.
Autograph: *Wgm* (VII 15419). 6 pages, ink.

6 THREE LÄNDLER

1.

2.

3.

Date: Ca. 1812.
Autograph: *KRa* (A 4380). 4 pages, ink.

7 [LÄNDLER] VARIATIONS IN G

[No tempo given]

Thema

Date: 1814
Autograph: Wgm (VII 15418). 12 pages, ink. Theme, 12 variations, coda.
Autograph sketches: KRa (A 4433). 2 pages, ink.
Ms. copy: WRt1 (Mus V=731). 31 pages, ink.

8 VARIATIONS IN A [FOR PIANO FOUR HANDS] ON A THEME BY SPONTINI

Date: Ca. 1816.
Autograph: KRa (A 4393-94). 45 pages, ink.

    (a) Fair copy: Introduction (4 measures), theme (from the Duo "Quanto amistà" from Act I of *La Vestale* by Spontini), and 10 variations, 23 pages.

    (b) Draft: Introduction (4 measures), theme, and 6 variations, unfinished, 8 pages.

    (c) Draft: Introduction (2 measures), theme, and 3 variations, unfinished, 8 pages; some pencil corrections in Beethoven's hand.

    (d) Draft: Introduction (2 measures), theme, and 4 variations, unfinished, 6 pages (piano primo part, 3 pages; piano secondo part, 3 pages).

Ms. copy: Wgm (Q 11427) ("Duetto dell' Opera la Vestale di Spontini con 10 Variazioni a quattro mani"). 26 pages, ink.

9 VARIATIONS IN G ON ROSSINI'S "DI TANTI PALPITI"

Date: Ca. 1817.
Autograph: Wgm (VII 15409). 12 pages, ink. Theme ("Di tanti palpiti" from Act II of *Tancredi* by Rossini) and 8 variations.
Ms. copy: Wgm (Q 15074). 22 pages, ink.

10 FORTY VARIATIONS ON A THEME ("O HOFFNUNG, O HOFFNUNG") BY BEETHOVEN

Date: 1818-19.

Autograph: *KRa* (A 4372-74). 72 pages, ink and pencil.

(a) Draft (Version I): Introduction, theme, and 40 variations, 26 pages. Extensive pencil corrections in Beethoven's hand.

(b) Fair copy (Version II): Introduction, theme, and 40 variations, 41 pages. Extensive pencil and ink corrections in Beethoven's hand. On an additional sheet glued onto page 3, in Archduke Rudolph's hand: *Aufgabe./von Ludwig van Beethoven gedichtet,/40 Mahl verändert,/von seinem Schüler./Rudolph Erzherzog.*

(c) "O Hoffnung, O Hoffnung" theme, ink; crossed-out pencil sketches, 5 pages.

Beethoven autograph: KRa (A 4375). 6 pages, ink and pencil. Corrections for the *Forty Variations,* 5 pages; suggested title (*Veränderungen/ über ein Thema von L. v. Beethoven/Verfasst von S^{er} kaiserliche Hoheit dem/Erzherzog Rudolph/Erzbischof*), 1 page.

Ms. copy: *Wgm* (Q 15057).

Editions: *Aufgabe/von Ludwig van Beethoven gedichtet/Vierzig Mahl verändert und ihrem Verfasser gewidmet/von seinem Schüler/R.E.H./[Opus] 1. Wien, bei S.A. Steiner und Comp. No. 3080.*
Wgm (Q 15076, Q 11428).
Wn (MS 36576).

Other eds.: Wiener Pianoforte-Schule von Friedrich Starke, Kapellmeister (*Auszug aus den 40 Variationen componirt von S^r. k.k. Hoheit und Eminenz, Herrn Herrn {sic] ERZHERZOG RUDOLPH von OESTER-REICH, etz. etz. etz. nach einer Aufgabe des Herrn L. van Beethoven...*).

Wien.
Wn (Ms 9909).

Cf:	*Allgemeine musikalische Zeitung* 3 (19 January 1820) 33-41.
	Allgemeine musikalische Zeitung 47 (10 June 1820) 369-75.
Recordings:	Musical Heritage Society MHS 3856 (Hans Kann, piano).

11 FUGA [ON A THEME BY DIABELLI] BY S.R.D. (SERENISSIMUS RUDOLPHUS DUX)

Date:	Ca. 1819-20.
Autograph:	*KRa* (A 4431); theme by Diabelli, 1 page, pencil; one variation sketch, ink.
Editions:	*Vaterländischer Künstlerverein/Veränderungen/für das/Piano Forte/ über ein vorgelegtes Thema componirt von den vorzüglichsten/ Tonsetzern und Virtuosen/Wien's/und der k.k. oesterreichischen Staaten/2. Abtheilung/Eigenthum der Verleger/Wien, bey A. Diabelli et Comp. (No. 1380-81).*
	Variation No. 40, by "S.R.D." (Serenissimus Rudolphus Dux).

12 CAPRICCIO

Date:	Ca. 1820.
Autograph:	*KRa* (A 4383). 2 pages, ink. Some pencil corrections by Beethoven.

13 ANDANTE

Date: Ca. 1820.
Autograph: KRa (A 4381). 6 pages, ink and pencil.

14 MENUETTO AND TRIO IN B

Date: ?
Ms. copy: KRa (A 4450). 3 pages, ink.
Autograph sketch: KRa (A 4436). 1 page, ink (in key of C).

Other Instrumental Compositions

15A VARIATIONS IN F FOR VIOLIN AND PIANO [ON A THEME BY PRINCE LOUIS FERDINAND OF PRUSSIA]

Date: Ca. 1809-10.
Autograph: Wgm (XI 15410) ["Variations f. Clav. & Clarinette (*sic*) über ein Trio von Prinz Louis von Preussen"]. 41 pages, ink. Theme and 13 variations. Score.

15B VARIATIONS IN F FOR VIOLIN AND PIANO [ON A THEME BY PRINCE LOUIS FERDINAND OF PRUSSIA]

(Theme identical with that of 15A above)
Date: Ca. 1810-11.
Ms. copies: Wgm (Q 17755) ["Variationen/Für das Piano-Forte mit Beglei-tung einer Violine/über den ersten Trio,/aus dem Quatuor, Oeuvre VI; vom Prinzen Louis Ferdinand/von Preussen./ Seinen Andenken gewidmet/ von/Rudolph Erzherzog von Osterreich." 47 pages (score, 33 pages; violin part, 14 pages), ink. Theme and 7 variations.
Wgm (Q 17763) ["Variazioni/F dur/"]. 38 pages (score, 29 pages; violin part, 9 pages), ink.

Wgm (Q 17764) ["Variazioni"]. 40 pages (score, 30 pages; violin part, 10 pages), ink.

Go1 (Mus. pag. 14 d/6) ["Variations/sur un Thème tiré d'un Quatuor/du/Prince Louis Ferdinand de Prusse/pour le Piano-Forte/avec l'accompagnement d'un Violon/composées/par/Rodolphe l'Archiduc d'Autriche"]. 30 pages, ink (piano part only).

16 VARIATIONS IN A-FLAT FOR CZAKAN AND PIANO

Date:	March 1810.
Autograph:	*Wgm* (XI 15414): *Variations/pour le/Piano Forte avec l'Accompagne-ment d'un Czakan/sur un Duo Tiré de L'opéra Das unterbrochene Opferfest/composées et dédiées/à/Monsieur le Comte Ferdinand de Troyer/par/R.A. d'A./ce 28 Mars 1810.* 8 pages, ink. Theme, 8 variations, and coda. Score.

17 DIVERTISSEMENT IN A-FLAT FOR CZAKAN AND PIANO

Date:	May 1810.
Ms. copy:	*Wgm* (Q 17756) ["Divertissement/pour le Piano Forte/avec/l'accompagnement d'un Zakan/Composé et Dédié/aux/Comtes Ferdinand et François de Troyer/par/R.A. d'A./ce 31 de Mai 1810"]. 30 pages (piano part, 18 pages; czakan part, 12 pages), ink. Introduction; Theme, six variations, and coda; Tempo di Menuetto; Marcia; Pollaca (*sic*).

18 [WALTZ] VARIATIONS IN A-FLAT FOR CZAKAN AND PIANO

Date: Ca. 1810.
Autograph: KRa (A 4404). 8 pages, ink.
                 (a) Czakan part: Theme, 8 variations, and coda (complete), 4 pages.
                 (b) Piano part: Theme, 4 variations (unfinished), 4 pages.
Ms. copy: Wgm (XI 15413). 26 pages (piano part, 19 pages; czakan part, 7 pages), ink. Theme, [8] variations, coda. Some slight differences between this copy and autograph of czakan part.

19 VARIATIONS IN B-FLAT FOR CLARINET, VIOLA, BASSOON, AND GUITAR ON THE ROMANCE "VOUS ME QUITTEZ POUR ALLER A LA GLOIRE"

[Clarinet in B-Flat]

Date: Ca. 1811-12.
Autograph sketches: KRa (A 4415). 12 pages, ink.
                 (a) Theme, 4 variations (some missing pages after Var. 1), 8 pages. Most of viola part in brown ink in another hand.
                 (b) Theme, 2 variations, partially sketched, 4 pages.
Ms. copy: Wgm (XI 15421). 6 pages, ink. *Variations pour Clarinette, Viola, Fagotto, et Guitarre sur la Romance: Vous me quittez pour aller à la guerre.* Theme, 6 variations, and coda. Erroneously catalogued as an autograph.

20 SONATA IN F MINOR FOR VIOLIN AND PIANO

I.   Allegro

II.   Adagio

III.   Scherzo: Allegro
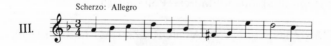

IV.   Finale: Allegro assai quasi presto
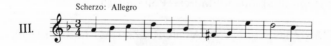

326

Date:　　　Ca. 1812.

Autograph:　*KRa* (A 4405). 32 pages, ink.

(a) 1st movement (Allegro), 15 pages. Score.

(b) 3rd movement (Scherzo: Allegro), 2 pages. Score.

(c) 4th movement (Finale: Allegro assai), 15 pages. Score.

KRa (A 4407). 9 pages, ink.

(a) 2nd movement (Adagio con espressione), fair copy, 5 pages. Score.

(b) 2nd movement, draft, 4 pages, unfinished. Score.

Ms. copies:　*Wgm* (Q 17754). ["Sonate/pour le Pianoforte/avec accompagnement d'un Violon/par/Rodolphe Archiduc d'Autriche"]. 45 pages, ink. Piano part.

Wgm (Q 17757). 66 pages, ink.

(a) piano part, 46 pages.

(b) violin part, 20 pages.

Wgm (Q 17758). 67 pages, ink.

(a) score, 55 pages.

(b) violin part, 12 pages.

GO1 (Mus. pag. 14 d/7). ["Sonate/pour le Piano-Forte/avec/ l'accompagnement d'un Violon/Composée/par/Rodolphe Archiduc d'Autriche"]. 54 pages, ink. Piano part.

(The four manuscript copies listed above, all virtually identical, show considerable revisions of the autograph, among them changes in movement titles and tempo indications as follows: 2nd movement, "Adagio"; 3rd movement, "Menuetto: Allegro molto"; 4th movement, "Allegro assai quasi Presto.")

21 SONATA IN A FOR CLARINET AND PIANO

Date: Ca. 1812.

Autograph: KRa (A 4397). 53 pages, ink.

   (a) Draft: [Allegro]; 15 pages; [Minuetto], 5 pages; Adagio, 4 pages.

   (b) Fair copy: Allegro moderato, 12 pages; Tempo di Minuetto, Adagio, Andantino [Theme and variations], 17 pages.

Autograph sketches: KRa (A 4433-38). 16 pages, ink.

Ms. copies: Wgm (Q 17759). Piano and clarinet parts.

Wgm (Q 17760). 64 pages, ink. First page in the hand of Wenzel Schlemmer, the remainder by one of his students. Numerous pencil corrections by Beethoven. Metronome numbers added in ink.

Wgm (Q 17761). Score and clarinet part, 65 + 19 pages, ink. GO1 (Mus. pag. 18/1). ["Sonate/pour le Piano-Forte/avec/ l'accompagnement d'une Clarinette/composée/par/Rodolphe Archiduc d'Autriche"]. 48 pages, ink. Piano part.

Editions: *Wgm* (XI 3497). *Sonate/für/Pianoforte und Clarinette/von/R.E.H.*
              [Rudolph Erzherzog]/II/dem Grafen Ferdinand Troyer/gewidmet./
              No. 3240/Wien/bei S.A. Steiner und Comp.
              Archduke Rudolph of Austria (1788-1831)/Sonata/for/Clarinet
              and Piano/ [Ed. H. Voxman]/Musica Rara/London, W. 1/ [1973].

Recordings: MUSICAL HERITAGE SOCIETY MHS 3856 (Ottokar Drapal,
              clarinet; Hans Kann, piano).
              MPS-Records, CRO 839 (Consortium Classicum: Dieter
              Klöcker, clarinet; Werner Genuit, piano).

22 SERENADE IN B-FLAT FOR CLARINET, VIOLA, BASSOON, AND GUITAR

Marcia: Allegro

6.

[Cl. in B-Flat]

Date:	Ca. 1812.
Ms. copy:	Wgm (Q 17762). 46 pages, ink.
Recordings:	MPS-Records; CRO 839 (Consortium Classicum: Dieter Klöcker, clarinet; Jürgen Kassmaul, viola; Karl Otto Hartmann, bassoon; Rolf Hock, guitar).
	TELEFUNKEN 6.42171 (Dieter Klöcker, clarinet; Heinz Otto Graf, viola; Karl Otto Hartmann, bassoon; Sonja Prunnbauer, guitar).

23 VARIATIONS IN E-FLAT FOR CLARINET AND PIANO [ON A THEME FROM ROSSINI'S "ZELMIRA"]

Introduzione: Andante

[Cl. in B-flat]

Thema: Allegro moderato

[Cl. in B-flat]

Date:	Ca. 1822-23.
Autograph:	Wgm. (XI 8244). *Cavatina von Rossini/aus der Oper Zelmira (Sorte! secondami)/mit/8 Veränderungen/für das/Piano Forte, mit Begleitung/einer/Clarinette.* Introduction, Theme, and 8 Variations. 70 pages, ink. Score. Numerous corrections and emendations, pencil, in Beethoven's hand.
	KRa (A 4400-01). 67 pages, ink and pencil.
	(a) Draft: 31 pages. Score.
	(b) Clarinet part (complete): 12 pages, ink.
	(c) Clarinet part (through part of Var. 4): 5 pages, ink.
	(d) Sketches: 19 pages, pencil.
	KRa (A 4432-38). Sketches, ink and pencil. 18 pages.
Editions:	*Variationen/über ein Thema von Rossini/für Klarinette und Klavier. Erstdruck.* Edited by Otto Biba. Diletto Musicale 696, Doblinger, Wien (1981).
Recordings:	ELECTROLA 1C187-30202/05 (Dieter Klöcker, clarinet; Werner Genuit, piano).

Compositions for Orchestra

(See Thematic catalogue number 4C)

Compositions for Voice

24 "WENN IN DES ABENDS LETZTEM SCHEINE"

Date:	Ca. 1812-13.
Text:	Friedrich von Matthisson *(Lied aus der Ferne).*
Autograph:	KRa (A 4422). 4 pages, ink. Voice and piano.

25 "JE VOUS SALUE"

Date:	Ca. 1816-17.
Text:	M. de Florian.
Autograph:	KRa (A 4423). 12 pages, ink. Voice and piano.
	(a) Fair copy, key of F, 3 pages.
	(b) Sketches, key of F, 5 pages.
Ms. copy:	2 pages.

Other version in key of A:

Autograph:	2 pages, ink.

331

26 "LA PARTENZA"

Date:	Ca. 1818.
Text:	Pietro Metastasio.
Autograph:	Wgm (VI 42159). *La Partenza. Canzonetta di Metastasio.* 8 pages, ink. [Bass] voice and piano. Seven verses; piano accompaniment in first and seventh verses only.
	KRa (A 4421). 10 pages, ink and pencil.
	(a) Fair copy, 8 pages, ink. Seven verses; piano accompaniment in first and seventh verses only. Numerous corrections, pencil, in Beethoven's hand. Above staff on page 1, in pencil: ♩=80 *Metronome de Mälzl.* On page 8, in ink, the theme of "O Hoffnung, O Hoffnung" (see Thematic catalogue number 10) is written out.
	(b) Sketch, 2 pages, pencil.
Ms copy:	Wgm (VI 15408). 12 pages, ink. Erroneously catalogued as an autograph.

27 "LIEBER BEETHOVEN ICH DANKE"

Date:	1820.
Text:	Archduke Rudolph.
Autograph:	KRa (A 4376). 2 pages, ink. Introduction and canon for four unaccompanied voices.
Cf.	*Zeitschrift für Musikwissenschaft* 4 (1921) 99-100.

II. UNFINISHED WORKS

Compositions for Piano

U 1 THEME WITH TWO VARIATIONS IN F

Date: Ca. 1809.
Autograph: KRa (A 4384). 1 page, ink.

U 2 THEME AND VARIATIONS IN A

Date: Ca. 1811.
Autograph: KRa (A 4389). 8 pages, ink. Complete through part of Var. 8.

U 3 POLONAISE IN E-FLAT

Date: Ca. 1812.
Autograph: KRa (A 4378). 1 page, ink.

U 4 THEME AND VARIATIONS IN A [FOR TWO PIANOS]

Date: Ca. 1813.

Autograph: *KRa* (A 4391). 8 pages, ink. Theme is complete; Variations 1 and 2 are incompletely sketched.

U 5 [MARCHES[FOR TWO PIANOS

Date: Ca. 1816-17.

Autograph: *KRa* (A 4395). 32 pages, ink and pencil. No. 1 is complete; Nos. 2 through 7 are incompletely sketched.

Other Instrumental Works

U 6 COMPOSITION IN B-FLAT FOR WOODWIND OCTET

[Clarinet in B-Flat]

Date: Before 1809?

Autograph: KRa (A 4417). 3 pages, ink. Scored for 2 oboes, 2 clarinets, 2 bassoons, 2 horns.

         KRa (A 4433-38). 1 page, ink sketch.

U 7 LARGO IN D FOR STRING QUARTET

Largo

[Violoncello]

Date: Before 1809?

Autograph: KRa (A 4417). 2 pages, ink. Fragment.

U 8 GANZ NEUE DEUTSCHE [FOR CLARINET]

Date: Ca. 1809.

Autograph: KRa (A 4382). 2 pages, ink. 24 dances, each 8 measures. One voice.

         KRa (A 4433-38). 1 page, ink. 6 dances for "Clarinetto in B."

Ms. copy: KRa (A 4417). 1 page, ink. 6 dances.

U 9 MARCH IN F [FOR VARIOUS ENSEMBLES]

Date: Ca. 1809.

Autograph: KRa (A 4410). 6 pages, ink.

         (a) Violin and piano score, 2 pages.

         (b) Piano four hands, 2 pages.

Ms. copy: Solo part (violin), 1 page.

         Solo part (violoncello), 1 page.

U 10 VARIATIONS IN A-FLAT FOR CZAKAN AND PIANO

[Czakan in A-Flat]

Date: Ca. 1810.
Autograph: *KRa* (A 4403). 6 pages, ink.
  (a) Theme and 6 variations, czakan and piano score, unfinished, 4 pages.
  (b) Czakan part, complete, 2 pages.

U11 VARIATIONS IN B-FLAT FOR CLARINET, VIOLA, BASSOON, AND GUITAR

[Clarinet in B-Flat]

Date: Ca. 1811-12.
Autograph: *KRa* (A 4412). 8 pages, ink. Scoring partially sketched.

U 12 [VARIATIONS] IN B-FLAT FOR CLARINET, VIOLA, BASSOON, AND GUITAR

Andante

[Clarinet in B-Flat]

Date: Ca. 1811-12.
Autograph: *KRa* (A 4413). 4 pages, ink.
  (a) [Introduction]: Andante.
  (b) Theme, Var. 1, part of Var. 2.

U13 VARIATIONS IN B-FLAT FOR CLARINET, VIOLA, BASSOON, AND GUITAR

[Clarinet in B-Flat]

Date: Ca. 1811-12.

336

Autograph: KRa (A 4414). 16 pages, ink.

(a) Theme, 3 variations, part of Var. 4, 8 pages. Scoring complete.

(b) Theme, 3 variations, part of Var. 4, 8 pages. Scoring partially sketched.

U 14 VARIATIONS IN B-FLAT FOR CLARINET, VIOLA, BASSOON, AND GUITAR

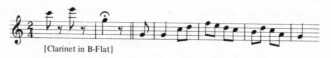

[Clarinet in B-Flat]

Date: Ca. 1811-12.

Autograph: KRa (A 4417). 4 pages, ink. Theme, 4 variations, partially sketched.

U 15 COMPOSITION IN E-FLAT FOR CLARINET, VIOLA, BASSOON, AND GUITAR

[Clarinet in B-Flat]

Date: Ca. 1811-12.

Autograph: Kra (A 4433-38). 4 pages, ink. Scoring complete.

U 16 VARIATIONS IN B-FLAT FOR CLARINET AND PIANO

Date: Ca. 1812.

Autograph: Kra (A 4406). 18 pages, ink. Theme complete; variations partially sketched.

U 17 COMPOSITION IN B-FLAT FOR ORCHESTRA

[Clarinet in B-Flat]

Date: Ca. 1813.

Autograph: KRa (A 4417). 7 pages, ink. Scored for: "kleine Flöte, 2 Oboi, 2 Clarinetti, 2 Fagotti, (2) Hörner in F, Trumpette in F, Contra-

fagott, Triangle, Cinelli, kleine Trommel, grosse Trommel."
Scoring partially completed.

U 18 COMPOSITION IN C FOR VIOLIN AND PIANO

Date:	Ca. 1813.
Autograph:	KRa (A 4408). 9 pages, ink.
	(a) Beginning of work, 2 pages.
	(b) New beginning, 7 pages. Scoring complete.

U 19 TRIO IN E-FLAT FOR CLARINET, CELLO, AND PIANO

[Clarinet in B-Flat]

Date:	Ca. 1813.
Autograph:	KRa (A 4514-15). 38 pages, ink.
	(a) Draft of 1st movement, unfinished, 10 pages.
	(b) Fair copy: Allegro moderato, 14 pages; Larghetto—*Theme von Prinz Louis Ferdinand von Preussen aus dem Ottetto,* 8 pages; Scherzo—Allegretto, 5 pages.
	(c) 2 sketches, themes for a finale, 2 pages.
Editions:	*Archduke Rudolph of Austria (1788-1831)/Trio/for/Clarinet, Cello & Piano/[Ed. Dieter Klöcker and Werner Genuit]/Musica Rara/ London, W.1 [1969].*
	[In this edition, the editors reversed the order of the second and third movements.]
Recordings:	MUSICAL HERITAGE SOCIETY MHS 4527 (The Nash Ensemble: Clifford Benson, piano; Antony Pay, clarinet; Christopher van Kampen, violoncello).

U 20 COMPOSITION IN F FOR PIANO [AND TWO OTHER INSTRU-MENTS]

Date: Ca. 1813.
Autograph: KRa (A 4392). 3 pages, ink.

U 21 [MINUET] AND TRIO IN B-FLAT FOR STRING QUARTET

Date: Ca. 1816.
Autograph: KRa (A 4411). 1 page, ink.
Autograph sketch: KRa (A 4433-38), 1 page.

U 22 VARIATIONS IN B-FLAT FOR CLARINET AND ORCHESTRA

Date: Ca. 1817.
Autograph: KRa (A 4419). 11 pages, ink. Theme ("Di tanti palpiti" from
               Rossini's *Tancredi*), Var. 1 (complete), partial sketches for Var.
               2. Scored for: "Clarinette in B, Violini 1 and 2, Viole, Basso,
               Flauti, Oboi, Fagotti, Corni in B."
Autograph sketch: KRa (A 4433-38), 1 page.

U 23 THEME AND VARIATIONS IN A MINOR FOR PIANO, VIOLIN, FLUTE, VIOLA, CLARINET, AND CELLO

Date: Ca. 1818-19.
Autograph: KRa (A 4409). 8 pages, ink. Theme ("Violino" and "Forte
               Piano"); Var. 1 ("Flauto" and piano); Var. 2, (Viola and piano);
               Var. 3 ("Clarinetto in A" and piano); Var. 4 ("Piano Forte
               solo"); Var. 5 ("Violoncello" and piano).

U 24 [SONATA MOVEMENT] IN B-FLAT FOR CLARINET AND PIANO

[Piano]   [Clarinet in B-Flat transposed]

Date: Ca. 1822.
Autograph: KRa (A 4399). 8 pages, ink and pencil.
(a) Sketch with pencil corrections, 2 pages.
(b) Sketch with corrections made, 4 pages.
(c) Sketch with opening phrase in clarinet, 2 pages.
Autograph sketch: KRa (A 4433-38). 1 page.

U 25 SONATA IN B-FLAT FOR CLARINET AND PIANO

Adagio

[Clarinet in B-Flat]

Allegro

[Clarinet in B-Flat]

Andante

[Piano]   [Clarinet in B-Flat transposed]

Rondo

[Clarinet in B-Flat]

Date: Ca. 1822-23.
Autograph: KRa (A 4398). 39 pages, ink and pencil.
(a) Fair copy: Adagio—Allegro, 18 pages; ink, with numerous pencil changes and corrections.
(b) Fair copy: Andante, 6 pages; ink with pencil corrections.
(c) Fair copy, clarinet part (1st and 2nd movements), 6 pages.
(d) Sketch, "Rondo," pencil, 9 pages. On final page, pencil sketch of "Salve Regina."

U 26 VARIATIONS IN F FOR CLARINET AND PIANO

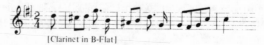

[Clarinet in B-Flat]

[Clarinet in B-Flat]

Date:	Ca. 1822-23.
Autograph:	KRa (A 4402). 29 pages, ink and pencil.

(a) Draft: Introduction, theme, and 10 variations; 24 pages, pencil. Scoring partially sketched.

(b) Clarinet part: 5 pages, ink. Complete.

U 27 COMPOSITION IN F FOR CLARINET AND PIANO

[Clarinet in B-Flat]

Date:	Ca. 1822-23.
Autograph:	KRa (A 4402). 8 pages, ink.

U 28 VARIATIONS IN F FOR BASSET HORN AND PIANO ON "TO JSOU KONĚ"

Introduzione: Andante

[Basset Horn in F]

Thema: Allegretto

[Piano]

Date:	Ca. 1823.
Autograph:	KRa (A 4509-13). 42 pages, ink and pencil.

(a) Draft: Introduction, theme, Variations 1 through 7, part of Var. 8 (KRa A 4509): 8 pages, ink with pencil emendations.

(b) Draft: Introduction (KRa A 4510); 4 pages, pencil.

(c) Draft: Introduction, theme, partial sketches for variations (KRa A 4511); 8 pages, ink and pencil.

(d) Fair copy: Introduction, theme, Variations 1 through 8 (KRa A 4512); 16 pages, ink and some pencil corrections. On page 16, new time signature for a final variation.

(e) Basset horn part (through part of Var. 8), 6 pages, ink.

(f) Basset horn part (through part of Var. 7), 2 pages, ink with some pencil markings.

Autograph sketches: KRa (A 4432); 23 pages, ink and pencil.
KRa (A 4398); 2 pages, pencil.

KRa (A 4402); 3 pages, ink.

Ms. copy: *KRa* (A 4513); basset horn part; 4 pages, ink and pencil. Comparison of the four versions above (a-d) by Vladimír Helfert, 4 pages, ink.

Recording: MUSICAL HERITAGE SOCIETY MHS 1182 (Heinrich Fink, basset horn; Richard Laugs, piano).

Compositions for Voice

U 29 [SINGSPIEL] FOR SEVERAL VOICES

Date: Before 1809?

Autograph: *KRa* (A 4425). 8 pages, ink. Parts for "Amarone," "Robert," and other voices. Text undecipherable.

U 30 REQUIEM (FRAGMENTS)

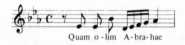

Date: Before 1809?

Autograph: *KRa* (A 4426-27). 23 pages, ink. 4-part chorus, 4 solo voices.

    (a) *Requiem aeternam:* 4 pages.

    (b) *Kyrie eleison:* 11 pages.

    (c) *Quam olim Abrahae:* 8 pages.

U 31 TE DEUM (FRAGMENT)

Date: Before 1809?
Autograph: KRa (A 4427). 2 pages, ink. Three 4-part choruses.

U 32 ICH DENKE DEIN (DUET)

[Piano introduction]

Adagio

Ich den - ke dein

Text: Friedrich Matthisson *(Andenken)*.
Date: Ca. 1815-16.
Autograph: KRa (A 4424). 15 pages, ink. Two soprano voices and piano. Piano accompaniment complete in introduction, partially sketched thereafter.

U 33 LUX AETERNA (FRAGMENT)

Andante

Lux ae - ter - na lu - ce - at e - is Do -

Date: After 1819.
Autograph: KRa (A 4426). 2 pages, ink and pencil. Bass voice with bass line accompaniment.

U 34 REGINA CAELI

Re - gi - na cae - li lae - ta - re

Date: After 1819.
Autograph: KRa (A 4427). 8 pages, pencil. 4 voice parts, 2 instrumental parts (soprano and bass), partially sketched.

U 35 SALVE REGINA

Sal - ve Re - gi - na

Date: After 1819.
Autograph: KRa (A 4398). 1 page, pencil (on final page of U 25). 4 voices.

Collections of Miscellaneous Sketch Fragments

KRa (A 4431-32).   177 pages, ink and pencil. Loose sheets.
KRa (A 4433-38).   [Membra disjecta]. 218 pages, ink and pencil. Loose sheets.
KRa (A 4450).   [Membra disjecta]. 14 pages, ink. Loose sheets; some pages in another hand.

III. TRANSCRIPTIONS AND COPIES

(Note: All of the following are autographs).

T 1	Bach, C.P.E.	*Allegro in G [for keyboard]*. Copy. KRa (A 4431).
T 2		*Allegro in A [for keyboard]*. Copy; unfinished. KRa (A 4431).
T 3	Bach, J.S.	*Fugue in F Minor* from Book II of the *Well-Tempered Clavier*. Copy; unfinished. KRa (A 4433-38).
T 4	Beethoven, L. van	*Septet, Op. 20 (Menuetto)*. Transcription for clarinet, viola, bassoon, and guitar; unfinished. Kra (A 4390).
T 5		*Quintet for Strings, Op. 29 (first movement)*. Transcription for violin, cello, and piano. KRa (A 4390).
T 6		*Sonata in C Minor for Violin and Piano, Op. 30, no. 2 (second movement)*; violin part only. Copy. KRa (A 4433-38).
T 7		*Piano Sonata in F Minor, Op. 57 (second movement)*. Bass line only, as a figured bass exercise. KRa (A 4432).
T 8		*Symphony No. 5 in C Minor, Op. 67 (first movement)*. Transcription for piano solo; unfinished. KRa (A 4387).
T 9		*Overture to "Egmont," Op. 84*. Transcription for piano four hands. KRa (A 4433-38).
T 10		*"Clärchen's Lied" from "Egmont," Op. 84*. Transcription for piano solo. KRa (A 4433-38).
T 11		*Piano Sonata in E Minor, Op. 90*. Copy of Beethoven's autograph. Wn (COD 16570).
T 12		*Overture to "König Stephan," Op. 117*. Transcription for two pianos; unfinished. KRa (A 4433-38).
T 13		*Marsch für Militärmusik in F, No. 2, WoO 19*. Transcription for piano solo. KRa (A 4433-38).

T 14	Diabelli, A.	*Waltz.* Copy. *KRa* (A 4431).
T 15	Ellmenreich, J.	*Marsch aus dem Singstück "Der Kapellmeister."* Copy. *KRa* (A 4384).
T 16	Gluck, C.W.	*"Che farò senza Eurydice,"* from *"Orfeo ed Eurydice."* Transcription for piano solo; unfinished. KRa (A 4385).
T 17		*Music of the Furies* from Act II, Scene 1 of *"Orfeo ed Eurydice."* Transcription for piano solo; unfinished. *KRa* (A 4387-88).
T 18	Handel, G.F.	*Sinfonia* from *"Messiah."* Figured bass parts and two complete realizations for keyboard solo. *KRa* (A 4431).
T 19		*"Comfort ye," "Ev'ry Valley Shall be Exalted," "The People that Walked in Darkness,"* from *"Messiah."* Figured bass parts and keyboard realizations. *KRa* (A 4431-32).
T 20		*"Dead March," from "Saul."* Transcription for piano solo. *KRa* (A 4385).
T 21		*Water Music.* Transcription for piano solo. *KRa* (A 4385-86).
T 22	Mozart, W.A.	*Quartet for Piano and Strings in G Minor, K. 478 (first movement).* Violin, viola, and cello parts transcribed for piano. *KRa* (A 4387).
T 23		*Sonata in F for Piano Four Hands, K. 497 (first movement).* Transcription for woodwind octet: two clarinets, two oboes, two horns, two bassoons; unfinished. *KRa* (A 4420).
T 24		*Sonata in F for Piano Four Hands, K. 497 (third movement).* Same as T 23 above; unfinished. *KRa* (A 4416).
T 25		*Overture to "Don Giovanni," K. 527.* Transcription for two pianos. *KRa* (A 4430).
T 26		*Overture to "Die Zauberflöte," K. 620.* Transcription for two pianos. *KRa* (A 4429).
T 27		*Fugue from "Kyrie" of Requiem, K. 626.* Transcriptions for piano solo and two pianos. *KRa* (A 4441).
T 28	Spontini, G.	*Overture to "La Vestale."* Transcription for two pianos. *KRa* (A 4387-88 and A 4433-38).

(Note: As this book goes to press, a performance of a Septet [for violin, viola, cello, bass, clarinet, bassoon, and horn] attributed to Archduke Rudolph took place at the 1988 music festival at Hohenems, Austria. Attempts to see the manuscript [purchased from a dealer in Prague] were unsuccessful, but I was able to obtain a tape of the performance and a sample of one page of the manuscript, which had been reproduced in the program. Several issues strongly suggest that this attribution to Archduke Rudolph is questionable: the manuscript is not in Rudolphs hand; its four movements are not stylistically in keeping with Rudolph's other large-scale compositions, notably in regard to instrumental writing and handling of formal structures; no sketches for the work exist, nor is it entered in Rudolph's catalogue of his own compositions; its supposed date of composition [1830] is six years beyond his last known completed work. Any further judgement on the authenticity of this Septet must be deferred until the manuscript is made available for study.)

Index

Page numbers in italics refer to illustrations.

Albrecht, Otto, 55n

Albrechtsberger, Johann Georg, 54, 260

Alexander, Czar of Russia, 6n

Alexander's Fest (Handel), 282

Aline (Boieldieu), 7

Allgemeine Musikalische Zeitung, xv, 37, 75, 323

Altensteig, General Haager von, 3

Anderson, Emily, 3, 153

Anleitung zu Clavierspielen (Marpurg), 67

Anton, Archduke of Austria, 34, 63

Anton, Prince (later King of Saxony), 35n

Artaria, Domenico, 75

Aschenbrödel (Hummel), 11,

Attwood, Thomas, 54

Bach, Carl Philipp Emanuel, 54, 57, 67, 273, 344

Bach, Johann Baptist, 21

Bach, Johann Sebastian, 57, 59, 66, 74, 344

Backofen, J. G. H., 186n

Baumeister, Joseph Anton Ignaz, xvi, 3, 6 passim, 19, 23, 34–35

Beethoven-Handbuch, 16n

Beethoven Jahrbuch, xv

Beethoven, Johann van, 21n, 26n, 27

Beethoven, Karl, 21, 72, 74, 109

Beethoven, Ludwig van (passing references omitted: for main discussions of Beethoven's relations with Archduke Rudolph, *see* Beethoven entries under Rudolph, Archduke.

(Beethoven, cont.)
Works cited:
Chamber Music
Piano Trio in C Minor, Op. 1, No. 3, 174
Piano Trio in B-flat, Op. 11, 106, 172–73
Sonata in F for Piano and Horn, Op. 17, 19
Septet in E-flat, Op. 20, 62, 64–65, 215, 344
String Quintet in C, Op. 29, 63–65, 344
Sonata in G for Piano and Violin, Op. 30, No. 1, 172
Variations in E-flat for Piano, Violin and Violoncello, Op. 44, 172
Sonata in A for Piano and Violoncello, Op. 69, 193–95
Piano Trios in D, Op. 70, No. 1, and in E-flat, Op. 70, No. 2, 15, 17, 19
Sonata in G for Piano and Violin, Op. 96, 16, 29–30, 31, 205
Piano Trio in B-flat, Op. 97 (*"Archduke"*), 15, 16, 106
Sonata in D for Piano and Violoncello, Op. 102, No. 2, 105, 144–46
Variations in G for Piano, Violin and Violoncello, Op. 121a (*"Kakadu"*), 78, 172, 174
Grosse Fugue, Op. 133, and piano arrangement, Op. 134, 16
Concertos
Concerto in C for Piano, Violin and Violoncello, Op. 56 (*"Triple"*), 5
Piano Concerto No. 4 in G, Op. 58, 14, 16

(*Beethoven, works, cont.*)
Violin Concerto in D, Op. 61
(piano arrangement), 16
Piano Concerto No. 5 in E-
flat, Op. 73 ("*Emperor*"),
16, 198
Opera and Oratorio
Fidelio, Op. 72b (piano arran-
gement by Moscheles),
16
Missa Solemnis in D, Op. 123,
16–17, 288
Orchestral and Incidental Music
Symphony No. 5 in C Minor,
Op. 67, 63, 344
Overture to *Egmont*, Op. 84,
17, 61–62, 344
"*Clärchen's Lied*" from *Egmont*,
Op. 84, 61, 344
Overture to *Ruins of Athens*,
Op. 113, 20, 344
Overture to *König Stephan*,
Op. 117, 20, 61, 63, 344
Marsch für Militärmusik No. 2
in F, WoO 19, 61, 273
Piano Music
Fantasie, Op. 77, 13
Sonata in C, Op. 2, No. 3,
143–44
Sonata in C Minor, Op. 13
("*Pathétique*"), 147
Sonata in A-flat, Op. 26, 135,
180
Sonata in D Minor, Op. 31,
No. 2, 180–81
Sonata in C, Op. 53
("*Waldstein*"), 106
Sonata in F Minor, Op. 57
("*Appassionata*"), 56, 344
Sonata in E-flat, Op. 81a ("*Les
Adieux*"), xix, 15, 16, 159,
198–99, 251
Sonata in E Minor, Op. 90,
19, 65–66, 344
Sonata in A, Op. 101, 283
Sonata in B-flat, Op. 106
("*Hammerklavier*"), 16
Sonata in A-flat, Op. 110, 106,
111
Sonata in C Minor, Op. 111,
16

(*Beethoven, works, cont.*)
Vocal Music
"*Andenken*" (Matthisson), WoO
136, 250
"*Lied aus der Ferne*" (Reissig),
WoO 137, 273
"*Resignation*" (Haugwitz) ,
WoO 149, 283
"*Seiner kaiserlichen Hoheit ...
Alles Gute, alles Schöne*,"
WoO 179, 17, 252
"*O Hoffnung, O Hoffnung*,"
WoO 200, 17, 69–72, 70,
234
"*Erfüllung*," WoO 205e, 17, 73
Berlioz, Hector, 260
Biba, Otto, 154n
Boettcher, Hans, 71
Boieldieu, F. A., 7n, 252n
Bonaparte, King Jerome of
Westphalia, 14
Bonaparte, Napoleon, 10, 13, 35n
Brahms, Johannes, 87
Breitkopf & Härtel, 15, 17, 27, 78n
Brentano, Antonia, 16n
Brentano, Franz, 21n
Catalani, Angelica, 8
Cherubini, Luigi, 252n
Choron, Alexandre, 283
Clementi, Muzio, 108
Colloredo, Anton Theodor von,
Archbishop of Olmütz, 6
Coupigny, A. de, 252
Croll, Gerhard, xviii, 153
Czerny, Carl, 141n
Diabelli, Anton, xii, xvii, xix, 55, 56, 67,
105n, 140, 141, 345
Dobenz (Tobenz), Franz Heinrich, 13
Don Giovanni (Mozart), 8
Drechsler, Joseph, 20
Dussek, Jan Ladislav, 108
Ellmenreich, J. B., 66, 345
Erben, K. J., 164

Erdödy family, 13, 15n

Esterhazy family, 13

Field, John, 108

Florian, J. de, 247, 331

Franz I (of Lorraine), Emperor of Austria (grandfather of Archduke Rudolph), 1n

Franz I, Emperor of Austria (brother of Archduke Rudolph), xiv, 1, 2, 21, 34, 63n, 131

Friedlowsky, Joseph, 6

Frimmel, Theodor, 16n

Fröhlich, J. F., 186n

Fux, Johann Joseph, 54, 260, 291

Gesellschaft der Musikfreunde (Vienna), xvii, xix, xxi, 33, 34, 36, passim

Giuliani, Mauro, 213n

Gleichenstein, Baron Ignaz von, 13n, 22, 27

Glöggl, Franz Xaver, 29, 30

Gluck, Christoph Willibald, 57, 66, 138, 345

Graun, August Friedrich, 234

Grünbaum, Theresa, 7, 8n

Gyrowetz, Adalbert, 154

Handel, George Frideric, 12, 36, 57, 59, 74, 138, 276, 345

Hanson, Alice M., 14n

Haslinger, Tobias, 54, 75

Haydn, Joseph, 2, 28, 137

Heberle (Eberle), Anton, 167

Helfert, Vladimír, xvii, 165–66, 342

Henriette, Archduchess (wife of Archduke Karl), 128

Hoffmeister, Franz Anton, 66n

Hohenwort, Graf Sigismund Anton von, 3

Hummel, Johann Nepomuk, 11, 108

Johann, Archduke of Austria (brother of Archduke Rudolph), 34

Johann von Paris (Boieldieu), 7

Jommelli, Nicolò, 12

Joseph, Archduke of Austria (brother of Archduke Rudolph), 34

Joseph II, Emperor of Austria (uncle of Archduke Rudolph), 1, 75

Kapellmeister, Der (Ellmenreich), 66

Karl, Archduke of Austria (brother of Archduke Rudolph), 13, 34, 128n

Karl VI, Emperor (great-grandfather of Archduke Rudolph), 2n

Kinsky, Prince Ferdinand, 14, 20

Kinsky, Georg, 16, 72, 234

Kirnberger, Johann Philipp, 54, 55, 234, 283

Koch, S., 186n

Köchel, Ludwig, 3

Kollowrat, Bishop, 9

Kraft, Anton, 20

Kramer, Richard, 54n

Lany (clergyman), 13

Laurençin d'Armont, Count Ferdinand von, 6

Lemberg, Archbishop of, 9

Leopold I, Emperor (great-great-grandfather of Archduke Rudolph), 2n

Leopold II, Grand Duke of Tuscany, later Emperor (father of Archduke Rudolph), xiv, 1

Lichnowsky, Count Moritz, 19n

Lichtenstein family, 13

Liszt, Franz, 140

Lobkowitz, Prince Joseph, xvi, 5, 14, 20, 28, 29, 30, 31, 205

Louis Ferdinand, Prince of Prussia, 11, 29, 225, 226, 276, 324–25, 338

Ludwig, Archduke of Austria (brother of Archduke Rudolph), 3, 21, 34

MacArdle, Donald W., xv

Maelzel, Johann Nepomuk, 8n, 20n

Mahler, Gustav, 137

Marcuse, Sybil, 169n

Marek, George, xvin

Maria Ludovica of Spain, Empress (mother of Archduke Rudolph), xiv, 1

Maria Ludovica, Empress (third wife of Franz I), 35, 63n, 131

Maria Thérèse, Empress (second wife of Franz I), 2

Maria Theresia, Empress (wife of Franz I of Lorraine), 1n

Marie, Duchess of Weimar, 139, 140

Marie Louise, Empress (wife of Napoleon Bonaparte), 35

Marpurg, Friedrich Wilhelm, 67

Martini, Padre, 3

Marx, Adolph Bernhard, 71

Mathilde ou les Croisades (Pichler), 8

Mattheson, Johann, 12

Matthisson, Friedrich von, 243, 250, 331, 343

Maximilian Franz, Elector of Cologne (uncle of Archduke Rudolph), 2n

McGuigan, Dorothy Gies, 2n

Metastasio, Pietro, 234, 332

Moscheles, Ignaz, 16

Mozart, Franz Xaver, 140

Mozart, Leopold, 291

Mozart, Wolfgang Amadeus, 28, 54, 57, 60, 61, 137, 152, 178, 183, 185–86, 197, 206–207, 208, 223, 234, 273, 345

Musikalische Zeitung für den Oester-reichischen Staaten (Linz), 29

Nägeli, Hans Georg, 27

Nettl, Paul, xvii, 153, 166, 253n, 255

Newman, William S., 111n

Nohl, Ludwig, 72

Nottebohm, Gustav, 54, 55

Novotny, Alexander, xv, 2, 3

Orfeo ed Eurydice (Gluck), 66, 345

Österreichischer Beobachter, 36

Paer, Ferdinando, 8

Parkar (clergyman), 13

Peters, C. F., 17n

Pichler, Caroline, 8

Racek, Jan, xv, 77n, 165n, 251n

Raimund, Ferdinand, 8, 10

Rainer, Archduke of Austria (brother of Archduke Rudolph), 34

Razumovsky, Prince Andrey, xiii, 6n

Reichardt, Johann Friedrich, 29, 234

Rendall, F. Geoffrey, 185n

Ries, Ferdinand, 7n, 17n, 18, 21n, 22, 26, 32, 108

Rietsch, Heinrich, 140, 141n, 142n

Riotte, Phillipp Jakob, 283

Rochlitz, Friedrich, 36

Rode, Pierre, 11, 30, 205

Rossini, Giacomo, 32n, 128, 129, 130, 151, 154, 156, 159, 161n, 198, 321, 330, 339

Rudolph von Habsburg (Pichler) , 8

Rudolph, Archduke Johann Joseph Rainer
Archbishop of Olmütz, 17
as artist, 34–35
Beethoven
dedications by, 15–17
generosity to, 14, 17–21
relations with, 13 ff.
study with, xiii-xiv, 3, 22, 26, 28, 31–33, 54–55, 69 ff., 182, 264
birth of, 1
dating of compositions, xx-xxii
death of, 53
ecclesiastical career of, 12
education of, 2–5, 53–55
Gesellschaft der Musikfreunde, Protector of, 33–34
health of, 5, 9–10
music collection of, xiv, 34–35
as pianist, 28–31
pseudonyms of, 75, 140
Works discussed in text:
Exercises and Transcriptions
Counterpoint exercises, 56–57, 58

(Rudolph, works, cont.)

Beethoven transcriptions, 61–66, *64*, 344

Handel transcriptions, 59–60, 345

Mozart transcriptions, 60–61, 345

Transcriptions of other composers, 66–67 , 345

Chamber Ensemble

Septet (doubtful), 346

Serenade in B-flat for Clarinet, Viola, Bassoon and Guitar (Them. cat. 22), 214, 216–19, 329–30

Theme and Variations in A Minor for Piano, Violin, Flute, Viola, Clarinet and Violoncello (Them. cat. U 23), 222, 339

Trio in E-flat for Clarinet, Violoncello and Piano (Them. cat. U 19), 183, 338

Variations for Clarinet, Viola, Bassoon and Guitar (Them. cat. 19), 220–22, 326

Orchestral Music

12 *Ländler* (Them. cat. 4C), xix, 139–40, 319

Piano Music

12 *Allemandes* (for piano four hands) [Them. cat. 4A]. *See* 12 *Ländler*

Canone all' ottava ("*Ach du lieber Augustin*") [Them. cat. 1], 146, 314

Capriccio (Them. cat. 12), 147–49, 323; Beethoven's corrections in, 147–49

Deutsche Tänze (Them. cat. 4B). *See* 12 *Ländler*

Forty Variations on a Theme ("*O Hoffnung, O Hoffnung*") *by Beethoven* (Them. cat. 10), xvii, xix, 59, *68*, 69 passim, 119, 159, 184, 200, 322–23; Beethoven's corrections in, 76–77, 93–95, 99–101, 103, 106–108, *112, 113*,

(Rudolph, works, cont.)

114, 115, 116, 117, 118; Beethoven's fingering in, 110–11; Beethoven's letters on, 72–75; *Wiener Piano-Forte-Schule* edition of, 108–11

Fuga on a Waltz Theme by Diabelli (Them. cat. 11), xvii, xix, 55, 56, 67, 140–46, 323

3 *Ländler* (Them. cat. 6), 138–39, 320

20 *Ländler* (Them. cat. 2), 138, 314–17

Menuetto and Trio in B (Them. cat. 14), 324

3 *Polonaises* (Them. cat. 5), 140, 319–20

Variations in G (Them. cat. 3), 120–25, *122*, 317

(*Ländler*) Variations in G (Them. cat. 7), 126–29, 320–21

Variations in G on Rossini's "*Di tanti palpiti*" (Them. cat. 9), 128–30, 321–22

Variations in A on a Theme by Spontini (for piano duet) [Them. cat. 8], 131–36, 321; Beethoven's corrections in, 136–37

String Music

Sonata in F Minor for Violin and Piano (Them. cat. 20), 205–11, 223, 225, 326–27

Variations in F for Violin and Piano (Them. cat. l5A and l5B), 225–29, 324–25

Vocal Music

"*Ich denke dein*" (Matthisson) [Them. cat. U 32], 250–52, 254, 343

"*Je vous salue*" (de Florian) [Them. cat. 25], 247–50, 331

"*La Partenza*" (Metastasio) [Them. cat. 26], 85–86, 233, 234–38, 247, 260, 332; Beethoven's corrections in, 238–43

(Rudolph, works, cont.)
    "Lieber Beethoven, ich danke"
      (Thcm. cat 27), 252–55,
      332
    *"Wenn in des Abends letztem
      Scheine"* (Matthisson)
      [Them. cat. 24], 243–47,
      331
    Sacred choral fragments
      (Them. cat. U 33–U 35),
      256–60
  Woodwind Music
    Divertissement in A-flat for
      Czakan and Piano
      (Them. cat. 17), 175, 325
    Sonata in A for Clarinet and
      Piano (Them. cat. 21),
      xvii, xxii, 6, 151, 183–204,
      327–29; Beethoven's cor-
      rections in, 199–204
    Variations in A-flat for
      Czakan and Piano (*"Op-
      ferfest"*) [Them. cat. 16],
      168, 169–74, 325
    Variations in E-flat for
      Clarinet and Piano on a
      Theme by Rossini
      (Them. cat. 23), 32, 152–
      64, 165, 198, 330;
      Beethoven's corrections
      in, 159–64; dating of,
      152–54
    Variations in F for Basset
      Horn and Piano on *"To
      jsou koně"* (Them. cat. U
      28) , 164–67, 341–42
    (Waltz) Variations in A-flat
      for Czakan and Piano
      (Them. cat. 18), 178–81
      325–26
Rust, Friedrich Wilhelm, 234
Salieri, Antonio, 11, 234
Sammler, Der, xv
Sargino (Paer), 8
Saul (Handel), 59
Scarlatti, Domenico, 11
Schindler, Anton, 3, 18n
Schlemmer, Wenzel, 73n, 185, 328
Schlesinger , Moritz , 16

Schott und Söhne, 18, 32
Schubert, Franz, 6, 14n, 28, 139, 140,
    243n, 246n
Schumann, Clara, 87n
Schünemann, Georg, 55n
Schuster, Ignaz, 8
Schwarzenberg family, 13
Schweiger, Baron Joseph von, 6, 20
Sehnal, Jiři, xviii
Seidler, Ferdinand August, 29
Seyfried, Ignaz von, 29, 54
Shackleton, Nicholas, 185n
Simrock, Nikolaus, 22, 26n
Sonntagsblätter, xvi, 11n
Souppé, Canon, 9
Spaun, Josef von, 28
Spontini, Gaspare, 57, 66, 131, 134, 215,
    321, 345
Stadler, Anton, 185, 186n
Starke, Friedrich, 108–11
Steiner, S. A., xvii, xix, 19, 69, 74, 76, 87,
    108, 110n, 184
Stuffler, Bishop of Brünn, 9
Stumpff, Johann Andreas, 36
Tancredi (Rossini), 128, 321, 339
Tayber (Teyber), Anton, 3, 13, 28, 53,
    57, 182
Teyber, Mlle., 8
Thayer, Alexander Wheelock, xv, xvii ,
    1n, 17 , 18, 182
Tiedge, Christoph August, 71
Trauttmannsdorf, Cardinal Maria
    Thaddäus, Graf zu, 9n, 12
Troyer, Count Ferdinand de, 6, 12n ,
    151, 169, 175, 184–85, 186n,
    205, 325, 329
Troyer, Count Franz de, 6, 12n, 151,
    169, 175, 205, 325
Türk, Daniel Gottlob, 54, 283
Tyson, Alan, 13, 14n
Unterbrochene Opferfest, Das (Winter),
    169, 172, 325

Vertraute Briefe geschreiben auf einer Reise nach Wien und den Österreichischen Staaten zu Ende das Jahre 1808 und zu Anfang 1809 (Reichardt) , 29

Vestale, La (Spontini), 66, 131, 132, 215, 321

Vetterl, Karl, xviii, 77n, 151, 153, 165n, 251n

Volkmann, Hans, 71n

Wanderer, Der, 36

Wegeler, Franz, 7n

Weigl, Joseph, 172n

Weissmann, John S., 167n

Weston, Pamela, 185n

Wieck, Friedrich, 36

Wiener Piano-Forte-Schule, 108–111

Winter, Karl, 21

Winter, Peter von, 168n, 169

Winter, Robert, xxn, 154n

Wranitzky, Anton, 164n

Wurzbach, Constantin von, 5

Zauberflöte, Die (Mozart), 60, 345

Zeiler, Franz, 13

Zeitschrift für Musikwissenschaft, xviin, 332

Zelmira (Rossini), 152, 154, 156, 161, 330